MISTER, MISTER

MISTER, MISTER

GUY GUNARATNE

Pantheon Books, New York

Copyright © 2023 by Guy Gunaratne

All rights reserved. Published in the United States by Pantheon Books, a division of Penguin Random House LLC, New York, and distributed in Canada by Penguin Random House Canada Limited, Toronto. Originally published in hardcover in Great Britain by Tinder Press, an imprint of Headline Publishing Group, an Hachette UK Company, in 2023.

Pantheon Books and colophon are registered trademarks of Penguin Random House LLC.

Library of Congress Cataloging-in-Publication Data
Name: Gunaratne, Guy, [date] author.
Title: Mister, Mister : a novel / Guy Gunaratne.
Description: First American edition. New York : Pantheon Books, 2023
Identifiers: LCCN 2023014388 (print). LCCN 2023014389 (ebook).
ISBN 9780593701423 (hardcover). ISBN 9780593701430 (ebook).
Subjects: LCGFT: Novels.
Classification: LCC PR6107.U55 M57 2023 (print) | LCC PR6107.U55 (ebook) |
DDC 823/.92—dc23/eng/20230407
LC record available at https://lccn.loc.gov/2023014388
LC ebook record available at https://lccn.loc.gov/2023014389

www.pantheonbooks.com

Jacket illustration and design by Jack Smyth; (suit and tie) Getty Images

Printed in the United States of America
First American Edition
2 4 6 8 9 7 5 3 1

For my mother Deepa
and my daughter Liah

Contents

I

1990–2005

Idiot Boy

Mister, I have lost my tongue. A quick cut with a cinch, little jerk of the wrists. Easy, clean, deed done. I suppose you'd say it was madness, psychosis, insanity – but no, not likely. An act of liberation, that's what. Permanence is what I was after. A final, effective riddance at the root – so, *snitch!* – since tongues do not grow back.

I've little pieces of cotton packed into my cheeks now, Mister. And a cup of salty water to soothe my blackened mouth. Magic beans to heal the rest of it. And them nurses take regular swabs of my sutured pits. The discomfort is nothing. Not compared to the satisfaction I feel from knowing that I've won back – no less, with an act of bloody violence – what has always been mine. By which I mean, of course: the right to tell my own story.

I can put down what I really mean to say now, God willing. And this time, Mister, you may even have my consent. You may listen. Though, I know, you'll be wary. Not least, because you'll have no control over what's to be said. But then, what's left to a person after speech is lost to them? Recollections and memories alone. And what harm can these silent things do, really, without a tongue to lift them to other people's ears?

1. LETTERS I intend now to write down the rest of it. Get scribbling on these here pages you've sent me. I do this in the spirit of reconciling what has happened. Naturally, there are questions. But you should know there will be no half-truths to my telling. Nothing invented, nothing untrue – you should mark that in your official report. And I've agreed, honestly, to tell you all this, not because your bully courts frighten me, or because you have Her Majesty's crest on your pin, or because you, yourself, intimidate me, Mister, sat there fiddling with your pen. It's because I am guilty of everything you say that I did. Guilty of treason. Guilty of inspiring bad men. Guilty of all of it. And more. So, do me in after I've finished. Have me drawn, quartered, stoned into a pulp for all I care – have at it!

But for now, I just want you to listen.

I have plenty to say.

2. GREAT BRITAIN To return to your question, well – likely is, you've already made up your mind, Mister. I can tell from the sorts of questions you've already asked me, like why I hate your country. I don't doubt it seems a little strange coming from me, but believe me when I say that I do not, not really.

Truly, I have missed your Great Britain. I've missed your old

British mores, Mister. Your pasties and that. Your cuppa-teas. Your John Cleese. And your poets.

This country has always been a home for me. Only place that's ever really claimed me, or that I could ever claim. I think about my childhood, my rambling half-cocked education, and then, my rise into fame and fortune.

It all happened here – right here for me, in this city, in this United Kingdom of the Great British Isles.

Nostalgia, call it. Remembrance maybe. I'm pining for the parts I was raised in. East Ham, that is, East London. Among local muftis, many mothers, wide boys, punters and clerics. Wouldn't call the feeling patriotic – nothing as waxy as a word like that – but it does beg a better question. One that I'd quite like to put to you now, Mister, and that is this:

If the greatness of your Britain remains so assured, then why is it so difficult to hear someone hate it?

Everything I've ever written, from the poetry to the long stories I've told – a litany of my many offending verses – every word was written under this same English sky, Mister, under which I was born, same as you!

My uncle Sisi Gamal – him, the old soapbox muezzin, who was always so clear about these things – said to me once: *Boy, there is nothing great about Britain – it's a madhouse! A place only fit for slumlords, field hands and rabble.* I didn't know what he meant by it then. I was young. Too busy making faces in the mirrors, shadows on the walls, to notice your taste for bully justice. But now, here I am. Sat in this cell. Enduring a barrage of questions as to *why this, why that, why whatever hatred,* and *why now* . . . when to me, it's obvious. As it should be to you.

It brings to my mind a saying, one from where my father

is from, which translates from the Arabic like this: *As you sow, you shall so reap*. It's a saying that graces all scripture.

So, let that be my answer, Mister. For any more, you must ask my Allah. Since mine is a life He chose for me, and at a time He chose for me to live. Otherwise, you're better off asking the times for answers. Since it was the times that also made me. Made my tongue. And by *times* I mean the world out there, the big bright-wide: the West. Into which I was born, raised upright, lived an antic life, and did my best to scribble a little poetry and pray.

3. NAMES You asked my name. I've had so many over the years. I collect them like stamps or old stones. Some names were given to me with love and seriousness. Granted by those who wished I'd grow old and become rich and famous in the world. Other names were given to me in spite. Along the way I've discarded old names like old hats and borrowed new ones to replace the ones that grew tired.

It was your newspapers, all them red tops and magazines, who gave me my many aliases. The *Jihadi Boy-Poet*, they called me. The *Hateful Fanatic*, they said. I was the *Internet's Ayatollah* for a time, and the *Pound Shop Prophet of Stepney Green and Newham* . . .

Now, I know these titles were only ever meant to mock me, ridicule me, sway public opinion against me. But knowing what I know now, Mister, I'd say your papers didn't go far enough! At the height of my fame, I was the most widely read poet in your England. And it's my verses today, my own particular poems, written under any number of monikers, that have me sat before you now, scribbling away.

My first – that is to say, the name my mother gave me – was

Yahya Bas. Bas comes from my father. I was Yahya throughout my youth. I've had others, but most know me by my *nom de plume*, my *nom de guerre*, my Arabic *kunya* – my poetic name: *Al-Bayn*.

But where do I begin?

If I'm to unravel my life, I'll begin where I like.

So, here's the order we'll follow:

A birth, then a death, then rebirth, then death and birth again.

First, birth . . .

4. BIRTH (MYTH) *Bismillah ir rahman ir rahim.* As a child, I was told I had no origin. I was moulded out of existence itself. A rush of swampy nothingness – *and then pop! Birthed under moonlight along an estuary in paradise* . . . Or at least, this was the myth told me. The first myth of many others. One had me born blue. No breath in the chest. Cold to the touch and silent. An almighty smack was administered to me then, upsetting the boy into a gasp of new breath. And yet another: I was told that I came into the world feet first, Mister, and all bloody, bent a little too, at the hip, with my legs limp like watery jelly.

Which of these stories comes closest to the truth, I don't know. Most likely there's a little bit of truth to them all. Most likely, Mister, I was born *breech* as it's called – pulled by the ankles out my mother's womb. A stubborn, slippery creature, delivered gnarled up. Goes some way to explaining my hip. A disjointedness at the sides, Mister, which has burdened me with a wide and irregular gait. To this day I imagine myself meeting the world this way: half in this world and half in another. And then some panicky smack forcing a cry out of me, forcing me to swallow great gulps of air, Mister, my first proper breaths in fright and pain.

In all probability, I was actually born on a white-tiled floor in a bathroom stall in our communal home in East London. My two acting *doulas*, my Mother Sadaf and Mother Miriam, would have been there alongside my uncle Sisi Gamal. It was my own mother – my white, English mother, Mister, her name was Estella Stevens – she was the one who kept up my more fantastical myths. Her, with her powdery pallor, fingers like clawed-at white candles, who'd sometimes whisper to me, when she was lucid enough to speak, saying softly: . . . *and then pop! Along an estuary in paradise* . . . in that thin, thrown voice. After which she'd stop, cover her mouth, as if she'd let slip some shameful thing.

Nobody else confirmed my mother's telling of it. Nobody denied the story either. But then again, Mister, my mother was an unwell woman. She was a liar. Though, even in her lies, she made my beginning, all beginnings, sound beautiful and bright.

5. BIRTH When I picture the first days of my new life, I see others gathered around me like moon-faces, squatting in them stalls, clearing blood from my mouth, hands coddling me, ringed fingers patting me down worriedly. And me there, squirming, smarting from that cold hard slap to the arse.

Were they charmed or repulsed when they first set eyes on me?

Well, I remember my Mother Sadaf telling me once – no, telling me a few times – that I was never a pretty child. I had paler skin than my mother. *As white as a bone*, she said. I was cursed with a sour white nose, fleshy nostrils, a fat lower lip which sagged as I suckled on my bloodless little fingers, and large, black, empty eyes, Mister, which must have struck my other Mothers as monstrous.

I heard their voices before anything else. My Mother Sadaf first – my dark Mother with arms like big black boughs, and her terrifying mouth always open – tossing me over, cleaning my folds, cutting my cord and then saying: *Boh! – see this baby – whiter than milk – just look!* And then my Mother Miriam there too, gentler, sweeter, quietly muttering prayers to herself, while peering over them shoulders to look: *Oh . . . oh, see his father's nose – yes, your nose, Gamal! – See how he stares and stares and stares . . .*

And then probably my uncle, my Sisi Gamal, would have spat on the floor and declared he recognised more of my mother in me. I imagine the old man stroking my mother's tired and silent head, his round-rimmed glasses reflecting back her blank gaze. It was at this moment, as I now recall the story, that my mother stirred and whispered the name into my uncle's ear: *Yah . . . Yah . . . Yah . . .* To which he nodded, added *Bas*, before saying a short prayer.

6. JINNA In Arabic, the word for foetus is *janin*, which shares a root with demon, ill-spirit or invisible creature – a *jinn*. I think because both are *jinna*, meaning hidden. So, I imagine my uncle's prayers were meant for all things concealed. And probably, Mister, my uncle was also thinking of my father – his foolish younger brother, whose name was Marwan Bas, born, as he was, poor in Northern Iraq – long gone by then, lost to the desert and presumed, on all accounts, to be dead.

7. GOD'S OWN My mother survived my freakish birth. I was laid out on top of her, onto her low sunken stomach, after making my first little stifled mumbles. It was one of the few moments she ever held me close, Mister, or even seemed to notice me there.

In her eyes I saw myself reflected – or should I say *refracted*? A better word, more tricksy and suggestive of my untidy beginnings – the sight of me seemed to offend her. She picked me up, looked at me, and quickly moved as if to push me aside and turned to the wall.

I don't blame her, Mister. Apart from the purpling bruise at my sides, my face was also riddled with conflicts. My eyes were too far apart. My poking-out ears were somehow ungainly and weird. And my skin, glue-like and thin, must have revealed enough to suggest something unseemly.

Mine then was a face unwelcomed by the world. The old seers in them mountains had a term for boys like me – *God's Own*, they called them. Offering the phrase for babies born disfigured, Mister, misshapen, or else left orphaned by the war. My Sisi Gamal adopted it for me, saying: *You are God's Own, Yahya*. It was easier to claim me for Allah, I think, than to offer me some tidier origin.

8. EARLY MEMORIES These early memories appear in the mind, Mister, tucked away in my head alongside scenes I'd rather misremember. But don't believe anyone who tells you the thoughts of newborns are too flimsy to retain. I can recall them early days in rude little glimpses . . .

. . . like the cloth my uncle wrapped me in, how I'd cry into that cloth, and how, after a while, the colour in my uncle's eyes began to darken. It was difficult for him. One hand on my mother's ailing shoulder, the other under my wailing head. Lucky for me, Mister, that my other Mothers were near so that he could lob me off when he wanted. *Ach! Away from me! This bloody child's bloody bawling . . . I will send a letter! This bloody arrangement will be done!* – it might have been obvious to anyone watching that my Sisi Gamal could not cope.

I'd started crawling and scuttling about after that. I started exploring, Mister, and then everything began to arrive at me with lightness, loudness, flashes and bangs and floods. Tempers flared and turned solid and stuck. Figures fashioned themselves into shapes and colours and form. I got the measure of how days would follow darkness. How smells swapped from body to body, from room to room. I remember the taste of sourness on my tongue, the sweetness and texture of tepid milk. I recall even my uncle struggling with the bottle. He'd hold me in the crook of his arm while at the same time leafing through a novel.

He'd hold me there for far too long, Mister. I'd sometimes turn and start suffocating in his armpits. It'd often take my Mother Miriam to snatch me away from him – *The boy cannot breathe your underarm stink!* she'd hiss, to which my uncle would throw a finger – *Ach!* – and return to whatever page he'd been interrupted from reading. I believe all this left me with the impression, Mister, that the world was a precarious place. Crowded with put-upon faces and desperate fits of impatience.

9. LOVE You asked if my uncle really loved me. Well, who's to say, really? My Sisi Gamal never wanted children. And I don't blame him for finding it difficult. I was told it was a difficult time to have been born into. This was circa '91, Mister. This was your Thatcher in decline, poll tax and riots, and robber-barons scheming to starve the needy and the weak.

So, have pity on my poor uncle. Sentenced to a lifetime of picking up the pieces after his brother. But then again, lucky him too – lucky the both of us, Mister – for having been surrounded by these women. The ones I'd end up calling my Other Mothers. And, in particular, my Mother Sadaf and Mother Miriam.

So, now, a little on them . . .

10. OTHER MOTHERS There was some anxious clucking about the boy. The neglected bruise at my hips had developed into a sort of protrusion. And my skin had turned a worrying yellowish hue. Even the whites of my eyes had turned yellow. *Too much blood in the blood*, was how my uncle described it, before stepping aside for my Mothers to take a look.

I can imagine my Mother Miriam poking her head into the kitchen – only a child herself at the time, about nineteen – she'd have been there, Mister, pulling at her scarf, fingers pressed against her plump wetted cheeks, chewing on stray strands of dark hair. My Mother Sadaf would have looked closer, that coal-coloured crone. She'd lay me out sprawled on a tabletop next to her blackened wooden spoon, Mister, her crusted measures and her dried rotting roots which she'd picked and forgotten about from the garden. There I lay – a baby born deathly blue and now a sickly yellow – staring up at them, unblinking and blotchy, my breath uneven. They'd prod at my belly and shake limbs, examining me for strange little marks or further discolouration.

– Maybe he will not die, muttered my Mother Sadaf, clicking her tongue, maybe not death, but not a good life, anyway . . .

She announced the diagnosis with a sweep of her burly arms, scratching her hair pinned back in a bun, and then, in some fit of irritation, scowling at my Mother Miriam, whose face was looking down in dismay. She flicked a hard finger at the younger Mother's forehead – *flap!* – cussed at her, and then attempted another – *flap!* – which was dodged, and then she cussed at the air, thumping the floor with her foot.

– *Boh!* – I've had enough of your face always dripping! Go now and take your tears elsewhere! I will deal with the child in my own time. Go now and get out!

These aggravated gusts were ignored, Mister. Once my Mother Sadaf had made her exit and was considered to be out of earshot, my Mother Miriam shuffled up to my Sisi Gamal to talk about what was to be done.

– The boy doesn't take his mother's milk . . .

– You must persuade Estella, Miriam. She is still – *ach!* – she does not want him. Does not let me close enough to bring him. Maybe . . . yes, maybe you try with her tonight?

With his usual pleading growl, my Sisi Gamal made my Mother Miriam promise. She bundled me up from the kitchen table and went to try again with Estella.

My empty-mouthed, doe-mother Estella, Mister. She was being kept alone on the uppermost floor at the time. Her habit of staring into walls and into ceilings and fiddling along with her fingers were only the first signs of descent. Her long periods of silences predated me by many years. And it's important now to mention, Mister, that my mother was on medication. A bucketload prescribed off the NHS. Dizzy pills you needed a proper doctor for, Mister. And somehow my mother – owing to a mystery I hadn't quite grasped at the time – had managed it. My Mother Miriam did the sorting of cups and ensured the cocktails were spilled into her every morning. My Mother Miriam was also the one who regularly checked on my mother. Noticed if she needed washing, nails needed doing, or if her hair was out of place and needed braiding. She'd sit up there for hours just brushing and braiding. And it's why, I think, the vision of Estella Stevens appears to me now so immaculate.

Sat there dressed in them warm white jumpers, Mister, her long plain skirts, and her hair so tidily combed as if posing for a photograph, a still-life painting, a mountain of clutter all around her in that room.

I remember my Mother Miriam made a face as we entered. *Tet-tet* . . . she went, looking over them moth-eaten blankets, clothes and old shawls, nappies too, sour-smelling wipes, left after my uncle's attempts at keeping me changed and fed.

– Estella . . . ? whispered my Mother Miriam as we stepped inside. My Sisi Gamal came in behind us. My mother was sitting facing the corner, Mister. My Mother Miriam bent down as we came nearer, and I was placed into my mother's arms in a folded cloth. My mother turned her head to look down at me. But she moved slow, like some battered and matted-haired doll come alive, with her eyes like two big pools showing no hint of recognition.

– You see? went my Sisi Gamal, leaving a foot out the door, it is like she doesn't – *ach!* – doesn't want to know him, Miriam . . .

– *Tet-tet* . . . went my Mother Miriam. And lowered her eyes.

I'd imagine her eyes did truly lower, Mister. Probably with disappointment and pain and a kind of heartache. I can picture her muttering prayers, pleading with my mother to accept me into her arms. For the woman did have the warmest of hearts, Mister. She wanted the best for me. Even when all them other Mothers asked her – and there were many other Mothers at the house, Mister, who I'll get on to in a bit – when they asked why she let my Mother Sadaf treat her so badly, since she was so kind and sweet to everyone, and why she let her bully her and cuss her out and so on, my Mother Miriam would only reply with a quiet little smile: *Owf . . . sticks and stones, my sisters . . .* Less about language with her, Mister. It was acts of unkindness, and cruelty, that upset her most.

My Mother Miriam reached for my bottle when my mother refused. Her quiet prayers became like lullabies for me. She waddled me about outside my mother's room for the rest of them first few years. She kept the bottle at my lip, her grey eyes staring down at me, pinching my gummy cheeks, making sure I was never alone.

My uncle, meanwhile, was released.

I see . . . he'd say, stepping away from the room, *I will leave it to you, Miriam . . . I will go downstairs, to be –*

And he'd scurry downstairs as if my mother's arms were reaching for him. I'll write to you now, Mister, about how my mother Estella and uncle Sisi Gamal were subsumed for a while, under the whirling clamour of the place – this madhouse – which was more circus than home.

11. MOTHERS' HOUSE The old Mothers' house stood like a beached trawler, a proper barnacled palace, on the end of Forty

Road. It stood close to the cemetery there, opposite the Cash & Carry and the skips. And like most communal homes, Mister, its story was maintained with far better care than its crumbling walls and the foundations on which it stood.

And so the story went they'd used the old house as a women's centre decades back, for them *ayahs* and *amahs*, so called, brought over by English families who'd returned from your colonies. This was circa early 1900s-odd. Them ethnic cleaners, childminders and cooks. Dark-skinned women from South India, Chinese nannies, sisters of Lascar domestics with gold rings in their lips. Most had been mistreated by their masters – *masters*, Mister, so called – soon as they arrived.

Many were dismissed shortly after. These poor women had no safe passage back to wherever, so they stayed. Ending up in *ayah* houses, which were dotted all over the place at the time. Ours was the only *ayah* house in East Ham. Most would move on a few weeks after arrival. There were many rooms. Eleven rooms in all, and allotments, where they could grow tomatoes and turnips and that. But then, over time, many of the houses were converted into employment ex-changes. Ours was one of the few houses that didn't. It was taken over by the local Islamic association instead. This was the seventies, still. Them imams were the ones to turn it into a refuge centre for *women of low to no means* – women like my mother, Mister, and my other Mothers – to help get them back on their feet, say, or at least offer them a place with a bit of company.

The only exception to the tenant women was my uncle Sisi Gamal, Mister – him, whose sole task at the house, it seemed to me, aside from being my mother's minder, was to keep me out of sight of the rest of them. Once I became old enough to doze on my own, I slept next to him in the basement. He put me in a second-hand cot, Mister, and he'd lie next to me. He slept with no pillow, preferring his arms to the floor. And I'd watch him snore through the bars, I remember. His lips jabbering with every drawn breath. I used to imagine his teeth like little blackened pearls too, glinting behind his moustache, and his giant nostrils like caverns in his head. I'd stare at spots on the khat-stained floors if I couldn't sleep, and at them hundreds of shelves crowding around, bursting under the weight of a thousand stacks of paper, and my uncle's hundreds of precious books.

I imagine my ears must have been stirring. Listening to them surly voices upstairs. And the telly going. The music playing somewhere, and the laughing. Whenever I pretended to sleep, I'd listen along till my Sisi Gamal rapped his knuckles on them wooden bars, waking himself up to scold me: *Hrmph . . . close eyes, boy . . . close . . . eyes . . .*

12. PERFUMES The figures of my other Mothers come vague to me now. I remember the sound of them more, the shapes they made against them corridor walls. Colours thrown against windows. The rush of bodies up and down stairs. Jingles coming off the radio, sung along like opera tunes, eruptions of sudden laughter, crazy, clamorous harmonics, Mister, of squabbling and crying together, crowded into their rooms.

The ones that stuck around became familiar. These were escapees mostly, Mister. Some thrown-together sisterhood of rough sleepers, younger runaways and moody aunties. They'd all fled their families and found shelter here. I knew them from perfumes. Cheap bottles of scents were like a mania for my Mothers. Perfumes in giant bottles kept inside drawers, and caskets. They were bound in elaborate gold and green ribbon. The bottles held a kind of mystery for me. I'd watch how my Mothers would dab their necks with them, these accords that always hit you hard in the head.

Sometimes I'd sneak into their rooms and spy on them. Fumes came swirling as I crawled. And then one of my Mothers would spot my arse up in the air and would pick me up: *Here he is, the little mutt!* And then I'd be passed around, and so I caught good whiffs of their myriad infusions, making mental notes as to which ones I liked, and which I didn't.

There was Mother Aneesa, for one, with her fat nose, thick eyebrows, and a vinegary funk, which she'd always try and hide with a scent of lemon. I'd take a sniff whenever she held me above her, extending her arms away from herself, or when she'd giggle into my belly: *Joo-hoo – you little mutt!* She was the opposite of her name, Mister – Aneesa, meaning *consoling companion* or *one who is gentle with others*. She was never gentle. And rarely consoling. And as her story went, she'd arrived at the house having left some crotchety old Yemeni husband, some older man, three times her age, who was still somewhere back in Slough. I heard he'd thrown her out, onto the street, Mister, with nothing but a pair of sandals and a pocket mirror. My Mother Aneesa's high, joggling voice sounded always caught in surprise, or as if tipping into heckling laughter, *Come here – ha-ha! – you stupid mutt! Joo-hoo! – look at your little tail, you little animal!*

And then there was my Mother Shahnaz, who together with my Mother Sofiyya shared a room on the second floor. This was the room that had a near-collapsed balcony, Mister, winched up at the sides from the outer wall. These two had arrived at the house together, and were determined to leave together too. Keeping themselves primed, prettied and ready-made for some second husband to appear, and provide an escape.

My Mother Shahnaz spent most of her time pining after photographs in faded beauty magazines. Pining after her younger self, I think, some lost image of her youth. She'd been plucked from a life in Pakistan in her teens, by a man who, having plucked her, then left her. She still wore a fragrance of strong peaches and orange, Mister, and she never once lost that look of frustrated expectation.

I'd often catch a glimpse of my dolled-up Mother Shahnaz, attended to by my Mother Sofiyya at all times, out on the balcony. That little perch was like a pedestal for them, a slightly tilted stage from which they'd present themselves as if on a pageant. Mother Shahnaz, her chin lifted as if to survey the Forty Road, and my Mother Sofiyya, much the younger, thinner, but with a set of jagged teeth, trailing a lighter scent of honeyed rose. They sat there most mornings gazing down half longingly, half resentful, at the parade of steady prospects below: delivery men, homeless men and other aged, shiftless, stumbling drunks, going in and out of the Cash & Carry. My Mothers would pose like a pair of sham idols, but never deigned to look any man in the face.

My own presence brought nothing but offence, however. Both were petrified, I think, that my meek little hands might make a grab for them. As if my existence alone, Mister, spoiled the illusion they'd created for themselves. My Mother Shahnaz pointing a painted nail: *Kiss-kiss! – Away from here, you little mutt! Sofiyya! Sofiyya! Take the boy back to Miriam – where is Miriam?* And then Mother Soffiya, snarling at me, hissing out from behind her kicked teeth: *Come, little goat-boy – esh-esh! – find somebody else to carry you!*

I'd get dropped then – most likely booted or pushed, Mister – from her hennaed hands, into the lap of my Mother Fareeda, who stayed a few doors down the hall.

Much the gentler, although a little mad herself, my Mother Fareeda seemed always distracted. It was this Mother's habits that fascinated me early on. She always went about muttering to herself, as if never alone in her head. She had a very thin, gaunt-looking face, and wore her greying hair tied up in a kind of poking bun. She was always costumed in the brightest of light-coloured shawls, patterned in the colours of her beloved Lebanon. She was very kind to me, Mister. And always sent a crooked smile at me whenever I came near. She told me once – her voice high and thin, as if coming out the top of her mouth and whistling out the sides of her nostrils, and calling me *dauling* with her *da*'s sounding like the Arabic *daud* – *We pity you, dauling, boy – how is it to be so alone, so lost and wretched as you are?* And then she'd close her eyes and petition the Almighty for me: *God give you protection . . . God give you light . . . Together we pray that our prayers are heard for you . . .*

That there was one of her odd little habits, Mister. My Mother Fareeda spoke in doubles. Her *we* and *us* and *me* and *she* were used even when speaking alone.

The story went, my Mother Fareeda had had a sister, some other Mother named Fatima, who'd vanished from the house many years ago. It was her sister's presence she felt when my Mother Fareeda spoke. *Lucky I had my blameless Fatima,* she'd say to me, *my love was my sister, it was she who kept me fed, and healthy – while this boy here can barely speak* . . . and then I'd watch her tilt her head. She'd give a sad little smile, pinch her withered fingers at my gummy cheeks, and then wander away to sit alone in her room.

Strange thing was, Mister, nobody could remember any Fatima. Nobody could even swear they'd ever seen her. Not in person, nor in any picture. I'd once heard my Mother Shahnaz and Mother Sofiyya whispering about it – both like inseparable sisters themselves – speculating whether this Mother Fatima couldn't have been made up. *She is cracked in the head* . . . *yes, she is crazy – yes, of course, Fareeda sees things* . . . *always has* . . .

My Mother Fareeda wore a patchouli scent which smelled like Vimto to me. And aside from my Mother Sadaf, no other Mother had lived at the house for longer.

It was only Mother Sadaf and Mother Miriam who went about smelling like themselves – one a warm scent of powdered milk, the other a ground sweat of earth and vegetation. One picked me up and threw me only kisses while the other was more likely to brush me aside with a mud-covered boot or flick a finger at the back of my head.

Of course, none of their rooms were left open for me. I'd only catch glimpses through cracks in the doors. All that colour, bright sequins and mirrored lights, Mister. I sometimes managed to get inside and climb over their cushioned pillows and clothes. I'd even make grabs at their perfume bottles, Mister – some devilish fit inside me wanting to hurl and smash them to pieces on the floor. Just to see my own reflections in the shards, I suppose. And let the scents overwhelm me with gorgeous air. I'd only get to knock a few over before I'd be chased away. And then I'd cry, Mister. My Sisi Gamal would then come after me, like some irritable ogre. He'd collect me under his arms, pinching his nose as we came down the stairs – *Bloody stink with these women . . .*

13. STAMMER My uncle's basement offered far less for the senses. *You watch where you are knuckling!* he'd shout at me, seeing me crawling over piles of unsorted books. *These books are priceless, boy – precious works – be careful where you crawl!*

My uncle seemed to prefer it when I wandered away, Mister, and I learned to look for attention elsewhere. I'd soon find myself huddled up on the first floor with my Mother Miriam playing draughts with Mother Aneesa. They played on a paper board, Mister, with squares drawn out in biro, and coins as playing pieces. Copper pennies, brass counters with milled edges. I liked biting their thumbs as they played, savouring the taste of metal money.

Sometimes I'd steal a coin off the board, and my Mother Aneesa would cover her mouth and laugh at me. *These coins are from home, goat-boy – ha-ha! – not for swallowing, you little shitter!* And she'd swipe them back and *tupp* the back of my head with her elbow.

My Mother Aneesa would get a lot of joy out of making fun. She'd point and laugh at my shambling hip. I was a lot plumper by this time, and still unsteady whenever she held me upright to do a dance for her. *Goat-boy! Goat-boy!* she'd goad – and here, I'm translating, Mister, she'd call me *mutt* as in *hajin*, and *kharoof* as in *dirty goat*, or *sheep* more precisely – she'd pull at my untamed hair and call me these things. *Dance for me, goat-boy! Go over there and dance – ha-ha! – spin around, you little mutt!*

I tried to dance, Mister, but managed only half a spin before dropping hard on my arse again. My Mother Aneesa would fall on the floor with laughter, rattling all the cupboards around me as she fell: *Goat-boy! You are a very bad dancer!* These Mothers regarded me as a kind of grotesque, I think. A little monster they could mock and throw about. This was, at least, until I got a little stronger and started running.

A year or so later, at the age children are expected to chatter, I sensed my Mothers growing concerned with me. I was slow to speak. Only repeating a few syllables by then. The beginnings of words mostly, or the endings. I'd catch the words before they fell out of me, Mister, and the habit produced a kind of stammer.

– What is this boy saying? went my Mother Shahnaz once, as I sat balanced on Mother Miriam's fat knees.

– Like a stone in his mouth, said my Mother Aneesa shouting from the kitchen, this boy will never speak!

My Mother Fareeda appeared and swept me up to hold her ears to my mouth. *What do we hear? What do we hear, dauling?* She shook me firmly and stared at my lips as I stuttered.

– We hear . . . the child is saying something – it is coming out – no, what is it?

My Mothers Shahnaz and Sofiyya looked from the hall.

– *Doh,* or *Dah* or *Poh Bah?*

– See how he struggles? But – *esh-esh* – don't let him cry! Give him back to Miriam!

My Mother Fareeda tossed me back to my Mother Miriam and I gave a cough at their patchouli and peaches and rose.

14. TEARS I grew bolder, began slipping their grasp, scaling the several floors of the house on my own, despite my uncle's wishes. I realise now, Mister, that they must have seen me as a bad omen at the time. From the moment I emerged, feet first into the world, with every milestone missed. I must have reminded them of the world's ugliness, its brokenness, with all its monstrous afflictions, that didn't spare anybody, not even the likes of me, some lonely *mutt*, whose presence nobody could explain.

Then again, they were the only family I ever had. My Sisi Gamal and me, my mother and my other Mothers were bound together with tears rather than blood. And theirs was a deeper sisterhood borrowed from something far more elemental than anything I could describe here, Mister. Their rooms, which were like little universes to me, with their secrets and magic and enchantment, were the only places these women could exercise a vulnerable, cat-like kind of freedom.

15. ESTELLA' S ROOM It occurs to me now, writing all this out for you, Mister, that I almost certainly spent more time with these other women than I did my own mother. Hidden away under lock and key, she drifted further and further into the background. I'd hear my mother, sense her instead. I'd listen out for her feet on them boards, or the sound of her tossing about in bed.

She lived in the only occupied room on the uppermost floor, separated from the rest of the house. That entire floor was strictly forbidden for me. And if I sneaked up two out of four flights, one of my other Mothers would haul me down by the ankles. *Don't you try it, you little mutt! You'll never make it up all those stairs by yourself!*

My Mother Miriam would have me stand at the door of my mother's room sometimes, while she tucked clean bedding into my mother's mattress, and tenderly persuaded her to swallow her pills.

I watched it all, lopsided and silent as I was, and stared into her odd, shrine-like little chamber. The room itself, Mister, looked so different to any other. There were hundreds of little portraits hung on the blue walls. Floor to ceiling, Mister, portraits of women in long dresses and shawls, mostly ink-like dark tones, a handful of them in faded colour. Each face seemed to look out in a different direction. The frames were lined with dust, as if they'd hung there for years, untouched. Nobody remembered who'd put them up there, or the little mirrors, nailed to the walls in their ornate gilt frames. And my mother – sitting in bed as I watched her, gazing at them frames, or from time to time sitting by the smeared glass window to watch the sky – seemed at home here, and perfectly calm. There'd always be a heap of black fabric beside her. And whenever she was alone, Mister, or thought she was alone, no matter what hour of the day or night, she'd be sitting there in that chair and begin sewing.

I'd sneak up sometimes – in the evenings, this was, and then regular visits whenever my other Mothers were away – and if I was lucky I'd find her door left ajar, and I'd watch my mother Estella going at it with her needle.

I'd see how the lines of her mouth quivered as she stitched, and realised how she talked to herself, or else quietly sang. She seemed so different when she was alone. I remember sitting there for hours just watching her. I wanted very much to go to her and ask her: *What's wrong?* Why would she never speak to anybody? I wanted to ask her about them portraits on the walls. All them faces that were staring at her, and her own reflection staring back. I was desperate to mark some resemblance between my mother and me.

Bolder still, I began inching further into the room until I could see over my mother's face properly, and she, in turn, realised I was within touching distance of her.

16. ESTELLA'S SEAMS My mother didn't really bat an eyelid when I came near. She only looked up to notice me there, before going back to her sewing, Mister. But it didn't matter. All I wanted was to watch her. See them lines at her mouth begin to tighten. See them eyes dart about as if chasing a vision in the light. I watched long and hard to find a likeness. Her nose wasn't as fleshy as mine. Hers was thin and narrow and chalk-white. My mother looked like one of them stitched figures in them old English tapestries, Mister. The ones in your village museums, pinned to stately parapets and church walls. Them courtly Roundhead women, I mean, with square hems and gloves at the waist standing alongside knights and kings and foreign princes.

Obviously, I realised why my mother looked like that. I knew why both our cheeks showed red in the cold air while my other Mothers' didn't. Me and my mother shared a whiteness at birth. And I suppose we were haunted by the same things. My white gummy skin had always seemed to repulse my other Mothers. It was confusing to see Estella's own whiteness shine so brightly in that dark little room. She looked beautiful. I began to compare her long braided hair with my own. I'd sidle close and smell her unwashed skin to see if I could recognise anything of my own odour on her. I'd search every inch of her face as she sat sewing, and from these little measurements – the curvature of her ears, slender hands fiddling away, them long porcelain feet – I found an intimacy with my mother despite the distraction in her eyes, and her refusal to let me touch her.

Only later did she confide in me, Mister. And by this I mean she eventually did start talking to me – or, at least, sometimes, when I felt she acknowledged my presence in the room, she spoke as if she knew somebody was there listening.

I drew even closer to make her out. It sounded as if she were offering stories into the air, little riddles, in weird metre. Strange, scattered speech. I could trace no meaning in it: *Dear one . . . hear the one, the one about Tamerlane . . . gave his men robes. Nice and clean robes. Not cheap! Stitched gold threads and gemstones . . . Marwan, Marwan opened it and found a blanket . . . blanket for an ass . . . serves him right, the idiot, the fool . . . give him an inch . . . coat off his back . . .* and then she'd shake a needle in the air before getting on with her sewing.

Mister, it was as if the whole world hadn't waited on her tongue.

It might be hard for you to hear it, but this random speech of hers, and her voice – low, and hot, and thrown about – was at once troubling to me, and exciting.

Who was she speaking about – her *Marwan, Marwan* – my father?

Even now, I can't be sure.

At other times I can recall how she held one hand up at the light, flashing a quick smile at the window as if somebody had appeared and had caught her eye in the glass – *No, I'm waiting, I'll wait . . .* she'd mutter, giving a little shake of her head and returning to her sewing.

I'd try and get her to repeat what she said. I'd try whenever my Mother Miriam was there. I'd tug at her skirt and tap at her arms to get her to tell it. But she wouldn't, Mister, not a word. My Mother Miriam, seeing all this, could only sigh and give a sympathetic look, ushering me away from my mother with a soft little *tet-tet . . .*

My mother Estella saved them riddles for me. And it's for this reason that I call my mother a liar. For as young as I was, Mister, I could see the dumb silence was a wilful ruse on my mother's part. Some performance played out for reasons I couldn't understand. I didn't think bad about it then, and in fact I was grateful to have a secret to share with her.

I spent all the time I could just watching and waiting for her to speak again. I was still small enough to crawl under her blankets. And whenever I'd find her asleep, I'd creep into a ball and tuck myself under her thighs. I lay hidden, Mister. Careful not to wake her. And I'd look over, studying her body for little marks. Like serrated lightning across her stomach. I'd follow them with my fingers, and I'd tell myself – here, this is where her skin snapped from mine, here, her hands like mine, nails like mine. Her skin seemed to shine even under covers. Even with her stubborn silences, I felt I could really see into my mother. I could touch her veins, almost. See the blood flow inside. I could press my ears against her, hear the beat of her heart, the heave of her breath. I felt I could even hear her thoughts. And there were parts of my mother, Mister, that bore a sink-water whiteness that tasted of tears to me, and just as bitter.

17. SHELTER My mother Estella might as well have been mad. Might have been Scheherazade, for all I knew – the woman with no breath, having run away from her past. So far back, at least to before my father had left her. Nevertheless, she became like a shelter for me at that early age, against the crazy carousel of my other Mothers – them, with their endless rushing air, battles over hard soap and splashing water. My own mother never tried to coddle me, let alone wash me. Never tried to temper my tantrums. And whenever Sisi Gamal would find me there, and try to take me off her, I'd cling to my mother for all my worth Mister. She was the only thing I could bear to love at first.

18. FIRST WORD Maybe I was after something more definite, I don't know. If not a word, then a gesture. Something that said to me: Yahya, this is your mother, and she feels for you as you feel for her. But my mother lived beyond measurable things, Mister. And it was into her silence that I poured my own imagination.

Beginning, of course, with my first word – which, as my Sisi Gamal revealed to me later, shaking his head in that ox-like slow bow – spoke of what I'd been grasping after, trying to tease back what I'd lost.

My first word came in Arabic – *ab* meaning *father*.

19. ABSENCES *Father*, imagine . . . The long-lost *abba*. My other Mothers were appalled at the utterance. They hadn't spoken to me about Marwan, Mister, and were never aware of my secret visits. I realise now – and it's obvious in hindsight – that they'd decided never to mention my father in the house. And this, despite the fact, Mister, that missing people, lost histories and past troubled lives were thick in the air at the time. This was a house cluttered with the past. Stretch out a leg, reach out a hand, and you were sure to find some bit of something left behind by an earlier occupant.

By this I mean it was a hoarders' house, Mister. The middle floors, where the rooms mostly stood vacant, were filled with piles of discarded junk. *Not up there!* came my uncle's cry, *there are nails in the wood, broken beams – ach! – things will fall on your head and end you!*

It was true, there was plenty to bang my head on or scratch my knee. There were clothes and umbrellas, worn-out old coats, stuff heaped into every corner. Entire rooms were left colonised by mountains of broken furniture, sofa cushions, collapsible chairs. There were black bin liners filled with moth-eaten rags, tinker toys with knobs and levers on. There were books and brassieres, Mister, and much besides, all left to rise like the sediment of the house's history.

At first, when my Mothers caught me sifting through this trash, they'd have to trudge upstairs to fetch me. They gave up, soon enough. I discovered too many hidey-holes, Mister, and became too good at covering my tracks. *Fine go then – go!* they'd shout back up, *you go and stay – pfft! – and roll in your mess all the day, you goat-boy!*

My favourite thing to do, once I was old enough to climb,

was to tumble into these heaps of trash head over heels. Mostly there were women's clothes up there. I got a lot of joy out of them dresses, sequinned costumes and boxes of cheap jewellery. I found ruby-red brooches and chain bracelets. I liked to put on these silky things and watch the cheap gems gleam in the dusty light. I'd wrap my arms around discarded *kameez*, make puppets out of long socks and black fabric. I'd make masks out of wicker baskets, Mister, build forts out of wooden chests, and climb great ziggurats of suitcases and jump and I'd soar. I'd spend long afternoons like this, Mister, climbing over mounds of wire cable, and then, whenever I heard a scurrying under clothes, I'd follow the sound of chasing rats under floorboards.

The days felt very big to me. In my memories they feel limitless. Sometimes I'd sit for hours, crossed leg-over-leg, under a pile of mattresses, Mister, or inside some bunker I'd fashioned out of old chests and broken drawers. I imagined my escape into that darkness. Getting lost someplace where my Mothers or Sisi Gamal would never find me. And I've often wondered, Mister, why such leftover wares made me so happy. Stuff was worthless after all. Any real value had disappeared, along with the lives of the women who'd left it all behind – but then again, maybe that was it, Mister – maybe their absences left me all the space in the world to roam and to play.

So, there I was – a child whose beginnings were mysterious enough, whose reflections were never clear – making hidey-holes among other people's cast-offs: clothes, ruby necklaces, leather belts. I imagined myself into their shoes, affording myself new names, new voices, play-acted the parts of them women on the walls. I was the possessor of everything left unclaimed. And I believe, also, that these flights of imagination first kindled a sense of poetry in me. I'd everything any young poet would need – my boredom, my imagination – and these absences surrounding me, Mister, which felt like a gift.

20. BRIGHT-WIDE You can read from my recollections that I spent a lot of time indoors. Until the age of five or six, the world outside – the big bright-wide, as I thought of it – was at once forbidden and frightening. Whenever my Mothers threatened to take me out to the mosque say, or the Cash & Carry, or the park to expend some energy, I'd kick and snap and bite back at their wrists. The world beyond the house seemed a place people only went to quietly suffer and disappear into, Mister. And as a child, I wanted nothing to do with any of it.

My other Mothers plodded into the outside world every day. Cleaners or cooks, mostly. They took buses into the far ends for pay. It was left to my Mother Sadaf to mind me. And even she'd spend most of her time in the allotments outside, returning in sweat and mud and her same earthy stink. My Sisi Gamal, meanwhile, had a habit of disappearing every morning. He never told anyone where he was going. I remember seeing him hauling out a wheelbarrow often, heading out there with his books. *Gamal has gone to sing into bad weather . . .* was all my Mother Miriam would tell me. The old man returned in the evenings, head lowered, dog-tired. And my Mothers too, collapsed over the sofa, in similar states, Mister, somehow lesser in body, as if they'd left parts of themselves behind.

Who would blame me for drawing my own conclusions – and then drawing closed the curtains in every room? I tucked them in at the bottom too, Mister, insisting that daylight only threatened. I preferred the darkness inside the house. And my Mother Sadaf cussed me out for it. She'd stomp after me, dashing from one room to the next. *Get out, you little mutt, leave these curtains – boh! – I will give you big beating . . .* I ignored her threats, Mister. I'd watched my uncle spend an entire afternoon nailing little prayer plates to the walls. By the end of that summer, he'd fixed an *al-fatiha* above every door except for the ones that led outside. I considered the matter sensibly, and presumed that any door fixed without a prayer was a threshold I was never going to cross.

That's not to say I wasn't curious. And in fact, I scoured the entire house for a proper vantage. I used a kitchen stool and set it on the counter. I could sit and look out from safety. I could see the allotments. I watched my Mother Sadaf shambling about with her basket and shears. It was here that I realised what a proper bounty grew outside. My Mother Sadaf would have her neck bent in a full hedge of parsley, Mister, and thyme, and great big rows of green peas and self-sown poppies. There were mint plants and fennel. Wallflowers mauled over by slugs. And masses of ivy, spread over an entire outer wall, Mister, as if holding the house upright.

My Mother Sadaf very much prided herself on that allotment, Mister, which she'd been nourishing for decades by then. Most of what we ate was grown there. She even tried planting a salt bush, and a *ghaf* tree once. Even bedded a date plant, though she blamed its fibrous roots for wilting everything else around it. Even now, there was a patch at the back of the grove where nothing else grew.

– God perish this child if he does not bring his head out the window . . .

My Mother Fareeda sat with a white shawl covering her feet. She turned her gaze from me over my other Mothers, Mister, standing around the muddy allotment. My Mother Aneesa, sat squat on the hardened concrete, looked up and stifled a laugh and spat.

My other Mothers, Shahnaz and Sofiyya, were heard playing their radio out the second-floor window.

– Miriam! Miriam! came my Mother Shahnaz's quick voice. Bring the boy out with some milk and some bread. He will come *surely* if there is food!

– And Sadaf! Sadaf! called my Mother Sofiyya, shrill over the music. Have you checked the boy's teeth? You go! Go and check the boy's teeth in his mouth, the little scammer he is, you will *surely* match the bites in your weeds with the ones on my wrists, the *bitey bugger*!

My Mother Miriam appeared then, rubbing the blotchy window I'd been staring out of with her sleeve.

– Why don't you come out? she whispered softly. Get some air . . .

It was summer, Mister. Everything was in bloom in the yard and the cluttered kitchen had started to reek of rotten veg and stale bread. I banged against the glass with my fist, crying defiantly No! No! No! before barricading myself into the hole under the sink.

I could hear my Mother Aneesa's laughter. I could hear my Mother Fareeda whistle and mutter. And later, Mister, when we were all together at the kitchen counter, passing each other bowls and dipping ladles for soup, it was my refusal to step outside that they blamed for my developing limp.

– *Ach!* – there is no limp on the boy, went my Sisi Gamal as soon as the problem was pointed out, with a jutting of my Mother Sadaf's chin, at the table.

– Are you blind, Gamal? spat my Mother Sadaf. Look how he goes crooked!

– We think the boy may be bow-legged, said my Mother Fareeda wide-eyed at me.

– He is not lame! Not bow-legged! went my Sisi Gamal angrily, throwing a hand.

– He is walking to one side, pointed out my Mother Sofiyya.

– To the left side, added my Mother Shahnaz.

– Yes to the left, like the ground on this side is heavier.

They all put their bowls down to look over. I was standing with my fingers in the door jamb rubbing at the sides. My Mother Miriam then stepped forward and called me closer. When I approached she turned me around and peered at my knees. Gave a little twist at the hip, which felt tight to me, and sore when she twisted the wrong way.

The others crowded in.

– See the one leg – *pfft!* – it is bowed, sputtered my Mother Aneesa agreeing. He swings like this – *ha-ha!* – like a rubber band, he swings. Like a – *ha!* – like a little goat . . .

My Mother Miriam whispered for me to walk in a circle so they could get a proper look. I made one round in the room. They all watched, Mister. And there was an exchange of looks. In the end, even my Sisi Gamal had to admit it. I was walking in a kind of violent, jerking shuffle, which made them all recoil and mutter darkly.

– *Ach!* went my Sisi Gamal once I stopped. So what if he

walks this way? Let other boys walk in straight lines! This boy will walk in circles!

They all turned away, pulling faces, but went on filling their bowls. Despite their looks, Mister, I was determined never to set foot in the open. All this time, I'd been watching them. Seen them rush out into it, only to come back all sullen and dull in the eyes. Even my burly Mother Sadaf, Mister, who worked the yard so busily, clipping branches, spreading black soil under an ancient rake. The way she groused and complained at the earth gave me the morbid impression that I might sink into it, that someday the ground itself might swallow me whole.

My thoughts went to the locked-away Estella. And the way my mother, Mister, with her stillness, looked out the window sometimes at them blackbirds. She'd follow the lines of their flight in the sky, suggesting to me that there were elements to that bright-wide that were far worse than bad weather.

21. MOTHERS' SOUPS It never occurred to my Mothers to take me to see any doctor about my hip. They had their own special remedies. I remember how they'd creep past in the yard, and come back with some cup of muck-water say, sprig of elderflower, or even a bit of chipped bark. *Put these things – pfft! – put them in with yeast, and – ha! – celery in with his bathwater . . . or else . . . good rub with khafaf . . . No! The bones will grow as they will . . .*

All these mad panaceas, Mister, and sheer invention. It's a real mystery as to why the same creativity couldn't once have been brought to the kitchen. The only thing we ever ate were variations of terrible soups.

My Mother Sadaf might have been a gardener, Mister, but a

cook she was not. My old burly Mother cooked soup in huge batches in a big black pot she called her *cubby*. She made leek and lentil soup for our lunches. Carrot soup with a mountain of butter at bedtime. Breakfast was always bread and butter alone, with great fistfuls of salt. Salt went into everything. I remember sitting on the kitchen counter imitating the way the long slow sound of red Saxa with its *shhhhhh* . . . came pouring into the pot. That amount of salt, Mister, consumed as it was, every day for so many years, rendered all our tongues a little numb.

One of my Mothers would call us and bash a ladle come dinner time. I'd hear the others rattle down banisters, their bangles and bare feet going, their perfumes mingling with the steam coming off the pot on the stove, and then they'd all arrive with a bowl in hand to dip and to serve. They'd fly in and out of that grubby kitchen. Scooping mouthfuls between cusses, insults and bursts of sudden laughter. No table to sit around. And never any room besides. Not with all the filthy laundry, bits of machinery and gardening tools left leaning on doors, old chairs, and picture frames stacked against sad-looking cupboards. Instead, we slumped into spaces left on the floor in the telly room. Legs stretched out in front of the set – and oh, what about your British telly, Mister? Your bunk-spilling, myth-making machine . . .

Yes – so many memories of them early days appear to me now, with the lot of us, sat in front of the telly. It was more an education into what lay beyond my Mothers' house. Beyond the allotment even, and into the proper bright-wide. All them British plots. Them bawdy British comedies and soaps. Them repeats of your *Open All Hours*, say, or your *'Allo, 'Allo*, and

Steptoe and Son on BBC2. My Mothers used to wrestle for the remote, throw spoons even, and spill tea over the cushions, just to decide what to watch.

My Mothers Shahnaz and Sofiyya, for instance, preferred American melodramas to them soaps. The ones with waxy faces and flashy clothes, Mister – your *Dynasty*, say, or your *Dallas*. My Mother Aneesa preferred the savagery of animals or people – gameshows like *The Crystal Maze* or *Ready Steady Cook*. My Mother Miriam enjoyed *Dr Quinn* and *The Darling Buds of May*, while my Mother Sadaf, whenever she appeared from work in the yard, never really took any notice. Most evenings, my Sisi Gamal would emerge from his basement, all squinting and irritated by the light, to try, usually in vain, to convince my other Mothers to switch the telly to the *Nine O'Clock News*.

No matter what was on, Mister, I enjoyed how everyone spoke over one another. All that muddled English over the telly, mixed with Arabic and bits of Dari. They all tore at each other's plates, dousing hard bread into watery soup. I'd slurp whatever they'd poured for me. And then my Mother Sadaf might come around with her ladle looking to spill the last of her dregs, and I'd offer mine. I'd always laugh at the way she'd accidentally dip a tit into her bowl as she served out. She never noticed it herself. She'd just carry on boot-faced, orange blotches darkening the ends of her enormous breasts. Nobody else spoke up either. It was enough just to watch it happen, night after night, giggling and nudging at each other, but saying nothing.

After dinner, we'd wash our own bowls in the sink. My Sisi Gamal often stayed on with me on the sofa. If he still hadn't won over my Mothers, he'd storm off and head back into the basement: *Ach! – I've had enough of your idiot-box! You women watch what you want . . . You can forget me!* My Mothers would barely register, Mister, sitting glued to the set. The little aerial sticking out the back of it. That cold blue glow against their faces. My Mother Miriam looking down at me going *Owf . . . your uncle is so dramatic.*

22. IDIOT-BOX Your British telly taught me a lot, Mister. Not just because I couldn't read or write at that age – and it was, honestly, my only way of finding out what was going on in the world – but also because it was in front of that telly that my Mothers began to reveal themselves to me.

My Mothers' house was not a quiet place. It was laughter one night, weeping the next. Although, my Mothers tended never to dredge up the pasts of their own sob stories. What they complained about was lives here in Britain. How miserable they all were. How they loathed their jobs, Mister, the nothing-ness each day offered, in the kitchens, minding other people's children, and cleaning rich people's homes.

It was through the telly, Mister, that I learned how my Mothers saw themselves – or at least how they'd like to see themselves and each other. Programmes which never reflected their own likenesses, not really, but in the fortunes of your Penelope Keith, say, or Lynda Baron, my Mothers still found their own refractions.

For instance, I was very confused when once, Mister, in an episode of *Open All Hours*, your Granville and Arkwright pretended to be Chinese. They put bin lids on their heads and started speaking nonsense. My Mother Aneesa and Mother

Shahnaz started doing the same, balancing parathas on their heads and falling about in laughter. At other times there were scenes that brought a strange kind of nostalgia. *I remember this one*, went my Mother Miriam once, *when the old man falls in the stairs and hurts himself . . . my abba was a drunk like him. Sad like him too.* And my Mother Aneesa, Mister, would laugh and reminisce about her uncle Faris anytime *Mr Bean* was on. *Faris was good in the heart*, she'd say, *but he could not talk because – ha! – the policeman shot him in the neck!*

These stories were a way for my Mothers to tell of their lives, Mister. To speak of things they couldn't or wouldn't otherwise mention. They'd even assign British types to one another. Mother Sharnaz was Mrs Bucket as she was forever on show. And Mother Sofiyya was her lustful sister Rose. But they all had their stories, Mister. Some sibling cousins in Ramallah say, some Mohammad and his brother Hamed in Nablus, some Farouk and brother Jabir from Jenin, who reminded them of Del Boy and Rodney flogging cheap wares off a lorry in their youth.

23. WIDOWS I also noticed how the telly started patterning my Mothers' speech. Little expressions, say, that were once so beautifully mangled now began to flatten out into imitation. My Mother Sofiyya, for instance, after coming home from scrubbing floors, make-up smeared and eyes all baggy, made mention of some so-and-so, some high-waisted woman she'd worked for all day.

– *Esh* – such a pain, she'd say, bloody woman thinks she is a *queen-bee*!

– What's the pain, this *queen-bee*? my Mother Shahnaz would ask.

– Bloody *fussy, fussy* when there is nothing to *fuss*! She wears the white slippers, *ah*? I don't hear when she comes. And when she comes I am resting. For *two minutes* I am resting! But then she comes and says if I want to rest, I should go-home . . . *Bloody-cheek!*

– *Esh-esh!* You tell her *buzz-off*, bloody *bucket-woman*! Bloody *feather-duster*!

And they'd laugh, Mister, with their noses upturned in the air. At times it was this simple. Just the odd bit of idiom: *bloody-cheek, queen-bee, not-on-my-eiderdown*. But then there were other storylines in them endless soaps and period dramas and so on which seemed to stir old memories. Stories involving adulteresses and scheming wives sent cushions flying. Soups were left to go cold and spill over. I remember my Mother Sofiyya screaming at the telly once *Chi-chi! – this little bitch!* before barricading herself in the toilet, where we could all hear her crying.

You might put this down to sentimentality, Mister. I'm not so sure.

I say this because whenever a heroine ended up with what she wished, some love story ending in marriage, say, their moods would blacken. They'd sit with hands tucked in their laps, just shaking their heads at the impossibility of happiness. I'd even go further to say it was tragedy alone that satisfied them. When Samir was killed just before marrying Deirdre Barlow in *Corrie*, my Mother Fareeda tutted at the telly, as if to say he had it coming. I remember my Mother Aneesa too, her thick eyebrows trembling: *Good, the Samir*

boy is dead – ha! – with this bloody white cow? – Yes, yes,
better off dead than married . . .

My Mothers wanted to cast themselves as widows, I think.
Tragic widows, Mister, with cobwebs, and dead flowers in
their hair, surrounded by ruin and rubble. But I never knew
who or what they were mourning. I learned to listen, anyway.
To how it all came out in borrowed metaphor and phrases. In
stories that were not their own, but in which they made room
for themselves regardless.

24. WILE E. COYOTE As for me, I was all about them
cartoons. Your Bugs Bunny, Porky Pig and Wile E. Coyote.
I do remember acquiring a proper dislike for your Coyote,
though. Something about that Coyote, Mister, that felt rotten-
hearted and mean. He never spoke. Never said a word. Only
snarled and pulled out them placards. The others had little
catchphrases and tics.

I'd have liked to have heard Coyote speak, just once – so I
could hear if there was any good in his voice, or just badness.

My own tongue was supple then, receptive to rhyming
whatever. I'd hoot a few *beep-beeps* like the Road Runner as I
made my circles. I'd developed a habit of running around the
house, Mister, trailing my hands in every room, repeating
the odd expression. I'd speak into ornaments, stained chairs
and groaning cupboards.

My other Mothers couldn't stand my constant mutterings.
Even my Mother Fareeda, with her hair sticking out the back
of her head, would hobble out from her room just to scold me:
Dauling, dauling – we pray your mother sews your mouth
shut! – God willing! Even at such a young age, I understood

42

that, in their minds, Mister, my distortions were already bound up with Estella's, as well as the eccentricities of my Sisi Gamal – and in fact, I must tell you a little more about my uncle before we move on . . .

25. SISI GAMAL He was an odd bird, my uncle. It was my Mothers who used the word *eccentric* for him – *eccentric airs*, they said of him. Which I always misunderstood, Mister, as meaning something to do with his speckled beard. I know now they meant that he could never hold down a job. Of course, he'd never try. The old scholar was happy enough pounding the streets with his wheelbarrow and books, or else reading alone in his basement. But my uncle didn't seem to mind my whispering, Mister, and his shelves offered shelter for me to hide and mutter away under. There were no slaps or cusses to dodge in that basement, and so I began to spend more time in his company.

The library was my uncle's hideaway. The shelves smelled strongly of cigarettes. My uncle used to hold them cigarettes in the European style, between his third and fourth finger. It was the only Western affectation he had on him, Mister. Otherwise, he'd style himself to be an *ancient man of Erbil* – even though he couldn't have been over fifty years old: *I am like the venerable reciters of the Muqaddimah*, he said as he lit himself another, lifting his dried lips from a book, *who would breath in leaves of tobacco, and breathe out eternal works . . .*

Then, of course, there were his daily disappearances. I used to watch my uncle bolt out the door with his wheelbarrow of books, on top of which he balanced a foldable table and chair, all of it covered with a green cloth. I couldn't imagine any job where these things would be useful. Nor could I imagine him cleaning and minding the way my Mothers spent their own busy hours. He was too proud a person for that. And otherwise, useless.

I'd watch as he'd fuss over his basement library of books. Cataloguing mostly, placing titles in an order decipherable only to him. My uncle – together with my father Marwan, as I learned later on – had shipped these old books from Erbil. *Saved these books*, he liked to tell me, *from getting lost under bombs and bastard evils.* They'd all been packed away in the basement of my Mothers' house, and now stood in haphazard towers, Mister, some towers reaching the ceiling, and around the floor, ready for my Sisi Gamal to consider carefully and shelve away. I remember the smell of them, the dust, Mister, and how he'd always play music while he worked. Wild pealing strings, which sounded to me like a constant whinnying, playing off an old cassette recorder he'd balance on a pile near his desk.

My uncle was an impatient man. And he sometimes spoke very brusquely. But I think he enjoyed having me around. I was a pair of empty ears for him to throw a verse into if he wanted. And there was a need in him, I think, to perform for me. He'd call me over sometimes, and I'd skip to the shelf he was nosing. *Listen to this . . .* he'd say. And I'd watch him lift his heels, hear him clear his gruff dry voice, and lift his bedraggled chin. He'd hold two fingers in the weak light, I remember, and only then would he begin: *I am whose books are seen by the blind and whose words are heard by the deaf . . .* but then, as quickly as he'd taken another breath, he'd snap the book shut, sending a swirl of dust into my eyes, and begin shaking a finger at my nose, sending me staggering.

– And this is who – *ah?* – whose words are these that I have just recited?

I'd stutter, knowing nothing, rubbing my eyes – as if I could have possibly known!

– Fool, boy! Indolent! These words – *ach!* – this verse is by *al-Mutanabbi*, boy!

He'd always say these names as if part prayer, Mister – names I'd yet to discover on my own. But I can recall even now how whenever he quoted from one of these ancient poets, my uncle was able to conjure a forcefulness from inside him, Mister, something bigger than himself, and with far more vigour than his voice could normally allow. He could seem terrifying to me, but also impressive.

Back in Iraq, my Sisi Gamal had been an orator – some famous reciter of poems. He'd known poets in his time, as well as musicians and actors and so on. He told me he'd once been part of some travelling show, carousing through Lebanon and Libya, performing for rich barons and sheikhs, on desert stages and stately palaces in Syria. It was some grander side of my uncle I'd only ever catch fleeting glimpses of, Mister. He never liked to say all that much about it. He tended, like my Mothers, to be very careful when calling back the past.

And, oh – about the things I should and shouldn't have known . . .

Over the next few years, Mister, my Sisi Gamal took my education upon himself. He seemed genuinely alarmed by my ignorance at times, as if he'd simply assumed that his passions would become my own eventually – how exactly he thought this might occur, I don't know. By virtue of the musty air we shared together, maybe. And now, after years of baulking at what my Mothers would consume off the telly – the *idiot-box*, as he called it – it was clear he wanted to save me from similar contamination.

Fair to say, I think, that my Sisi Gamal believed he knew more about the world, Mister, because he'd studied it, just like he'd studied them books.

26. NOTABLE EVENTS This brings me to my uncle's more eccentric methods. That is to say, Mister, that my Sisi Gamal had made a routine out of recording events off the telly.

These recordings, Mister, made on VHS tapes – tapes which he seemed to have an endless supply – were clipped from daily reports and dispatches off the nightly news. If there was a crisis, say, another war, some piece of terrifying military footage, a media swarm over a famine or natural disaster, my uncle would point the remote and stiffly press the red button.

These tapes were collated together in rows of chronological order. He would stuff them, I remember, on a small shelf in the basement where the label read: *Notable Events*.

Such was the mass of stored footage, it must have gone back to the early 1980s-odd. And yet, again, nobody really questioned it. Even my Mothers, who surely must have seen how diligently my uncle worked, crouching near that VCR every night, searching for something worth retaining, said not a word about it.

It was another mode of his obsessive study, I think. My Sisi Gamal was always fixed for it, and his eyes grew squinty and dark, thanks to the dimly lit basement and having to sit watchful in front of the news. The only time I ever saw him at ease was just after the *Ten O'Clock News*. After he was satisfied he'd done all his watching and waiting for the day, and when your BBC2 sometimes aired old repeats of *Hancock's Half Hour*.

My uncle loved your Tony Hancock, Mister. That was the only exception to the regular British fare he used to chide my Mothers for. I think it was because that Tony Hancock used to utter lines of poetry, Mister, during them little asides he used to do. Hancock would look wistfully up at the camera while the lens zoomed in, and then he'd recite a bit of Auden say, or a bit of Omar Khayyam. My uncle liked when he did Khayyam. *Do you hear that, boy? – This Hancock! – Did you hear?* I don't think my Sisi Gamal saw himself in Hancock, though. Not like my Mothers did with their own heroines.

27. LADY DI There's one moment that sticks in the mind when it comes to this, Mister. It was in August that year. My Sisi Gamal called everyone down to the telly. The commotion of my Mothers rushing the stairs stays with me. All in their nighties, hair still in nets, legs smeared with night cream – that smelly *bitu* which I used to dip a finger into. And how they all came around and stood near to watch slowed footage of a crushed Mercedes under a tunnel.

– Princess Diana is dead, my Sisi Gamal said, matter-of-factly, drawing a line in the air with his cigarette, and then coughing.

Cannot be! came the chorus of my Mothers' cries.

– Dead. She is dead.

They watched the newsreader – might have been your Peter

Sissons, Mister, or that Alastair Stewart on the ITN News –
and my Mothers started saying prayers for the princess, all
kneeled and bent down, crawling to the telly with panting
incredulous breaths.

Mother Sofiyya started mouthing *How could it be . . . ?* and
my Mother Miriam brought me close to her chest. I noticed
her hijab had come loose and her hair had fallen over her
shoulders. I sleepily pawed taking some of it to chew on. She
held my hand away distracted, saying *She had two sons . . .*

Everyone fixed their attention on that rolling circus on
the news for them following weeks. Between prayers, and
over meals, my Mothers were completely gripped. The usual
chatter was replaced by doleful murmurs, sniffles and tears.
I barely understood the significance at that age. But then,
slowly the bright-wide began to feel a bit more real to me. It
became peopled with princesses, prime ministers, speeches
and sorrowful celebrities playing piano. Diana's death coloured
the air inside our house, the same way family tragedies do.

I started fetching my Sisi Gamal whenever any new footage appeared. Sometimes he even let me press the red button.
It's how I learned to take notice, I think. As I realised my
uncle never recorded repeated reels – the crushed black car, for
instance, the Union Jack at half-mast, the flowers piled high
over the gates, and the hearse heading up the M1. My uncle
taught me to develop a more discerning eye, Mister. See them
regular faces, people laying wreaths along that Paris bridge, for
instance, resting a million bouquets outside the palace gates,
ten-hour queues to sign the book of condolence, lit candles
along the kerbside, hanging pictures in the trees.

All of this we captured and logged, Mister, using blue biro

and labels, marking each completed recording: *1997: Death of Lady Di*.

My Mothers even took an interest in what we chose to record. Whenever the image of Dodi flashed up, say, my Mothers would always insist the red button be pressed.

– Royals are never allowed to marry Muslims, said my Mother Fareeda.

– She was killed for her Dodi, went my Mother Aneesa.

– Yes, yes – last month, I saw Lady Di in *Hello!*, said my Mother Shahnaz. She was in a boat with her Dodi. Another time holding hands with her Dodi . . .

– Britishers – *ach!* – bloody plotters schemers, villains! blurted my Sisi Gamal.

There was a murmur of grim disapproval around him.

– One day they wave their *merry-merry* hands at us. Next day knives will be drawn at your heart – *ah?* – at the throat, at the back – *Ach!* – this country . . .

– Of course, and see . . . said my Mother Sofiyya, see how they cry for their princess? But who cries for her Dodi? Tell me who sheds tears for Dodi al-Fayed?

28. MARTYRS What was I to make of your rituals for honouring the dead?

I've watched similar spectacles since – the death of a royal, a bad end to some tabloid celebrity. I've also seen how quickly everybody forgets. It happened with your Princess Diana too, Mister. And it's why I can never take it so seriously. These rituals are never private affairs, but public. You mourn your martyrs in masses, Mister, as if it were easier to revel in a spectacle than to acknowledge any pain of your own.

29. 1991 Which brings me back, one way or another, to my Sisi Gamal. The day I turned six years old, my uncle stood over me and went:

– Come, boy – I want to show you the world when you were born.

He handed it over then, another cassette labelled *1991: Gulf War I.*

– You play it, he said. And be careful.

I went to the telly, Mister, and slotted the tape into the machine. There were murmurs all around as my other Mothers watched on. My Sisi Gamal waved a hand at them, switched off the lights, and went to sit near my Mother Miriam.

I watched the tape draw itself in with a mechanical whirr, and the screen flickered. First, a quick series of images. Fast and continuous, which only lasted a few seconds. Then bursts of colour and low, measured voices speaking over one another. It was a sequence of clippings from the news of the world, Mister, crudely curated by my uncle.

– *Blip!* – *Cyclone in Bangladesh* – *Helicopters in Iraq* – *Crosshairs over desert bases* – *Scud missiles in Dhahran* – *A vehicle explodes* – *A house disappears into smoke* – *A hospital ward is splattered with blood and white powdered dust* – *A woman mouthing the letters A-N-O* – *Lockerbie, Lockerbie, Lockerbie* – *Yeltsin is elected* – *Freddie Mercury is dead* – *Smart bombs kill hundreds in Baghdad* – *Black smoke rising from a flat desert* – *Blip!* –

Faces interrupted the stream. Peter Sissons, Moira Stewart, Jill Dando, all with their different outfits, hair and the same stern expressions under studio lights.

For a few seconds there was only white noise, before again:

– Blip! – Apartheid is dismantled – Yugoslavia dissolves – last bit of the M40 is opened – Iranian Prime Minister is killed with a kitchen knife – Serbs murdering prisoners of war – Blip! –

And then over. The year 1991 faded to black.

When my Sisi Gamal switched the lights on, I found my cheeks wet with tears. I wasn't really sure why. I looked over at my Sisi Gamal and saw his face entirely unmoved by what we'd just seen. My Mother Miriam was the first to *tet-tet* at him. And then the others piled in, saying I was too young for such things. He shrugged then and went to retrieve the recording. He disappeared into the basement saying *This boy . . . he should know the world he was born into . . .*

30. CIRCLES It was the images of that hospital that lingered, Mister. There were circles of red on the white walls and the windows. I couldn't understand it – why anybody would bomb the sick and the dying and the already dead. I couldn't understand what my Sisi Gamal wanted from them tapes. But I knew, Mister, that there was truth in what I saw cut together that day. Somehow I'd felt it in the gut. And I was grateful for it.

31. STORIES Slowly, as if stirred for the first time, I came to realise there were parts of my own story being kept from me. Silences, Mister. Missing pieces.

There was my mother and father, Marwan. As well as what my uncle went off to do with his barrow. These were stories I couldn't imagine myself into just yet.

And then, of course – there was God.

There was Allah, Mister. And the Prophet.

But all this appeared at the fringes of my experience back then. In my Sisi Gamal's prayers. Prayers pinned above doors. And my Mothers' cusses. The Prophet was a notion. Like my father's absence. Hanging on, like some mysterious bird until I was ready for both to come and claim me.

32. EID I first came to suspect these silences hinted at something more when my Mothers took me to Eid. I remember how my Mother Miriam put a date in my mouth that morning. She told me it was Eid in preparation for breaking my fast. She told me that today was a special day for another reason. They were also taking my mother to see the Imam Ghulam.

Imam Ghulam was one of the venerated imams that looked after the local centre. He was the man my Mothers would go to whenever money was tight. They'd decided to ask the Imam to loosen the purse strings for us. They hoped, I think, that my mother's presence at Eid would help.

I remember trying everything I could to avoid going. I hid inside a suitcase in one of the upper floors. I knew my Mothers would have to clamber up three flights to come after me. My Mother Miriam had already gone ahead to help in the kitchen. And so, to my surprise, it was my wheezing Mother Aneesa who came and found me. She pulled me out from my dangling sock, shouting *I got you! I got . . . you!* between breaths.

I cried and bit her on the cheek. She dropped me and scolded me. She said I was a little *goat-boy worth nothing to anyone.* And I told her I didn't care. I didn't want to go outside. *Not in a million years, not in a millennium,* I screamed and flicked a limb at her. She threw me down and laughed. *Joo-hoo! – very big words for a stupid mutt . . .* and she hauled me away to get dressed.

She hung a white smock over me which reached my ankles, and a pair of boy's leggings which tucked into my socks. Then she palmed spit into my hair and combed it down both sides and pushed me in front of the mirror.

I looked like a tent.

– You must wear something new, she said. This will do it.

She replaced my dirty socks with a pair of white ones, and wagged a bitten nail saying I shouldn't run around with the other children at mosque.

I pulled a sour face and promised nothing.

The others were waiting outside, and I remember squinting stupidly into the daylight. They were all dressed in black shawls, Mister, and scarves, carrying food parcels on plates in clingfilm. Only after I stepped into the light did I see, Mister, standing there at the shoulder of my Mother Sadaf was my mother Estella. She'd been dressed in a long *chador* with her hair tucked under a cloth. I stared and stared at her. She seemed taller somehow. The cloth, black and plain, made her thin face look fuller. I didn't like that, Mister. She seemed so different from the distant busy-in-the-head figurine I was used to seeing sat by the unwashed window. She seemed changed, and a sickness welled inside me for having seen it. I watched her turn and follow my other Mothers past the hedges out front. It was as if she'd somehow betrayed our secret visits. She'd stepped outside into the bright-wide without me.

Go now, go! barked my Mother Sadaf and we started off toward mosque. My Sisi Gamal trailed a little way behind us. I kept looking back and saw the old man shuffling along in his traditional *thawb*, muttering to himself, and kicking at the ground. He had a carrier bag by his side, and it looked heavy. He kept squinting at the sky, waiting for some heavy shower to drop from above him.

Ramadan fell in February that year. It was grey and the streets stale and spoiled with puddles and rotten leaves. The closer we came to mosque the more coloured bulbs I noticed strung along lamp posts and trees. I clung on to my Mother Aneesa that evening. She kept pushing me aside, but I was scared. Everything along the short route seemed to frighten me. I felt my heart beating with every step. It was only when we came to them streaky-coloured doors, and seeing hundreds of other people shuffling in, some with other children, and as we stood in a line among the smell of old socks and bad breath, the noise of chattering families, and solemn greetings, did I settle down.

My Mothers went to take shoes off. *Give me your foot!* My Mother Aneesa wrestled my shoes off and tucked them into her own before pushing me forward. I noticed once inside that nobody came to greet us. A few older men said *salaam* to my Sisi Gamal and Mother Sadaf, but nobody approached my other Mothers. All them other uncles and aunties, Mister, some with other children, went about greeting each other like they were family. We seemed to be the only unfamiliar ones there.

My Sisi Gamal took me by the hand and began to lead me away. I tried to pull back to my Mothers, but I saw them filing in through a separate door. We were parted, Mister. I didn't know why. I realised I'd been deliberately left behind – ditched, really – and now I was stuck with my Sisi Gamal. I glared at him, angrily. I wanted to, but didn't dare, bite him.

For the rest of the evening, we sat listening to sermons and speeches about the local lot. There was an excitement about some announcement. But I was very bored and felt hungry during most of it. I could smell the steaming pots from the kitchen. My belly rumbled. And once prayers were done, my uncle led me back to the tables and went to greet some of the men he knew.

I remember getting a sense of what my uncle felt about these men, Mister, from the way he approached them. There was a man named Abdi, for instance, and when he came close my uncle squeezed my hand so tightly. And then another, an old man with a brown beard named Anas, my uncle delivered such a squeeze I almost shouted to stop.

These were little hints. Unconscious signals, I think. Letting me know: *This one – don't trust; this one – a friend.* I found it very useful to navigate the room this way. I heard my uncle introduce me as *Marwan's son* and he often gave a little tap near my wrist when he said it.

A few would smile when they heard Marwan's name. Others would look at me, and then look away, making some excuse and hurry off.

We broke our fast that evening. There were meals served on paper plates with samosas and coloured rice. There were other children about, but I avoided them. Instead, I watched close at how they'd finger their food, hang all over their minders, and just run about.

I sat with my Sisi Gamal in silence.

– Boy, went my uncle nudging me, why didn't you say *salaam* back to Mr Abdi?

I made a face like *what for?*

– *Ach!* – where did you learn such rudeness?

But there was no fooling me, Mister.

I knew my Sisi Gamal hated these people as much as I did.

After we ate, we went to wash our hands above the basin where there was a large framed photograph. The image was of these blurred figures in *salah*, some mass procession around a black cube. I pointed and asked my uncle what it was. All he muttered was *Ka'bah* . . . and shushed me. We went to put our shoes on, and I went again, asking what was under the black cover. My uncle explained to me, Mister, that it was a shrine in Mecca. He looked up, glancing around, and leaned toward me.

– And do you know, boy – what is inside the *Ka'bah*?

I shook my head, staring. His eyes glinted as he peered at them other men, bent down, slapping water, washing feet.

– Inside is . . . just a rock, he said and pressed his lower lip. It is a black stone Meteorite. From heaven above, boy! The rock landed in Mecca long before there were any Muslims. And now Muslims walk in circles around the rock. They walk in worship, boy, do you see?

I didn't see, Mister, but I didn't say.

– What does it mean, I said, the rock?

I watched my uncle collect the carrier bag from where the shoes were kept. He looked inside, checked, reached in with his hand, and then he put his trainers on.

– What means what? Nothing. Everything. It means what we make it, boy . . . *aha* . . .

My uncle held his palms at the people inside, praying, talking, eating.

He hurried me then, saying there was someone outside he

wanted me to meet. I was to give my name this time if it was asked for. And I followed him out into the alley.

33. WHITE FEET Outside it was freezing. That smock my Mother Aneesa had stuck over me was barely enough to keep warm. I moaned about it to my Sisi Gamal, who told me to stamp my feet to warm myself up. I went stamping the rest of the way.

In the alley behind the mosque there were large skips piled on top of each other. Litter was scattered all over the street. It smelled of rotten fruit back there, but it was too cold to hold my nose with my fingers. Further along, my uncle pointed to a man he recognised. When we made our way over, they shook hands very formally. I watched them turn then and stand beside each other facing forward. The man offered my Sisi Gamal a cigarette. My uncle declined and took one of his own, one of them thin ones. I followed the little ritual with fascination, Mister. They spoke Dari. I'd heard my uncle sometimes speak Dari with my Mother Shahnaz. They seemed to decide upon something. And my uncle handed the heavy plastic bag over.

I watched the man check, Mister, and bring out an old tape. I saw from the labels it was one of my uncle's. The bag was filled with my uncle's recordings.

The man nodded and said something I couldn't understand.

My Sisi Gamal turned and looked at me.

– Boy – say hello, he said.

I stopped stamping my feet and looked up at the man. He was younger than my uncle. Severe-looking too, with wrinkles at the eyes. He was feeling the cold as well and was bent rubbing the sides of his knees with his gloves.

– Hello . . . I said quietly into my chest.

– Hello, and how are you?

– I'm fine, I said stammering.

– I am Hamidullah Sayed, said the man. I know your uncle many years. I know your father long time back also. We all – your father, uncle, me – came together. In a boat!

He looked down at me and smiled. He said something to my uncle in Dari. My Sisi Gamal nodded. Then, seeing that I hadn't understood, the man bent down and whispered.

– I just say to your uncle that you do not look like your father, he said. But Marwan – he hated English weather – just like you, *ah?* – and me also!

I said nothing in reply. Just went on with my stamping.

My uncle and this man spoke a little longer while they finished their cigarettes. Then they said goodbye, and the man left with the bag of my uncle's recordings.

Only then, Mister, did I notice that this man – this Hamidullah Sayed, an ancient name belonging to my uncle and father's hidden history – had been standing all this time, talking, smoking, with no shoes on his feet. His trousers, which were much too long for him, were wet under his own heels. The wet ends were dragging now as I watched him crossing the muck with his bare white feet on the road.

I never saw the man again. I just remember my Sisi Gamal standing with me, Mister, watching him disappear into the alley before turning to leave. He took my hand and we walked away together. He squeezed very tightly as we stepped back inside.

34. IMAM GHULAM In the outer quarters of Imam Ghulam's offices, there was a small room with these dark wooden benches running along the aisles. I remember a great heap of shoes, boots and rolled-up balls of socks thrown into the entrance way. It was here that my Mothers had been asked to wait. My Mother Sadaf was inside with the Imam Ghulam talking things over. I remember thinking my Mothers all looked very tired after prayers. They were rubbing their calves, cupping their ankles as they sat about the floor, or on benches. My Mother Sofiyya sat with her legs stretched out by the door. Behind them stood my mother Estella near the window in her long dark *chador*. She was just staring, Mister, at the car park where people were saying their goodbyes.

Timidly, I went to stand next to my mother against the radiator. For a moment, Mister, with that confused little knot inside me beginning to tighten and turn, I thought she might lean over and whisper a word to me. Had my mother made a sound I'd have snatched her tongue and called out to my other Mothers to witness it: *You see – it's an act! She speaks!* But Estella, of course, didn't say a word to me. She didn't move. She stood there silent as ever, looking out the window and up at the sky.

The imam entered and the mood shifted. The imam was a very small man in a white *kameez*, and a cloth wrapped around a small forehead. He had on these half-moon glasses, which hung on a chain, perched on his crooked nose, with light speckled eyes behind them. One of his eyes squinted. His beard was brown and stiff, but also greyed at the edges. His right hand was balanced on a black wooden cane, which he quickly whipped at his feet as he entered.

Assalamu Alaikum, he said in a quiet, raspy voice. He stepped toward my Mothers, who nodded earnestly, and he put a trembling hand on his heart for each of them. When he caught sight of Estella still standing to the side, he went over to her, switching his cane to his left hand as he walked. He said in English how glad he was to see her. I thought a look of sadness crossed his face then, as if darkened somehow, when he turned to look and stare down at me.

My Mother Sadaf's heavy fingers came and pressed on my shoulder.

– This is the boy, Imam Ghulam – Estella's Yahya.

She nudged me forward with a knee in the back which made me stumble.

The Imam caught me by raising his quick stick and held me upright. He moved toward me then, bent down and peered, squinting over them glasses as if reading my face, my muddled features, but didn't say a word as he looked.

The Imam nodded, clearing his throat to speak to me.

– Say your name, boy, he said.

I was frightened, Mister. My breath wouldn't gather.

– Yah . . . Yah . . . was all I could get out.

The Imam drew down his wrinkled mouth then, and peered over at my Mothers.

– Old enough, but cannot speak, he said. And still he cannot read?

– No, no – not good enough, replied my Mother Sadaf quickly. He says some things, but it comes out wrong, Imam . . .

– But the boy must attend school, croaked Imam Ghulam. He should be with other children. Why he is not?

– It is difficult with him – you can see his mother. He is the same . . .

I looked up at my Mother Sadaf then. I saw how she raised a hand to the side of her head, making a circle with her finger, tapping the side of her ear. Imam Ghulam responded with a slower nod. They both looked at me then, with their faces hard and fixed.

– Idiot boy, said my Mother Sadaf.

It was as if all their eyes had fallen upon me at once, Mister. My Mother Miriam and Sisi Gamal, when I looked up, had a look of pity on them, and a kind of desperation that I'd never seen before.

And I'm not sure what happened in my heart in that moment, Mister. I only remember a feeling of hotness around the throat. It was shame, I think. As if someone had pushed my stomach too far down. I only looked at my feet and said nothing.

They all talked a little while longer. Imam Ghulam nodded in agreement over something my Mother Sadaf had pleaded for. And then we went to get our things after *iftar*. Later, I remember feeling very angry at what my Mother Sadaf had said. And I decided, Mister, then and there, that all my Mothers were liars. They'd have claimed anything if it meant squeezing a bit of money out of that old man at the mosque. And that Imam Ghulam – him, with his one good eye and breath like burnt toast – would have believed anything said about my mother and me.

35. LITTLE TRUTHS With Eid over, the house settled back into routine. The place suddenly felt very different to me after

that visit to the mosque, though the walls were the same, the ceilings still sagged, and the spare rooms were all still riddled with filth and mystery. The change had occurred within me.

For weeks and months afterward, I found the things that used to excite me no longer served. I stopped rummaging about upstairs. Stopped spying on my Mothers' rooms or swiping at their perfumes. Boundless and as bad-mannered as I was, Mister, I'd been given an odd glimmer of my own reflection. A vision of myself in other people's heads. I'd heard my name called among grown-ups. I'd been referred to as *Marwan's son*, and *Estella's Yahya*, and my Mother Sadaf's *idiot boy*. It all made me feel uneasy, Mister, as if I'd been marked somehow with a blot of permanence, or some dull colour on me, which I sensed might prove difficult to scour away, no matter how much I'd try.

I began to feel very sick of the old house. Its sad stories and names for me. It was what made me step outside at last, into the yard, for the first time on my own. I went along the allotments to help my Mothers Sadaf and Miriam clear the weeds out the back. I was given a garden hose and a can, and I'd wobble along watering the veggie groves and plants. Our grounds were some sixteen square plots, I remember. And with my natural swinging gait, Mister, I was able to water the entire allotment faster than any of my other Mothers could.

I took pride in that. I got used to working with my bow-legged limp, as well as the bright skies and the air above me. By the end of that summer, I'd spent as much time outside as I had with all the junk I'd found indoors. And I still had time for new discoveries. I found time for worms, Mister, flies and stinging wasps. My Mother Miriam would see me dig up the soil looking for insects, and it'd draw a smile from them cheeks of hers, and she'd call out at me: *Oh . . . he has changed his tune . . . just look!* I'd whistle at her and repeat in a little mutter: *Chánged your tune . . . change choon . . .* , to which my Mother Miriam would pull her scarf and laugh, before getting on with her weeding.

I'd finally got over my fear of the big bright-wide, Mister. I enjoyed being in the muck and the mud. I liked the smell. It gave my lungs something other than my Mothers' perfumes and dusty tomes to breathe.

Also, as per the Imam Ghulam's instructions, Mister, my Mothers decided they'd send me to school the following year. They'd understood I'd been neglected. And to prepare for my first proper year my Sisi Gamal decided to sit me down every weekday and attempt to pour books into me. By then he'd catalogued a great number, and there were only a few shelves left to order. We'd spend most of our days together that summer. I'd help with his shelves, and with great enthusiasm my uncle began to teach me what he called *the rudiments of poetics* – by which he meant the beginnings of English, Mister, as well as an introduction to basic Arabic grammar.

I was a quick learner with both – which seemed to surprise my other Mothers. He taught me reading and writing using the Qur'an and children's books. A few Ladybird books and your Blyton. I enjoyed them stories, Mister. But had a harder time with the maths since I couldn't make the relations stick between numbers. Not in the same way I could with most letters. I spent my time now tracing my fingers along shelves, Mister, cracking open some old storybook, and even began reading aloud what I could. I looked over names dipped in golden lettering. Names that sounded to me as if broken into halves and quarters – like al-Akhtal, and Ibn al-Muqaffa and so on.

My stuttering eased eventually. I only assume my lack of speech made it all spill the way it did. Entire sentences began pouring out of me after that. I spoke most of it into corners and floorboards around the house. I hadn't imagined anybody would hear me.

That was until my Mother Sadaf caught me sitting under the kitchen table one morning, muttering away. She quickly lifted the tablecloth to stick her head underneath.

– You, boy – what is it? What did you say – say it again!

She startled me, Mister. I coughed at the dust thrown up.

– . . . *Fed-a-yeen* . . . *fed-a-yeen* . . . *fed-a-yeen* . . . I repeated.

I was expecting a hard clout around the ears, so I shut my eyes and held my breath.

– Where did you hear that? came my Mother Sadaf. Her voice suddenly softened – where did you learn this word . . . *fedayeen*?

I opened my eyes after hearing how she'd swallowed the word as she said it. I told her I heard the word fall out my mother's mouth, during one of her riddles.

My Mother Sadaf wouldn't hear it. She sputtered at me then, insisted I was a lying *little mutt*, and that she'd give me a hiding. But instead of giving me a hard boot, Mister, she went stomping about the kitchen. She kept saying the word over and over: *Fedayeen? Fedayeen?* – a word, Mister, meaning *those who sacrifice themselves* – and it was clear from my Mother's anger that it wasn't a word I should never have uttered.

She went on cussing into the walls, Mister. But the more my

Mother worked herself up, the more I began to think she might have believed me. She seemed to forget I was under the table. She started speaking as if to Estella instead, scolding her for having said it herself.

– Marwan? *Fedayeen?* – *Boh!* – nothing . . . nothing but a bastard. Bloody useless coward . . . left you . . . and you . . .

I watched my Mother Sadaf then trudge into the yard leaving me there, Mister, under the table. I learned, I suppose, that I should have paid more attention to what I let fall out of my mouth.

36. CHRISTMAS I'll recount for you one more story. And then I'll rest a little. My arm is getting tired, Mister. And I'm hungry. Today is Friday and they're bringing the good broth – but I wanted to tell you about Christmas. The second-to-last Christmas before the end of the century.

I remember waking up that morning to an almighty crash. Some angry clatter from the kitchen downstairs. It was followed by another, and then another, and then a miserable wail unlike anything I'd ever heard.

It was Estella, Mister. She'd been out of her room that day.

This was after a conversation I'd heard that morning between my Mothers Miriam and Sadaf.

There'd been a change in my mother's medication.

– It makes her anxious, said my Mother Miriam. She frets so much when she is stitching, sometimes her fingers are bleeding. Sadaf, I am worried . . .

My Mother Sadaf wiped her nose and tutted.

– I don't have to say what it is, Miriam – you know what it is. Estella is turning the same, *same*, just like my Dina . . . *fiyuu!*

And then she made a gesture like something had flown out her head. I didn't know who they were speaking about, Mister – who this sister of my Mother Sadaf was, this Dina. And my Mother Miriam wouldn't tell me anything. Whenever I asked about my mother too, she'd only ever say she was troubled because *it hurts to love someone so hard – see how she loves you, Yahya . . .*

But that sort of thing no longer satisfied me, Mister. I'd sussed there was some deepening problem with her. And I was convinced that all these borrowed words, obscuring notes, went to work like them perfumes my Mothers used to waft to hide the festering smell in the walls. And so, when I heard the sound of that sudden crash on the morning of Christmas Day, I came running.

My other Mothers were huddled near the kitchen listening to the wailing, the crashing, the sounds of desperate voices. My Mother Sadaf and Sisi Gamal were inside trying to hold her steady. It was my mother, Mister. She was standing there barefoot in her nightie, in the middle of the kitchen, shards of crockery at her feet. She was holding a plate aloft as I pushed in to see. I watched as she suddenly hurled the plate at the floor. Pieces went flying. My other Mothers, Aneesa, Fareeda, Shahnaz and Sofiyya, shouted in alarm, as pieces of chipped ceramic scattered at my shins.

My Sisi Gamal lunged forward to stop her doing it again. My Mother Sadaf held her arms, trying to pin them against the wall. My mother's fingers clawed at her sides, and she started chattering so impossibly fast, Mister, it seemed like she was repeating a prayer from memory. All the while my Mother Miriam stood in front of her, arms raised, straining in a whisper: *Sister, please . . . sister, please . . . be calm . . .*

66

And the strangest thing about it, Mister, I remember feeling not a bit afraid seeing my mother that way. I just backed into the wall in silence.

I came to help clean the mess afterward. My mother had cut herself and I was sent to fetch a large bowl for her. When I returned and handed it over, I could hear the sound of my mother weeping. Other voices were keeping her quiet behind the door. My Sisi Gamal handed back the bowl. Blood swirled in the water. I went to wash it away and tried not to spill any on the carpet.

You must understand, Mister, that I thought this was the way most families lived. And if, like me, you believe madness to be a kind of blood relative, you'd see how it paints a picture of the world. It was everything else that seemed crazy to me and least of all my mother.

Honestly, when I saw her smashing them plates on the ground, my reaction was more *Well, why not?*

Even if she was pretending, putting on some manic perform-ance. To my idiot's eyes, Mister, her actions seemed totally deliberate and right. There were bombs being dropped on hospitals, after all. Circles of red against windows . . .

Anyway, these are the scenes I remember. My white mother in a passion of colour and rage, and me, by her ankles, holding her black cloth. Little rooms smelling of perfume and powder. Portraits on the walls. Mirrors everywhere. Verses hung above doors. The spines of books in the basement. Books with dipped gold lettering, books kept near my mattress. My other Mothers' rags over banisters. All them watery soups. Rugs laid on the floor where we'd watch the blue telly. The smashing of plates. My own mother's tears, my own mother's anger. And there was I, Mister, wide open in the middle of it. Groping around for leftover stories. And images of warfare and carnage. Them bombs might have been falling outside my window for all I knew . . .

So what childhood, Mister? I had apparitions instead, and masks behind masks. And I can see now, as I've been carefully writing all this out for you, how inevitable it was that I became what I am now. It's just as your Wordsworth said: *The child is father of the man.*

And there – the call comes. The dinner bell, the warden.

Have you had dinner, Mister? Stay with me a while and eat.

You won't want to miss it, the broth.

Boukie-Head

On to my schooling then. Another blaring muddle – and I'll continue now, Mister, with your man, Tony Blair – him, with that middle-parted hair, on the telly everywhere, on posters and the sides of buses. My Mother Miriam said he reminded her of a sock puppet, or a muppet *with his mouth in a mawp – Education! Education! Education!* was his famous repetition. And, well, there was a truth in that slogan for me. For there were three rounds to my schooling, three educations drilled in with much purpose and instruction . . .

First came my primary proper. Doldrums to begin with, for a boy so used to bare feet and bounding alone. I could tell you about some exalted moment, when I found myself among other children, recall some early triumph maybe, some dew-eyed glee at winning some juvenile thing – or I could just as easily recount some traumatic scene, where my small world collapsed in on itself, Mister, when some childish terror surfaced to halt and blunt my progress. I experienced both at that age. Tossed between wild happiness and surges of fearsome rage. I remember running, arms linked, proper gabby, eight or maybe nine years old, plunging into friendships, only to emerge as spit-swear enemies by the afternoon bell.

My own indiscipline was too far gone by then. And your British schooling didn't do much good. Instead, it was with recklessness, and sudden bursts of rebellion, that I attended my early education throughout.

37. EDUCATION (1) The money Imam Ghulam had promised came with certain conditions, Mister. My attendance at school being one. There weren't as many faith schools back then. Only a few orthodox convents across the water. My Sisi Gamal said he'd rather have me *a bloody beggar in the roads* than attend any C of E – so it was the local primary for me, Mister.

See me then, cast in with the rest of them. Into overstuffed classrooms, Mister, into multi-culture and grief. Them top-knot turban boys, them coloured-print hijabis, green skirts and grey trousers, a proper East London mire. Them fairer girls and whiter boys too, poor and po-faced, with most other children born second- or third-generation. Mostly Bengalis around our parts. And Polish. And Somalis who kept their heads uncovered. See young Yahya among them, Mister, with his school bag large on his back, thickly oiled hair combed backward. Still bushy, spit-parted to the side. It was usually my Mother Miriam who dropped me off in the mornings. And if she was too busy helping out at mosque, I'd have to suffer under my Mother Aneesa, who took me in her absence. Either it was a quick kiss into school from one of them, or a shove and a boot from the other.

I remember the sound of the teacher's bell every morning. How we all were made to freeze where we stood. That high-fenced cage dividing us between an area for smaller kids and the larger grounds for older children. I'd hear a hushing of voices and the rustle of backpacks and coats. Older kids would slowly file in from outside the fence. Each year group, Mister, as their class number was called by a teacher, would then follow into the building after them. Ours was a black lady teacher, Miss Hosannah. She was nice. See her ringing the bell with them walrus arms, and gather us to follow her inside.

I was head down, Mister. I was wary. I saw myself as an ugly stranger among this other lot. Prettier faces, it seemed to me. Who already knew how to speak and how to be. How to smile. Make friends. Say please and thank you. And all the rest.

38. OTHER CHILDREN What was obvious was how crowded everything had become. All them others with their packed lunches, pennies for tuck shop and that. They went about in huddles, Mister. Moulting together in classes. Even during break-out hours and lunch. I was shy around them. More attentive to the stuff pinned to the walls than the faces sat around me.

An entire side of the room, I remember, was covered with a grand map of the world. All mirror-like and vast. There were animals pinned to parts of it. Penguins in Antarctica. Toucans from Colombia. I remember the walls plastered with hand-drawn art. Pictures of holiday homes and jeeps and safaris. I'd always colour too far outside the lines to make it up there. My own pink flamingo kept bleeding into the black water. But I remember it was one of them malformed maps. The one where the rest of the world crowded in around Europe. Your lot, privileged and plump in the middle, with mountains raised as bumps you could touch. I could feel with my fingers the peaks. They were glitter-capped with white. And I found a patchwork elephant raising tusks. Curly-tailed lemurs holding Madagascar in place.

The other kids might have spent only a moment looking up them countries and climates. They'd point at some part, name animals and oceans or anything else taught them as being strange and exotic. I would never join in. Sometimes Miss Hosannah even asked us to stand on our chairs in front of class and declare what animal we'd like to be. One would cry: *I am a golden monkey!* before another would step forward and say: *I am an eagle*! And another: *I am a Bengal tiger!* Or again: *I am a rhinoceros* . . . I never knew which animal to choose.

And then, with the skittering of plastic chairs and the clatter of lunchboxes, I progressed through into state primary, Mister. Aged seven I remember them rushing elbows and repeating colours, word games and cusses. Names like Omid and Afua, Gemma and Lucy, all crowded around Ishmael, Vicky and Rajesh. And teachers too, Miss Marks and Mister Oliver, straining to keep us from riling too fiercely. I remember feeling a thrill seeing it all come down. Paint thrown against walls, fists banging on stools like goblet drums. I was one of them, Mister. Just another noisy child who liked the sound it made to ruin a thing.

It was all so bright and boundless at first. I'd even go so far as to say I made my first friends there. Don't remember any names just now. But you can imagine: it was the sort of state school where you could guess the names from the news of the world. Plenty of Somalis and Slavs in my class. A fair few refugee kids too, who wouldn't speak a word of English. I fell into the groups of huddled brown boys mostly, harbouring one or two white lads, whose quicker English I felt at home hearing. I learned to play with them. Get on with their playground games. Keep my voice level with others. Games like Bomb-Drop or Had, where *home* was the window by the blue door. Rounders was the only one the pretty girls joined in. We played with open palms as bats. Nutmeg Rush, where we'd vie to kick a bottle between shins, and then deliver beats to the unlucky lad. Beats came in flurries, Mister, hard and fast, so you'd get bruises. I wasn't very good at the games owing to my swinging left leg. But I fought hard for points and did well when fielding short, long or chucking. And I gave and received my beats like anybody else.

Eventually, other differences started to show. I fell often. And after the first few times when somebody helped me up, after the third or fourth time they didn't bother. I was also the only one out of the lot of them, Mister, who couldn't just point to the map and declare some neat origin. Everyone else had a certain place. Or a place behind this place – behind Britain, where their parents, grandparents or ancestors had come from, having plotted a dashed line to London. Theirs were differences that were fixed. And it's that thought alone, Mister, that tends to cast a sourness over the memory.

There were also many times when I noticed differences in proximity. During the dumb silence of that morning bell for instance. When it was all bent knees, ready eyes and dry mouths in stillness. I'd see how they'd stick close together. The brown lads standing with the other black and brown lads. Them black girls all sitting in a circle. I'd watch them with my black eyes feeling some murmur of injustice at having to stand alone.

But it wasn't other children who gave me cause to feel wary early on. It was more during them classrooms, after all this knowledge came instructed into me by them teachers – it was these grown adults, Mister, with their dipped forked tongues.

39. MILDER HERESIES My other education had come along by then. My Sisi Gamal had me memorising parts of the Qur'an, Mister. I'd started practising proper scripts, which I took to like pictures on paper. I'd learned to read beyond Blyton. Now I went poring over them old tomes with my uncle's supervision.

It was here that I concentrated. And as far as my uncle Sisi Gamal was concerned, Mister, my proper schooling represented merely deceit and distortion. Anything I learned there wasn't worth retaining. *Bloody committed*, he'd tell me, referring to them teachers, Mister, who'd tried plying me with Western history, *to the realm of wickedness and contortion . . .*

My Sisi Gamal would often fetch me after the bell. I'd notice how he'd stiffen at the sight of them prim uniforms we all had to wear – black blazers, black trousers and striped, red ties. And he'd always squint an eye at the crest above the school gate. *Hands over ears,* he'd whisper to me, *they will corrupt you, boy – ach! – confuse you. Try swallow you whole with their lies . . .*

It was for this reason, Mister, that I felt very guilty when enjoying myself at all. I'd spot my Sisi Gamal coming to collect me – usually long after the other children had since left – and it was head down all the way home. He'd have brought along his barrow, of course. The foldable table and boxes of pamphlets and books. My uncle would have me push the thing alongside him at times, telling me he'd been pushing the *bloody thing all over* . . . He seemed so intent on guarding me, Mister, that the very sight of me in my uniform seemed to get under his skin – *Apparatus of oppression, boy! They will want to mould you into their merry-merry shapes – so you must cover your ears – you cover them!* And I'd nod along, half listening, worried about the weight of the barrow rather than his warnings.

The only exchange we'd ever have would go something like this:

– Boy, what colour did your Miss say is the sky today?

– Blue, I'd reply, to which he'd throw his head and scoff at me.

– Blue? And is she correct?

And sure enough, I'd look up and the sky was not blue, but grey and dark and ugly, where the grey clouds would meet them dull dark towers and estates. To my tin ears, Mister, my Sisi Gamal had the ability to prise some deeper knowledge out the muck. It came from a proper curiosity, I think, but confused with a twisted and stonier habit for suspicion.

In the basement, my Sisi Gamal would sit me down with denser texts after school. He'd really do this, Mister: open up some heady old al-Ghazali in an attempt to undo what I'd already learned. I'd get very bored with it and end up watching my uncle hurrying about instead. I'd watch him inspect his shelves, Mister, and sometimes take an old cassette out and tighten the spool with a finger. Other times, I'd watch him pray. He'd bring his old carpet out from under his mattress. And he'd go at it right there, next to my knees at the table.

It's worth mentioning, Mister, that my Sisi Gamal went by his own methods for worship. My uncle's faith was entirely his own. Some days he wouldn't pray at all. And when he did, it was never alongside others. He prayed alone, Mister. And to what he blasphemously believed was *his own Allah* – as opposed to that other *big-eyed Allah for fools, those bad-men at the mosque* – and he'd only fall to his knees when the feeling compelled him. *Prayer should rise out of the gut,* he'd say to me, *like holy recital, boy – recited aloud like belly-breath – like beautiful fires!*

Sometimes, when the impulse came, he would grab me by the arm, and I'd pray alongside him. I remember how he'd make me rise quickly and bend down with him. And his was a fierce kind of ravenous worship, Mister, with his eyes pinched, and his hands trembling at the wrists, as if whatever feeling had come upon him needed seizing by him and holding on to before being finally released and set free.

I suppose it was an imprecise method, but it was also his intensity that justified my belief in him. It was almost as if my Sisi Gamal required a hot temper for it. And even then he'd pray to an ad hoc Allah – some half-invented God; he disguised his Allah, Mister, so that no Western bully, nor exacting imam, could recognise his faith as proper faith.

Well, a bit of that concocted worship must have spilled into me, Mister, because I took it on as an excuse for my mutterings.

He caught me wandering the halls, and asked what I'd been saying. I quickly made something up telling him I was reciting one of the ninety-nine names of Allah. He leaned toward me, doubtfully, and asked which one. I gave a start and said the first thing that came to me.

– . . . The . . . the . . . Allah the Great at Dancing and Spinning Around . . .

And he'd laugh at that. Hold his neck back and laugh.

Then he'd have me recite more of my made-up names for the Almighty.

– Allah sings? Allah waves his hands with what? – *Ach!* – oh, His godly fingers – *aha!*

My uncle didn't mind my milder heresies, Mister. Just as long as they weren't formed at some *English-English* school, I was alright.

Anyway, had he told me to stop I would have. I took all of his advice just as seriously. I'd sit for days at my school desk with my ears cupped and eyes squeezed tight. I decided the less I read off blackboards the better. And while I'm sure my avoidance was noted, Mister, my teachers always turned a blind eye. Maybe out of indifference. Or maybe they figured it better to leave me alone than to intervene.

Most of the time I'd sit in them classes asking myself questions: *How high were the minarets in ancient Medina? Were they as tall as the spire on St Paul's? Had he appeared in Britain during the reign of Queen Victoria would the Prophet have worn a top hat?* And then I'd come home most days throwing my blazer to the floor in triumph, confident that my time outside the house had left me totally uncorrupted.

40. MULCH These are childish memories, Mister – one boy's idiot mind. You must think this rambling story, letter after letter, has so far little to do with my crimes. But it's important you know what sort of mulch I came from, Mister. I was just another state school lad at the time. No mullah-led madrasas for me. And I'd even insist that any learning that mattered came to me from outside any recognised curricula. In that basement alongside my uncle, I mean – with him, and his khat-coloured teeth, flicking his cigarette at me, saying things like *Poetry is prayer in the dialect of Allah!* – seeing him laugh, scratch his head, and then disappear into them shelves expecting me to follow.

41. DA'WAH My Sisi Gamal burst into my room one morning and shook me about: *Boy! No school today! You are coming with me – rise quick!*

I nearly fell off my mattress, Mister. He threw me yesterday's clothes and went on barking at me to come along: *Hurry up . . . Hurry now . . .* I threw the clothes on but managed to pull on only half a sock before he came again, and hurled me out into the road. The barrow followed. *We will take the buses – quickly, take these!* He thrust a few papers into my arms then, but didn't say where we were going. My uncle stamped with a quick glance at the sky – the clouds were their usual grey. I watched him mutter to himself, then scratch his ears, turn and shut the door behind him.

After we caught the 92, our wheelbarrow rammed alongside the prams on the bus, we sat together with him on the aisle. I realised it was all part of some pre-planned excursion, Mister.

– You will learn eloquence today, boy. That is the great

balogha – art of the voice, recital. Now tell me – what do they teach you in this school of the ancient world, the past – *ah?* Speak!

I rubbed at my eyes, still tired, and slurred something about Christian kings and Celts.

– *Ach!* – in those big English books, these Celts? *Encyclopaedia Britannica?*

I nodded. My uncle shook his finger at me. He was rambling, and only ever paused when other passengers, whom my uncle would attempt to stare down, pushed past and sat in the seats surrounding us.

He leaned into me, hushed and serious.

– *All of history must be recorded in order to make it.*

He was quoting, raising his finger, watching me keenly, expectant.

– Ibn Rushd? I guessed, hoping I'd recognised it.

– Rushd? – *Ach!* – fool, boy! It is Ibn Rashiq who says this . . . Listen to me – these poets were once feared more than Christian kings, but you will not read that in their *Britannica!*

The old man looked irritably at the grey faces on the bus. It was like the living dead with their snotty, sniffing noses. All dull, dark eyes and nothing lips. I looked around myself, and spotted an old man with a Sainsbury's bag sitting reading the races. Another woman fiddling with her bus ticket and a packet of mints. Another, whose anguish was clear, with her hair like a fountain, skinny wrinkled arms, and whose face seemed ruined beneath thickly painted make-up.

I thought about my Mothers. My Mothers would have taken this same route out to work. It almost seemed like the shunting, suffocating bus journey itself was reducing all these people into half-light, slug-like, and absent-bodied. I felt sorry for them, Mister. I was about to ask my uncle why everybody looked so sickly, but then the white woman's voice on the Tannoy sounded – *Edgware Road* – our stop.

My Sisi Gamal heaved the barrow out onto the street. I followed with my arms stacked with his cassette recorder and papers. We went toward the station, where the junction branched off into four directions, and the sound of our rattling barrow became drowned out by the cars, buses and cyclists. We positioned ourselves opposite the station's main entrance, between two crossings. I watched as my Sisi Gamal started pulling the foldable chair out the barrow together with the table and a small wooden box. He directed me, instructing me to arrange the books in an orderly pile, the tin cup on the green cloth, the pamphlets on the left side, and the cassette player propped up on the right. He pointed at the cassette player, snapping his fingers at me to look.

– Boy, when I ask you to press it, you press play – understand?

I nodded quickly without a clue as to what we were doing. As commuters appeared from around the corner, my Sisi Gamal glanced up at the station entrance, stepped up to take his place on the wooden box, and clapped at his chest, clearing his throat. As he raised his two fingers into the air above him, it slowly dawned on me. My Sisi Gamal was a proselytiser. He was a street preacher, some pulpiteer, who'd come out every morning just to bellow a bit of verse into the ears of indifferent Londoners.

– Now, boy! Press it quick!

I scrambled to the foot of his wooden box and pushed the button as quick as I could. Out came that slow melodious whine, Mister. The music scattered as the streams of people began to thicken and crush alongside us. They were all dressed in professional garb, suits and black coats. Lifting his heels now my uncle began to recite surrounded by the press of these bodies. His voice changed. His fingertips played the air. He even brought his palms down slow, in the same gesture I recognised from whenever I saw him pray.

He must have seemed a proper kook to some of the people walking past. But me, Mister, I couldn't keep my eyes away. When he stopped it took me a minute or two to realise my uncle had stepped down from his box. He was telling me now to *pack everything away.*

Next was a Morrisons. We took a bus there and set up next to the entrance. He began again. Two fingers in the air, that high steady voice, his eyes squinting shut, and again I sat near the table completely transfixed. I listened dumbstruck and delighted at how he could soften and undulate his voice like that. How his voice would rise and make itself heard above the traffic only to then mingle with the music.

The poems were from Ibn Sina most likely, or my uncle's favourite, al-Mutanabbi. But, of course, I wouldn't have known that then. At the time, Mister, it all just sounded like a series of melodic loops worked into a sort of operatic register, a sweeping, skilful eloquence. Not that any of them booted commuters took the slightest notice. The stream of busy bodies rushed onward while my uncle sang regardless.

Even when it got darker, and the glare of the supermarket lights was the only thing that illuminated my uncle's frame on the overturned box, he didn't seem to care when two Asian lads shouted from across the road:

Oi – da'wah man! Da'wah man – you ugly bastard!

My Sisi Gamal didn't bat an eye, Mister. And while he might well have been a ridiculous sight to them boys, a proper sad sack turning up to these spots every day to be ignored, he'd transformed himself into a vision of some imperious orator for me. Just like them names he'd always pluck out them books – he was Jarir for a day, he was Ibn Rushd on the Edgware Road – reciting great peals to the masses. He was your Tony Hancock too. That melancholy Hancock off your British telly, Mister, staring out as the cameras pushed in, reciting for all the viewers at home.

It was a strange lure, for sure it was. And I felt so inspired. When the rain pelted down on our journey home, I asked my Sisi Gamal if he could teach me. I wanted to learn how to throw my voice that way. My uncle nodded at me almost gravely when asked, and in an oddly distant tone said: . . . *Yes, I will teach you da'wah* . . .

42. EDUCATION (2) It's no wonder, Mister, that it was here my second education properly started. Out on them heaving street corners and shop fronts, but also down in my Mothers' basement with my Sisi Gamal. Down there, Mister, where it smelled of dead wood, spit-up tobacco and musty bedsheets. Where the smell hung over broken chairs, old mattresses, kitchen appliances and wooden frames. It was under all that clutter, Mister, that my uncle started revealing to me the mysteries of his vast library of books.

His library was organised completely haphazardly. Cloth

bindings, mostly. And what looked like yellowing, tapered files among others. Some were tied together with string and bits of tape. There were articles too, old clippings from newspapers, magazines and poetry anthologies, all stuffed between weathered bindings. I had to climb over some to find others. On the ends of shelves labelled *Notable Events*, my uncle set big atlases against rows of recorded cassettes. And it was so dark in there, Mister. You'd have to peer close to the spines to read the titles. There was also only ever a single bulb swinging over my uncle's desk. It gave the place a kind of steady stillness. As if the desk itself was the only thing protected against the darkness. From then on, it was the only hidey-hole I ever needed.

Begin again . . . came my uncle's whisper. I'd hear his voice from behind them toppling shelves. Sometimes all I would really see of him were his hands. I would glimpse his ringed finger stirring a pot of yoghurt. *Begin again – give it nostrils, boy! – Back of the throat – repeat again!* And see the changes in me, Mister, as I sat and listened and read. I'd gone from being some illiterate lad obsessed with that idiot-box, hiding under all that clutter in the house, to now having my head filled with ancient metre. And something deeper, something more fundamental, too. I could feel my body firming. Muscles in the throat, I mean, becoming reformed under new intonation – all that *daud*, *qaaf* and *ghayn* – which sounded out of me now, Mister, in notes of unfamiliar breath. And see my uncle in his usual habit, chin rested on his hands, his smeared muddy glasses, eyes small, dark and heavy, set on texts from them circular schools, *muru'a*, *qalam*, *qira'at*. – I can still hear his voice buttered with all that creamy yoghurt: *Like prayer, boy –*

like history – not enough to know the beginnings and endings of things – you must feel it echo in the telling, and the re-telling, and the re-telling again . . .

Poetry, Mister, was my uncle's method for explaining absolutely everything.

43. A POET'S DIPLOMA I thought I was the luckiest boy alive, honestly. For what followed was a hotch-potch history of poetic technique. Along with all them exhaustive readings from my uncle's Qur'an – which I began to read as a poet might, Mister, paying attention to the allegory, the shifts in the language, the use of metaphor and so on, and inversion – my Sisi Gamal would press a finger into my chest, alerting me to how each shift meant an alteration in delivery. *Must take a breath there*, he'd say to me, *there is a change in the tone, so change your breath again* . . . And so I'd breathe again, lift my chin, fill out and strain just to keep my shoulders from buckling.

Alongside the Qur'an, the first of many big books, the *Mu'allaqat* came next. All them poetic odes written in the *jahiliyya*, Mister – a time before time. The emphasis was on the sound out the mouth. My uncle had me memorise and then watch from the aisles, flapping a finger whenever I fumbled. The old man pulled a thousand years off the shelf at a time. It was like being shown a thousand histories at once, Mister. We went from the *Mu'allaqat* to the linguists. From al-Razi to Abu Ubayda. And then to the Ummayads and all them fierce, fouler-mouthed Abbasid poets, whose court scribes performed war stories for caliphs. I learned how them ancient poets did battle in oratory. Crowds would gather to watch a man pierce a heart with a bit of wordplay and a sharpness of style. They'd be-friended explorers and foreign Junkers. And they'd bring back stories from far-away travels. They all had such heroic names like Ibn Hazm, Ibn Zaydun and Abus Salt. And their words, Mister, were so admired that each of them had their own scribes dedicated to recording their every utterance.

I tried to recite these poems in the way it sounded inside my head. And while my voice, newly unleavened, could climb higher than even my uncle's, Mister, it was my crooked posture that bothered him most. *Too loose in your stance, boy – ach! – you will have to rid the rudeness from the sides.* He was relentless. I'd even receive quick whacks at the knees on occasion. And while it didn't hurt, it made my legs shake from the effort it took in toeing forward. He was always on at me about shaping my body. *You must let the sounds boom-boom through . . .* For there was a part of my uncle, I think, that expected them ancient rhythms to bring some realignment out in me. Problem was, my modest lungs could never draw enough air to imitate my uncle's busting oratory. And so, whenever I failed to match his measure, my uncle's hard eyes would stare down at me, Mister, out from behind them soup-speckled glasses, at my unbalanced posture, my slanted shoulders, at the way my whole body slumped to the left, with growing frustration.

I was trying, Mister. And while I couldn't control the dis-jointed manner in which my body had decided to grow, I'd now become an avid reader. Even then, my Sisi Gamal was always careful about what names he picked out the library for me.

Boy – did your teachers teach you how the devil was cast

out from heaven? I shook my head at this question, asked as my uncle returned from some rummage in the furthest aisle. He came back carrying something retrieved from some discarded heap in the back. He came carrying it with purpose. *Bloody shame*, he said, smacking his lips and tutting, *their Milton is close to Ibn Hazm – ach! – the fools at your school will do no good for nobody . . .*

He cracked open the book he'd found and showed me an illustration of Satan wing-split and fallen from some heavenly light. The ignorance of my schoolteachers often left my uncle horrified, Mister. It also gave him reason enough to introduce me to your Western writers. For instance, he demanded I get to grips with the proper canon as soon as possible. He handed me some chewed-up copy of the *Junior Works of Homer* once, stuffed with depictions of giant heroes and meddling gods. I remember reading a version of *The Odyssey* with children's illustrations of Telemachus stringing his father's bow. He even found ways to bring me bits of Shakespeare, Mister – at that age! Made me recite little bits of Viola say, from a Ladybird book of *Twelfth Night* – which, incidentally, I can still recall: *O Time, thou must untangle this, not I. It is too hard a knot for me t' untie . . .*

In his roundabout way, Mister, my uncle revealed to me texts he'd proper regarded. And was just as resolute with the ones he did not. He'd always tell me Shakespeare was a *genius the size of al-Mutanabbi*, and your Dante was *nothing but a plagiarist – ach! – pilferer of old spiral stories!* All he really wanted, I think, was to get me used to a variety of rhythms. Keeping me limber and elastic in the ear. Both Western and Eastern literatures, Mister – as well as the stories of them old

Ancient Greeks, who, with special exception, *belonged to everybody* . . .

I suppose it kept my tongue fluent too, and my brain useful. I concentrated on getting my posture right, imitated my uncle's style, sticking two fingers up in the air and swirling. A roll of my shoulders. Eyes upward. Deep breath in. And he'd stalk around me, inspecting and correcting my stance – *Good, good, speak up from the gut, boy – the belly, boy – You will attain a poet's diploma yet – now begin again!* I'd pose for him, while his tune played out from his cassette. And so, by the time I got to the *nahda* poets, Mister, I felt my tongue soaked in all colours and richness. As if a good sort of fate hung before me now. As if poetry had been there all along.

44. BLACK DEATH It'd be many years before I'd discover the likes of Rilke and al-Barudi, Mister, but my beginnings were here, during this invigorating year, when every book was followed back to the proper breathwork of the Qur'an.

But I'll admit here, Mister – my Arabic stalled somewhere around the nominatives. I just couldn't keep up with the language. Eventually, tired and irritated, my uncle relented and gave me English translations to read. He said I should be careful with translations, however. The quality of interpretation, he said, could mean the difference between *neighbourly embrace* or a *limp English handshake* . . . and any bad translation would be *no good for nobody* . . .

And, maybe, now that I think about it, Mister, this was what he feared might happen to me. That somehow *I* might become a *bad translation* – some half-baked boy, skipping along without any sort of justification. My teachers had shown no interest in what I could become. And I was so obsessed with my own education that I thought even less about them. I started bringing books into school. I'd open some translated work of folklore, say, about the monster Nasnas, for example, a creature with half a face and only one leg who'd leap about to devour his prey. I'd have it on my lap under the table, Mister, while all my classmates plodded on with their Pepys and the Black Death.

All this made it difficult for me to make any friends. Though, honestly, others my own age already seemed far distant. They'd all gone from playing rounders with their palms to playing Snake on their phones. Oily-skinned lads who'd exchange glances with girls, and them girls, Mister, collars looser around their necks now, would gaze back at them fitter lads, the ones with their shirtsleeves rolled up, forearms exposed and shorts hitched up to their arses. I was confused with these new lines of attraction. How they'd all sit during break-times buzzingly discussing who was for who, and what type was for them, while all I did was sit somewhere, crossed leg-over-leg, studying *usūl* cycles of Islamic orality.

I was bullied, yes – my differences didn't go unnoticed. There was this one bug-eyed boy with wet hair and freckled cheeks who liked to batter me in the back with his elbow. I'd started double-jumpering by then. Just so his beats wouldn't leave bruises. Craig was his name, a full ten inches taller than me. He'd sniff me out in them corridors, and him and his goons would call after me: *Oi! You faggot! Oi! You little spaz!* And they'd all walk behind imitating my limp, calling me out again: *Oi! Batty-boy* or *Oi! Boukie-head* or whatever. I learned to glare back. Push them off me. Run away and continue elsewhere.

So there – I'm not saying it was easy. Far from.

I turned very solitary after a time. Even at home, my Mothers would notice me skulking past the telly room. They'd call after me: *Yahya! Sit down and come watch with us!* Or else at the dinner table – where I balanced books on my knees under soup – my Mother Aneesa would flick a stubby finger my way: *See him? This one will not look up at us – pfft! – Look up from your books, Yahya! Boys should be outside – ha-ha! – playing with other boys!*

Eventually, my Mother Miriam would come find me. She'd ask if anything had upset me at school.

I'd lie and tell her I was fine.

– So, what did you learn at school today?

– Black Death, I'd say, without another word.

Ouf . . . she'd say and leave it at that.

I wouldn't have been able to explain, I don't think. All my Mothers assumed I was the same boy they'd bundled in at birth. The same goat-headed lad, Mister, who'd come into the world feet first, who'd stuttered in speech, and who'd drawn the curtains to keep in the dark. But now, my second education was proving different. They couldn't tell whether I was an idiot boy posing, or a scholar-to-be behind my uncle's books. My Sisi Gamal was the only one who knew better. He knew how much of a learned head I had on me now. It was one that, after tearing through countless texts and recitals, was starting to get filled with all kinds of ambition.

45. FORTIFICATION You asked if I was too young for it. Probably was, Mister. Much too young for half the stuff my uncle taught me. But age made no difference to my Sisi Gamal.

He aimed to fortify me, I think. Make sure I was equipped for a world which sought to bag me and turn me out.

He taught me to resist the slackening in the body, of course, but also when to give way in the mind, slip away, and be elusive. It eased his nerves to see me strap to my stomach some Ibn al-Walid or Bashar Ibn Burd – poems in a style of *badi*, Mister, relishing repetition, kinks, little knots in the language. He made me read the likes of Zaid al-Harb, a Kuwaiti poet. Told me I should read al-Harb to see why them oil fields had burned. And he'd sit me down, slot in a tape. *1991: Saddam torches wells.* And make me watch your Michael Buerk, long black plumes trailing behind him.

I had to figure it out for myself, Mister. He wanted me to understand that some things could be remade with poetry, while other things couldn't. *Your father would want you to know*, he said, *Marwan always told me: Don't look away, Gamal – read the world like you read faces . . .* I think he wanted me to see more than I possibly could at the time.

46. FATHER (MYTH) At this point, Mister, I should mention that I knew very little about my father. Sketches alone. Nothing you'd call a proper picture. I can list the few things I did know:

1. Marwan Bas was born in Erbil, Northern Iraq – same as my uncle.
2. The two brothers arrived as refugees in the UK – my uncle: *There was trouble at the border – we had to go by sea . . . British said: you are welcome! Come in!*
3. Marwan Bas was *handsome and tall* – my Mother Miriam.

4. Also, *no good for your mother, the coward, took liberties*
   – my Mothers Sadaf, Fareeda.

It about sums it up, Mister. Snatched fragments only. Over-heard conversation. Little hints of my father's life. Anything beyond that I read into my own mother's whispers: *Dear one . . . have I told you about . . . when my Marwan, Marwan met a liar . . . a liar he didn't believe wasn't dead . . .* Little of which I hoped to string into any sense.

I knew another thing: my father, like his brother, had been a hoarder. My Sisi Gamal would sometimes sniff out a book for me, hand it over, and then after a pause say to me: *This here belonged to your father . . .* eyeing me watchfully as he presented it.

It was during them bus rides out for *da'wah* that my Sisi Gamal started saying more. It came after a full morning of oratory, after I myself had climbed onto the wooden box and delivered something from one of my father's books.

– Did my father like this poem? I asked him.

Sisi Gamal glanced over at the book – Abdullah Pashew, a Kurdish poet.

– Of course – Pashew is from Erbil, our infinite city, a city written into songs. It was Pashew who translated the great Pushkin into Kurdish – *ach!* – it was him who did that! Your father and I, we lived on the same road as Abdullah Pashew. We did not know his family. But we were all brothers as boys . . .

My uncle took a moment to jam his mouth full of green khat. I listened as he leaned on his barrow. He was spitting while speaking, flinging great gobs of chewed khat onto the road – *thoo* – as he went on:

– Marwan was a good reader. But he was like you, boy. Like Sindbad too. Blowing this way and that. No discipline. Marwan went in all directions. Only *silly-silly* things he read when young – Nasiruddin stories, tales of Mamelukes and then, later, the Bedouin women with big *bazazz*... But in those days you could find anything in Erbil – if you wanted al-Farid, you could find him. You want even al-Radi or Dildar, you find them too...

The bus arrived and I followed my uncle. We gathered our things and sat while my uncle continued between chews:

– But – *thoo* – when we came to this country he changed completely. Lost his head inside more adventures and nonsense. He put down his Nasiruddin. Picked up bloody *Crusoe* – *ach!* – obsessive! Indiscreet! He became lost in these *English-English* novels – *thoo* – all about criminals, thieves and adventures – *thoo* – these stories, *ah?* These voyages by the sea, great cross- ings, life and times tales... Marwan went mad for big lives, always wanting to go so far...

He spat into his palm the blackened leaf. I glanced at the passengers, who ignored us. I was holding my uncle's pamphlets and cassettes. I drew them all closer to me.

– What happened after you came here? I asked.

– Me – I found work, but no good. Marwan, he could not work. He got sick.

– Sick?

– He got sick, boy – *thoo* – why all these questions? Wait a minute, I am telling it...

He looked around at the other passengers, peered and muttered a cuss, before returning to me.

– Marwan got sick. He said once he could sometimes see

things that were not there. I tell him – *pah!* – *look what you are reading!* A head sick with stories. But it got worse. He was with your mother. These two met when Estella was teaching. It was at a school for children in Tooting or somewhere – she helped filling forms, more. Anyway, she was completely in love with Marwan. Marwan could speak to her. He would tell her those same stories of Mulla Nasiruddin – stupid tales, boy, which you don't need to bother with, for children – but they made her laugh. I could hear it from the other room, this laughter. When Marwan got sick, the mosque took them both in. Gave room to live at Forty Road. Gave dishwashing, sweeping floors at the mosque, so they could be married. Estella converted for him. She was happy to do it. But by then, he became sick of everything. Even her. And she with him. This country, boy, it got him bad in the head.

My uncle fished a tissue out of his pocket and wiped the remaining leaf from his teeth. He wiped his soapy beard with it. He then settled into his seat and leaned away. The world had suddenly erupted outside. It was raining hard smacks against the glass, the sound of cars and buses tearing angrily past the window.

– Anyway, Marwan was not the only one. Many others went. There were no pictures back then. We knew nothing about the war – the BBC never showed pictures from the *fedayeen* side. We just heard stories. These men were warriors, they told us. Protectors of our women, building new lands in the desert. And so, when Marwan, like the others, heard this, they wanted good strong men to fight with them, for *Allah* . . . He heard their stories and wanted to be a hero like them. He wanted a bigger life, boy. Do you understand what I say?

The bus turned to stop at the centre. My uncle rang the bell.

– He went to . . . fight? I stuttered.

– *Ach!* – boy, your father was not a fighter . . .

My Sisi Gamal sniffed and peered at the turning clouds outside.

– He wanted to play his oud. Your father was a magnificent musician, boy – how he could play! He wanted to play for the *fedayeen*, for Allah he wanted to dedicate his gifts. But I said to him: *Which Allah wants you to play dead in the desert?* He told me: *There is only one Allah* . . . And then he said he will try for *paradise* this way – with his oud, and with his *other brothers on the path* . . .

The bus shunted and threw me momentarily. The cassettes I'd been holding fell and scattered across the deck. I gathered them in time to step off the bus, where my Sisi Gamal was stood waiting for me. He was shaking his head.

– Problem with your father, boy – he believed in paradise. Marwan came to believe these things existed in this earth. He lived for fantasies, boy. So easily, like nothing. Other people's stories became his.

He tapped his wet temple and snorted at the rain.

The rain was chucking down now, plastic bags floating in drains, strangers scurrying under shelters.

– And you didn't know, *ah?* he said, pointing at my chest.

– What –?

– The music, boy . . . the tapes – there, there!

My uncle was pointing at what pressed against me.

– There, boy. You have Marwan and his oud in your arms. The cassettes he recorded for all his *fedayeen*, and his *big-eyed Allah* and his Estella too. He made those recordings for her.

94

I stared down at the unmarked cassettes encased in scratched plastic.

My uncle watched me straining to make sense of what he said. Seeing me stand there, blinking and confused in a puddle.

– *Ach!* – this boy is still very dim-witted, he said sourly.

He moved off then, looking for cover to push the barrow under. The next spot was down the way. I followed him, trying not to crush the cassettes under my arm.

47. PARADISE (MYTH) Could you imagine, Mister? Learning a thing like that blundering out of a bus, arms piled high with cassettes from my father. I don't remember anything about the rest of the day. I don't recall what poems my uncle recited, nor what I fumbled with in my own readings. I can just imagine pressing my ears under that rain. All my attention drawn to them tinny songs, my father's oud, echoing out of that little speaker.

My Sisi Gamal told me later, Mister, that my father sent them back the first years he was away. This explained the faint numbers on the front.

Little scratchings denoting the years recorded: first, *1992*; *1993*, two cassettes reading *1995*, and another, a cracked cassette marked *1996*.

– Your mother never listened to them, he said. She refused to listen, turned away.

– And . . . no more after *1996*?

– Nothing, boy. *1996* was the last your father sent.

I immediately started my own system of classification. Borrowing a pair of scissors, Mister, and sticky tape, I listened to each cassette and added a description next to the year: *1992 (oud, drumming)*; *1993 (oud, flute, second flute, chanting)*; *1994 (just oud, no voice).* Most were continual sessions that lasted entire cassettes. It was *1996* that I liked best.

I remember finding an empty room in the upper floors to play them in. It was there, in one of my Mother's cluttered chambers, that I noticed the sound on that tape was damaged. Sections would skip as if a part of the film had been rubbed away. And there were other differences. The song on my father's *1996* recording was what's called an arhythmic *nashid*, Mister. A communal song sung to a jolting pattern. Voices could be heard in the background. None of them really singing. But I could hear them under the drums, reciting as if deliberately off the beat. Male voices. Shuffling bodies. The barking of dogs and birds trilling. All of it part of some low, disharmonious tune. A kind of *zoun . . . zeen . . . zeen . . .* recorded in the wild somewhere, at an unusual pitch, as if there was a deeper rhythm I couldn't quite follow.

I unwound my Sisi Gamal's headphones, plugged them in and pressed the foam against my ears. I cleared space on my Mothers' littered floor and lay back, Mister, and focused.

Quickly, I became lost in the discordant music. My eyes fell back. Off in a trance with it. Deep into wonder, Mister, at the fact that I was listening to my father's oud, his music, his memory, and – and that, as my uncle had said – did I hear right? – my father had been seeing visions before he'd left – *seeing things in his head,* was how he put it.

Difficult to know where my father might have been during that *1996* recording, Mister. There was no other marking on the cassette, and my uncle had told me nothing else.

But I could imagine – I could see faces as I lay there. The

faces of those who might have been sitting next to him – the flute player, the drummer. A circle of men sat around in the desert. Faces in shadow. Narrowed eyes. I could see them with me. Proper see – like a real-in-the-world vision around me. The scene played itself out as I listened. Each face emerging into that damp little room. Hands taking turns on the drum. A fire lit inside a cleft in some distant range in the wall. A ritual song. The repeating rhythm, taken over by a second voice, and the drums giving way to whistles. I pursed my lips to make the tune. And then the sound of dancers. Yes – I could hear bare feet over sand. I could see them too – throwing dust off the ground, the whipping of the cloth, the fast *thwap-thwap* on the carpet. Just as the cassette stopped and wound back. Leaving an abrupt silence.

I opened my eyes and came to breathlessly. My sight had to adjust to the room. The mess all about me. The cassette player next to my feet. It was performances on these dusty tapes, Mister – singing, dancing, sounds in the background – that arrested my imagination so completely. As much as the music itself, I enjoyed the visions my father brought out of me. These flights, Mister, these apparitions, plucked out my head like a new set of strings. It was exciting. I could feel myself changing. Like a further unfolding.

And I'll tell you now, Mister, it wouldn't be the last time I'd find myself locked in a room with nothing but my imaginaries.

48. REPAIRS, REPAIRS, REPAIRS Well, I had a new rhythm in my head. I heard it as I recited, practised and studied. The problem was, Mister, at the time I could barely think over the din surrounding me. The repairs had started. That summer it was near constant drilling, banging pipes, shuddering walls and my Mothers shouting over everything.

I'd complain about it. And got so irritated by the noise that I went all the way to them upper floors to get away from it. I sat with my headphones on and pressed, Mister, listening to my father's *zoun . . . zeen . . . zeen . . .* over and over again. My Mother Shahnaz came calling up at me sometimes: *Pick a nail and help with it – ah? Would it kill you to lift a bloody finger?* But I couldn't see the point in helping, Mister. It was obvious the house had given in.

Imam Ghulam's money had arrived too slow to save it. Delivered in envelopes too, in only part-sums, much to my Mother Sadaf's frustration. *Maybe you should ask Gamal to send one of his bloody letters . . .* whispered my Mother Sofiyya once.

I remember how everyone was brought into the yard. My Mother Sadaf was showing them what needed doing, urging them to join her and set to work. I remember seeing how she'd kick the dirt from the sides of the walls. Pointing at patches of ruined gutter. She cursed the earth with it, saying: *The ground here is sinking! The house is falling to one side . . .* And my Mother Fareeda, with an ear cupped, declaring in one of her divinations something that made all my Mothers turn black: *God give us protection . . . we know this soil will swallow us all with the house . . .* and despite her muddled confusion, Mister, my Mothers took her words as a kind of proper forecast.

They were frightened, I think. Especially them who'd settled in the lower floors. My Mother Miriam, for instance, in whose room the damp had so thickly furred the walls, where the leaks had become so severe that the swelling travelled to the ceiling.

My Mother Sadaf, however, whose own room had set to a rolling slant, decided there was only enough money to fit short buttresses to the eastern walls. Them greening pipes and crumbling stone would have to wait. And so inevitably, there were whispers about whether any of my other Mothers could bear to suffer another winter.

49. A HUFF Maybe it was my own juvenile throes, Mister, but I chose to ignore it at first. I stomped around, snubbing the work being done, ignoring my Mother Sofiyya when she went: *And there the goat-boy goes – off in a huff – esh-esh – and where would he be without us, ah? . . . In the road and bloody dead most likely . . .* I went and chose a spot between my uncle's shelves to sit alone. I'd imagined, Mister, with a certain degree of satisfaction, that it was the weight of them shelves around me, stuffed with heavy books, that had been dragging the house into ruin. I'd sit with my cassette player rested on a pile, and listened along, ignoring the rest, as if it were my own mode of stroppy rebellion. Like my silence, Mister, was a finger stuck up at the noise.

50. MOTHER'S REST Well, as it was, with each passing day, my Mother Fareeda's words began to sound more and more like a portent. It was Estella, up in her blue room, with all them hundreds of portraits and mirrors, that'd offer the first clue that our fortunes were turning. Something had changed in her. It was my Mother Miriam who found her. She called my Mothers to come up to her room and see.

– It's Estella, she said quietly to them, Estella's fingers are still. She has stopped sewing!

My Mothers hushed and gathered around her door. It was true, and obvious from even the slightest peek, that while my mother was sat where she had always been, alone by the window, something was amiss. Not only had she stopped sewing, she was also trying to undo what she'd already done. Estella was untying her stitches one thread at a time.

Fourteen years Estella had sat in that same animated pose. Every day she'd worked the same way, and now, suddenly – and unimaginably, from my other Mothers' point of view – she'd set her pale fingers to rest.

This change sent my Mothers into panic. My Mother Fareeda went about closely inspecting every crack in the kitchen, every broken buttress, making long sour faces at bits of discoloured plaster. *Hmm* . . . she said as she approached a peeling door frame, *we told you it would begin, did we not?* . . . *God knows we did tell you all* . . .

Mother Shahnaz and Mother Sofiyya had to console one another after that. Both disappeared into their room before appearing again, not more than two hours later, wearing entirely different outfits on the balcony outside. My Mother Aneesa, seeing them prop themselves up in their safety-pinned finery, cooing at passing strangers below, all in that same sequinned performance, stifled a laugh at them – *Joo-hoo!* – *The pigeons are perched again. It is all a bloody disaster* . . .

Eventually, rattling bangles to the troubling news, my Mothers hid away upstairs. It was as if all the worry thrown up by my mother was too much for them to bear. My Mother Sadaf and Sisi Gamal, meanwhile, were the only ones who appeared completely unfazed. The old woman occupied herself with her weeds, while my uncle hurried on with his shelves.

Wives are as close to their husbands as garments, he muttered. I knew my uncle was quoting the Qur'an. We were deep into our lessons on *tajweed* that night, and the quote about garments made sense to me. My mother had been working toward my father with her cloth. Same way I'd been poring over his tapes, Mister. Marwan was there, in them knots in her head, chased down between her fingers. My mother and I had resorted to an invented method, just so we could claim my father's absence somehow as our own.

51. PAH! PAH! You asked whether any of my other Mothers had pined the same as Estella, fallen as she had, into a kind of distracted obsession with Marwan. A lot of them had known men like my father, Mister – runaways, cowards, deserters. My Mother Shahnaz, for example, described how her own husband would hit her with a toothbrush – *pah!-pah!* – on the backs of her knuckles. She showed me where the bruises had been, *He would hit me when I did not do what he pleased – and what pleased him was so terrible . . .*

Others told similar stories of mean and ill-tempered husbands. This house had been their only haven. But now, with Estella having slowly turned crazy upstairs, this house had given them all the yips. They didn't want to end up like her, Mister. Not just alone, but alone and mad – which was a fate worse than anything they could have imagined.

Even my Mother Miriam, who was the only one who really cared for my mother, sat combing her hair and rubbing her ankles most days, and whispered at me, *I am afraid, Yahya . . . of what it means when someone like your mother changes and we all stay the same . . . maybe she is trying to tell us something . . . tell me something maybe . . . that I should change and go . . .*

52. DEPARTURES So – off they went. One by one, over the next few months, all my other Mothers committed to leaving the old *ayah* house after all. My Mother Aneesa was first. I saw her rummage around upstairs the day before she left. Her fat round nose rifling discarded clothing. She'd packed a dark woollen hat and a warm winter jacket, two sets of hardy-looking boots she'd found in a wardrobe, a big black bag of heavy sheets and warm blankets, as well as an *A–Z* retrieved from under a busted table. I don't know when exactly she left. And I'd have expected at least a clout around the head, Mister, or an earful before her departure. But it was Mother Miriam who told me she'd left. She hadn't said goodbye to anyone.

And then, that following month, on some blustery day when the draught kept me under blankets upstairs, I heard two white vans come and park outside the front gate. I heard my Mothers Shahnaz and Sofiyya running down the stairs. They had their hairdos tied into knots of multi-coloured hairclips with bits of shoelace and thread. I'd never seen them done up so lavishly. One wore a dark velvety dress, while the other's was a creased blue with a bow on the back. I saw my Mother Shahnaz at the door. She seemed to be fixing some brooch on her lapel, and ordered my Mother Sofiyya to open it. How she flapped at her tassels, Mister. Clawed at the baubles around her neck, strung in the style of some expensive garland.

The door swung open.

Two strangers had come to collect them.

Who these balding, haggard-looking men were, Mister,

I hadn't a clue. But I stood aside and watched as they went hauling my Mothers' suitcases into the backs of their cars. My Mother Miriam appeared and I asked where they were going. *I think these two are brothers*, she whispered. We watched them giddily fussing about my Mothers, as if neither could believe their own luck – sweeping my Mothers' dresses into separate cars, delicately shutting the doors, before getting in themselves and pulling away. *One of them works for the Cash & Carry*, said my Mother Miriam, *the other one . . . tet-tet . . .*

It seemed my Mothers' balcony pageants had done the trick. But whether these two balding brothers had been long-term admirers of my Mothers, I never knew. I'd never seen them before, Mister. I can only picture my Mothers on that balcony, staring down at the street, assessing each passing stranger, pointing at two – *this bugger here* and *that bugger there* – and choosing another life that way.

Anyway, the oddest departure of all was my Mother Fareeda's. My elder Mother, Mister, announced she was leaving the house a few weeks later. We were in the telly room with my Sisi Gamal, Mother Miriam and Mother Sadaf. She set down her bowl and declared that she'd made a decision – *finally, in communion*, she said, saying she was going to where *we better belong, she and me . . . going back to Beirut! . . .* We all glanced at each other in nervous recognition, thinking, honestly, that she'd lost it.

It was my Mother Sadaf who reacted. She went to rampage in the kitchen, grabbing pans, her *cubby*, hurling them against the walls and cupboards. She kicked a hard boot at the table which made all the tossed cutlery shiver, and then just went around, Mister, punching the air, the doors, and the backs of the chairs we were sat on.

– After all this house has given you! she went. After all these *bloody-hell* years – *boh!* – none of you can stay and fix this place, *ah?* Hold it strong with me? My own bloody hands in the mud and the weeds – so, go now, go! – All of you go now, and get out!

I clutched at my Mother Miriam as she began clearing the room of our bowls of steaming soup. We made to leave, Mister, but my Mother Fareeda stayed still. She raised her right hand and went to calm her. She said something which seemed to startle my Mother Sadaf at first. She nodded and gave a smile. I watched my Mother Sadaf wipe her brow then, breathe heavily, and go into the yard to be alone.

I didn't hear what was said. But a few weeks later, I watched my Mother Fareeda at the front door one morning. She was wearing a long, thickly lined coat, I remember. One I'd never seen her wear before. And she was holding a single cloth bag by her side. That greying hair was fixed in her usual bird's-nest bun, with them black eyes set along Forty Road, expectant.

The rest of us could do nothing other than to stand and watch alongside her. She hadn't called anyone. Nor made any arrangements. But we watched the road all the same. I honestly thought, Mister, that she might be standing there waiting for some gust of wind to pick her up. Lift her away from our doorstep, with her bag and her hat, like some mad Mary Poppins bound for some imagined Beirut. Send her up, Mister, into them clouds, where her dotty head seemed to be.

But then, hearing an approaching car, her eyes lifted. She quickly gave me a pinch on the cheek, made a whistle, gathered her things, and as if gratefully, with a loud sniff, firmly nodded at the others as if saying goodbye.

– God protect you, she went. God heal all of you. And may God have mercy on this house . . .

And then, just before my Mother Fareeda was about to step away from the door, I saw my Mother Miriam leap out in front of her, wrapping her arms around her neck.

– *Owf* . . . no, wait, Fareeda . . . come, please, inside . . .

She wanted to tell her, I think. Tell her there was nobody coming for her. That it was just a passing car, Mister, she was just confused. But my elder Mother shook her away, and walked out into the middle of the road. She raised her right hand at the car. A moment then, as my Mother Fareeda waved at the windshield. I saw her face crease in a kind of realisation. A woman came out to greet her. We all fell silent when we saw she was the spitting image of my Mother Fareeda. The same hat pitched to the side, and her face, drawn inward and thin, like a perfect mirror. We watched them sit close inside the car, embrace again and then, in another bizarre vision, both wave back at us with their hands in matching motion. The car turned and was out of sight the next moment.

Nobody mentioned the name Fatima afterward. But I could have sworn I saw my Mother Sadaf mouth the name in the garden. And when, eventually, we did the rounds inside them empty rooms, where we found more clothes, dirty bedding and so on, the ghosts of the scents were the only thing she'd left behind her. I heard my Mother Sadaf tell my Mother Miriam: *Leave these things to the house,* as if conceding defeat to the hoardings. *Fareeda is gone. Allah will not bless this place again.*

53. MIRIAM DEPARTS But, Mister, that was not the departure my Mother Sadaf felt most betrayed by. A little while later, after the worst of the winter months was over, the yellowing in the walls had receded and the rooms had returned to their regular funk, my Mother Miriam announced she'd met a man. She was getting married.

I'd remembered, having taken more notice of the comings and goings of the house, my Mother Miriam had been spending more time at the mosque. She'd been coming home later in the evenings. Sometimes dropped off by a stranger. I never caught sight of who it was from the window.

It was some young cleric, she said – and a convert at that – named John Muhammad, who'd asked. And she'd accepted. Imam Ghulam had blessed the union.

My Mother Sadaf cussed them all out when she heard and in her familiar hysterical pitch, Mister, threatened to never allow my Mother Miriam back to the house.

– *American* man? – *Boh!* – You stupid, stupid girl – *it will be a bloody disaster*!

– I just want a better life than this, said my Mother Miriam, I want to begin again. Begin with him – and I will!

– Begin again? Begin where? Stupid! Better you die and do your life over if you want to live again. You think you are any different? You are who?

I remember Mother Sadaf bringing her arms up suddenly, thundering toward my Mother Miriam with her thumb and forefinger pressed. My Mother Miriam managed to swing out the way sending my Mother Sadaf tumbling a few feet forward. She caught her breath and glared at her. The look on her face, Mister, it was as though my Mother Miriam had just committed the most egregious offence. She collected herself, nostrils flaring her great wide jaw jutting from under bluish lips.

– You are just the same as the others, she said, dusting her apron and smoothing her hair. Who were you when your mother left you? – *Stupid!* – And who – who raised you all these many? – *Shame!* – You had only me, me it was who fed you – *ungrateful!*

Mother Miriam turned to face her from the other side of the room.

– I am still young, she said. And yes, maybe stupid. But you are not my mother, Sadaf.

They didn't speak again, Mister. I suppose my Mother Sadaf felt they were abandoning her as well as the house. I'd never seen her so incensed. She was like some maimed animal charging after them. She spent her hours outside, muddied in the soil, completely alone, and allowing nobody near, or to speak to her.

I remember how my Mother Miriam left. Although, forgive me, Mister – I won't write how I felt about it. Sitting here now, I realise how painful it still feels to recall it. I was proper young. And it's difficult, even now, honestly, to write it out of me . . .

All I'll say is that my Sisi Gamal blessed my Mother Miriam for leaving. He understood she needed to leave – She saw her chance with this convert and took it. She told me I would see her again. And I believed her, Mister. She left alone on a Sunday.

Nothing else needs to be recorded about that sad day.

54. UPPER DECKS I came back to my recitation, reading and study – my only response to all the changes about me. And by then, Mister, the Millennium was approaching. I was nearly nine years old now, and I felt some need to deepen my learning before the new year. I also felt some anxious instinct to fill every empty room. I filled the silence with my muttered recitals, the echoes of my footsteps in the hallway, playing my father's tapes. I chose the low tones of *1994* for my Mother Aneesa. Tangled strings from *1995* for my Mothers Shahnaz and Sofiyya. I went stalking about in circular patterns, swirling my wrists in the empty air. There was nobody there to watch me or question what I was doing. And nobody to rap me on the legs and tell me to straighten my crooked shoulders or anything.

All pretence, meanwhile, of attending proper school, had fallen away. I started skiving, Mister. I started spending entire days on them buses now, and trains, just circling the city alone. I'd use my lunch money to buy myself several bags of Ready Salted crisps and I'd sip on Sprites all day long without a bother. I'd watch the windows, Mister, looking down at them moneyed boroughs passing beneath me.

This was Covent Garden, Regent's Park and Russell Square. All these marbled parts my uncle never ventured to for *da'wah*. The faces outside were all so hopped up, it seemed to me, busy with life. I'd watch performers. The buskers, bards on thin legs singing on shop corners. I'd admired this lot, Mister, how they captured crowds of tourists and onlookers with some raised voice above the traffic. I'd watch them gold-painted men. The ones holding cardboard mugs, claiming spare change for charity. There were people everywhere skipping effortlessly, or else dead in the eyes and troubled. Now that I'd seen so much more of the city, my own end of East Ham seemed so much smaller. And without my Mothers to spit-comb my curls behind my ears, Mister, I realised I must have looked a proper beggar boy sat there, like some lost-in-the-city beggar boy. I even got off to wander. I felt how easy it would be for me to disappear among this lot – all these tourists, fiddlers and street performers.

Then again, it's not like I was completely alone on them buses. I'd spy all them wet-faced boys, who'd clamber upstairs after school. I got back to East Ham and I'd watch the ones who'd sit in the seats around me. I'd stare at the back of their necks. I'd see how their collars were never clean, shirts always stained with browned sweat. I'd notice the good shape of their bodies when they bent down to take up their bags, or reached over one another to slap heads. All the talk was about girls. And a thousand other opinions about life. Some of these lot, I remember, snaffling crisps, and chugging back Cokes, sounded to me like proper fantasists. It was as if the world was about to roll over for them. As if *any day now* their entire lives would fall into place at their feet.

How could anyone feel this way about the world? This same bright-wide, Mister, which was only troubling to me and violent. It seemed almost boundless to them, and so much of it already theirs. I decided they were all posers. Fakers who were egging each other on about their place in it for laughs.

I withdrew into my reading. I'd sit there scratching my ears, slouched in my seat, muttering to myself and imitating these other lads under breath. I might not have been as upright as them, Mister. Not as carefree or unfettered. But I was quietly content with my lot. I knew, in the end, that I, Yahya – a little more pretentious, maybe, a mock-learned lad – stood whole universes apart from these others.

55. 2000 The Millennium had come. The few of us left, Mister – myself, my Mother Sadaf and Sisi Gamal – all apart from my mother Estella, who was still upstairs in her silence, were sat huddled in front of the television.

The ceremony had started. All them tailored Royals, Tony and Cherie, your mega-rich and glamorous, holding hands with your Queen. It was time for 'Auld Lang Syne' and fireworks for the nation. My Sisi Gamal had the machine ready to record.

Admittedly, I got quickly bored with it. I threw a heavy coat on and sat outside on the balcony. I spent the night with my head buried in some old poet instead, Mister, perched on my Mother Shahnaz's chair. Even when the colours flew up, I was reading al-Maari or similar, under them banging skies come midnight. I could hear my Sisi Gamal shouting up at me, *Boy – you'll miss the whole thing . . .* but I could see enough, Mister. And the fireworks allowed me to read much clearer in their light.

56. NITS! Events took a turn after spring. The pipes had frozen from the winter just gone. I remember my Mother Sadaf went about clattering the radiators after it, saying: *Plumbing's gone! Boy, you will have to go and shower at school . . .*

They sent me out unwashed, Mister. My unkempt hair started bunching. A thick layer of grease causing itchiness. Soon I started getting sores all over. My neck became very tender with a rash. And after a couple nights of terrible sleep, Mister, I woke to find a redness all over my shoulders and back.

I was scratching my scalp and armpits so incessantly at school that the stout Mrs Chow the nurse – her with her puffed cheeks and painted-on eyes – took me aside one afternoon and called my uncle. I remember the old man brought his barrow with him. Some of the other lads saw and laughed. And when my Sisi Gamal dragged me out, clipping both ears, saying *Stop scratching! Stop it, boy!*, they were already hooting, breathlessly laughing from afar.

We got home to find my Mother Sadaf bent over a hedge.

– He's got *nits*! Bloody *nits*! – *ach!* – those bastard children gave him the *nits*!

My Mother Sadaf looked up and threw her gloves.

– What *nits*? . . . What's this?

She came over and started pulling at my roots. I felt her slowly tease my greasy knots and watched her pucker her lips. It was then that I knew I was in for it. I was infested. I listened to them go at it for a bit longer. My Mother Miriam belting me into the soil she was so cross. My Sisi Gamal blamed the school and other children. My Mother Sadaf blamed my Sisi Gamal – *Nits might have jumped into his head at school, but – boh! – your filthy basement doesn't help!*

My Mother Sadaf took me into her bathroom and drowned me under a bucket of soapy mixture. She mixed whatever chemicals she found under the sink and I was soaked and kneaded and towelled, her calloused fingers cutting into my skin. I was naked on the bathroom floor, Mister, and so embarrassed. She scrubbed my head and back, doused my hair with what smelled to me like drain cleaner and detergent – *Be still, stop moving! – slippery little mutt* . . .

I might have shouted that it hurt, Mister, but no use. If I

screamed, my Mother Sadaf would have slapped me harder. If I went to pull away, she'd hold me back with a forearm at the neck. After that, my uncle sat me down on that toilet. Held my arms crossed, Mister. Telling me to set my head straight and went at my curls with his clippers.

How I cried, Mister! Threw my arms up, spat at my uncle's feet. My Sisi Gamal did his best to calm me. *Stop! Stop! Recite the Antar and Abla . . . hold still!*

Eventually, the old man released me wrapped in a towel. I ran up as far as I could, into the upper floors with my towel, Mister, past my mother's room, and I sat in an empty space running my fingers over the sore spots.

I found a small dirty mirror left behind by one of my Mothers. I peered at my skin, all puckered and torn, scratched and bleeding. I cried not for the loss of hair, Mister, but for the way my Mother Sadaf and Sisi Gamal had got at me. Jumped me like some child, some *nobody worth nothing*. I also knew my Mother Sadaf had planned to march me to them school gates in the morning. No chance of skiving off. I'd have to face the entire school looking like I'd been thrown into a bag of razors.

57. BOUKIE-HEAD I tried to make a go of it. Determined to put up a front of indifference. See me, shoulders pressed, chin to the ceiling. I was copying the boys I'd seen in school – them, with their backpacks half slung, all rolling arms, full of confidence. But then, all it took was them same lads to catch full sight of me, all them Waynes and Gavins and burly Craigs, gurning and hurling cusses: *Look at the faggot now – what a freak!*, and for others to turn in their seats to stare: *Raas, look* *at the state of you! Oi-oi, you ugly boukie-head!*, for my confidence to flounder fast.

All day they threw things, Mister – beats, spit-paper, erasers. Sent messages with my own face scrawled on crumpled paper. I felt myself recoil. I could feel the slant in my shoulders give in, and my head sink into my chest. I felt my legs tense again into their usual bow. I realised no amount of studied composure would have made me into something acceptable to this lot, Mister. By the end of that day, I think I just gave up trying . . .

I remember sitting there allowing the words I'd heard to fall into my mouth. I began repeating them to myself even louder – *faggot, boukie-head, stinking freak* . . . I don't know why it made me feel better to do that, but it did. Easier to sit, body limp and slouching, curled into the ugliness they'd assigned for me. Even when some Chinese girl, Janet or Jane or Joana, noticed what I was doing and asked if I had *fucking Tourette's*, I didn't hide or shy away from her. There was no *leave me alone* or *don't speak to me* . . . I only repeated the words, stirred under breath: *fucking Tourette's, boukie-head, freak* . . . as if some instinct had set in, Mister. I'd have to imitate my bullies to survive them.

58. THE TRACE . . . THE TREMBLE . . . Fair to say, this was a humiliation the depths of which I'd hardly known, and it affected me deeply. I remember wandering about the house during these weeks. My Mother Sadaf was usually out among her weeds. Sisi Gamal out for *da'wah*. I felt so alone and unhappy, Mister, and I think I ended up seeking answers in my old Mothers' house which still stood, for me, as the sump of collected mystery. I began searching, wandering, drifting about, hardly sure what I was even looking for . . .

I wandered the upper floors just as I'd done as a boy, revisiting them abandoned nests and hidey-holes, lifting broken headboards and dirty sheets. I threw aside the leather belts I'd hung from the ceiling beams, kicked open old bunkers I'd once so carefully constructed. All around me were relics of the *little mutt*, Mister. I even crept into my doe-mother's room. I crawled underneath her bed, pulling boxes of clothes and coloured fabric. I even went through her dressing tables. Prising opened jammed drawers filled with yarn, pin cushions and playing cards. Nothing more. As for all them faces, them framed portraits and foxed mirrors, none of it helped ease my rising doubts.

On the second floor, I pulled out old forgotten albums filled with faded holidays. Photos of sunny landmarks, people dressed in fine clothes draped across sofas, big hats, wine glasses pinched with fingertips. Memories of people I didn't recognise.

I went into the basement at last, and sat on my heels as I usually did with some book open in front of me. I leaned back and rubbed my sore patches against a row of my uncle's spines. I felt very tight in the chest. It felt, honestly, like I hated everything in the world in that moment. My own school had turned on me. My teachers had never even acknowledged me there. My bullies had torn at me all week. Even my Sisi Gamal and Mother Sadaf had left me humiliated and bruised.

I looked around at the towering shelves and suddenly something else rose out of me.

I got up and took a swing at them. I sent books and pages

flying. I got up and went over the loose pages that fell, trembling with a rising anger. I picked up a heavy tome and hurled it hard at a corner. Entire rows came cascading down. Falling binders missed my head by inches. I spat at them angrily. Swearing at them for falling. I started frantically searching the back shelves then, wanting names that sounded unfamiliar. Stuff I'd yet to read or hadn't been pushed onto me by my Sisi Gamal. Everything looked so ordered and fixed. All the same narrow set under that same yellow light. And now I felt my chest tightening further. I went into the shadows, into the corners beneath that low ceiling, and peered in. And there – under some far leaning shelf – I saw boxes stacked against the furthest wall. Behind the clutter. Behind all my uncle's shelves, tucked furthest back. There were so many left un-opened.

As I stepped closer, I realised the smell from the ground was growing fouler. The putrid damp had eaten at these boxes. Puddles had formed under the lowest stacked. Faint whitish spots had bloomed over their sides. These boxes had been left to bleed into filthy water. I crept forward, Mister, ducking under beams. I rolled my sleeves and covered my mouth. And then I lifted a lid to look inside.

Books. Just more books.

But different bindings on them. Some were bound with black tape. And the labels too, were written in unfamiliar handwriting – a long, beautifully girlish hand with flowing *y*'s and curling *q*'s. Kneeling then, in the stink and frothing puddles, I looked closer at the back of each label. The same initials were written on every parcel – *M.B.*

I couldn't have known it then, Mister. But I had the

irrepressible feeling that whatever I'd been looking for had finally found me.

59. FATHER'S BOOKS And I'd like to have said, Mister – given where I've ended up – that I recall some strum of fate when I lifted that lid. In reality, I held my breath, and went on my tiptoes to see, half terrified at the stench.

These were my father's books. Each cardboard box filled with what my uncle might have dismissed as junk and *written English nonsense*. I realised they were the same books my father had read upon arriving in Britain. Adventure stories with rowdy titles and garish covers. He'd been obsessed with these stories of battlers and big lives – and here they all were, stacked on top of each other, like some hidden library too crude or otherwise meritless for my uncle to bother with.

The volumes themselves were in okay shape. A little eaten and damp but otherwise good. Most were cheap paperbacks with frayed edges. Others bundled in no obvious order. I went and opened another box. Some of these were better kept. I whispered aloud the beginnings of long titles, lifting them one by one:

The History and Remarkable Life . . .
The Fortunes and Misfortunes of the Famous . . .
Travels into Several Remote Nations . . .
The Life and Times in Four Parts . . .

Bound with these tattered novels were little pamphlets from poets I'd never heard of. There was a dog-eared copy of *Briggflats* by Basil Bunting. *Songs of Innocence and of Experience* by William Blake. I mouthed these names for the first time, Mister, and set them down to read on. Some names really made me laugh – *Dickens*, *Godwin*, *Gooch* – names like cheesemakers and slave owners. Made me think of fox puppets and flags. And Ford Maddox Ford, William Carlos Williams – names like American cowboys or cops.

I flicked through a few more and found little scribbled notes in margins like little insects. I remember thinking to myself: no wonder my father lost himself to the bright-wide, Mister – just look at what he read!

There must have been a dozen boxes tucked away in that basement. English novels, American poets, European works with never-ending titles. I was so eager to read them all, Mister, hear them all in my head. I wanted to hear them like I'd heard them Abbasids and Umayyads and the rest of my uncle's lot.

I decided I'd return to the boxes when I could. I replaced what I'd found and retreated into the light. I stood for a moment thinking of my father. The fragments of him, his *zoun . . . zeen . . . zeen . . .* his scribbled *M.B. . . .* there were notes of his that, if I listened hard enough, I could still hear in the air that surrounded me.

I decided against sleeping in the basement that night. I crept upstairs, careful to avoid my Mother Sadaf and Sisi Gamal in the kitchen. I went into my Mother Aneesa's old room. I lay there resting on the sore side of my head. My whole body felt very tense. I was trembling. As if I'd been wound tight like a coil about ready to burst.

60. EDUCATION (3) Here, then – the third and final strand to my education. Snatched in secret this time, entirely of my own making, and without my uncle's supervision. I returned to that far corner, Mister, and over the next few months picked at them boxes at random. Stealing them away, tucked into my trousers and jumpers and my bag . . .

Forgotten were my uncle's rhythms and metres for the moment. All them bold ancient verses, Mister. I skived nearly every day during these weeks, fixing myself to them upper decks, and hungrily devoured my new finds. And these books, Mister – filled to the brim with tales of swashbucklers, pickpockets, sea captains and thieves, mad kings and squires, drunkard friars and impious priests – all these twisting, heightened lives, Mister, stained with the manias of some other age. I'd laugh at them old English stories. And these characters – some familiar to me, speaking in a tearaway cant, the sort I'd heard about East Ham – thrilled me, Mister. And aside from all them panting girls and disabled bodies drawn as villains always, which confused me, I began to enjoy my reading in a way I never could with my uncle.

I began to read parts aloud to myself on the bus. These ruddy-faced, collared gentlemen, say, with their passions, and intrigues, and their *I say, I say, I say* . . . And all them funny matrons, and their *ladies of the house*, as well as them washerwomen who chased beggar boys and orphans, who'd somehow outwit them all about the city.

After every reading, I'd catch myself staring out the window, Mister, blowing out my cheeks and muttering to myself in the style of Old Sally, say, or some muddy-cheeked sweeper:

Now that's a life! . . . Cor, what a life!

Imagine then, Mister – how I came to also discover the likes of your Robinson Crusoe and your Lemuel Gulliver, say, your

Poe, your Blake and your Wordsworth. These were the sorts of books my father had collected. Them, as well as a couple of Arab poets he'd favoured enough to bind – Taha Hussein, bits of Adonis I'd never read, and even Nawal El Saadawi. I was shocked by some of it. Shocked by the split-apart rhythms and messy formulas. Some had illustrations inside – I became enthralled, for instance, by Blake's 'The Tyger', which I read over and over with a growl at the mouth, *What immortal hand or eye, Could frame thy fearful symmetry* . . .

This Blake seemed the proper sort, Mister. I looked longingly over his paintings of *Albion*, that ecstatic white body on a rockface, in all his glory, arms out like a naked dancer.

I fell in love with these English prophets. All of whom my Sisi Gamal would have regarded as *bloody poison and polluters* and nothing more. And he was right in a way – I felt my insides burn while reading them.

Everything here felt so uneven, unfixed, fragmented and free. And you must understand, Mister, this stuff was everything I was taught proper poetry was not meant to be.

So then, I found myself thrilled at the idea that it could be. That anything could be. And that everything was.

And what it was, was all so different from them slab-faced viziers my Sisi Gamal had beaten into me. All them names who my uncle had claimed held history together. I suppose I'd learned that there was more than one way to write history into poetry, Mister. And there was no such thing as a poet's diploma.

61. IMPROPER LANGUAGE Like any heady poison, my father's hidden library might have been better gulped down in smaller doses. They wrought changes in me and I felt them in my body. I noticed, for instance, how my legs had grown a little longer. How my feet and palms had started to feel all the time clammy . . .

I arrived home one day and found my armpits swollen sore. My skin gummier. And my bushy hair had come back in tight little knots. I didn't feel sick otherwise. But I didn't know what to make of all these changes. There were parts of my body, Mister, that once I examined them, bent low in the mirror, appeared darker in places, and other parts that seemed smeared.

I could only put it down to one thing: them unruly forms I'd been swallowing. It was as if all them strange, irrepressible poets, Mister – sometimes rude, other times totally incomprehensible – had drawn me out somehow, and my limbs had started unfurling. There were even times, Mister, in the middle of my recitations, when my voice would suddenly break into some discordant surprise – jolts, halts, jumps in the breath. It was as if them hopping verses were giving out from inside. I realised, after this series of so many educations, that it was the learning I'd made on my own terms, Mister, that had truly taught me how to be. How, that is, to let go of parts of myself, just as other parts were letting go of me.

62. INTO THE WORLD Now, I know none of this would have amounted to any primary proper, Mister. I learned nothing of your Boudica and Stuart kings and I daresay you'd have had me down as delinquent. My education followed the busy course of my Sisi Gamal's erratic interests up till then, and now my own.

But I threw myself into each of them regardless. And this

last stage came in such a sudden frenzy that it sent me reeling through the rest of that pivotal year. My father's English books and all them heretical poets helped me recognise something important. Namely, that what I was feeling had been felt before. And not only that, Mister, but it had been *written down* before – here, in these fractious, scrambled rhythms. The dangerous lives I read in them old English novels felt so close to me, like I really knew them, like I'd lived alongside them. The effect this had on me was huge. It was the first time the world felt suddenly familiar. The next time I was sat on my uncle's sofa, Mister, watching his Moira Stewart, I could finally recognise the world as it was – and I was lucky then. Because it was around this time that my Sisi Gamal, having blustered in nearly catching me thrilled by some free verse Salah Sabour, informed me I was going to be sent out to a new school.

My Sisi Gamal explained that Imam Ghulam had made plans for opening a new Islamic school in Poplar. He was going to waive the fees for me to attend my first year. *Ach! – it is better than the one you have*, he said, *at least you will learn surah and continue with Qur'an* . . . And this school was going to be under the centre's direction, Mister, along with the council representatives from other mosques, including Imam Ghulam.

It was to be called the Ibn Rabah School for Islamic Study. With uniforms, a gated campus, courses in Islamic history and the rest. And to tell you the truth, Mister, I couldn't wait for it. I was dreading my last few years of primary, Mister, and mine was the kind that followed on from my primary. By then, I'd developed my way of skiving off to avoid the worst of it. But now, Mister, with my sudden involuntary sweating, flashes of thirsts and uncontrolled swells, smells and strange yearnings beginning to emerge, it was as if my sudden compulsions might burst at any moment. Perhaps I'd also hoped this new Islamic school might stay whatever my father's books had coaxed out of me.

Now that I remember it . . . there was one time in Maths, when some nosey girl – Gemma, Natalie or Claire, with a Blue Peter badge, and an Alice band in her hair – demanded I show her what I was reading. She snatched the book off me, began flicking through, declaring that I was a *fucking retard . . .* before giving me an offended look.

I remember staring back at her and thinking very seriously, Mister, about spitting in her face. The urge left me so disturbed – for I really felt I could hawk something filthy up to spit at her – that I quickly scuttled away and wouldn't dare look at her again for the remainder of that final term.

63. 11 SEPTEMBER Before I set my pen down for this part – before I go on to recount for you the years I began writing my first proper poems – you asked about the day in September. Except, I can't say I have much to offer about it.

I remember the dust clouds on telly. The Falling Man. Your Blair and your Junior Bush, their goggling faces everywhere, and on repeat.

I do recall what I was reading – an anthology of Abu Tammam, it was. One of my uncle's poets in preparation for the new term. We were out in the yard, Mister. My Mother Sadaf was pulling the weeds out the ground. Soil up to her elbows, her bare feet were brown. She'd left large bags of fertiliser in the hot weather and the stink had attracted flies. There were swarms of the pests all over.

As I recall it, the poem I was reading was an ode to the sacking of a city. The city was Amuriyya, I remember. A real place or imagined, I don't know. But the story went, the city fort was protected by two great towers and a single gate. The poem was in praise of the men who breached it. The martyrs who sacked the city claimed it was for the might of Islam – proper *fedayeen*. They'd fought and died bringing Allah to an unbelieving city.

I might even remember the verse:

Conquest of conquests, outside embrace of language
The day of Amuriyya was rich with bags of milk
Islam drove the confounders of faith down the slopes
It was worth the sacrifice of many mothers.

And I swear it, Mister – just as I came to the last line of this poem, a fly landed on the page I was reading. I snapped the book shut, instantly killing the fly. I opened it to see the bloodied yellow secretion smeared across the line between the words *sacrifice* and *mothers*. I think it was one of the most revolting things I'd ever seen, smeared across one of the most beautiful lines I'd ever read.

I didn't feel much for the fly. All I remember was thinking that if it wasn't for Allah aiming them *fedayeen* at the towers, they would have surely missed.

It was at that moment, Mister, with me sat musing, and my Mother Sadaf muddied and wheezing, and them flies buzzing around, that my Sisi Gamal appeared at the window of the kitchen with his elbows going, his hands up at the sky and yelling: *Quickly, boy – we must record! – Come quickly . . . Come, come!*

He looked like a madman to me. Flapping his arms as if announcing some shattering thing. I went inside and saw – two planes had crashed into the twin towers. Images of great clouds of smoke, fire and faces fleeing in terror. You'd have thought the world had just declared, in some spectacular way, the close of one century and the start of another. Though the only sound my uncle made, Mister, in his state of giddy ecstasy, was a cry made out and repeated with a chest full of elation and praise:

Allahu Akbar! Allahu Akbar! Allahu Akbar!

Yah! Yah! Yah!

And so, as my luck would have it, just when things had started to burst out of me in bodily shots and protrusions, the big bright-wide, Mister, which had always felt so distant, began to resemble my own inner life. 9/11 had transformed the world into a kind of lurching constant. Everything seemed so un-balanced. But I couldn't wait – it was time, Mister, having turned thirteen, to face up to the world as it was. And I'd have to face up, also, to the *big-eyed-Allah-in-heaven* – which was what my uncle called that one sharper God, who he'd credited as having delivered *an almighty sock to the West* . . .

After the initial euphoria at the pictures on the telly, my uncle had settled into an anxious recant. *You be careful now, boy*, he said, *these are dangerous times . . . must be so-so!* And he'd lift my wrists and let them drop to the sides of me. *But learn to speak up! Speak up and don't be afraid!*

Articulacy was what he wanted from me, Mister. My uncle

insisted that my words hold meaning. But as I found out later, that was like asking me to make sense of an idiot wind. On the news, on the street, everybody had started speaking in suspicious half-truths and spun realities. So, as it was, I'd have to learn to *Speak up! Speak up!* just as language itself was falling to pieces at the mouth.

64. FIRST POEMS Into the mess of them early aughts came Yahya – older now, and arched, string-armed and goat-haired again – putting pen to paper for my first proper poems. A few scratchings alone, Mister, nothing major. But it was clear I had something of my mother's gift for pulling old stories into unfamiliar forms.

My Sisi Gamal and I kept on with *da'wah*. Into them high streets now, filled as they were with gobby hatred. Afghanistan was being bombed to its bones that winter. There wasn't a single recital where we weren't either heckled or spat at in the street.

The sight of two Muslim proselytes, Mister, reading *surah* into the cold open air, seemed to animate the dumb fears in people. They'd pelt us with things. Some crushed plastic bottle hit me hard above the left eye. We were outside an Iceland in Newham at the time.

Fuck off Taliban! I heard someone shout.

My Sisi Gamal calling my name: *Yahya!*

I told him it was fine. Just another yob having a go.

Fuck off you Taliban bastards!

I continued with the poem. But it was incidents like this, when the world outside provoked in me new feelings – something nearest to rage, I think – that I tried to reproduce in my early scribbles. My poems arrived in fragments, however, amounting to nothing much on the page. But curiously, it was also what seemed to lure these words out of me. I even kept a notebook to record all them significant slights:

1. Another bottle (KA Kola) chucked outside a Boots.
2. A cuss: *fucking terrorist* from a boy on a bike.
3. An old woman calling my uncle: *Ay-Ay-Ayatollah!*

And so on. I'd already started to see everything in cruel little fragments. In shards and splinters. I wanted now to turn it over to my imagination, Mister. Strike these phrases down into rhythms livid with a kind of restlessness. A kind of poetry that'd fizz with the same stuff I was heckled with.

But before I go on and recount for you how I further developed my poetry, I have to re-introduce my Mother Miriam. For it was another sort of inarticulacy, Mister, that I was concerned with at first. The first poems I ever wrote were about her . . .

65. MIRIAM (MYTH) As far as my Mother Sadaf was concerned, my Mother Miriam had lost her claim on our house. She'd made her bed, married away, and my Mother Sadaf was a stony woman of her word. *The girl will not step one foot in here – boh! – not a foot!* And she spat on the ground, right there, on the floor of her own kitchen.

Not long after my Mother Miriam had left though, and once I'd started at the Ibn Rabah, I began to see her around school. Her new husband, the convert John Muhammad, whose name had become a kind of enormity around the school, had secured a job for her in his offices. She wore colourful hijabs now, yellow sequinned scarves, bright shawls, carrying papers past my window.

Sometimes, I went looking for her. I could never spot my Mother out in the open, in the square say, or that grand central court with the fountain. It was only when I walked onto the other side of the court, sat biting my lips on one of them stone benches, that my Mother Miriam came and found me.

– Look at this one! she went, with her hands under her belly. A man now, *nearly-nearly!*

I felt I could have embraced her there, Mister. But my Mother Miriam stood a few feet away. And I held my side as I stood.

– *Owf*, Yahya, she went, you are worried. Is it your hip?

I said I was fine. But my Mother sensed my unease.

– Come, come, she said. We can go and talk this way.

Once out of sight of the main square, my Mother led me onto another footpath behind a high white fence. I could hear whispering behind bushes, red flaring within the leaves, cigarette smoke in the air, and laughter. My Mother told me these back gardens were where she liked to sit sometimes. To get away from *all these nasty boys and men*, she said. We sat for a few moments on a bench. As far as I knew, Mister, we were alone. I kept glancing back at the path we'd walked down as if somebody might jump out the bushes.

– Tell me, she said. Are you worried about all this? New school . . . new friends, *ah?*

I nodded. There was a band on her finger.

– Nothing to be worried about, she said. These boys are not as clever as they think, believe me. And you are cleverer than them, *ah?* Braver than them . . .

Her skin seemed to shine as she sat there. She even smelled different. Her clothes looked new and expensive. Her eyes were clearer now and light.

– How is your mother? she asked with her voice changed.

I told her she was the same, *just like she was*. And then she asked about my Sisi Gamal and I said he was *still recording*. To which she clicked her tongue and sighed.

I waited for my Mother Miriam to ask about my Mother Sadaf, but she didn't. She talked to me about her new life instead. Told me about her John Muhammad. She spoke while looking up at the trees, the greening leaves, telling me *I think it is love* . . .

– His friends I cannot stand, she said. They say nothing to me, just smile and turn away when I come. These people – and – *owf!* – their wives . . . and then she jabbed a finger at the school. She imitated them: a little half-smile, a hand to the heart, *and still no baby?* Then she spat on the ground.

It made me laugh. And then she laughed and threw up her hands.

– It won't be for too long . . . John says he will leave the school. Too much politics. He says he wants to take me home, Yahya. *Home* – you know? My old house – can you believe? I want to see if the trees are still there. My mother's trees, *ah?*

My Mother Miriam had told me about the grove she held in her head since her childhood. Now she would get to see it again with her John.

I turned away and scratched my nose. The smell of her perfume began irritating me.

My Mother Miriam took my hand up to her belly and placed it there.

– And . . . after that, John says we can have children. He doesn't mind – boy or girl.

I felt the warmth on her fabric. Some stirring in me resting there.

– Do you think it would suit me? Here . . . a baby.

I quickly snatched away my hand. The sudden image of her body swelling made my lips curl. My Mother Miriam laughed gently – *Owf!* – with her shoulders falling forward.

– Yahya – *tet-tet* – I have plenty of time for that, she said and got up.

We walked back together and parted just before we came back to the square. When she asked if I felt better, I lied and told her yes. My Mother Miriam then made me promise to rest my hip when I could. Then she gave me a warm hug. And then she turned away from me. I watched her walk past all them other bodies in the court, and disappear as if upward into the sky, where I could no longer see her.

66. HEAVINESS I began to write about my Mother Miriam after that. I tried holding on to that strange stirring in my gut. Wanted to keep it, Mister. Just long enough to drip like metal into one of the many notebooks I'd been keeping.

But the thing about it was, Mister – the words, when they came, landed in ways that disturbed me. Anything I wrote circled only these sensations, the feelings that arose when I sat with her, watched her and listened. There were parts of my Mother Miriam now that felt unfamiliar to me. The stories about her new life. Them new, beautiful clothes she wore, and her scent. These new elements smeared against the things I found familiar. Her breath, her hands, her touch and laughter.

It was as if the intimacy we shared had now been excited by something else.

I'd close my eyes and think of her. And I started to see things: my flights again, real-in-the-world visions – these strange images, fantasies . . .

I imagined, for instance, what it would feel like to taste her. I imagined myself lowering my tongue onto her skin, tasting the salt from around her wrists. I imagined what it would feel like to press on her stomach again. To touch her there. These were wants, Mister, desires that came suddenly. But it wasn't as if these feelings surprised me. I wasn't taken aback by them. It was more that they'd been sounding inside me for the longest time, like drumbeats heard in the distance. They'd been muffled but were rising now, animated by some other measure.

There was nobody to talk to about any of this. Nothing I could read in any book that could explain completely – a kind of longing in the senses, a heaviness.

And I did try – I returned to my uncle's shelves to see what the poets had to say. Most made it sound as if the experience were a natural part of life, as if *wanting* things – other lives, other bodies – came as a relief or release. It didn't feel that way to me. This was grief and excitement and pain all at once. And it was the first time I'd ever felt anything like it.

I knew I had to find the language somehow. There were ear-splitting sentences, Mister, that stifled inside me. I knew if I wanted to make any sense of them – claim them somehow – I'd have to find some way to pour them out onto paper.

67. YELLOW PAGES I convinced my Mother Sadaf to part with a little cash that month. I went with my Sisi Gamal to collect a PC off a man in Yellow Pages. I'd already learned Windows in IT, and I knew, having heard a few whispers from other boys at the school, that the internet could provide me with what I needed. Soon enough, my uncle's desk became the site of our first home computer. The telephone line was plugged into sockets, wires trailing upstairs. And with everything set, I could now follow these wants and desires, Mister. I could search for anything I liked.

68. OTHER YAHYA It's no wonder then, that I came to find reflections in the strangest of places. As a boy, I remember holding up bits of broken glass, gurning at my own distorted reflection. I'd catch a sight of myself on the surface of a perfume bottle, say, nose spread outward, mouth swallowed in. I was always on the lookout for another reflection, which could, in the end, say more about me than me alone.

The feelings came back to me as I started searching. I learned to search a thousand sites, Mister, and what came up were other bodies. All pinned up like animals on the screen one after another. They were laid bare like out them biology books, Mister, limbs bent and held in contortions. These images seemed limitless to me. I sat there gawping at the sheer variety, the many shapes, and different proportions, everything just a click away . . .

At first all I did was watch. I sat and waited for these files to load, line by line, with my face nearly pressing the screen. I clicked through, clicked away, clicked again, and then, softly trembling, I began to touch, Mister. I was testing my boundaries, I think. Feeling my own inlets and that. Started pinching myself to begin with. Started kneading my thighs at the sides. I was taking measurements of myself against these other forms – these other fictions, I think.

And then, came revelation after revelation. You know the sort. Filled with that hotness and terror. When I learned how, it was like spilling milk over the rim of a pan. Gently at first, easily and carefully, and then profoundly and fast and forever. It was like I'd suddenly discovered another Yahya inside me. Some separate self, who was all eyes and sensation. I could play alongside him. Someone whose elbows could dig into mine, could fumble and twist taking turns. And while he might have only been a figment, Mister, it was his hands that fell languidly aside next to mine.

This Other Yahya – ghostlike, within me and without – was like a secret friend at times. And as I slept, Mister, it was his hands, I knew, that would take my pen, and would write my dreams out for me.

69. DAYLIGHT I don't mean to go too much into all that – but it did become like a mania for me. And, of course, any jottings down during my nightly ecstasies, I'd quickly press into scribbled poetry. But, inevitably, Mister, upon waking up all parched and irregular, I'd tear these verses to pieces.

I destroyed them, Mister. I must have realised somehow that whatever had excited me in the night, whatever gross transformation had occurred inside me – which I traced back to that first dizzying of the senses – had begun bursting out of me now, manifesting in some cloying apparition outside my own head. It felt like a disaster to me. And it scared me. For whenever I read what I'd written the previous night, it felt so angry. As if this Other Yahya, Mister, could only ever express himself in fury. Every sentence, as if written in a hard mocking tone, every word aimed like a cuss or a cry, or a heckle.

I know all this makes me sound a little demented. But anyway, I tore them up. Out of shame and resentment, I think. And I'd spend the rest of the day bleary-eyed, wandering around the house. I'd worked myself into such a state that I went pulling cables from their sockets, cussing at the computer; I covered everything under bedsheets and hid myself away between shelves. And I know, again, it sounds stupid, Mister, but I also sometimes went and picked out a bit of poetry bound to my uncle's stricter metres. The *adab* rhythms, say, the rigours of them ancient poets like al-Jahiz or al-Mutasim – I thought it'd do me good! No sooner had I started, however, than I began to feel the trembling again. And I'd return to the screen, plug everything in I'd yanked out, and go again, and again, and again . . . and surface only for soup.

My Mother Sadaf sensed something was up. She saw me stir my bowl in distraction. I was slurping, silent, listlessly, and then she went:

– You, boy! What were you doing so long in the dark – *ah?*

That low voice – like she'd already sussed.

– I was studying . . . I sputtered.

– Studying . . . she said, repeating.

I quickly lapped the rest of my soup. Shamelessly I'd then return again to the computer, Mister. I'd spend the entire night searching again, and then morning would come, revealing the dull knot in my stomach again. And another appalling poem.

I'd spend the rest of the day in defeat. And even now, I can't entirely explain what came over me. All I can say is that I suspect I was terrified of this new and uncontrollable energy.

The great shock of being thrown into the Ibn Rabah, as well as the torturous changes inside me, Mister, it was enough to make anybody lose a sense of themselves. My body no longer felt like my own.

And while I knew mine was a loneliness that was necessary and difficult, I also knew that my desires needed announcing. I was so desperate to feel good and impressive again. But I came out stumbling. And in the end, it was among other lads, other budding poets at my newly established school, that I'd find my confidence, and a proper outlet for all my rampant wilding bents.

70. IBN RABAH Now we come to my attendance at the Ibn Rabah. The school you assumed was the great radicaliser, chock-full of fanatics, red-pillers and rubes. I suspect you're wanting to know, Mister, what this school in the middle of East London was like. Though I expect you've already made your assumptions.

It actually took a good number of years before the Ibn Rabah developed into what it later became. From a handful of classes in them first years, to then having an entire faculty of sheikhs dedicated to proper study. That meant classes in linguistics, Mister, world history without gaps, even courses in eloquence, oratory and *tasfir*. The place was similar to your own public schools in a lot of ways. All quadrangle doorways and long hallways, packed with long-necked posh boys in buttoned-up collars. Strange to think now that this school was the first of its kind in all of England. And in Poplar, imagine. Down the road from the little Lebara shop where my Mother Shahnaz used to buy her magazines.

The only thing we had to pay for was the bus fare. Everything else, much to my Sisi Gamal's relief, from textbooks to meals and uniforms, was offered free for local boys who'd come from low means – chosen scholars called *talebs*.

I was among that first year. I got to watch the transformations come rapid around our ends. Early on, I saw them neighbouring buildings get renovated, scaffolding put up. The school expanded, Mister, converting old office buildings into classrooms and prayer halls. In my second year, a large golden sign appeared at the front gate. A fence put up around its perimeter. By the third year, I watched all them outer walls get worked into patterns of floral arabesques, ceramic glyphs, big stone arches at the entrance.

To see it take shape was really something. At the time the Ibn Rabah became like a monument at the heart of East London. Built in the style of them old majestics, Mister. Same as the pictures I saw in my uncle's textbooks. All vast courts, fountains, geometric designs and so on. Them four main buildings, with their separate spires and flowing lines, appeared so large and imposing, Mister, that its proximity extended a kind of spell over everything. The Kwik-Fits and pubs closed down. Locally owned businesses moved to take their place. Shopkeepers arrived, old uncles and aunties speaking all kinds of dialects – ones who'd fled broken windows in some other ends, ugly scrawls in some other borough telling them to *get out, go home* – were invited to relocate here.

I remember sitting on the bus watching it. Sitting there, in my new uniform, my long white *thawb*, soft topi and lengths of white cloth, noticing the rising number of legal practices, halal butchers, convenience shops, and sellers of Middle Eastern goods. The Ibn Rabah in the middle of it became like a local attraction. Altering the face of the area in them three short years. And it was thrilling, honestly, to see it happen. It turned the eyesore it used to be – all them drab garages and coffee chains and Safeways – into a kind of flourishing immigrant end packed with local businesses. Islamic bookshops moved in next to phone shops and kebab shops. And with all them shisha houses, Mister, the streets started smelling of heaven. The school was generally welcomed around them ends. I got the impression that the muftis acted as kinds of benefactors for people. I'd sometimes see passers-by looking up at them intricately drawn walls and speak with a kind of reverence, Mister, in the same way most tourists might have had for your old English abbeys, say, or your cathedrals elsewhere.

71. ELOQUENCE So – not just any school, Mister. It was a new world I was entering into here. And I'd still be starting my first term as a lad proper plagued with insecurities. My awkward gait, my trailing limp, my knotted hair and pastiness – it was all bound to mark me out against them other boys.

I realised my Mother Miriam had only been placating me when talking down the other lot. At first sight all these other lads seemed to be smart and all well mannered. The majority were a posher lot from some rich international set. Saudi families, say, or the olive-tanned Egyptian sort. And a few soft-chinned *talebs* who went about like UAE aristocracy. Most spoke in a kind of glassy high English. A sort of drawn, sort of long in the throat, accent like the ones I'd hear around Knightsbridge or Edgware Road. Even the lads who'd travelled closer to home had better shoes than me. All these Ibn Rabah boys seemed to walk with a more confident step.

I'd look over my coarse hands and common shoes, and my socks with worn-away holes. I wanted to ask why my uncle hadn't found a minute to acquire better supplies for me. And it felt mad to think how I'd be learning to call *adhan* with that lot, Mister. Under proper *hafiz* clerics and so on. What kept me going was the thought all this might, over time, come to something, Mister. That I might even amount to some significance here. Me, some idiot boy from nowhere good, had at least made it to a posh school in muddy East London.

During my first class it was all bony huddles again. All them Mohammads and Mehdis over in one corner, the Femis and Abdis over there. Everyone folded into certainties, Mister, and it was difficult for me to find where to fit in. All my old torments came rushing to the surface. But then, slowly – having been bored stupid during them dud lectures on algebra and science – finally came linguistics, and at last poetry. These were wonderful classes where I'd sit and discuss patterns of poetic *kalam* and religious verses of the Mutazilites. I remember looking over at them others sitting in rows of four in front of me. All listening hard to the sheikh in that circular room. My holed socks were left tucked at the door with the others, together with our Reeboks and Converses lined in rows at the entrance.

Some classes felt more formal than others. In linguistics classes it felt as if we were treated as young amanuenses, Mister, like in them pictures in old books. Them ancient scribes in the courts of a caliph, our papers all illuminated by lamps. I could easily imagine, say, plush benches for us to sit on. Thick carpets and copper cups. But our classrooms were mostly big empty spaces. We'd sit around blue embroidered mats and were asked to compose verses. The sheikh would then have us perform. I'd often back away, Mister. There was no way I'd reveal what I'd written. And I'd often bluff it. I'd dash off a few glib lines, and palm them off as my best.

I'd listen instead. I watched for various styles and stances. I noticed how at ease these other boys were. And what became clear, Mister, was that some of these lads were far more serious about their faith. I could hear it in their voices – the ones from Yemen say, or Sudan, or Bangalore, or Karachi – the way they'd strain their metaphors in delivery. How they'd invoke *surah* into every bit of imagery, Mister. So eloquent and cool, and far more impressively versed. Meanwhile, locally born lads like myself, for whom the Qur'an bore down like a measure of balance, but not much else, couldn't help but feel a little inadequate. It was as if we lacked that brainy, fiercer tradition. A sort of intensity in speech which them foreign-born lads gave out so effortlessly.

Then again, all that hot religiosity was not for me then – not yet. It was enough to know that there were others taking all them conventions as seriously. Or like Ibn Rabah himself, say, who the school was named after. That's Bilal Ibn Rabah, Mister – the first to have called prayer at Medina. The first muezzin taught by the Prophet himself. Circa some early AD.

72. BEAUTIFUL THINGS It took a little longer for me to find my feet. I spent the time between classes with my ears plugged, Mister, drawing circles around that airy school court, not saying a word to anyone. Mostly, I sat alone with my father's *zoun . . . zeen . . . zeen . . .* with the rest of East Ham, with its shabby degrees of grey, disappearing out the window. My head became stuffed with beautiful things. Beautiful pretension, I suppose – ecstatic poetics, stylistics, proper *deen* – and Him with the Beautiful Names.

73. **SPLASH!** How lucky was I, then, to find a set of quickly rising lads to fall in with? Three boys who became a band of my brother-peers that first year. Ibrahim, Hass and Moazzam – one lad gifted with the gab, the other an entrepreneur and another a self-styled seer. But where was it that we first met? – the court, the fountain. I remember I'd stopped to rest at the round centre. Other students were flowing in matching dress past me. I'd closed my eyes for a moment to rub the soreness at my hip. I heard a pair of sandals brushing up behind me. It was Ibrahim.

– Salaam, cous'. Do you mind if I . . . ?

I remembered the face, Mister. I'd watched this Ibrahim perform in class. He was a Somali lad who everyone knew as one of the only students who could grow a decent beard at thirteen – it was waxed at the end, a pointed tip. His recitals were usually too much for me. He fidgeted too much with his face and I found it off-putting.

– I know you, he went as he swept his keffiyeh back and sat beside me. You're the one that's always at the back of the class with your blank pages, yeah?

I nodded at Ibrahim, and moved over.

– We seen you, cous'. You put not a blot on that paper. How you get away with it?

He grinned at me with his pink gums and wide white eyes. He stopped when he noticed I was staring. He whistled –

Oi! Oi! Come! Two other lads approached. There was handsome, fat Moazzam. That black thickness of curls around his cheeks. And Hass, who was hunched, squat and stony-faced with both hands in his pockets. They perched on the fountain. Moazzam had a pile of books with him. He balanced them beside me on the stone. I read the spines. It was the comparisons, the linguists – al-Zamakhshari, Ibn Qutayba, the *Majaz ul-Qur'an*.

I was impressed, Mister. This lot were reading the heaviest stuff, the prosody and so on.

– I'm Moazzam, said the big lad, with a massive hand toward me.

We shook and I said my name. Hass nodded from the other side of Ibrahim.

– Hass, he went, and sniffed.

– I was telling Yahya, said Ibrahim, that we know him as the boy of blank verse . . .

– Yeah, I seen that, said Moazzam. Yeah, how come none of them sheikhs says nuttan when you hand in? Must be a nephew or suttan, *alie*?

– Ask him, ask him if he does any of the reading, went Hass, nodding at the books.

– Must fake like he does, said Moazzam. Do you do them, brother?

Truth was, I ignored most of what them sheikhs set for us, Mister. I hadn't thought they'd have noticed me. These three were usually huddled together in the corner, sat on the blue mat spinning lines together. Moazzam always used to swing his arms when reciting, as I recall. Had a loudness to his voice. Sometimes it'd come off soaring, mostly it rang so hard he made the windowpanes clatter. Moazzam was from Cairo by way of Croydon, or somewhere like that. Hass took to performing in a shallower mode. He was quickest to perform when called upon but usually dashed once he got there. Like a spring release, he was. Launching his lines like a slam-poet would. All bent knees and flying fingers. His poems were never really any good. And I noticed how each of them, including Ibrahim, would snatch a quick glance around our faces before sitting back down. They were each expecting applause, I think, which we were never allowed to give. Sometimes they received it if they did well. But nobody would have heard me speak until that point, I suppose, let alone recite.

I swallowed hard, Mister. Sucking back a stutter as I replied:
– I have, yes, I said.

I looked back at the thick reference books, all creased yellowed spines.

– But you can't have read all of them already, said Hass stepping closer.

– I have, I said. Read them before – but the *Majaz ul-Qur'an* I had to read twice – I forgot some. But the Ibn Qutayba is better. That one is about detecting harmonies in *surah*, and . . . how the words might flow out the breath. And this –

I stopped when I noticed them staring. I felt somehow self-conscious, and I shrank backward as I sat, covered my legs with my shawl.

Moazzam leaped to his feet and lifted the books from me.
– Out the way then . . . He went.

I ducked as he hurled two of the books into the fountain – *splash!*

– What you do that for – you fool! went Hass wiping his chin and shoulder.

– Easy, Moazzam! went Ibrahim.

Moazzam stood holding up the copy of Ibn Qutayba. Around us other students were staring, pointing at the water and at us.

– You heard the lad, said Moazzam. This one he says is worth reading. The others would have taken me a whole year. What you say your name was, bro?

– Yah . . . Yahya, I stuttered, confused.

– *Yah? . . . Yeah-yeah?* he mimicked. Well, you've saved me a waste of time, bro.

That was Moazzam, Mister. The boy who loved nothing more than making a splashy spectacle. I was confused at the time as to why anybody would want to ruin a book. But I laughed when them others laughed. And for the rest of that term we became inseparable.

74. BROTHERHOOD So – there I was, Mister, eager to head into another school year having made friends with a rangy sort. These lads seemed so exciting to me, so full of life. All came from good families too, and proper gabbers. At first, they really brought me out of my shell, Mister. I even began to pay attention in class, composing, inventing and practising new rhymes at recitals. The problem was I was still hopping with my giant urges, Mister. And there were parts of myself I felt I couldn't reveal.

I was too impatient to impress, I think. I'd attempt to cook up a few sanitary verses to show the next day. I'd go into my basement, stick a pair of headphones on, turn the sound way up and scribble a few lines measured to my father's metre. But every time I read back what I'd written, Mister, I found myself so repulsed that yet again I'd end up tearing them all to pieces and apologising the day after.

All this is not to say that everything with my brothers was easy. These lads were definitely better combed than me, more controlled, and comfortable in their own skin. And although none of them seemed bothered with anything like the same convulsive terrors, the sort that left me emptied and ashamed, they had their own inadequacies, for sure.

We'd often sit under them white arches in the square, going over set texts. I was usually the only one who did the readings, so they'd often ask me questions. They'd ask about using the *iltifāt* as a device, for instance – which involves, incidentally, a quick shift in the grammar, singular to plural, while referring to the same person. Moazzam asked about it but then seemed confused by my explanation, giving a shrug.

– Bro, just give me the quick version, he said. Aren't there any easier *tricks* to pull? I just want to get the *gist* before tomorrow's appraisal. I'll die if I get shown up by Fahim again.

– Me too, said Hass, looking similarly exhausted, I'll die if I get laughed at one more time. Can't allow that Fahim, bro. Can you, bro? Seems suss to me, that Fahim . . . *wallahi-mums-life.*

I shrugged and scratched my ear, saying nothing.

They didn't consider style, Mister. Although they cared very much about how everybody was going to receive them. Even Ibrahim, who did seem to want to better his method, was usually left deflated once he realised he couldn't get ahead fast enough.

– No, no – I'm done with this, cous', he said, getting up and packing his things.

Ibrahim was the one who'd often organise events around school, Mister. He'd give us flyers to hand out. Seemed more interested in *making a scene, cous', we have to publish, need to be seen to be taken seriously* . . . so he was always trying to whip up interest in our writings. He'd print pages, publicise them, pinning poems to cork-boards and leaving them out on canteen tables and so on. Even going so far as trying to convince them sheikhs to let him put on a public reading.

I gave no hint that I knew better, Mister, or felt irritated by their distractions. Although I did, and I was. For all the warmth and affinity, I also never shook the sense that whatever formed between my brothers and me – and however much I wanted to believe it was a true thing, that closeness – it still smacked of performance at times.

An odd thing to say, I know, to claim my friends were only posing, but maybe that was all we were capable of at that age: posturing, play-acting, pretence. The affection felt real. But it was also a kind of pose, I think. All another way for the four of us to say – look! Here we are, a little band of brothers – against them other, foreign-born flatter lot.

Ibrahim, Moazzam and Hass were all from wealthy families, Mister. When any of them spoke about their childhoods it was like hearing they'd been raised in beautiful idylls. Ibrahim's four elder sisters looked like queens to me in pictures, dressed in traditional Somali finery, and were doctors. And his parents were doctors. They had holiday homes in the richer parts of Mogadishu, he said, although Ibrahim himself had been born in London. Hass was born in Manchester. His dad had founded an energy company and was usually away with work in Karachi. Manchester seemed as far away as Karachi or Mogadishu at the time. And even the gruffer, loud-mouthed Moazzam, who'd previously gone to no better state primary than mine, had boasted how his father was *pretty famous back home, you know*, and had been on Egyptian nationalist telly for years.

In that sense, I saw no difference between my brothers and them other lads. And yet, I could see how quickly them others brought their ends up. It was as if they still couldn't measure up – *Nah, that lad there is a proper boot-licker, brother . . . Ah, they're only posers, cous', we can do better* – and then I also saw how they'd imitate them. Moazzam would always raise his chin to press a point just like Fahim. Ibrahim would make the same severe turns of phrase as Samir. And Hass, watching Midhat, would copy his jerking gestures during recitals, shucking his arms back and forth like a skinny pigeon. It was all such see-through stuff, Mister. And it irritated me, honestly.

I think part of the problem was that, like me, Ibrahim, Moazzam and Hass had been born in Britain. Had lived most of their lives here and had gone to British schools. This other lot had only seen the West from the outside. It sometimes felt as if they regarded any kind of Britishness as embodying the threat of the bully West – and so even being born here was seen as suspect.

My brothers sensed that, I think. Ended up feeling ashamed, and making new versions of themselves to fit in. And while it did bother me, Mister, I understood it.

My own estrangements wouldn't be so easily erased. My

awkward gait was enough to keep me outside that measured set. There was nothing I could do about it, Mister, and I'd come to terms with it, I think. My brothers made it easier. They'd known I'd been marred at birth. Even Moazzam, with that bad mouth and bluster, made a proper show of helping me any time I stumbled.

Thinking back now, I can see how completely invested everybody became in *putting on . . . making airs . . .* and the theatrical. From the flowing uniforms we had to wear, to them long white shawls, matching satchels, sandals and that high-minded speech. And our huddling in little groups even. I'd say my brothers and I might have speared our palms that second year. We could have marked ourselves with blood, Mister, like them boys in all them Nordic myths, and made a big show of our brotherhood – except, again, I doubt this lot would have seen themselves in any Gunter, Högni or Sigurd . . . My brothers wouldn't have managed to reach that far, Mister, for their metaphorical tricks.

I suppose, watching everybody send themselves up helped me discover my one advantage: I wasn't as concerned about being seen. And I doubt anyone at the Ibn Rabah had suffered the kind of loneliness I'd felt. Nor had they been made to spend as many hours reading. None of them had been forced to fill every empty space with mutterings just to feel less alone. And as troubled and unsteady as I was, Mister, at least I was used to being ignored.

75. DOUBLING DOWN I resolved shortly after that to stop feeling sorry for myself. I felt able to leave my Mothers' basement, Mister, and them classrooms behind me. During the half-term holidays, I began to write all day and my head came singing with new formulations. I'd made use of the school library – so much so that I no longer searched by the author, Mister, but for the translators themselves, names like Humphrey Davies, Denys Johnson-Davies, and Paul Bowles, whom I revered just as much as them masters. It felt as if I was finally putting some substance to the flash.

I still wrote listening to my father's cassettes. But the sound came imbued now with a sort of restless, boundless energy. The poems I read back still frightened me, however. And they still felt strange spoken aloud – like some chaotic voice when reading.

When I returned for the new term I met up with Ibrahim, Moazzam and Hass. We began to practise our verses together. It was obvious that I'd come on in leaps and bounds over the holidays. Obvious to me, at least. As for them – and at this point, Mister, it became more than a little irritating – none of my brothers seemed to acknowledge our differences in ability. They focused instead on my form and muddled posture. Moazzam, for instance, liked to suggest things to me: *Just do suttan with your hands. Do anything, bro, instead of just standing with your skinny arms up.* And then Ibrahim would join in with a jibe: *You'll never be a poet, cousin!* And then he'd lift a hand, going: *Joke – just a joke!*

I kept my patience. Saying nothing. Nodding along and muttering *Okay, yeah – I'll try* . . . But my doubts had lessened by then. My confidence had grown. And although I hadn't shown it in any classrooms, I'd not a doubt that I'd have outshone them all in private.

76. INVISIBLE BOY (1) I returned to them upper decks, Mister. On weekends and evenings, I'd pick a pair of jeans, T-shirt and a bucket hat from a pile of discarded clothes, and went out for a few hours to write on trains and buses.

The intention was to disappear, Mister. Go invisibly into them sweaty crowds of strangers. Commuters packed onto the Tube and the DLR trains. The noise of them all, a constant chattering lot.

It was during one of these happy first outings that a group of lairy football fans boarded the train. England was due to play a minnow that night. The carriage was suddenly crushed with sweaty arms and the noise of chanting: *We're gonna scoooore one moooore than yoooou . . .*

The sight of this damp rabble, Mister. All them knee-length shorts and football shirts. Women with their striped leggings and faces coloured. All them drunken wide boys bare-chested and *proper-ammered*, beer at their *froffin moufs*, elbows out, voices loud – *givin it laaarge*.

I sat there mouthing what I could. I watched how they smacked each other's shoulders, fell into each other's arms, staggering about, red-faced and blotted.

One of these lads, square-shouldered in shorts and a cloth belt, came over to me. He sat down and slapped me on the thigh, shouting: *Oi! Score more than four, mate?*

The lad was drunk. He had blonde messy hair, and eyes crinkled with laughter. Name like Jamie say, or *Jambo*. He was slurred and silly-eyed, Mister, but he was handsome. He had a charm about him which made me want to forgive his spilling beer on me. There was a girl with him. Some Sharon say, or Vicky or Tracey. She sat next to him like a riot of red paint.

I stared at them both feeling the sting of the hard slap on my knees.

Score, mate? He said again. *Score more than four?*

I shrank away, looked out the glass. There were wires running along the outside of the window. In the reflection I saw the girl make a gesture at me. I heard her whisper the word *moos-lim* into the lad's ear. Then she pointed at me, the stray hairs on my chin – my barely-there beard – a giveaway. It was enough to offend him, Mister. The lad burped in my direction and laughed. The girl laughed. I pretended not to hear them with my earphones on. They both left me then, and started singing *who-are-ya* at some other boy.

It might have been the smell of the beer, Mister, or the gentle drum of the train, but the whole scene transfixed me. See their mouths, chests and burned red skin. The singing, the cusses and laughter. One of the girls, some Denise or Charlene, clutched at the arms of another lad, twisting in her little white top and jeans. And him, some proper Onslow-looking lout – some Robbo, say, Liam or Dave – see him fondle her so openly. And them other lot, paunch bellies, loud gravy mouths, swaying with the train, cheering them on.

I couldn't tear my eyes away from them, Mister. I couldn't help imagining them in sweaty collapse. The white boy's red lips, how he grasped the girl's neck with one hand and an empty cup with the other. The girl, barely upright in his arms, one hand clinging on to him, the other clutching a lighter.

I knew that I hated them, Mister, but couldn't help but feel my body caught up with theirs as I watched them. I sank into my seat completely inflamed, trying hard to shake the feeling. I looked down at the ground. I couldn't bear to catch any glimpse of myself in the glass.

77. BODIES ON THE TRAIN I returned home that night and went into the basement. I just stood there for a moment letting the slow ache at the bottom of my stomach settle. Deliberately then, with a pen and paper in front of me, I recalled the sight to my memory. Bodies red from burning. All wet and shining and white. My fantasies emerged. Another flight.

I saw bodies over mine. Other backs, muscular chests, fingers running over my skin. I closed my eyes then, and, absurd as it sounds, I recalled their voices around me sounding inside the room. I heard their slurred singing. It felt so real in that moment. I could smell the beer on their breaths. I could picture my own body among theirs. I imagined strong arms around me, a mouth, a kiss. And then a jolt. Sounds as if screaming. I suddenly saw myself thrown over the railings. And a train, thrown. There were limbs now lying around all bloodied and splayed. Some explosion. Torn bodies and metal strewn all about. More screaming. And then a blankness.

As the dream faded, I felt myself sit upright. I laughed, I remember, as if everything inside of me had been released. And I gathered myself, began putting what I'd seen onto paper. I'll recall a line here for you now – which I'm sure you already know – the one ending in a bloodied flag:

Eng-ger-land! Eng-ger-land! Eng-ger-land!
I'll paint your white bodies black again
With the blood flooding up from your flag

Just a fragment, Mister – though I've read countless interpretations of this one verse since. I can tell you now, it came out of nowhere at the time. All I remember is the sense of triumph at getting it out of me.

Probably, you have a clipping of this poem in your bag. Maybe you have it cut from one of them papers say, them fearmongering red tops, Mister, who took what I'd written and claimed it eventually, as intolerable, hate-filled and properly prophetic . . .

But all that comes later.

78. MANIAS There were times when it'd felt as if I was the only boy in the world whose insides felt so uncontrollable. It's easy to dismiss and say it was just a flush of teenage obsession, Mister, but I also had the suspicion that my manias were bound to me by blood.

Part of my *fitra*, if you like – a kind of inherited jinx.

I'm reminded now of that very summer. My Mothers' house had become unbearable in the heat. The suffocating air had brought on another of my mother's episodes. And this was after my Sisi Gamal and Mother Sadaf had hoped her fits had passed, and that maybe she was getting better. But then, one evening, the sound of loud moaning came from across the hall, and the rattling of metal. My mother was banging at the radiators. I went to see and stood by the doorway looking in.

My mother was crouched in a corner, arms writhing, almost naked, and my Mother Sadaf crouched beside her, trying to settle her. She was almost embracing, Mister, trying to pull her hands away from the radiator, burning her skin. The humidity was enough to make smears on them grubby windows, Mister, while my mother kept pressing her wrists against the heat. It was as if the pain somehow relieved her.

Eventually, the crisis passed. I heard my Sisi Gamal suggest they confiscate anything in the room she might harm herself with. All that clutter in her drawers, them mirrors. The small blue room seemed ghostly after that. There were marks on the wallpaper where the mirrors had been. A few portraits remained, and her knitting needles. Her needles were rounded enough to keep safe. I don't know why them photographs were kept there. Them faces seemed like spectators to me, waiting to watch my mother's next re-enactment.

79. THE BLACK POT My Mother Sadaf and Sisi Gamal seemed to become unsettled after that. My uncle had the news constantly on – *Blip!* – *Ten-year-old girls go missing in Soham* – *Statue of Thatcher has its head hacked off* – *Blip!* – and sat there as if he were watching the world fall off a cliff. Everything seemed to irritate him: *Ach!* – *whole place is going to pot . . .*

My Mother Sadaf would sometimes even join him. More often than not, their conversations were about Estella. My uncle wanted my mother to be sent into residential care, but my Mother Sadaf was having none of it. She'd stomp around in while my uncle shouted after her. *Sadaf! You must listen, we cannot take care of her alone – you must think of Estella . . .* and then every so often, Mister, pushed by my Mother Sadaf's protestations, he'd ultimately threaten to write a letter – *I will write one, Sadaf! I will write one and it will bring an end to it . . .* To which my Mother Sadaf would thunder back at him, threaten him with a battering, and go, *You just try with your letters, Gamal! And you will see – your letter will bring an end to you!*

The sight of them burly arms, Mister, clutching her *cubby*, and the knowledge that the old Mother had become even more un-predictable – maybe even madder herself at her ancient age – the threat alone was enough for my Sisi Gamal to change the subject.

80. ECSTASIES Mister, you asked if what happened next was the result of my own early misfortune. I suppose it was in a way . . . How else could I have interpreted the world, other than through manias, obsessions, mirrored images, and mad-ness? The only difference, Mister, was that my own manias came out in borrowed language, into poetry, springing out my head in heckling, bullying tempers. I was scared of my inside Other, that's for sure. But like Estella, I began to feel the same compulsion, Mister, to bring my red fingers to the heat.

81. IRAQ (1) I'm sure it was no coincidence that my voice announced itself, just as the world had begun to focus on the region into which I'd lost my father, Mister.

A country that always sounded to me like a dry seed in the mouth: *Iraq! Iraq! Iraq!*

It was April, I think. Your Blair and Junior Bush had just decided to lead half the world into war. Baghdad was getting bombed from the skies. And at the time, Mister, I remember having been sat on the sofa with my Sisi Gamal, both our eyes fixed on the telly. The VCR had its red light on, recording. My uncle rarely left the sofa. Shoulders sunk, glasses sliding low on his long nose. And there, his trembling finger poised above the button . . .

When the war started, Mister, I noticed how quiet my uncle became. I kept glancing over at him, waiting for him to say something about it. Maybe even cuss at the telly, say, the same way he cussed at them commercials. It was only when Saddam's face appeared on the telly did he even raise an angry fist. He shook his head at your Blair, though. For your Junior Bush, he could only laugh – *Ach! ha!* – tossing a hand at the telly as if his laugh were a shoe.

I remember thinking to myself that maybe my uncle was just exhausted by it. Even I'd seen them pictures before. On a tape labelled *1991: Gulf War, bombings, beginnings etc* – the year of my birth. That was when them American planes flew over Baghdad the first time. Missiles, smart bombs, helicopters and your Senior Bush. All them sandblasted faces, Mister. Little dots in the desert. Markings on a road where vehicles had crossed, bodies strewn like garbage. And now, having recorded so many wars, so many outrages and atrocities, my uncle might not have been able to muster any anger for a war he'd seen before.

Some nights I'd join him on the sofa. We'd have the window open even after dark. Hoping the stuffy air in the house would drift into the evening. My ears would drift with it sometimes, through the window, Mister, out to where my Mother Sadaf would be crouched, clipping at her roots.

I began to wonder what it might be like in other people's houses. Other people's sofas. Seeing it all unfold like that on the telly. Pictures of tanks, planes and the blurred-out dead bodies. All these people baffled by an enemy they hardly knew. And you, Mister – what did seeing your lot going off to war feel like for you?

155

I can hazard a guess. Must have felt like a release of sorts for you. Like on a valve, a little. To see yourselves as the heroes, I mean. It must have been nice to see your boys in such a respectable light. British armies rolling into Basra, Najaf, Kirkuk – *giving the world what for* – after so many years deprived. Like the most natural thing in the world to go off and bomb your way into *decency*, *dignity* and *good*. Into freedom, Mister. Priced-up freedom, sold like mouthwash, chewing gum or nice, clean, impeccably white trainers. Packaged in USAID, say, or so many cans of Coke.

For my Sisi Gamal it must have seemed like taking the piss. As if it were a sham – a big bright nothing. I remember the way he stared at them crowds. Them children in particular, and their scruffy dads, who welcomed them soldiers on the BBC. They were blowing kisses at the tanks, I remember. He leaned forward to watch. My uncle was neither surprised nor offended by it, I don't think. Although I did notice his hands set down. He'd withdrawn his stained fingers from the remote.

Even when the tape expended and wound back, he only sat there and stared and listened. My uncle usually asked me to fetch a new blank tape whenever one was out. But, this time, when all them smiling Iraqi children came out shouting *You-ess-ay! You-ess-ay!* he just sat there without a hint of feeling on him.

Maybe the news had changed, or maybe he had, Mister. I don't know. But my uncle watched that evening news as if it were one of my Mothers' soaps. Completely unmoved. Or maybe, with all things considered, he'd decided for himself that this was a bit of history not worth recording. Like it was just another war story. And one told badly, at that.

82. IRAQ (2) Mister, I can't say anyone else acted as if the war was for show. At school it was all anybody could talk about. No one believed your BBC. But there were other sources my brothers could look to now and get the news. At the same time there were these unfiltered images that started to stream into our phones, and on certain websites, and school forums. All them news reporters on telly became irrelevant after that. We started logging on to find out what we needed.

– Is this for real? went Hass, huddled near the screen.

We were under them arches, Mister. It was a kind of ritual every morning. We'd trawl through the latest photographs posted up from the war. Images of awful devastation. Roads strewn with charred bodies. Anguished families running barefoot from their homes. We'd scroll looking for the most graphic. I remember a series of pictures from inside some Iraqi mall. Heaps of bodies. One close-up of a man lying twisted on a marbled floor. He had on a checked shirt, I remember, and a digital watch. His arms were folded over one another, as if the person taking the photograph had placed them there. He was dead. And though it was difficult for me to make out his bloodied head, it seemed to have fallen to one side, like a severed limb.

– Proper real brother, said Moazzam, zooming into the mass of red pixels.

– I don't believe it, said Hass throwing his hands up. No verification.

– Verification for what? went Moazzam. You want a name tag on the poor fucker?

Moazzam snorted and scrolled on. These images were from the aftermath of an aerial bombardment. And for weeks,

Mister, there was nothing about it on the news. It was like being shown an alternate reality. Another world revealed on our screens. Some darker and hurtling world. Fires in the sky. Mountains erupting. These images came thick and fast and from our point of view told a better story. Only time I glimpsed the turbaned fighters was online, there in our palms. Bloodied faces, and wrapped around arms, not much older than we were. The world seemed so much more desperate and cruel and exciting. None of us had any words for it. Only short breaths: . . . *wallahi* . . . *Allah* . . . sat there every morning under the fountain. Just watching, scrolling, clicking through.

83. PROTEST! A season of protests followed. Everyone at school had seen the same pictures. Students started carrying slogans, chanting and putting up placards and that. One group after the next started picketing at the gates.

Each morning I'd shamble in with my backpack and bushy hair. I'd hurry past them placards and signs declaring the latest atrocity and numbers of the dead. Full of outrage, they were. Against your Blair. The bloodshed and occupation. And they were chanting. You could hear their shrill voices echo all across the court – *Not in our name! – End the illegal war in Iraq! – Blair! War criminal!*

And so on. Months like this it went. And it's important to mention, Mister, that the Ibn Rabah had become such a local marker by then that all of Poplar came to watch. Passers-by even joined. White women carrying shopping bags and that. Old men wearing woolly scarves and leftist buttons in their caps. A younger crowd took pictures on their phones, though they didn't linger.

The protests continued the following year. Most students had drifted back into class by then. Though, as the war rumbled on, Mister, the temper of them rallies began to harden. The ones left were the meaner-looking sort. The *proper devout* as my brothers would call them, *with their tongues in sheikhs' ears*. They were an older lot from the school, ones I recognised but didn't really know. There was a certain seriousness about them. And though there were fewer gathered now, they were loud and could fill the court with the sound of their slogans.

The echo of anti-war chants was eventually replaced with recitation. Many of them had studied in class, and so these readings were often very beautiful. Along with *surah*, they'd read pages from more obscure works like Sayid Qutb. The stuff praising Allah for protection at first, and then dragging the West for murderous corruption. I remember them sheikhs' disapproving any time we heard their chants.

How quickly it all changed, Mister. I didn't know these boys. But each morning their eyes seemed to follow me in as I brushed past them through the gate to get into school. Reproving almost. Most of us ended up using other entrances into the square. But over time, Mister, the relentlessness of these recitals provoked more than interest. There came a kind of admiration.

– What are they saying now, bro? went Hass as we sat at the fountain with our eyes at them at the gate. I can't make it out.

– They're saying names, went Moazzam standing up to take a look. They've been going at it since yesterday. Just saying names. Same names. Over and over.

– Whose? I asked.

– Just names, bro. Of the dead.

It was a long list, Mister. The protesters were reading out a list of civilian casualties from the past week. My brothers and I had seen pictures. Bodies scattered from an airstrike. Some of these bodies had been wearing schoolbags, Mister. Them at the gate had found their names and were reading them aloud in a kind of remembrance.

– That's inspired though, muttered Ibrahim, pinching the ends of his beard. Who is it singing? Abdallah, is it?

– No, Samir, went Hass. Singing about the path to paradise.

We all nodded having heard that boy before. He was a small lad, light-brown hair covered by a cowl. His voice rose sweetly as he pronounced each name.

– Him, he's proper *akh*, proper *Salafi*, now . . . said Moazzam and nudged Hass, who sneered at him.

– Samir? *Salafi?* How would you even know? Samir doesn't even talk to you, bro.

– Got eyes, bro. I can see with my own eyes they're *Salafi*. Not just *religious-religious*. Look and see how they've shaved their heads and top lips. Beards up to here too. Same as Abdallah, with them three plaits at the back. Samir's shaved his head bro, and he's only from Edgware.

– I think we should join them, said Hass getting up to face the gate. Offer them our voices too – maybe Ibrahim can put a show on?

– Yeah that's an idea, you know, said Ibrahim.

They were all standing now looking over at the gate. I noticed Ibrahim begin to step toward that side of the square as if drawn to it. When he spoke again it was with a sort of loaded manner I'd heard before at his recitals.

– No, you're right, cousin, he said with feeling. Should be –

should be doing something for our brothers and sisters in Iraq . . .

He nodded as he spoke, about the suffering that was obvious in pictures. *Can't help but think about my own mothers . . . my own sisters . . .* and that we had *a duty to raise our voice for the voiceless.* He nodded and pinched his beard. The other lads had quietened as he finished. They seemed genuinely moved by what he said.

I suppose it's why I spoke up myself, Mister. I glanced at the gate, all them lads in heavy dress, black *thawb*, black puffa jackets and trainers, backs turned against us. Before I knew it I'd started to speak, unable to catch the words falling out of me:

– My . . . father was from Iraq. I said. Marwan. He went back, actually, to fight – went ages ago. Might . . . still be up there. I don't know – never really knew him . . . yeah, nobody knows . . .

I felt my fingers cover my mouth. I realised almost immediately that I hadn't spoken about my father before, not with them. It almost sounded like a lie when I heard myself out aloud.

– Wait . . . Your dad went to fight? went Moazzam, stepping toward me.

– Far as I know . . . I said.

– When did he –? And he went to fight? Ibrahim asked.

– Before I was – I don't know, like 1990, '89 . . .

I sat down again and felt the warm stone bench with my fingers. My brothers said nothing.

Strange thing was, Mister, it was after my claim that I noticed my brothers started treating me differently. They started making space for me in the square. Made sure I'd get a seat in class and so on. Even started asking how I was keeping – *How you keeping, brother, you alright, yeah?* And then one day, when Moazzam arrived with another grisly picture – *You won't believe this one, brothers* – Ibrahim told him to leave it. *Put your phone away,* he said and pointed at me with his chin. Moazzam held his hand in apology.

I think they might have thought it was a deeper bereavement for me, Mister – all them images of bombing, shelling and death. But my origins were murky enough. And it was easier, I think, for my brothers to fabricate their own relation to it than it was for me to cross the real distance back to my father's Iraq.

84. YEAR OF THE GOAT I'm trying to explain it here, Mister but it's difficult. There was a drive in all our hearts to pitch up against the war. All us students felt we had to have a say, and we had to do so confidently. Like them bearded lot at the gate with their religious rites and slogans.

I'd sensed more of an uncertainty among my brothers. They really didn't know how to feel, or what to say. The images seemed to have forced a kind of paralysis. They were angry, I think, and didn't know what to do with their anger. They were also ashamed of not knowing how to act. I heard them sometimes repeat slogans they'd obviously heard chanted at the gate, No, *that man is a war criminal, cous'* . . . *say nuttan* . . . *whole political class need shutting down, alie* . . . though somehow the words fell flat in their mouths.

As for me, I stayed quiet.

Like my Sisi Gamal always said: *Boy, you must always take breath, before saying anything true* . . .

After glaring at the telly for so many weeks, my uncle's simmering ire had finally found an outlet in *da'wah*. He began performing more hostile verses in the street. Even on them buses, he'd gurn at other passengers. These grey faces snatching nervous glances at our boxes and books. My uncle would turn and cuss if they looked too long. And then he'd turn to me, Mister, and whisper quietly: *Regard their prejudices, boy – they shape us in their heads.*

We were at a Poundland in Turnpike Lane, next to the station where all the buses were parked in rows. I'd hear him muttering to himself even while sorting out our table. And then he turned toward me again, saying:

– Did you see . . . they destroyed the library, boy – *ah?* – the national library gone. Looters. They could have stopped it. But – *ach!* – what are these things to them. Our language . . . it is like the barking of dogs to them. Like braying of goats . . .

He brought his wooden box to the side of the table. He cleared his throat, wiped his lips. And then he stepped on without his usual poise. He clambered up, Mister. Tossing his arms to his side and, with a hacking cough, spat at the ground. He took a breath. And even then, as he brought his forearm to his chest, he glanced over at me suddenly, widening his mouth to show them khat-blackened gums, and in a hiss said to me:

– We will show what a noise we beasts can make!

He caught sight of a passing couple on commute. He made a growl at them. Something like an animal might. Then he rose loudly: *Ne-eh-eh-eh! Ne-eh-eh-eh!* And he gagged and coughed, falling into fits of hacking laughter.

The couple were startled, stepped away, thinking the old man crazy. He went at them again: *Ne-eh-eh-eh! Ne-eh-eh-eh!*

And it seemed absurd, Mister. Then he lifted his arms and began a loose, kind of cawing, ecstatic recitation – a spiralled crying with breaks in his breath – making his poetry sound like some terrifying din.

I didn't know what to do. People were beginning to look over and stare. It wasn't long before two policemen approached from inside the station. I went to pull my uncle's arms down, telling him to stop. My uncle did come down, Mister, but went on with his laughter, still muttering, and making great swirls with his arms. We barely had time to gather our things before them uniformed coppers, pushy in hi-vis vests and down faces, started moving us on, telling us *Get on your way, leave off now . . .*

My uncle didn't even look at them. He didn't even bother with the barrow. He just lit a cigarette, looked up at the sky still laughing, and left me there to collect what I could. Some books I had to leave behind, Mister, left scattered on the road outside the shops.

85. ABU GHRAIB I'm sorry it's taken me longer to send you another letter. There was an accident – one of them nurses took a swab of my cheeks and tore a stitching. I've been in the worst kind of pain, as you can imagine, Mister, though I feel no anger toward your nurse. I'll have to write through this next letter in discomfort.

My story had come to a turning point, as I've already recounted. And so, it's with my uncle at Poundland, after being shooed away by them coppers, that I'll continue . . .

Maybe my Sisi Gamal actually had gone mad, Mister. Or maybe he'd got to the point where he decided he'd become exactly what they wanted him to be, what they all saw in their heads. I don't know. Either way, that afternoon in Turnpike Lane seemed to stir something inside me. And actually, all of my uncle's subsequent *da'wahs* were performed just as madly. All that boisterous flailing about on his box. I'd never seen him that way, Mister. I remember having to prop him up on the way back home. But then listening to what he delivered that day, I'd finally come to conclude something for myself too.

I'll write and tell you now, how I did it.

That following day these photographs started doing the rounds. New photographs, Mister, had made it on the proper news this time. Even your BBC and CNN had chosen to show them. These pictures were so shocking, Mister, so appalling, that, for a moment, it was as if the world my brothers and I had glimpsed on them forums and phones had at last broken through. Outrage in the press. Condemnation from across the globe. It seemed that everybody finally believed that there had been atrocities committed by Western troops. Them pictures from Iraq had proved it.

These pictures, Mister, had been taken by a group of soldiers themselves, showing how they detained Iraqi prisoners and forced them into degrading positions in their cells. *Advanced interrogation*, they called it – *torture*, by any other name. Men piled on top of each other naked and beaten. Men held in stress positions. Men tied up and bleeding, bitten by dogs. There were captions to each of these images, and it was there that I read it had all happened in an Iraqi prison called *Abu Ghraib*. Abu Ghraib was a place on the outskirts of Baghdad, Mister, some dungeon there, at the edge of the world.

It looked like hell to me. The images published in your

papers were censored, and I had to look on them forums to find originals. And I swear it, Mister – I found hundreds of them. Someone had dedicated an entire board to Abu Ghraib. I spent hours clicking, reading replies, waiting for new pictures to surface. The comments and attachments were endless.

Sooner or later, Mister – and I don't know which exactly provoked me first – I started taking notes from comments left by users. I could hear them in my head as I read. They sounded to me like students at the Ibn Rabah, though it was a public forum, Mister, and could've been anyone. Names like @nasim88 and @abu_dun_dun while their messages sounded a kind of manic tone. All threaded together it read like a mad cacophony – *Look at these rabid murderers bastards fucks!* – *American soldiers, see? American dreams* – *See, these look like somebody's nightmare!* – *EXPOSED!!* – *So, now the world sees the WEST – Sadists! Fascists! US Dogs!* – I sat there and read aloud, Mister, copying down, mouthing the words as I wrote them. And then, slowly, some beginning would feel itself out.

O Western wind . . .

Names speaking from behind pixelated silhouettes. Anonymous identities, talking in turns, avatars and 'O's' trailing along endless annotation: @sashy_habiby: *how can human beings be so cruel?* – replying @sashy_habiby: @abu_salut: *these ones are not human! what are you expecting?* – I'd mutter again, read it over, clicking, copying, scrolling on – @umer9: *the kufr are incarnate, brothers, look to His seed* – @haseebpr0: *is she holding the leash? bitch is a torturer, look at the detainee –*

replying @haseebpr0: @rfv556 *the detainee is in a puddle of his piss* – I made notes absently, looking, writing, reading again – *when will it stop, when will they stop . . .*

O

Western wind
When wilt thou cease

I started noticing, Mister, after the long thread reached multiple pages, how similar expressions kept coming up – @abu_cutee: *Death to America!* – @gr17: *Fuck Bush!!* – @hassanc33: *Fuck them all and FUCK her with the leash!* – It sounded like spits, scratches more than language – @diselkhal: *Fcok Biush!!!* *%3G09awfsvdEeurm!!!* – @bakhtin5: *Death to American Dogs!* – But I'd trace the words that were not words, carrying their sound instead.

O

Western wind
When wilt thou cease
That the red and blue may burn, may burn, may burn

Comments came in great floods after them pictures emerged. These ones showed American soldiers posing with their thumbs up against bloodied and beaten bodies. They were enflamed on the forum – *replying @samirkhdr: @salfaizul: no kill your-selves!! who r they??? degenerates, freaks* – @no5elay55: *Americans, fucking kufr whores and fucking killers!!* – I read on and it became more difficult to tell if there were real people behind the names – @zadim_zadim: *no – trust me this is all*

staged – @vice50: US have a history of this, check the dates,
meta data shows discrepancies in the – or whether they were
even being serious – @matejramzy: *these are paid actors, check*
the names that bitch was on tv two years ago –

O

Western wind
When wilt thou cease
That the red and blue may burn, may burn, may burn
Allah! Allah! Let my hand take the leash!

It was the next flurry of posts that made me feel the poem
finally taking shape. The names of the soldiers were revealed in
the press. Names like *Lynndie, Sabrina* and *Ivan* – @fatouKRT:
all American names, find their all American families, find
their American homes – @said_said: *'Sargent Smith' yeah?*
'Sargent Fred' scum!! – And then there came stories that the
guards had given the prisoners nicknames. See a picture of
a man standing naked with his arms stretched out to the
sides, his feet crossed like a dancer, like a saint, in a pose.
Except when I looked closer, faeces were smeared all over his
body – @saeed007: *they called this one 'shit-boy' the papers*
say he was mentally ill – @grrt9: *no words, no words . . .* –
@barduk2: *Death to America! Death to America! Death to*
American dogs! – Still, I copied it down, ran over it, clicked on.

O

Western wind
When wilt thou cease
That the red and blue may burn, may burn, may burn

Allah! Allah! Let my hand take the leash!
I'd have these white bodies beaten faced

And then – there came a trace, Mister. I'd been sat at that desk in the basement for so long, days by then, and in the end the rush of another idea felt like a dream. I realised it was the terror and fear that I needed for the poem. Not a lyric, nor a song – but a heckle. A shout that could provoke some kind of flinch, say, or some sudden turn of revulsion. A poem that could recall the braying of goats and barking dogs – like all them voices I'd found here on the forum.

O

Western wind
When wilt thou cease
That the red and blue may burn, may burn, may burn
Allah! Allah! Let my hand take the leash!
I'd have these white bodies beaten faced
Down into their own shit and piss

I scanned for one photograph in particular. A man stands in a peaked black hood. A cloth covering his head and upper body. His arms are outstretched. Dummy wiring attached to electrodes at his fingertips. He looks like an angel standing there. Like a prophet. Them same sadistic guards had given him a nickname too – *Gilligan* – after a character on American TV. He reminded me of an angel, Mister, but also Blake's *Albion* – him, with his arms stretched out, naked, in all his glory. I went back to what I'd written. And suddenly it was as if the poem had found its own form, and its own significance.

169

O
Western wind
When wilt thou cease
That the red and blue may burn, may burn, may burn
Allah! Allah! Let my hand take the leash!
I'd have these white bodies beaten faced
Down into their own shit and piss
Death to America!
Death to America!
Death to America!
And they call us, us
Beasts!

The joy, Mister! A breakthrough at last!

It's always a beautiful thing to recognise yourself in your writing. And it's a relief to see it here again. For there I was at last – the traced outline of me. Hidden still, but there between the lines. I posted the poem, Mister. Right into that comments section with all them others. But then I needed a moniker. An anonymous signature to go with it. And after a moment's deliberation, Mister, I found one. Not a proper *kunya* nor some ready *ism*, but rather a preposition. I chose the word *bayn*, meaning *in-between* in Arabic. I liked how it sounded in the mouth. *Al-Bayn. Albion.* The hooded man in the Iraqi prison made me think of England.

86. GOING VIRAL Whether anyone on that forum actually read the thing, I didn't care. What mattered to me, Mister, was that I had it out of me at last. And all while listening to my cassettes in order – *1992 (oud, drumming)*; *1993 (oud, flute,* *second flute, chanting)*; *1994 (just oud, no voice)*. By the time I'd got to *1996*, the poem was done.

Only later did I notice the little number change beside my new moniker. That ticker, Mister, began to flash as others on the forum began sharing and replying to my poem. But it was out of me at last. And it was now beginning to spread.

87. GRATITUDE Can I say now that none of it felt real to me – probably that new name, a kind of mask, or disguise made it easier. I sent as many as four, five poems out the next day. Started early and wrote a couplet for every current event. A small following quickly grew around my Al-Bayn. Hundreds began to reply to anything I posted. Other commenters even started doing the same, in similar styles. But that didn't bother me. I felt relieved, honestly, and lifted. And, Mister, this was the same month I'd started praying alone.

Yes – I'd started praying again, Mister. On my knees after every completed poem. I'd go at it by the table, pressing down, rising, kneeling, in some half-remembered method. Same way my Sisi Gamal had taught me so many years ago. And there was a great swell inside me now. Something like gratitude. Gratitude for my own singing, spinning Allah, Mister, whose graces had finally done me good.

88. FORTUNE COOKIES I met with Ibrahim, Hass and Moazzam soon after my night of revelation. In my head it feels like it was the very next day, but in fact, it was a few weeks later. And while my Al-Bayn was the most widely shared on the forum, Mister, none of them knew this suddenly popular poet was me.

It was at a Chinese takeaway, Harry Wu's, that I met with them. There was an old, melted-looking man behind the counter who served greasy chicken in little plastic boxes stained like the man's yellow teeth. I'd got a Coke while the others devoured chicken and bean curd as if it were a Mile End delicacy – which it was, in a way.

They'd been talking about an event that'd been organised. It was to be a recital that coming weekend. The school hadn't given permission to host it, so he'd ended up putting it on publicly in a park for free.

I wanted desperately for Ibrahim to put me on the billing, Mister. I remember feeling impatient about it. All my brothers had already performed for large-ish crowds by then. I was yet to make a bow. And even though my uncle's *da'wah* had offered me plenty practice, this felt different. I'd be reciting my own proper poems.

– Didn't order for you, bro, said Hass as I sat down. Didn't know you were coming.

I waved a hand saying it was fine. Hass had grown a beard, Mister. It made them dark stony eyes look menacing. Moazzam too had grown his thick curls out. They were all having to wipe away the dribbles of sauce with their napkins and sleeves.

– How long you want mine? Moazzam went to Ibrahim, slurping a Coke. I got a few other names, mind. If you're still looking. What about Samir?

Ibrahim nodded, his lips tight around a straw.

– I have a few more slots. Need them filled by Wednesday. Friday I want confirmed. I managed to get hold of a few from the forums but –

Moazzam gave a start, swallowed and leaned over his food.

– Nah, nah, nah. Don't want them ones, he went. Don't know who the fuckers are online. Could be anyone. Could be a fed.

– It's true, went Hass, waving a chopstick in the air. But not knowing adds to the thing, yeah, the mystery – I read some of them forum lot, have you, bro? I've read enough.

– Point is, said Moazzam, it really could be a fed turning up at them recitals. Some Prevent arsehole looking to ruin.

– Online names bring crowds, said Ibrahim. You sure you can't do five, Hass?

– I can't brother, no. Interview next morning.

Moazzam jutted a smeared chin.

– For what? Proper job, yeah? Full-time?

– Part-time, just deliveries. For my uncle.

– *Mashallah!* said Moazzam. Got your licence then, is it? Good for you, *akhi*. Face like mine and yours – *beardies* now. Lucky your uncle has vacancies, *alie*!

Hass ignored him and started picking broccoli off his meat.

I had to wait, Mister. For these two to pack their mouths before getting a word in.

– Um . . . Ibrahim, I said, steadying my voice. Actually, Ibrahim I'd like to do a few minutes myself.

Moazzam and Hass nudged each other, looking over.

Ibrahim wiped his beard and looked up.

– You –? For the –

– Yes, me.

I felt a hotness at my cheeks, Mister. I didn't like the smell in the place. I didn't like having to sit and listen to these lads chew and slurp through horrible food. All I wanted was an *okay, yes* so I could get on with it. And so I stared at Ibrahim until he spoke again.

Ibrahim nodded. Glancing at the others, and then back at me.

– Of course, cousin – yeah, he went. Can you do five minutes, four . . . ?

I nodded. I didn't want to tell him about my *Al-Bayn*, Mister. They'd find out soon enough. I snatched at the Coke and finished the rest with a gulp.

– *Hah!* – Like it, brother, Moazzam said after a moment. You've loosened up, look at you. Less tense. Less in your head. – Oi, Hass, see how Yah's coming and you're not?

– I can't, bro, said Hass, I want to be in the book though. There's a book, yeah, Ibs? Gotta get on this now, *chop-chop* . . .

– I'm speaking – I'm talking to printer people on Friday.

– Need a name for the group too, said Moazzam, leaning back to think. What do we call ourselves, brothers? The four of us, needs suttan like –

– Yeah, us four, we can wear all black, yeah? All black.

– Yeah – good, good – we'd be like The Beatles, bro . . .

– Yeah! Like The Beatles – us four. Ringo, John and Paul and that.

I stood to leave as the others laughed and finished up. Hass started fishing into the plastic bags. He was looking for the fortune cookies tossed inside.

– Hass, you're obsessed, cous', said Ibrahim.

Hass began gently cracking open each strip. This was customary, Mister. It was the one thing I enjoyed about coming to Harry Wu's. I leaned forward and watched. Hass never usually revealed what them fortune cookies made of our fates.

He'd keep it for himself, Mister, only giving us knowing nods. But this time, one cookie seemed to have left him confused. *What's this . . . ?* He brought the offending note into the open and left it there for the rest of us to read. The fortune was written in Chinese, Mister. None of us could figure the lettering. Hass could only shrug. But we all saw his frown. Then he threw the note into the remains of the meal, like it was nothing.

89. FIRST RECITAL What should I write about my first public performance, Mister? Admittedly, it wasn't the momentous occasion I'd hoped for. Wouldn't have turned any heads, so to speak – not even your own, Mister, had you been there.

A crowd had gathered at the famous Speakers' Corner. Maybe fifty or so bunched and shivering. I'd dressed myself in a long black shawl, I remember, some itchy fabric. I wanted to disguise my sloping shoulders, adding layers to appear bigger than I was. My brothers were there, similarly dressed in black, matching new beards. And we stood waiting for our names to be called.

My eyes were on the gathered crowd. The usual anti-Iraq War lot had come. Some faces I'd recognised from the Ibn Rabah. A few groups of lefty white lads too, badge wearers and banner men. Ibrahim had set up tins to collect donations. *For bereaved families*, he said. Ibrahim had set the tins alongside pamphlets and CDs and other things to purchase. I saw him running about before we started. He was sorting out the mic and the speakers himself. And when it was time, we shuffled in then, like a band of curious priests.

The first few performers were the ones Ibrahim had handpicked from elsewhere. These lads I didn't know. A few earnest appeals among them. Poems pledging calls for conscience and solidarity and so on. Difficult to hear them at first. The softer-spoken lads especially, given the streaming buses and cars on the busy roads nearby. I was more interested in the crowd reaction, honestly, than that early lot. Miserable faces. Heavy coats. Beanie hats and scarves. They were looking around at each other mostly. Holding placards and standing aside, allowing dog walkers and other old dears to cross the walkway.

I was among the next set of poets. A boy named Ahmed went first. Then Moazzam. The big lad went bold with it too. He made his chest large, filled his big cheeks and sent his short barrelling poem over everyone. He seemed disappointed with the limp claps he received. And then it started to drizzle, Mister. And when the next lad went up, the crowd were too busy with umbrellas and hoods to really listen. Ibrahim went after him. And I remember he'd chosen a poem we'd worked in class together. It had a *buraaanbur* style to it, a sort of lyrical Somali strain. He began as he'd done in class too, with a prepared introduction. He stood there for a full two minutes explaining how the poem was written in reverence to Ismail Mire – *who fought in the expulsion of gaalo* . . . He spoke the thing aloud rather than performed it. But it was too intricate, Mister. Too obscure a thing for that gathered lot. I remember when it ended, he was agitated too, his skinny elbows pointed as he stepped off the stage.

I was to follow Ibrahim, Mister. I'd decided on a poem I'd written the night before. It had a cast of hundreds of voices though nobody would know it. All plucked off the forum with them carping voices. It was a poem about the killing of Izz al-Din. All I remember was I'd approached the microphone with my arms raised, and then let my wrists fall to the sides as I started. *My poem is to commemorate a martyr . . .* I said, steadying my voice. I performed the poem, Mister. And it was over in a few minutes.

I wish there was more to it than that. I'd like to say that I'd left more of an impression. Some hint that I'd made a mark. I even picked out a man in the front row wearing a green jacket, and delivered my last syllable at him. His reaction only came when I rose sharply and stared hard as I closed – there was a flinch. I saw it.

Other than that, nothing. Polite claps from the back.

When I stepped down, Moazzam huffed and offered a rub of my shoulder. *You did well, brother*, he tutted, *but the crowd was proper dead.* We left the park in relief, honestly. And then we threw ourselves into the 240 bus and headed home happy to get out of the cold.

90. KUNYA I was very quiet on the way back. Moody impatience spilling into some harder feeling, I think. Ibrahim came and sat next to me and said he wanted a word. The lad was already thinking of the next event, the next move.

– Cous', listen, he went, tonight was just a start of it . . .

– I know, I know, I said.

– I was thinking about a book – about publishing. We should all be published poets next term. And cous', I think your stuff was among the strongest – and I can tell these things, cous'. I have an ear for it – *wallahi*, it's true. Yours was the strongest.

I looked over at him and nodded thanks.

– You got more where that came from, yeah?

– Yes, I said.

91. ESTELLA LEAVES Sands were shifting. The sky was shaping around me. I had wondered, Mister, what my Sisi Gamal had been scheming during them past few weeks. In all that time I'd spent in the basement, I hadn't seen him. I'd hear the old man busying himself in them upper floors. Talking to himself in my mother's room, talking about *a letter, I will write a letter . . .*

Not long after that, I found out my Sisi Gamal had made arrangements on behalf of my mother. She was to be sent away. There was a care home that would look after her. *All arranged, boy – at last! But – ach! – do not say a word about it to anybody!* He'd done it all behind my Mother Sadaf's back.

She was leaving the house. And honestly, I don't know how I felt about it when he told me. I'd been praying, of course, and I felt as if my Allah had magically cast aside my mother. It was a selfish thought, Mister. But it's how I felt at the time.

My Mother Miriam returned briefly to help my Sisi Gamal pack up for her. She arrived concealed, I remember, out of sight of my Mother Sadaf. I'd watched them both from the top of the stairs, quietly shuttling bags from her room to the landing. The day she was to depart, my uncle booked a cab for her. He said he was going to settle her down. And he flapped his hands once the cab arrived, and we bundled several bags, heavy black ones filled with my mother's fabrics, into the driveway outside.

– *Owf* . . . it is cruel to do it this way, said my Mother Miriam. Her eyes were wet and reddened, and she'd stopped in her tracks. She was a sister to Sadaf, she went on, Sadaf should have the chance to say goodbye –

– *Ach!* snapped my Sisi Gamal, you know what is *cruel*? It is keeping this woman inside with the door locked! While she gardens, seeding, digging, planting things that will not grow . . .

My Sisi Gamal hissed for us to hurry. My Mother Miriam wiped her cheek and carried on to the cab parked down the road. I rolled the luggage over the potholed drive. Most of my mother's things fitted into a single bag, Mister. Them long reams of fabric – which my Mother Miriam insisted my mother would be lost without – took several careful trips up and down the stairs to gather. When we'd finished loading, my Mother Miriam took hold of my arm as if to steady herself, and walked with me.

It's an odd thing to remember now, Mister. But even in that moment, even if she too believed we were doing it for the good of my mother, my Mother Miriam's thoughts, as gentle and big-hearted as she was, were toward my Mother Sadaf – the woman who'd fed her, cared for her, but had also flicked, spat and cussed her out for her entire life until she'd left. *Sadaf is not cruel*, she said. *It is the only way she knows how to love is to bully*. Her forgiving words stirred me somehow as I watched my Sisi Gamal come pushing my mother out in a wheelchair.

The chair was an old wreck he'd retrieved from the clutter. I remember my mother sat bundled, feet wrapped in bedsheets and old clothes. She was leaving for good, I realised. It sent a turn in my stomach. Her breath showed in the cold. My Sisi Gamal lowered her into her seat and stepped into his own.

My Mother Miriam went to say goodbye. I hesitated behind, Mister. I stood by the bushes with my hands in my pockets. It was only when my Mother Miriam asked me over that I dared get closer. Estella's face – them eyes clear under that white light, staring absently ahead of her – sent another lurch into my stomach, Mister. I moved past my Mother Miriam and crouched down by the door. I looked over her hands and noticed how pale and thin they were, delicate pink at her fingertips. I felt myself falling forward then, pressing my head against her, pulling her close with my arms. And as the swell of hotness came to my cheeks, I realised I felt no movement from my mother, no response. It was like holding a wooden doll, Mister. My need to hold on suddenly turned into revulsion. I staggered to my feet. I wanted to run back to the house, but I stayed and watched my Mother Miriam close the car door.

My breathing began to ease. I realised that a period of my life was ending, Mister. That sight of my mother, my Mothers' house, them decrepit corridors behind me, even my uncle, who waved at us from inside the cab. *Just for the first few months*, he'd said to me when explaining why he was going along. *I can find a small flat and get Estella settled. Better weather in the south . . .*

My Mother Miriam and I stood silently for a while afterward, next to them overgrown bushes and peeling fences. She looked down at me, eventually, and saw my face.

– Mr and Mrs Stevens of Kettering, she said.

I looked at her, questioningly.

– Estella's mother and father, Yahya. It was they who sent the money. They have always sent money for her. Never to see her, not once since your father . . . just letters, numbers, account names – *Mr and Mrs Stevens of Kettering* . . . I saw the letters once when I went to get your mother's prescriptions.

My Mother Miriam looked so sad, Mister. And as she spoke it became very clear in my mind how my Sisi Gamal had never needed to work for his room, and his basement at the house. And how all three of us were allowed to stay on for so long. We'd been taken care of. *Mr and Mrs Stevens of Kettering.*

– I think she will be happy by the sea, said my Mother Miriam, saying *happy* like it was a borrowed word. She smiled, as she turned to touch my cheek.

– Go inside, she said to me. And listen – one day you will leave this house too. And you must promise me, Yahya, you must promise it will be *you* who chooses. No matter who says otherwise . . . my *goat-boy, my boy* . . . Sometimes the only thing to do is to abandon a dead thing.

She bit her lip, looking at me and then glancing up at the house behind me. I watched her turn and walk away into an unlit road. Her arms wrapped under a black shawl. It was the last time I spoke to my Mother Miriam. She was like a stranger. Her shawl, her scent, smelled nothing like her.

92. SALT I won't go into how my Mother Sadaf reacted to being deceived about my mother. She'd been distracted when I told her. I said my Sisi Gamal had sent my mother away at last. And all she did was nod along wearily, mumble something, and hobble off, looking for a trowel out in the yard.

Some months later, my uncle returned to meet my Mother Sadaf at Forty Road. It was May, as I recall it. Only giant mounds of brickwork remained. Splintered beams and concrete left behind. The council had given permission to pull the house down at last. It was gone, Mister. When we came to see it one last time there was nothing.

Neither of us said a word. We only looked. The allotments

at the back had been cordoned off from the main site. My Mother Sadaf swatted away the *Caution* tape and walked right in through the wire fencing. I followed her around the plaster and broken roofing. What was left of the house was piled into different lots. As we walked through I recognised parts of what remained. Old prams, boxes, picture frames and footstools. Everything lay on the grass alongside broken cement. The gardens behind were mulched over and trampled. Metal piping had been strewn all across them ruined beds.

From there, my uncle and I let my Mother Sadaf walk ahead. See her trudge on with her sunken neck into them weeds and rotten vegetables, Mister. This woman who raised countless strange roots and turned them into even odder soups. I watched her walk out inspecting the ruin. She spat. Kicked a few overturned pots and walked on.

We'd been worried about what would happen to my Mother Sadaf now that the house had gone. She was never going to join my Sisi Gamal down south, that much was clear. When he offered, she said the sea would bring only wet air – *bad for my bones* . . . and so on.

I watched now as she produced a small box from her pocket. It held what looked like white powder or dust. She emptied the contents over a patch of soil.

It was salt, I realised.

I watched her sprinkle spoiled cabbages with it. The wilted mint beds too, and the crushed flowerpots and torn leaves. She dusted her palms, spreading the last. Everything the house had meant for the old woman, Mister – for all of us, over so many years – was now an empty waste. And my Mother Sadaf, socks hitched up to her swollen knees, was reminding us now, in the only way she knew how, that there was no use crying over such unforgiving soil.

She didn't say goodbye as she left. Only walked past us both, Mister. Brushing her palms at the earth, fixing the knot in her scarf, and kicking the dirt up as she went.

93. ENDINGS (MYTH) The memory of that day – seeing the old woman salting the earth, stomping the ground in them ugly boots, and then turning away – has stayed with me. Like some half-demented fairy, my Mother Sadaf vanished completely after that. To have recorded her name with her voice – with all her cusses and stuttered *bohs* – brings me a bit of satisfaction, Mister. I feel I've laid her to rest on these pages, here.

The memory itself reminds me also, that sometimes life moves from one stage to the next quickly and haphazardly, and at other times with so much finality and purpose.

It reminds me that stories, like silences, have a way of enveloping a person. My Mother Sadaf knew the significance of that. She knew how rituals, gestures and actions make up a person. I knew it too, I think, even then, having learned most of my truths from her. I knew a consequence would arrive to replace this period of my life. I was confident that I'd sent the right intentions into the world. Some new and shattering occasion would be just around the corner. An event, say, that would send me hurtling into a new and louder life. And it did arrive, Mister. I only had to wait another month before another vision became reality.

94. 7 JULY This day I remember perfectly, Mister – you needn't ask if I do. Bent metal burning. Rubber tyres. An old childhood memory of a rhyme: *wheels of the bus go round and round* . . . These pictures were on telly in an endless repeat. Tavistock Square. Aldgate Station. It was only a few weeks into that summer. Right down in them tunnels there, in the Tube, near them *da'wah* spots Sisi Gamal and I used to stand and recite.

This was Edgware Road. Near the station. Where everyone saw them thin lines of blackened ash rise into the air.

I'd moved to my new dormitory a week before. I was now at the Ibn Rabah, Mister, my uncle said he'd talk to them muftis and took care of it.

I remember sitting, Mister, crossed leg-over-leg on that carpet just watching the telly report – *blip!* – *four British-born lads – backpacks strapped to shoulders – three separate blasts – fifty-four dead – blip!* – London streets filled with debris, bodies fleeing, sounds of sirens, trains, reporters filming at the scene. It all sounded so familiar to me. Like a memory. Like I'd seen it all before. It was a strange, unsettling feeling, Mister.

I set about writing as quickly as I could. Words came once I heard them names on the news – names, again, Mister. But not of the victims this time. What caught my ears were the names of them four Bradford boys. The bombers. With their mugs like mine and my brothers'. All four names were mispronounced, I remember. Every newsreader on the telly got them wrong, even that Moira Stewart fumbled beside them blurry shots of them boarding them buses and trains.

I can't tell you why these names sent a tremor through me, Mister. Ibrahim messaged me about it later, and I couldn't even tell him why, when I heard the names of the bombers, I'd felt inspired. I could hear the excitement in his voice, Mister. How he kept telling me: *You'll go viral for this one, cous' – didn't I tell you – didn't I say* . . . I used Al-Bayn to post them, Mister. Because it was Al-Bayn, made of the collected mass off them forum voices, that I heard read out the poem in my head. I'll write just a fragment here. I know you've read it before. A poem as tribute to four unmourned men:

> *Let British tears salt British soil instead!*
> *As we sing the names of our martyred dead:*
> *Mohammed Siddique Khan!*
> *Shehzad Tanweer!*
> *Hasib Hussain!*
> *Germaine Lindsay!*
> *For in His name Their names are:*
> *Holy! Holy! Holy! Holy!*

I remember the same murmur at the mouth as I'd finished it. I posted the poem straight away. And then I just looked out the window and peered, waiting to see if the sky had changed – and it had. The clouds had parted. There were shades now of some impressive new light. And can I say, Mister, despite the mess that followed – all the noise that has landed me in it, into this here hot water – I saw no other way of reflecting the bright-wide back on to itself.

So – *chop-chop* – Al-Bayn it was who'd send me off into fame and misfortune. And I think I'd understood also, Mister, that my bristling, teeming-under-the-skin, flower-bud Yahya was no more. I was no longer *goat-boy*, Mister.

And I would never, could never, go back.

II

2010–15

Al-Bayn

To fame, then – notoriety, and disagreeable celebrity. For what did it mean, Mister, to see the sight of my own irregular face, to hear my own indecent speeches suddenly cast back at me now, refracted again, into so many circulated recordings, photographs and imitations?

Five barrelling, spinning years had passed since the posting of that last poem. That ode to the 7/7 martyrs made my name. I daresay by then my Al-Bayn had become the most widely read poet in your Great Britain. Had I known where I'd end up, I might have preferred obscurity . . . As it was, I was self-styled and out there now – with my curls pinned back, tucked under a short cowl, wearing a sort of black keffiyeh, and a thicker, blacker beard, dyed dark, combed and pointed at the end. I'd assumed the form, you could say, of an improper poet: Al-Bayn.

In truth, I was a stranger to myself in these intemperate years. I began to reject my fame almost as quickly as I'd found it. For when it arrived, Mister, fame came like a flood for me. Nearly swept me away with it. Fame nearly drowned me. First for my words, then my *kunya*, and then my body. I'd have gone under had I not found a way to escape . . .

95. AL-BAYN! AL-BAYN! So – my youth lay behind me now, while the years of adventures and bold escape to come – the next period of my life, Mister, spent beyond your British borders, out in exile and so on – lay ahead of me still, and waiting. But before I get into that, I'll write to you about the year preceding, the year that ended with my abandoning your Great Britain for good.

How quickly them poems started circulating. I was republished and reprinted many times during the five years since. People read me in little pamphlets, Mister, press magazines and papers. I began hearing my name – repeated endlessly. Out on the streets, strangers would come up, yell at me: *Al-Bayn! Al-Bayn! Al-Bayn!*

And so, imagine me – once the slack-jawed *idiot-boy* born to a mardy household – catapulted now into a celebrated figure of sorts. And as the years passed, many of the faces I'd known, and had known me by my first name, had become lost to me. Moazzam and Hass, for instance. Both left after finishing studies. Them lads never got to see my fame arrive, or my rise into notoriety. And after my Sisi Gamal had also sped away with my mother, Mister – that doe face sat in the back of the cab, and him waving out the back of it – my days had become so busy I had no time to visit. My uncle, too, had stayed for the entirety. Choosing instead to live by the sea, to be close to her, and be shot of East Ham, at last.

Incidentally, the old man left me with a caution: *Eyes open, boy! – And remember: no telling what their beliefs will have them do . . .* And he was right about that, Mister. I began to be surrounded by strangers wanting to please me and bend over backward for me. It was an odd feeling, as though my own poems had overrun me, Mister. Or caught, like little fish-hooks, inside other people's ears, and had somehow become animate in the world without me.

Ibrahim was the only one who remained at the Ibn Rabah. And it was his idea to record me. He'd sussed the demand to hear my verses, Mister. And so it was him – my brother Ibrahim with his canny eye for an opportunity – who started publishing my oratory online. There were videos now, audio clips and so on. Ibrahim burned CDs off a computer. He sold them over websites with my name emblazoned in bold. And the ads he made were something like *Al-Bayn! Hear the Voice of a Generation!*

I began drawing proper crowds. Proper numbers, Mister. Over the next few years, what started as a few nights slowly turned into shows every weekend. And soon, barely able to keep up with new poems, I was being shuttled from one recital to another. From community halls in East Ham to outdoor rallies in Dagenham, I was delivering my poems directly to crowds of hundreds.

My life, Mister, from being nobody's boy to being cheered upon stages, had totally transformed.

96. FAMOUS You asked if I enjoyed it. Admittedly, I did – at first. I liked the attention. I don't mean to say my mug was suddenly daubed on the sides of buses. It was nothing like that.

But around them ends, and especially that corner of East London – Poplar, East Ham, parts of Shadwell and Mile End – there were some who'd come and stop me in the street. All these peaked caps and hoodies. They'd come and give me salaam, bow their heads at me: *Bless you, Al-Bayn . . . Brother, I've read you, read you all over . . . You're the only one telling it like it is . . . You! You're the one blowing up, brother . . .* And they'd take their phones out, Mister. Quickly snap a picture of me just standing there, squinted and startled. And then I'd look up and they'd be gone, having made off with my likeness.

97. PHOTOGRAPH Five years later, I could barely step out my dorms without getting accosted by some pack of followers who'd recognised me. A few might have seen me recite. Others had heard the name. Making me out wouldn't have been difficult. That long black shawl down to my ankles. And my hood, which I'd wear most days, and covered often. It wasn't like I had other clothes I'd care to wear, Mister, but it felt more appropriate now. I was dressed for the part. Same with my beard, which I'd only dyed because Ibrahim had said it'd suit my new routine.

Anyway – there I was, Mister, out on a walk one evening, when I stopped at a wall covered in fly-posters. It was a shop front, or similar. Shuttered now and serving as an advertising board for local businesses. Between them ads for estate agents, theme nights, music events and the rest, I'd recognised my own mug staring back at me.

Al-Bayn – black smock and scowling.

Mouth wide in mid-recital. One finger in the air, a little to the side, a sort of hectoring pose I'd practiced.

The photograph was taken at a performance. It wasn't big, the poster. But then I glanced across the street and spotted more. There were others plastered up behind me. Replicates of Al-Bayn, Mister, pinned on lamp posts, the sides of walls and windows. That barking black-and-white apparition had been papered all the way down the main road.

I was struck with a sudden nausea. Five years of this, Mister. The ground, the street, seemed to rumble beneath me. I reached to grasp hold of something and catch a breath. I quickly looked around to see if anyone had seen. Rows of parked cars. Bags of stinking rubbish. I reached for the first poster I saw. I tore it off and revealed a bright streak of colour underneath. I stuffed the offending poster into my pocket.

I stood there for a moment then, deciding whether to tear at the others. Hundreds of Al-Bayns glowering out at me. I looked up at them heavy clouds and wondered how long it would take for the rain to wash them away. I muttered a short prayer for it.

It occurred to me – and the sense came with a feeling of dull hotness, Mister, like a hoarseness in the breath – how repulsed I was by them pictures. I decided to go and see Ibrahim. To talk to him about these photographs, tell him I wasn't happy. I'd hated what he'd turned me into – an image, not a person.

98. IBRAHIM'S PRAYERS Them five years seemed to have fixed him too. Everything about Ibrahim seemed hard and serious. He'd often have me wait whenever I came to see him. He always had something else to attend to. Rushing around, scanning papers or open books, or staring into his laptop, putting his phone down in irritation, picking it up again in relief. When I showed him the poster he'd batted it away, saying, *One sec, cous', let me just –*

His rooms were large, Mister. All big windows, with wooden ornaments displayed like gilded plaques on the walls. He'd been lecturing a little at the school. And this room with an awning, a view overlooking the main court, came with his new posting. All that half reading and pretend, Mister. He'd still managed to get them sheiks to regard him as a proper sort. It looked to me as if Ibrahim's bluffing had come good.

– You don't look well, cous', he said at last. You should sleep better. Creative minds need sleep. Did you see – did you look at the schedule?

Ibrahim's beard was as tidy as ever. His hair was receding, but there was a polish to him now. Everything about him so neatly pressed.

– Haven't slept, I said, rubbing my cheeks. And this don't help.

I dangled the poster in front of him again. Ibrahim slid it over and gave it a look. The lad seemed to feign annoyance at the image. He tutted.

– Not much we can do about that, he said. If you knew the sorts of budget operations I have to deal with, cous' – *amateurs.* Spend all the money on booking you, don't they.

Ibrahim had been on at me to start producing and posting more regularly. I'd only written a handful of poems that week. He'd been setting targets for me. Four poems written and two posted a week. I wasn't even sure what he did with them, honestly. But I knew they went somewhere. He'd shown me screens full of numbers.

– Major, major plans for us this year, he said, tucking his

hands under his elbows. Pay zero mind to the rest. We can't bother with trivialities, bro. The world is here, now, changing, cousin. Don't talk to me about no posters, please.

Ibrahim smiled, and pulled on his beard, scratching irritably at his ear. He came around and perched himself on the desk.

– One problem though. I'm already looking to sort, so you shouldn't worry . . .

– Go on . . .

– It's the sheikhs, cousin. I got a letter saying they decided against your stay. Want you out by next week. They see you as a troublemaker. Until now, they turned a blind eye to all the attention you were getting. But now – but since . . .

– Since . . . ?

– It's yesterday's problem, cousin. Nobody comes to their sermons, that's all. They've seen all the crowds flocking to you up in Lewisham, in Barking. It's not their crowd. They call them *activists, polluters, perverts* – but even still, it offends them to see the younger generation take a different path to *deen*. People would rather watch you online, watch a video at home and then do *dua*. Let them sheikhs cry about it, cousin. We move.

– But where am I supposed to go, Ibrahim? Where am I supposed to –

– You're anxious, cousin. You shouldn't worry. I'll take care of you . . . Better this way, anyway. Let that lot scare, cous'. Get your bags packed. I'll find you a temporary –

The phone beside him began buzzing. He looked, mouthed a cuss and took it.

Ibrahim was back to other tasks, Mister. I sat there scratching my head for a moment. Looking around the room at all the good furniture and strong shelves of bound books. In the corner there, I saw several boxes of newly printed pamphlets marked *Al-Bayn*. There were stacks of video tapes too. And hard drives next to them. They were labelled with masking tape and left like paperweights on his desk.

Ibrahim glanced up at me, disappointed I hadn't left.

– Alright – come. If you're here we might as well pray together. They've given me a prayer room, my own. You'll feel better after. And I'll show you out after that.

This was the same Ibrahim who might have scoffed at Moazzam anytime he'd leave us for *dhikr*, Mister. This same lad was now leading me through a small door in his office to pray. Inside were two intricately woven mats lying on the floor beside each other. I was hesitant stepping in, Mister. I hadn't prayed alongside anyone since my Sisi Gamal.

Ibrahim was neat with it. His motions well practised. As tidy and clean as that pointed beard and them line-like eyes. He knew the manner, Mister. And with them oiled feet and his flowing garb, he looked the part. A proper devout. I made do with my own shuffled motions. Keeping an eye out, Mister. Watching my brother mouthing his prayers with such easy effort.

99. 'WHO IS AL-BAYN?' It became obvious the sheikhs at the school had known what was coming. Maybe they'd been offered a tip, Mister, I don't know. The following week, after all my Ibrahim's *don't worry's* and *I'll sort it's*, the national papers had my Al-Bayn plastered all over their pages. They'd used the same picture from that poster. With the headline going like: *Who is Al-Bayn? – Britain's newest hate-preacher.* I couldn't believe it, Mister. After spending all this time sourcing

the papers and telly for my poetry, it was Al-Bayn who was now staring back at me.

Every word, of course, was slander against me and lies. Some British journalist, Mister, had framed what I'd written, inserted a few quotes and listed them in a spew. I remember marching around my room fuming at it – *Al-Bayn . . . this ghoulish figure . . .* – appalled at the caricature: *. . . anti-Western hate spills from the preacher's mouth . . . mosques up and down the country . . .* The entire article, Mister, painted me as a big-mouthed cleric. As if I were up near a street corner somewhere, some any-sort fanatic, pushing oratory. My poems, they said, had been greeted like *sermons*, my recitals like *jihadi bile . . .* And though there was no mention of the Ibn Rabah by name directly, Al-Bayn's schooling was noted as having taken place at *a popular East London madrasa . . .*

Them sheikhs must not have liked that. Ibrahim had only once previously mentioned a fuss over a poem. *That one about the cartoons, cous', was strong, very strong – published last week.* Some cartoonist had had a poke at the Prophet. The whole thing had provoked such an uproar online, I'd made a verse from what I read. The poem had come out flying, Mister. Like so many I'd written at the time. And, honestly, I wouldn't have remembered had they not been reprinted in the paper: – *let them mock! – let them ridicule! – clowns! Apologists! – our kitchen knives are mightier than their armies! –*

My words were taken out of context. It offended me, honestly.

This cartoonist had started appearing in papers himself, saying he'd received death threats and so on. The article claimed my poems had something to do with it. As if I'd egged them on, Mister. As if I, myself, had been calling for the doodler's head!

I couldn't bear to read the rest of it. I took out my bag, Mister, and began throwing my clothes into it. The thought occurred to me that Ibrahim must have known about the article. He must have, Mister, and yet he hadn't warned me about any of it. I felt aggrieved. I started stamping over my notebooks and that, sending papers flying with a swift kick and a cuss. I was angry at Ibrahim. Angry at the article. Everything felt so unjust.

100. PANTOMIME Of all things, Mister! Your papers chewing me out for what? For a few lines on a cartoonist. The whole thing felt like a pantomime to me. And the maddest part: the article only made my Al-Bayn more popular. Life during the next few months became even more like a parody for me. More like a cartoon than any real life. I became just as they'd drawn me, Mister, caricatured with my glowering eyes, black mouth and black beard. And I soon came to realise – after Ibrahim saying: *Don't worry about it, cous, look at the numbers! Look at the crowds!* – that all this had gone far beyond my control.

101. CROWDS, CROWDS, CROWDS See me drawing mobs in places like West Harrow, Slough and Tower Hamlets. See me out there, Mister, in front of all them baying faces. Every crowd I performed for felt both larger and more rabid. Scrawny young men, mostly, with hungry expressions on their faces. They always seemed to stare, fish-eyed, jostling and elbowing each other, as soon as I took a breath to begin . . .

Oh – a little on the quality of my performances, Mister. You should know how much I'd come on. I made sure to serve it *out the belly*, just as my uncle had taught me. But there was no finesse to how I performed – that wasn't what they'd come to see. I let my body slouch almost, sloping to the side, and carrying the same finger-wagging style as my Sisi Gamal. I knew my silhouette alone was enough to unsettle some in the crowd. And I also knew the mystique made them want to hang on my every word.

Off to the likes of Birmingham, Bradford, Leeds after that. I'd never travelled so far, Mister. I was loosed and newly minted. My Al-Bayn had become top billing, and there were even times when it felt good giving these people what they wanted. The real uneasiness came later.

It was after my recitals, when I came down from them stages, that a strange surge started to worry me. There, among them sweaty bodies, Mister, I always felt a revulsion. A sudden physical nausea that I couldn't quite explain. It might have been all them skinny arms reaching out at me. I was surrounded. They'd shove things onto me, into my hands. Bits of papers, receipts. Sometimes it'd be little scribblings of me. And they'd demand my name, that I write it out for them. I couldn't stand all that babbling hysteria, Mister. It was as if they envied something inside of me, sensing something monstrous, out- rageous even, that they now wanted for themselves.

Ibrahim had me staying at a bedsit with a boy named Zenab. Another white-boy convert, Mister. One of a group of volunteers helping to distribute flyers and so on. Ibrahim told me: *The boy Zenab's a proper sort, cous'. Best stay with him until I can find better . . .* Zenab was a runner, Mister. As well as a driver, a recorder and whatever else Ibrahim would have him do. His name hadn't always been Zenab. He'd been some Christopher or Lawrence or similar. Ibrahim had told me he'd converted when he'd reached this side of Mile End. He had that same strange vacancy in the eyes, Mister, that odd dimness to him, as if in awe of me, maybe, or totally bewildered.

It was this Zenab who recorded my recitals, Mister. Always had a contraption on him too. Some camera strapped to his shoulder or a wired up mic propped on a pole. His thin *English-English* accent would follow me about: . . . *Yeah, yeah, I did Media Studies at uni . . .* and so on. Prattling away behind me, Mister, showing off a new bit of kit. *No drama,* he went, *if the crowd go off on one again. This thing will catch your voice perfect.*

All that electrical equipment stuffed into an enormous rucksack, Mister, kept him hunched as if on expedition. It made him look bigger than he was. I'd watch him in the evenings when we returned to his dingy rented bedsit to-gether. I'd watch him as he'd kneel to pray on the carpet as soon as we got back. I'd ask him how he'd managed it, following me around for the entire day. *No drama,* he said, which was his usual refrain, *I eat on my feet when I'm able. It's an honour anyway, a duty.*

It was Zenab's job to follow me, Mister. Everywhere I turned I'd find the lad pointing a scope at me, recording my every gesture. I'd see his shaven head tucked under his beanie, them crooked eyes fixed on me. Like the rest of that begging crowd, Mister, he did seem lost in that same daze of unnatural adoration.

102. 'GERMANY SOON, COUSIN!' There was one night in Manchester. We were very late getting back in the car. Ibrahim had been driving, giving Zenab, who had driven for the last few hours, a break. He was in the back now, sleeping with a coat over him. I was tired, Mister. Sore in the head. My throat feeling tight and there was traffic as we came into London. Them red lights seemed to stretch for ages.

While he slept, I remember asking Ibrahim how long I was expected to stay with Zenab.

– Few more weeks, cousin, he said. Just until –

He seemed distracted, Mister. The radio was going. He kept nudging me to listen.

– See Tunisia on the news, cous' – it'll drive hits for our stuff for sure. Libya next and then, maybe –

Ibrahim pressed the volume on the radio. I'd been making a habit of bringing along notebooks on these rides out of London. I liked to jot down phrases, little terms I could turn into verses.

1. *it is the end of everything, mashallah!; the old and very old.*
2. *there is hope, gathering in masses; people are rising!*
3. *we are connected; this is not your revolution!*
4. *spring; hope springs.*

– The world's a madness, cousin, Ibrahim went.

There was a giddiness about him suddenly. Fidgeting behind the wheel. He quickly glanced behind us at the sleeping Zenab.

– You're too restless, you know. Shouldn't worry about Zenab. The boy's just eager. Says he wants to make a documentary about you – about Al-Bayn. Has he asked? . . . I told him unlikely. All these younger lot, all they want to do is be the next – some are not bad, actually, the poets – all these *next-next* Al-Bayns.

Ibrahim scanned the side mirrors and turned into another lane.

– And there's the other project. I can tell you a bit about it if you want – about Hamburg. Yasir and I spoke. Last week. Yasir wants you to come in, cousin, meet people, wants you to talk to people there. They're serious there. The path out from places like Belgium, Germany is all set . . .

I was listening to the radio, Mister, trying to ignore him. The news was Iraq again. Some border town had been sacked by a new militia. The newsreader's voice came low as I listened, shifting in my seat, making a few scratchings on my pages, facing away from Ibrahim and toward the window.

– Cousin – is there something I've done to upset you?

1. *how long will they stay?; forever – and who's we?*
2. *a rupture is a breach is an opening, of sorts*
3. *emptiness breeds opportunists*
4. *the future holds uncertain forms.*
5. *Paradise and –*

Another switch of lane. And then, Mister, I felt something rise and choke at the back of my throat. As the lights flashed I started to feel light-headed. Slumped backward then, I held my head as the car shifted a third time. Ibrahim seemed not to notice . . . *You're not saying anything, cousin. You're not talking to me. You're silent* . . . The sound of Ibrahim's voice, the voices on the radio, seemed to circle in my head . . . *I wish I*

had what you have – but I do what I can . . . Germany soon,
cousin! . . . I felt a sudden convulsion. A sharp tang at the roof
of my mouth. Gripping the lever, I wound down furiously.
Ibrahim clutched my shoulder as I stuck my neck out the
window. Hot watery mouthfuls spewed out of me and into the
rushing motorway outside.

103. METAMORPHOSIS What exactly made me vomit out
half my insides, Mister, I can't say. I do think, though, that
language, like rivers and seas, get polluted with what's expelled
into them. And that sort of pollution goes both ways, Mister. It
sickens you. And when it's used to carp and cuss, and degrade,
the sickness can snag at the senses.

Words change the perception of things and other people. At
its worst, in a kind of crazy regurgitation, whatever you say
ends up defining the world. Making actual and true what once
you'd only imagined. I'd been reciting, I think, for so long and
for so many years, that it'd made me sick.

After washing off Ibrahim's window, I realised I didn't like
what language was making of me. Didn't like what I was
becoming, Mister. I'd become a kind of gobbler, a consumer of
the world's bad news, and I was sick of the feed. I wanted it
over.

I was frightened, Mister. When I returned with Zenab to his
flat, I fell immediately into prayer. I ignored Zenab, who knelt
beside me. I uttered my own prayers quietly, saying whatever
came into my head. No proper surah or hadith. I spoke in half-
prayer, half-nonsense, Mister. Because I knew my own Allah,
for whom I knelt this time, had made me up just as unevenly.
I was *God's Own*, after all. And so, as surrounded as I was by

Zenab's empty boxes and stale plates on the floor, I let the words spill out of me in relief.

I think, also, invention became a method by which I could cope. I continued the habit. During my performances, Mister, I began making up verses on the spot. I'd stare out at the crowd, at them angry young bodies, all with an ache in their bellies, and I offered whatever came into my head. It didn't seem to bother anybody at first. They continued to chant, shouting back my moniker in syllables only: . . . *Ul-ba-yeen! Ul-ba-yeen! Ul-ba-yeen!*

I thought I'd got away with it, Mister. But then . . .

104. OTHER AL-BAYNS It had come to the point when all your newspapers had to do, Mister, was splash my ugly likeness over them grubby pages and crowds would come and gather and grow ever larger and louder. The only way I could stop myself feeling sick afterward was to drown everything away. So, along with my spontaneous, spur-of-the-moment recitals, I also started covering my head with a dark hood, and shielding the glare from them constant lights by holding my palm up at them. I posed the part, Mister. But paid no attention to the words, or the manner in which I spoke them.

Of course, soon enough, people began to notice. And it wasn't long before things started to take a turn. There was one night in Waltham Forest, I remember, when boos and heckles started to ring so loud from a crowd. This was the same lot who'd lapped up them poems about your Junior Bush, his *dubya-em-dee* . . . and your Tony Blair and his *blood-splattered tie* . . . and now they were jeering me, calling me out for being an imposter.

This was some dark, dingy town hall, Mister, and it was packed that night. I could feel a sense of violence and confusion. My eyes had been closed, I remember. I'd been babbling away trying not to feel nauseous again. But then I felt the square stage beneath me begin to lift. Arms started reaching after me. And these angry, heated faces, Mister, were staring up at me, growling, spitting. It was like seeing a hundred Al-Bayns come at me at once – and it occurred to me that maybe these were my imposters, Mister, my pretenders. The ones who'd come to every recital of mine just to hurl my poems back, as if my voice was their own.

It's difficult to tell whether all this happened in my head or out of it. But I do remember them climbing onto the stage that night, pushing me aside and grabbing hold of the microphone. As I heard these others, these stick-figure Al-Bayns, jumping about in raving imitation, bellowing out some half-remembered verse, I quickly grappled away and off stage.

Zenab was waiting for me, puckering his eyes from behind the camera. His lens squarely aimed at all the commotion, trying to capture every moment on video. I remember pulling him back with me behind the curtains. I leaned into him and shouted:

– Zenab! I sputtered, give me some money, quickly.

Zenab, confused and frightened in that moment, rifled through his pockets, and, as if by miracle, Mister, which I can only now attribute to my Allah's graces, the lad turned up a handful of coins and paper notes. I snatched the money off him. Pushed him away and thanked him. Then – in the best semblance of a runaway I could manage – I made for the exit and escaped.

105. INVISIBLE BOY (2) Not two hours later I found myself on a train bound south. I'd run away, Mister – finally fled my noisy fame and left my ugly Al-Bayn behind me.

The only place I could go now was south. I had my Sisi Gamal's address written on a postcard. All I knew was that he lived now in some flat by the sea. *I am here, near your mother,* he'd written, *come and see me, come and see your mother . . .* But, of course, I hadn't visited, Mister. And tried not to think about how my uncle would insist we go to her. It'd been years and I was anxious about it.

I'd found an empty carriage and a tattered seat to slouch. There were nervous glances, I remember. Looks and little flinches from the other passengers whenever they passed. They were eyeing my black clothes, beard, and bag beside me. I ignored them and fixed my gaze on the window.

Eventually, graffitied tunnels gave way to muddy fields, forests, great pylons cutting past. Mister, it was all the country beyond the city. I didn't know what to expect. The only thing I wanted, honestly, was to be with my uncle again. Some quiet corner with him. I wanted to read in the same room as him and have him ignore me. Same way I'd been ignored a boy.

106. SOUTH *Puh!* The old man spat out his cigarette when he saw me. Like he'd seen a ghost, Mister. Screwed his face up like he'd caught a bad smell. And then his features turned into a half-smile before he embraced me.

– Look at this, he said, the boy has shaved his lip . . .

Five years, Mister. I muttered and brushed at my beard. I let the bag slip to the ground, and we embraced. He'd felt very small as I held him.

It was dark by the time, Mister. And he made me take off my shoes once we got to his flat. My uncle's flat was on the fifth floor of some mouldy court with a stairwell. The scent of his cigarettes was almost welcoming. Laminated pictures with no frames hung on the wall. A little painting of scripture. And a familiar image of the *Ka'bah* leaning against a box near the landing.

– Inside! Inside! came his gruff weary voice.

It was a poky little place, Mister. Sofabed next to the radiator. Two armchairs with worn armrests like cratered skin. There were packets of samosas and crisps strewn all over. The telly was going in the corner. But there were no books, Mister. Not that I could see. Nor any newspapers or anything else to read.

– Milky-tea? came his voice again.

My Sisi Gamal was pottering about in his socks. He had on a woollen jumper that didn't seem familiar, and a pair of baggy brown trousers. He poured in water and put the kettle on the boil. I saw utensils and unrinsed plates in the sink. The counter behind him, too, was cluttered with unopened envelopes. The peeling surface was covered in tea rings and brown stains.

My uncle shuffled toward the little window and coughed.

– I have been growing greens, he said and waved a finger under the light.

There was a dish on the sill with another small glass.

– Cress, he said. And one onion. I eat in the mornings.

His back was turned to me, and I said nothing.

– The allotments in the old house . . . fed us for years. But now the Tesco here is not twenty-four hour. Aldi is too far to walk. So I make do with cress and a bit of butter on bread.

He turned to look at me again. I noticed white spittle at the sides of his mouth. His beard was cut short, but was still patchy.

He beckoned me into the next room, where he lowered himself into one of the armchairs. I sat in the one opposite. The steel coils rang underneath as I sat. I watched my Sisi Gamal brush sweet wrappers from the side table and point the remote at the telly, pressing mute.

I really didn't know what to say, Mister. Had the old man not spoken first, we might have easily sat there until the kettle whistled an end to it. As it was, my uncle suddenly jabbed his finger at me and pointed at my shawl, keffiyeh and dyed beard.

– What have you been doing, boy? You come to me dressed like a mullah?

– It's . . . what I wear for recital, I said and swallowed.

My Sisi Gamal rested his chin on one hand, his attention drifting toward the telly. I could just about make out the low hum from the evening news. Muffled voices too, from the upstairs flat or below.

– Yes . . . yes I know about your recitals, he said.

I glanced around. There really was not a single newspaper or magazine anywhere about. Not even discarded or left on the side. I took a breath, and the kettle began whistling.

– How did you . . . ?

– *Ach* – you ask because it is not you who has written me. I heard nothing from you.

– In papers, you must have read about me in the newspapers?

He paused and lifted the remote and pointed at the telly. He switched it off.

– News? Not much of anything down here.

He slowly got up and switched off the stove, lifting the kettle, letting it hiss into the sink with the dirty water. Apparently changing his mind about the tea.

– Visiting hours in the morning, boy. We will go to see your mother. You sleep here – anywhere here.

Before I could protest, Mister, the old man gathered his slippers and shuffled toward the next room. He paused and turned, pointing at the peeling walls.

– Here, boy – do you like this wallpaper? This, here –

Dull running bands of lavender, stained at the skirting board. Everything about seeing him so reduced, in this little flat, was totally depressing. I shook my head, no.

– Me neither. I will have it changed. There is a man at the shops – Jerry. His brother also named Jerry. He does renovations. With him, I will have it fixed.

My uncle coughed and scratched his chin. He disappeared into another room. I heard the groan of his mattress springs then, before a few shorts breaths. Then the sound of snoring. As tired as I was, Mister, I must have fallen asleep in my uncle's armchair.

107. LITTLE ENGLANDER We left early next morning. I hadn't packed any clothes, and I wondered what my uncle had made of my hood and long black shawl. He seemed to hate my get-up, Mister. But then I realised my uncle had also changed. How effortlessly he seemed to walk about them cobbled streets for instance. And had admired the pebble seafront with them wooden moorings which reached into the sea like long rulers. *This is not a short way*, my uncle said, *but more pretty this way than the other . . .*

The breeze and the sea were so loud, I remember. It seemed quiet otherwise, all empty chippies and wooden alcoves. Even them quaint little beach huts nestled into the side of the promenade. Everything was painted in such an overbearing white. Just the shine off everything had me squinting.

But my uncle didn't bat an eye.

– Look there, he went, pointing to a row of teashops and confectioners.

– Over there lives the other, he said. His name is Guru Dutt – like the filmstar. He sells teacakes and *cosy-cosy* things. But anyway, me and him don't talk.

His expression turned to a scowl as he stared.

– Don't you speak to anyone else here? Know anyone else?

– Know anyone? For what? I told you – this Dutt is the only other . . .

– It's such a small place. Easier to get to know people.

– No, no . . . I go and see your mother only. Talk to her every day.

We stopped near a little mount with 'scopes to peer over the seaside. I stood with my hands in my pockets. That wooden decking, them scrubbed-down surfaces, Mister. Rows and rows of clean white houses. I looked up and saw seagulls in a shining overcast sky, and circling above some shuttered ice-cream stall with rows of peeling benches. An old coconut shy too. And a rusted lock on it, with strings of old bunting twisted round the frame. It all looked sad and tired to me, Mister. Like a fairground or the memory of one. But it wasn't really anything.

– Don't really like it here, I said, facing away from the sea.

My Sisi Gamal coughed into his collar. He looked at his watch and prodded at the side to walk on.

108. ESTELLA'S WARD When we came to the hospital, Mister, I noticed these coloured lines on the floor. My uncle followed the red. We ended up in a room where we were told to wait for a nurse to collect us. There were stools where I sat and fingered the rough cloth of the seat. It smelled of soap and harsh chemicals. Everything looked so washed clean and sterile. People were rushing about them following lines. Suddenly my cheeks felt very hot. I couldn't help but glance along the corridor, where some of the doors were gridded behind painted grey barriers.

I was about to see her again, Mister.

I wondered if she'd changed. Or if I'd find her just the same as she'd always been. Them sad empty eyes, fine hair and ageless skin.

One of the cardiganed nurses found us. Some kindly Petra or Pauline. She led us down a second corridor with a green line passing yellow doors. When we came to my mother's room the nurse held the door for us, Mister. She turned, smiled and said: *She should be waking up around now* . . .

I watched the nurse step forward and move to a figure sat inside. My mother's shoulders. My mother's hair. There she was, Mister, facing the far wall.

The nurse touched her at the back of her neck. She was there dressed in a blouse and cardigan. Her hair combed and even. The nurse leaned over and whispered.

– Estella, dear – visitors for you . . .

The cotton cardigan. Pleated skirt. White cotton leggings. Even two rounded brown shoes, Mister. There was something all too neat about her appearance. Her skin gleamed as if her cheeks had been swabbed with the same washcloth as them windows.

The nurse left us. There was only one cushioned chair and Sisi Gamal set it in front of a small chest of drawers beside her.

I looked closer. Her eyes were the same. Same uneven mouth. The only window in the room was on the far wall, too high for her to look through. My mother was simply staring at the wall in front of her. Her fingers were still and lay together on her lap.

– She's different, I said quietly.

– *Ah* . . . but she is a good listener, said Sisi Gamal.

He was peering from over his glasses. He'd never doted on my mother before, Mister. It seemed as if these five years had kept her as the centre of my Sisi Gamal's thoughts. It was tenderness. Care and attention worn out of habit and routine.

– Does she . . . say anything? I asked.

– Say anything? No words . . . But . . . sometimes she hears me.

I watched him take out a handkerchief. He unfolded it and laid the contents on the small table beside the bed. Inside the cloth were two round cream-filled biscuits. He left one biscuit beside my mother's lap and took a bite from the other. He brushed his beard and glanced at me.

– Did not bring one for you, he said.

It was strange. My uncle seemed so at ease around my mother. Seemed almost pleased to see her in that tidy room. It made me remember my mother's previous one, Mister – that blue room in them upper floors, where she'd sat spinning her fingers.

I looked at her fingers. They were perfectly still.

– What happened to her needles, her thread? I asked, looking at her hands. And your books? What happened to . . .

– Those things? Some we sent as donations. The books I sent the mosque.

He took another nibble. And then he gave a start like he'd remembered something.

– Some of Estella's things we kept . . .

He slowly knelt at the chest of drawers beside my mother's bed. He tugged, bending with a hiss, and pulled out an old shoebox.

– Boy – see. I found this when we were clearing her room. And we decided, me and her, to show you this when you came.

My uncle took the lid off and felt with his fingers. It seemed filled with pieces of notepaper. Thin little candles. Earrings and pins. He pulled out a worn-looking piece and handed it over. It was an old photograph.

Two men. The man on the left had a large face. In his thirties say, with a thick brown beard, and an instrument in his right hand held at the stem. It was an oud, Mister. The other man was much older. Bald and withered-looking, freckles on his chest. Both were smiling and standing in front of a bright blue wall. There was a house. And a tree with white bark and dark notches.

The first man's face had been scratched, it looked like to me, like the eyes had been torn away with a pin.

I looked curiously at my uncle.

– This is your father, boy. The one with no eyes, there. Taken when off on his bloody *who-knows-where* adventures.

I stared, dumbfounded. Letting my breath out as I looked. My father was brown-tanned and bearded. He was holding some long-stemmed oud in his hand. I brought the image closer to me. My father and this other man were standing with what looked like great hills behind them. Some blurred distant mountain. A magnificent valley shimmering below. There was a line there of blue water. And a bright smudge burned in.

I looked up and my Sisi Gamal was sat watching me. My mother, meanwhile, was turned away. Her biscuit untouched by her side. They were both silent, Mister, waiting. As if it were my turn to speak.

109. MARWAN'S EYES Mister, my uncle and I left my mother's room with that photograph of my father.

I went to touch my mother when I left. Just softly, on the back of her neck, the same way that nurse had done. I touched her there because I couldn't think of anything to say to her, Mister.

– She's not there, I said to my Sisi Gamal as we left.

– Not here, he admitted. But at least not alone.

We walked to a cafeteria near the main station. I couldn't say a word, even after my uncle ordered a plate of chips for us and some milky tea.

I stared, Mister. For the longest time. I didn't see a resemblance. His broad shoulders, for instance. And so tall. The creases in the photograph had turned my father's face into a wrinkled map. I drew my fingers along the mountains behind him.

The voice of the waitress brought me back:

– Anything else, lovelies? she went.

She had blue hair, I remember. Two studs in her cheeks like dimples. I looked past her at them handwritten signs on the wall. Little ketchup bottles on the other tables. Paper napkins inside metal nets.

– Nothing else, replied my Sisi Gamal.

He sprinkled salt on the chips.

There was an inscription on the underside of the photograph. I hadn't seen it until I sat turning the thing around in my lap. I recognised the same girlish scribble as I'd read on the labels of his *English-English* books. My father had written: *Abdallah's House, Ayn Issa. 1996.*

I turned it over, peered at the narrow strip of colour to my father's right side. The blue wall, Mister, and there, the small tree behind him: *Abdallah's House.*

– It is Syria, said my uncle. A town called Ayn Issa. Northern region – it is on *the path.*

– Syria? My father was in Syria in 1996?

My uncle dropped his head, making his glasses slide, and ate some chips.

– Maybe. Last thing he sent was this. A cassette before it.

– The one labelled *1996*?

– Yes – it's the one.

Of course it was, Mister. That strange whining tune. That wildness in the voices.

– He . . . we don't look anything alike, I said quietly, spreading the image on my lap.

– No, no, said my Sisi Gamal, sipping some tea with his chips. You are like her, boy. But you disguise yourself like him. See now, how you dress like Marwan.

He lifted a chin at my black smock, my beard and upper lip.

– And Him, said my uncle, pointing upward, Allah brings you here for a good reason. But why do you think? Tell me.

I thought a moment, Mister. Reading his eyes as if there were some right answer.

– Maybe to stay here. With you?

At this my uncle burst into laughter. He brought his palm down so hard the table shook.

– And do what, boy? Do you think these Berties and Betties want to listen to your verse? And what would you sing – the *Mu'allaqat*? Or maybe your own about bombs and bullies and such things? And where will you sing them? There? . . . There? On these roads, on these *Peter-Paul* roads? Believe me, you cannot . . .

My uncle dusted his hands and gestured for the photograph. He brought it close to read the inscription.

– Good that you came, boy. Good that you came and saw your mother. The woman has suffered. But she does not need you here. And me, I do not need you here.

– Where do I go then? I leaned foward, swallowing my breath. There's nowhere left.

My uncle shushed me and gave the picture back. I sat there quietly and ran my fingers over the marks on the photograph. I noticed the brightness of the sky behind the two men. The sun. And them scratches at his eyes, Mister, which felt violent to me now, and frightening.

– My mother made these didn't she? I said.

– The scratches? Yes – she said to me once, *Marwan smiles with his eyes* . . . So – *scratch, scratch* . . .

He imitated, clawing at the napkins.

I looked at the photograph, where my mother's nails had pierced through.

– She used to talk to me, you know, my mother – she used to say things to me.

– *Hmm?* What are these things she said, boy?

– I couldn't understand her. She'd mention him a lot, say his name – like whisper it. And then she'd tell me other things. I couldn't understand any of it.

My uncle turned and looked out the window. There were people on the promenade, old dears wrapped in windcheaters, earmuffs and hats. Others with scarves knotted at the chin. The sky was darkening. It was about to rain, though these people looked prepared for bad weather.

– Your father . . . my uncle began. And your mother . . . Estella loved Marwan, boy. But she could not understand him. Did not want to put up with his *dreaming – ach!* – they would fight like dogs when he would tell her . . . And Estella could be unkind, boy – she knew what to say, how to say it. But even after, with his foolishness, and her, with her words, they only had each other . . . And then, she knew you were inside. *Hmm* . . . So she was going to convert for him. But by then, Marwan told me his dreams were like *fire at his feet* . . . so he left. He was selfish. He ran away, boy. Marwan wanted *paradise.* And he believed it – really believed like those other men, fathers, brothers, who left to fight in the desert . . . Marwan believed in paradise more than what he had. Because what he had was this country. And Estella. And they would not believe in him any longer . . .

My uncle sniffed, looked away.

– What about the rest, I said. What about your letters . . .

– *Ach* . . . he went, raising his eyebrows at the glass. I don't know. I never met Estella's father and mother. They sent me a letter, asked me to take care of her. It was after you were born, boy – they sent enough to take care of you both.

He looked at me stonily. Measuring me with his eyes.

– They sent money, boy. Not love. That is this country.

The waitress came and left a saucer. My uncle fished for coins. I felt with my fingertips over the edges of the photograph and with my thumb at the scratches.

– What colour were his eyes? I asked.

– Marwan's? His eyes were black. Like mine . . . see.

He gurned then, taking his glasses off, and making his eyes into scoops. Them rheumy irises, Mister, like marbles in his head. They might have been black at one time, but were only a dusty grey now, and small. He dropped his coins into the dish. I went to help him out of the booth. He came out hissing, cussing, complaining about his *aching arsehole* and *buggered spine*. He then told me, between breaths, that I'd be catching the five o'clock train to London – *fast train, boy, you are better off . . .*

110. ZOUN, ZEEN, ZEEN . . . I think it was right my Sisi Gamal leaving me there at the station. The last thing he asked was for me to send a picture from one of my recitals. *Something in the light – ah? I want to see you in the light, and see if you slouch when you stand . . .*

I said I'd send him a photograph. I left watching for a moment from the ticket gates. My uncle stopped to light a match. He coughed and a blue cloud lifted up around him. Then he turned the corner and was gone.

I found a seat in the last carriage next to someone's luggage. I sat with my back turned and my hood covering my ears. I reached for the cassette – the *1996* – but then stopped. I wanted to conjure that *zoun, zeen, zeen* . . . from memory, Mister. The sound of them drums. With my other hand I felt for the photograph in my pocket. Tracing my finger along its edges.

Them lines in the folds. I couldn't have possibly imagined where them same lines were to lead . . .

. . . but enough with the mystery, Mister. It's time to write how I came to leave your Britain. How I escaped my Al-Bayn and even gave Ibrahim the boot. How I went off, at long last, into the far-flung, Mister, committing myself into exile.

111. 'YOU'RE A SELFISH PERSON' Well, I knew I'd have to have it out with Ibrahim. It's an episode I won't dwell on for too long. It's enough to mention here that my brother fumed at me, Mister, before finally accepting my choice.

I met him in a kofta shop near school. Ibrahim didn't speak to me at all, at first. He was sore at having heard of my antics at the last recital. Making up nonsense verses and instigating only heckles and commotion. It didn't bother me, Mister. I wanted to tell him I was out. I knew it would most likely mean an end to our friendship. But Ibrahim seemed so distracted he barely registered I'd said anything. It was only after I repeated myself that he set his plastic fork down.

– Come on, cous'. Don't overreact – you're too sensitive. So you bombed your last recital, so what? Won't happen again. Not if you stick to the set-list. Make sure on Thursday –

– It's not just the recitals, Ibrahim. It's all of this. Everything. I'm done, really . . .

– Easy, cous'. Be mindful what you say – *muraqabah*, remember – you can't be rash with these things. You're so anxious. You're so restless –

– And why wouldn't I be? Can't you see that I don't like doing this, Ibrahim? I'm up there every night, nearly. I'm sick of it – I really am.

– No – can't stop. Not now, cous' – I'm sorry. Six events I've planned for June. Two in August. July we're in Hamburg – there's a recital tonight up near – up near Finchley Road ... But I'll see once this eases, once things lessen up. I'll look after you, don't worry.

I held up a hand. He looked across at me.

– No, Ibrahim. No more.

Ibrahim sat up staring at me. He shook his head perplexed. It was like I was trying to deny him something that was by rights his own. Him, sat there in his nice clothes now, and shining cheeks.

– How do you mean done, cous'? And how are you saying this to me now – now, with all the plans I've – what's supposed to happen now? What am I going to say to Sohail? Idries?

– I don't even know who these people are Ibrahim!

– Who do you think publishes you, cousin? Has it occurred to you that this is bigger than you? Bigger than just you on a stage in Barnet, or Bradford, or wherever?

I wanted to get away, Mister. To leave the lad to his kofta and anger at me. But then I relented and took a breath.

– Look, if you want me to do tonight, I will. But it's the last, Ibrahim. I swear it. It's the last one I'll do.

I watched as he went on shaking his head at me. He looked at my ruffled shawl, my matted beard, and hood. It was as if he wanted to laugh, Mister, but he was so desperate.

– You're a selfish person, he said.

I could see more than anger now. He was hurt.

– Not so many others have what you have, he said. Allah blessed you. Gave you – gave you a gift! So many people you put on *the path* and now you want to throw it away like . . . like . . . it's nothing. Go against His will – go against Allah's will . . . you want to go against Allah's will, cousin!

I wanted to ask *which Allah*, Mister. But I didn't.

– No, I said. You have my poems, Ibrahim. Go to my rooms if you want more, take the lot, I don't care. Take my notebooks if it'll make you happy.

Ibrahim stared at me blankly. His mouth fell open as if to reply but he swallowed it. And he was watching me now, his fingers scratching at his trimmed pointed beard, and his eyes narrowed, as if figuring out some calculation in his head.

– And – and you said you'd do tonight? he said quietly.

– I will if you want me to. And then it's over.

I remember wondering, Mister, in that moment whether Ibrahim hadn't always been a pretender all along. Him, who always plucked at his pointed beard, which seemed to me, now, only shaped to conceal his weak chin.

I can't recall what he said to me after that. But I hadn't lied to him. I'd no intention of writing poetry again. And as far as I was concerned, Mister, it was already over.

Al-Bayn was a dead name to me now.

112. LAST RECITAL See lights illuminate the rows of mostly men. My last recital was at some domed mosque in Edgware. A beautiful place for my last. It was packed to the proper rafters for me, I remember. Fierce applause began as soon as I arrived. I noticed the walls were tiled with delicate blue lines, letters curling around the sea of upturned faces.

The stage was positioned so high that I felt I could almost touch the centre. My eyes lingered there for a while. I stared and waited for the applause to end. I closed my eyes and said a short prayer.

I was praying for forgiveness, I think.

For I knew my own Allah would be up there, watching me, tutting, rolling His eyes, disapproving of me . . .

I did at least have the dignity, Mister, to stand there on that stage and deliver the proper thing. I acted the grotesque, hunched and leaned into all their very worst refractions – some split-apart djinn, some gobbing apparition, their red-lipped King Bollo, Mister, their greedy-eyed Golem, their slavering Saladin. For one last show, I watched them thrash about for me, appalled by me, enraged, call to me and reach for me. I gave them three written by Al-Bayn, and then a fourth, invented by me on the spot.

Picture me holding one finger up in the air, Mister. Giving the crowd whatever spilled out of my head. I knew it didn't really matter. They went wild for it regardless, tongues like eels as they shouted up. They were so loud. The sound came back at me so hard that I held my ears against it, Mister. People in the stands were stamping. Fingers at the edge of the stage scratching, and others making little circles in the crowd, shaking at the knees, and their arms outstretched, mouths wide and wet . . .

I stumbled away after that. I fell back as the lights came down and headed backstage. I'd fulfilled my promise, Mister. I flew out now, into a back alley, covering my face with my shawl, and let my breath steady itself in the darkness. I made a vow to myself as I went: I would not recite another word.

Not a word, not a word . . . not a word . . .

113. THE GATE As it was, I was afforded one last bit of grace. I arrived breathless, doubled over, my sides throbbing with pain, and having stumbled into the streets in confusion. I'd found myself at the giant gates at the Ibn Rabah again, Mister. Back in Poplar, and exhausted. I might have said a short prayer for myself. For it was then, out of the blue, that I felt a touch at the elbow.

I turned and saw them same squinty eyes on me – it was Zenab. The lad was alone, reaching out and calling my name. His lips moved but I couldn't hear him. And all of a sudden, Mister, I felt faint, a familiar stirring in the belly. I felt myself fighting against myself. And I began to slide, sinking to the ground, before Zenab held me upright. The lad took me by the arms. I made no complaint as he shuffled me away with him.

114. 'THANK YOU, ZENAB . . .' Memories become vague as to how Zenab got me back to his flat that night. He must have carried me over his shoulder, Mister. I remember spotting the bright lights above the Kentucky Chicken window. And the smell of the hallway stinking of chips.

Once inside, Zenab brought my legs over, and I winced, feeling the pinch at my sides as he lowered me. The dull pain had grown at my back, Mister. I could hear his voice in the relative quiet saying something like *Take these . . . for the pain . . .* and I felt him push two tablets between my lips. I remember his fingers lifting my chin to swallow lukewarm water. And then nothing.

It was morning when I awoke. I managed to shift myself slowly over to the window. Parked cars and strewn rubbish, men going in and out of delivery vans carrying crates. It was early. I heard someone open the door and come inside. It was Zenab again. He had two carrier bags from Kentucky Chicken.

– Better you keep away from the windows, he went, as he brought two containers out to the table, with two Cokes, and held two plastic forks out to me. You hungry, brother?

I ate as if I hadn't eaten for weeks, Mister. And as I devoured them wings and dip, coleslaw and chips, I glanced around Zenab's apartment, a dark earthy-smelling space. His prayer mat was placed near the far wall. It was the only spot which wasn't occupied by electric wiring and heaps of other heavy equipment. There was a spinning, hissing computer, which seemed always to be on, in the middle of his desk, which he'd linked up with external hard drives and a colour-coded keyboard. There was also a sort of labelling system he'd created for himself. Several towers of neatly stacked Mini-DV tapes surrounded his computer.

These were my recitals, I knew. The ones he'd so eagerly recorded on behalf of Ibrahim. I realised after the first few weeks living there, Mister, that this lad had been running a one-man operation from his flat. He'd been the one printing posters and editing slick-looking videos of my recitals, the ones I'd seen doing the rounds on them forums.

Whenever we ate together like this – and usually it was the same chicken and chips from downstairs – Zenab would talk between mouthfuls about his latest edit. He seemed quieter that evening. He sat hanging his head over his food, and kept glancing up at me, staring, nodding as he slurped his Coke.

– What's wrong, Zenab? I asked, my voice still hoarse.

He swallowed. Looking away at first, at the floor and then the window. He looked worried, concerned after me.

224

– I've got to tell you something, brother, he said. There were people doing the rounds this morning. Asking after you. At the school. A few were in your old dorms. Poking about, I heard.

– Who said?

– Volunteers, same as me. We went looking for you after we heard. They were police. Didn't look like police, mind. But you can tell. I stayed here looking for you, brother. And then I found you. By the gates.

He stuck a fork into his chips and breathed in relief.

– Does anyone else know I'm here?

– No, brother. If you want I could –

– No – Nobody can know, Zenab.

He looked up at me then, curiously. And then nodded his head, Mister. He understood that all that stood between me and them police was him – him, this shaven-headed, pimpled convert. He was the only one I could trust.

– Of course, brother, he went, and swallowed again.

I told him thank you. To which he offered a thousand thank yous back. Saying it was his honour, his pride, his only duty to shelter me, Mister, and so on and on.

115. ZENAB (MYTH) That following evening, Mister, I couldn't sleep. Zenab had left in the early morning to volunteer. I was worried somebody might come and find me. I stood and went walking in circles around the mess. I was trying, I think, to settle my nerves and occupy my mind with other things.

There was a second desk near the kitchen where Zenab kept clippings, labels and video tapes. He'd been labelling tapes of me, I knew. Marking them up with titles like: *Al-Bayn – East Croydon (17.6.12)*. There were even a few photos of Al-Bayn pinned to the wall. And photocopies of articles. I didn't see any pictures of his family.

Zenab had converted one year ago, I learned. He'd found himself pushing pamphlets, chugging donations for the cause – *the path*, as he called it. Each evening, I'd watch him come back tired from volunteering. We'd eat leftovers, and he'd talk to me about one of my recitals, Mister, and how I'd deeply influenced his approach to *deen*. It was always some recital I barely remembered. And then he'd always ask to record an interview with me. I always declined.

His was a strange infatuation, Mister. And I knew it had nothing to do with me, but rather whatever he'd felt and seen in Al-Bayn.

Zenab had once shown how he'd edit clips together. Ibrahim had asked him to make these flashy edits to publish online alongside my poems. *What is it?* I'd asked. And he'd shown me a few heavily filtered videos he'd made of Al-Bayn – see me there, Mister, mid-verse against a backdrop of a hundred bodies. *Easy for me*, he went with a little note of pride, *I'm quite good at it, as it happens – on Final Cut Pro, I mean. Got a trial version off a uni mate. It does the job – no watermarks, obviously.* He showed me another video, where he'd used a bootleg instrumental score as background music. Some of these edited clips reminded me of a film trailer, Mister, or promo, say, for some Hollywood movie. It was all so fast-paced, slick and professional. I was impressed by Zenab, the boy was a proper whizz.

On another night, he brought me to a desk where he showed

me some of the stuff other volunteers had made. Images, screenshots, audio clips, taken from his many videos. Zenab encouraged remixes and reproductions from his work. *We don't even have to ask, brother, most of it's just Photoshop, anyway. It inspires them. Allows them to get creative . . .*

There were several images, Mister. Al-Bayn spliced into different backgrounds and overlaid with different captions. One showed Al-Bayn against a sky with clouds formed into palms in prayer. Another showed Al-Bayn's face pasted – slightly awkwardly, amateurish – onto someone else's body. One had an enormous chest and a sort of bullet-belt from Hollywood action movies. A painted-on skull covered the muscles. Arabic letters spelled out *Al-Bayn* from my gaping mouth. Zenab clicked another image. *Yeah, I think he used Punisher for this one – from the comic books?* It was a sloppily edited gif, Mister, repeating the same message in English this time: *Join the caravan! Join the caravan!*

Zenab laughed nervously, hesitantly, when I asked what it meant. He just repeated the words back to me: *Caravan, brother – the caravan . . . the path . . .*

It was a call that'd been pasted into every poster, Mister, tacked onto every one of my poems posted into the forums.

It occurred to me not long after I'd come back after my last recital, that *the path* might have been the same my father had taken all them years ago, Mister – a route out of Britain. Zenab began telling me about it. Explaining that this path was meant to lead Muslims to *paradise on earth*, a real place, which lay out there in the desert, where defenders of Allah were building a new state in His name. I realised then, that what Zenab was offering me was an escape.

I watched him picking at his fingernails, scratching his shaven head. He finished his Coke and stared. His eyes became saucers when he was excited.

– I don't need to tell you, brother. Of course, you know.

Zenab shuffled his papers and showed me another. A small poster, Mister, crumpled and torn. It had small printed lettering along the top reading: *Join the caravan* and then a verse written in large text across the middle:

A new nation! For which Kings will abandon
Their Kingdoms for His!

– This . . . is one of yours, brother, said Zenab to me, with a mad kind of smile. I know you need to disappear, brother. I think I can help you do it . . .

I didn't recognise the verse, Mister. But Zenab was so insistent that I almost believed him. He explained it to me: young people all over the world, especially across Europe, were leaving the West in search of that same paradise.

Zenab seemed suddenly charged, Mister. He started drumming his knees as he spoke. He asked me to sit next to him on the filthy floor. The curtains were drawn and the glare from the computer screen illuminated our faces.

– My friend Asad went, he said. He went last year. He's doing well, brother, as it happens – he writes to me online. And this year, some of us have been planning. Umer and Deena went just recently, and others are getting the money, but they'll go still – for sure, they will. We're all helping each other, brother. It's so beautiful . . . all us volunteers.

There seemed to be a flash of boldness that crossed his face then, Mister. Zenab reached out and pulled a black bag from underneath his bed. He looked at me and opened it.

Inside, crumpled paper notes bound by little rubber bands were set into stacks at the bottom. British pounds, Mister. In stacks of tens, twenties and fifties. Zenab's passport, the little burgundy book bearing your Queen's golden arms, lay across the money.

– It's enough, he said, And a fortnight on Friday – it's set.

Zenab leaned closer, Mister. He shuffled in front of me, sitting there next to the bag with them tired eyes of his, and them pitted cheeks, imploring me.

– It would be my honour, brother – I mean to say, if you'd do me the honour, of taking my place. Then it's yours . . . it's all arranged. I will do this for you, brother.

116. ZENAB'S PRAYERS Probably – and I say this now, since you'd never have known how the rest of it transpired, unless I'd written it here – but if I'd have hesitated with it, Mister, or discussed it with Zenab a little longer, I might have missed the opportunity to get out as quickly as I did.

Maybe Ibrahim would have come and found me. Or some other lot who'd been poking after me might have found me and caught me, and I'd be talking to some other Mister now instead of you . . .

As it was, Zenab was so desperate to claim a purpose for himself that he'd now found one in me. I'd no choice at the time but to say yes. I'd heard my own calling of sorts too, Mister. One that impelled me, called me out to them golden mountains, that sliver of blue below, the shining vision in the photograph of my father. But I didn't tell Zenab about any of that. Instead, I let him fuss, organise, and prepare everything for me.

First thing was a change in appearance, Mister. I needed to match the mug in Zenab's passport. He looked much younger. Thin cheeks and eyes cool and rested. I'd also noticed his name had been misspelled under his photograph. It was written as *Zeinab*, the feminine form of *Zenab* – like Bint Ali, or Badawi – but when I asked about it, Mister, the lad said he hadn't known any better. *I just wrote it how it sounded . . .* he said and laughed.

But, Mister, it was a surprise to me when I returned from the bathroom, having taken his clippers and shaved off my locks and thickened beard, to find Zenab and I looked very much alike. I'd returned to my boyhood face, and it was in that guise that I resembled him in other ways too. His slouching meekness, say, and the paleness around our eyes.

I can say I was excited by the thought of assuming another face – and I was very grateful that Zenab had given me his. When the lad asked that night if we could pray together, I told him we could. He'd been so meticulous in the last few weeks. Making sure everything was ready for me. I'm sure now that I'd underestimated the lad entirely. There was something in the way he prayed that seemed so resolute also. How he rose so emphatically, as if lifted by his very breath. And when down, how he spread his palms and fingers so widely that they reddened as he stretched. Zenab seemed as if he were praying for his life, Mister. Whereas I, with my buckling sides and tired breath, could only mutter a few untidy verses.

My and Zenab's faiths had very little in common, I think. The lad would have recognised very little in the Allah I was praying to, Mister. My own Almighty, who might have been sitting there beside us at the time, while his Allah was very much up there, *big-eyed* and still in heaven. Truth was, Zenab's devotions were just as mad as my own, Mister. And I doubt he'd have claimed me as Muslim proper. But then, I'm not sure I would have called him Muslim either. And yet we knelt together. Praying up to our separate inventions.

117. ONE-FINGER SALUTE It was that evening that I made good on my promise to my uncle. I picked up one of the pictures from Zenab's desk. It was my Al-Bayn in his scolding pose, mouth open, finger held in rebuke.

I took the picture and used a pencil to score out the teeth with the tip. I scratched the mouth away, Mister, until the tip went right through the paper. Just as my father's picture had been defaced, now my Al-Bayn was missing the part of him that might reveal too much. I folded the picture and wrote my Sisi Gamal's address on the other side. I didn't leave a note. I just left it there for Zenab to send and then tried to get some sleep. There were only a few short hours before departure.

118. EXIT Zenab had organised it all, Mister – a cab to Harwich, Stena Line to Holland, Germany, then Greece, then Turkey, then out. The lad had put it down on a map for me. It was raining that morning. And I remember kissing Zenab on both cheeks as I left. I recall the yellow light from the chippie reflecting off the lad's face. The way he stood there on the pavement as the cab arrived. I whispered a short prayer for him as I lifted my heavy backpack into the boot and climbed in.

I had the boy's passport, Mister. And his clothes. He'd given me his name too. And now, I watched as we parted, and as the cab turned away from him.

See the familiarity of East Ham passing outside the window, Mister. I was about to leave your Great Britain for good. I recalled what my Mother Miriam had said: *Sometimes the only thing to do is to abandon a dead thing*. And how true it had felt then. It really did feel like I was taking control of my life at last. Circumstances, events, other people's made-up myths would hold no authority over me now. I wasn't only abandoning a home, but also my body, my name, severing any continuance with what I'd known. All to step into what I didn't know, Mister: an *unknown-unknown*. And a bit of adventure, maybe . . . in exile.

Zeinab

Begin again! – The only difference, Mister, between this life and the next is a matter of slippage. An interrupted sentence, a snatched breath, a mispronunciation at most . . .

In the Qur'an, there's no question that death is a part of life. There's the mention of the *al-ūlā* and the *al-ākhira* – the First and the Last life, Mister . . . And the *al-dūnya* and the *al-āhira* – the Nearer and the Latter life. These words are tied together like threads at both ends. Even in speech, it's impossible to invoke one without the other. And the words *dūnya* and *ākhira* each appear with the exact same frequency in the Qur'an – some 115 mentions.

Well, I might have crossed as many borders on my journey out. The road, this *caravan path*, marked the beginning of this period of my life – my great and grand adventure.

119. EXILE! It was a hard, tumbling road with split rocks, divots and scrapes. Weeks of travelling on a sore arse, continually changing transports, riding for miles before getting told to transfer into another unmarked van, busted car, a seat to struggle into and hold tight. The last transit city was out of Urfa, and the last border crossed was from Turkey. I kept myself to myself, trying not to complain too much, or spew as we turned out into some anonymous city, then into a border town, and finally into the great arid desert. I did as I was told, Mister. I gave my papers at each proper border. Answering only to *Zeinab* whenever some uniformed guard demanded my name. And while all these drivers, Mister, these old men, with their dusty half-tucked-in shirts, picking their noses, barking, shouting at me to get out, get in, and picking up other passengers who'd sit and stink next to me – similarly drawn faces, tired from travelling out from who knew where – I kept my own eyes solely on the horizon.

120. THE OATH I might not have exchanged a single salty breath with anyone had I not also shared seats along the way. I was no longer willing to share my real voice with strangers – *not a word . . . not a word . . . not a word . . .* but I'd pray with them. The rest I'd disguise and only ever reply under breath.

I focused my thoughts instead on my father, Mister. Asking myself what Marwan might have made of this land. This nothingness and flatness outside. I wondered if he too might have been troubled, as I was now, by sudden visionary surges in the desert. My waking flights seemed to seize me more violently here, filling my head with all kinds of flashes, shapes in the dark. Proper dizzying sights appeared before me, Mister, even when all I could see from the window was the road reaching on, and the empty earth passing either side of me. But then I also thought: here I am, in the desert, where my next life awaits me. Where it might so nearly have ended too, at the other end of it, at the sea.

121. THE OGRE My silence lasted, maybe, until the end of that final stretch of road. I was rudely awakened, Mister, by the giant bulk of someone clambering into the van beside me. He was all pungent arms, black armpits, some gigantic chest and butcher legs. He looked like a sack of heavy meat to me, Mister, and he took hold of me and shook me. I'd suddenly found myself in the hands of an ogre.

I started up in a panic. I began flapping at them fleshy hands. This enormous round head was staring, Mister. Shining bald, and as toffee-brown as the ground outside in the desert, with these wild glaring eyes. Dark curling hairs, like little black whirlpools, covered his body. He seemed to take up all the space in the van.

His voice came at me in a shout. Something like: *Show! Show!*

All I could do was babble, saying I didn't understand him. He sat back then, and in a loud barking English went:

– Country! What country? Where are you from?

He started jutting his finger, pointing at the rucksack stuffed between my legs.

– Show, now! Show, he went again.

I hesitated before reaching into my bag for the passport. I'd hidden it inside the zipped pocket, Mister. And as I pulled it out, the ogre's hands went to snatch for it, but I drew back. I saw him turn his head and read the cover.

– UK . . . he said. His mouth hung like a bag of rocks. He

slowly opened his hand to me. Cautiously, I handed the thing over.

I watched as he inspected the unchecked pages, finding the photocard, reading the name. He smirked as he came to it. And peered hard at the photo.

– Salaam . . . *Zeinab* . . . he read laughing. From *Oxford – hurmp – shire . . .*

He tossed my passport back and turned his attention to the spare thin trees whipping past him.

I'd no idea where we'd picked him up, Mister. And I'd no idea how long I'd been asleep. The last person I'd had to share the cab with was let off a few days before. The next stop would be my last, however, out near them golden mountains. At which point I assumed I would be transferred to another truck.

I put the passport back into the zippered pocket. I tucked the bag under my knees, Mister, held it there with the back of my heels. I hesitated again, hearing the lad sniff and give a little low chuckle.

– You carry your things, he said, like they are very precious.

He stared as I brought my hands to my belly, my chest.

– My passport, I muttered. They were the first words I'd spoken in a number of weeks. My throat felt thin and parched. The lad made another drawn face at me then, and pointed a stubby finger at the window past my shoulder.

– Useless things. No need for papers here, he said.

I looked out at the empty land, Mister. All sweeping on and upward, everything toward them mountains in the distance. There was no sign of any other vehicle, or structure, around us. Nothing in the sky. Not a cloud. Just a heavy blue span burned white near the sun.

– What . . . country are we in right now? I asked.

The lad snorted again, sweeping his fingers at the window.

– Country . . . what country . . . ? he said, as if the word had lost meaning.

But then he brought his massive palm out at me again, leaving it open.

– I am Bilal, he said. I am from Quetta.

Nervously, I rested my hand in his.

– I'm . . . I began.

– You – you are *Zeinab*, he said, clucking his tongue as if the name amused him. And you are from? From UK! – *hurmp* – you see, Zeinab? My English is very perfect . . .

He watched for a moment, as if he needed acknowledgement and so I nodded, agreed.

– It is okay, he went. We make it far, *inshallah*. Not easy road – see there, see, nothing in the desert – but we can be friends, Zeinab! We can help each other here – no problems . . .

I watched him shift his mighty weight, moving across to the other side of the cab. He rested his head, yawning, completely unaffected by the rattling shell of the truck, the splitting rocks, the rumbling on. In a matter of seconds, he was snoring.

122. NEW PRAYERS The elderly driver who was taking us that last stretch – him, whose name I never knew – had a habit of waking us at dawn for *fajr*. I'd hear his belching, the shudder of his door slamming closed before tapping the window to wake me. It'd become part of the ritual, Mister. The old man's spitting, pissing, groping about outside preceded our prayers. And between him and this Bilal, Mister, I rarely slept more than a few hours a night. We were nearing the border when the driver woke us again with another call from the front, sucking his cheeks in with a *ch-ch-ch!*

We were coming to a stop near another checkpoint with a spare concrete shelter, some ancient generator tucked under a plastic chair beside it. We usually blew past checkpoints along the way, but here we'd slowed to a stop.

The driver indicated to Bilal that we bring our bags out the back. I glanced and realised the big lad had already got everything together. The driver laid our prayer mats outside. It was just after dawn, Mister. Bilal made a fire and left it going as we came to our knees and faced the horizon. I did the best I could with my positioning, and began by listening to the breeze in my ears and the soft utterances either side of me.

For a moment, Mister, I sat and looked out at the dotted plain. It seemed like such a frightening space when we were barrelling into it. And whenever we'd come out for nightly prayer, I was struck by the way my mind tended to make forms where there was really nothing. I was grateful to have been able to come so far. It called to mind a memory from when my Sisi Gamal was showing me a map. He'd drawn a finger over the parts he'd travelled – *The golden parts are deserts*, he said, *which were our first fountains* . . . I'd stared and stared at those blank parts as a boy, where the names were spare, and the lines to mark frontiers were fainter and dashed. And now, here I was staring out into one of them.

In my exhaustion, I could still draw into my prayers with conviction. I was also half delirious, I think, and it felt as if the deserts were demanding new prayers from me.

It's difficult to explain to you, Mister, but I was wary again of how I held my body as I prayed next to these others. I knew that if either Bilal or the old driver had seen my unwieldy method they'd have accused me of being a pretender or worse. Thankfully, they prayed with their eyes closed. I'd no doubt the ogre, with his massive head bent low to the cloth next to mine, was one of them fiercer devouts. And now, without the transport going further, I knew I was going to have to walk the rest of the way alongside him. It made me less eager to find out what was beyond them mountains, honestly.

I stole a glance at him. I was reminded again of how much the big lad's body seemed hewn out of the same horizon. Like he belonged here, Mister. Like he was built for this journey. And as I began my prayers, I was more conscious of the discomfort I felt when kneeling and rising alongside him.

I tried a few new words. Uttered whatever came into my head. I felt as if let loose all of a sudden, free of any designation that had felt like a weight only a second ago. It was a mixture of *surah*, but with my own meanings muddled in, and then offered quietly into the wind. I'd spoken similarly during previous prayers. Prayers made to no measure. And only whisper-spoken now to my own Allah.

I allowed myself to feel more, I think. Every ounce of pain as I knelt, turning my back against the sky. And there was an ecstasy in it too, Mister. Everything I didn't care to deny myself any longer. The burning I felt going at it, submitting myself, and everything it aroused inside me. Everything my previous life had left me ashamed for having felt was all perfectly permissible here, Mister. I felt clean here, in the desert. I was opened up.

123. BURNING After prayers, Bilal searched his bag and brought out a small package. It was wrapped in foil and tied with wire. He saw my face as he approached and snorted, gesturing for me to follow.

There was nothing around except the shelter and its corrugated roof. The generator lying in the sand looked more like a rusted troll. The road ended here, I realised. The rest of the path had been made by cart tracks and dusty feet. I followed on, Mister, behind Bilal, who looked just as enormous out in the open. We came opposite the driver, who had stepped aside for us. There were black marks on the ground, the smeared remains of fires.

When Bilal crouched and removed a bottle of lighter fluid from his bag, I realised, Mister, that it wasn't only for prayers we'd stopped here that morning. Even the air, tinged with the scent of petrol, hinted at the purpose for which others had stopped here before us. Some ritual was expected of me, I knew. I'd have to mark my own way before going further.

– Zeinab, went Bilal, beckoning me over with a thumb.

He had a small fire going now. He'd made it from what looked like heaps of old clothes drenched in oil. There was only a little warmth. And the smell was awful.

– What are we doing? I asked.

He pointed into the distance. I'd only heard snatches of names passed between Bilal and the driver – Sarrin, Raqqa, Tel Abyad, and a mention of the Euphrates.

– After this, Zeinab – we are alone. We burn our things here.

I stared at him for a moment. Stared at the fire. And then at the driver who was standing at a distance, smoking a cigarette.

Neither of them offered further explanation, Mister. Only that it was expected of me here, to burn my possessions before daybreak.

I looked up and saw the subtle blue creeping behind the mountains. I glanced around at all the black marks and noticed the remains of clothing, backpacks, the bindings of old books. My eyes drew back then, to Bilal, who sat there next to our fire unmoved, waiting.

I brought my bag around and emptied it. A towel. Some spare clothes. Zenab's maps, documents from the crossing. There was a frayed toothbrush and an empty plastic bottle.

Bilal threw my things together with his, wrapping them into a bundle which he then soaked in lighter fluid. He tossed everything into the fire.

The flames flew up, Mister.

Bilal approached me then and pointed at my bag.

– Passport, he said.

– What . . . ?

He spat my name – *Zeinab!* – his lips red from the firelight.

– It is only we two here, he said, No papers, no ID . . .

Bilal reached into his pocket and brought out his own passport. The book was green. There were no second thoughts, Mister. The lad threw it in, and gestured at me to do likewise. I felt for the zippered pocket and brought out the passport. I swallowed hard and moved to hand it over to him. Bilal stepped back. I went over then, and crouched near enough to the fire for the scent of the lighter fluid to sting the insides of my nostrils. I threw it in. The flames flew up again. Bilal reached for my emptied rucksack and tossed it in with his own. We both stood back. The road stretching behind us, daylight clearing in the distance. The only identification I'd had on me was now slowly turning black at my feet.

124. TO AYN ISSA Later, once the driver had turned back the way we'd come, Bilal and I were left scratching about in the dust. We huddled under the shelter together. Hard to describe the size of the lad, Mister. He was a giant, and he spoke in a booming tenor. Sometimes he'd take these breaths as he spoke, sucking his words into him, like a *hurmp*, as if a muscle had pinched in his throat. I imagined it like a giant's gasp, Mister, like he was swallowing back a *fee fi fo fum* . . .

We sat there for maybe another hour before Bilal finished plotting our path. The big lad said he was able to find a direction without a map. It was his gift, he said. He could divine it from the sky, the sight of them mountains, and the horizon. We were to head north. And he seemed to want to encourage me before we set out, saying, *I will explain these things to you, Zeinab. You must take only clothes you need. Carry in your hands. Because why, because look – we walk with easy, easy breath . . . you understand? – But walk quickly . . .*

Despite the heat, I'd taken enough to not freeze to death in the night-time. I tied extra layers to my arms and shoulders, Mister. Then I took off my coat and tied it around my narrow waist. I checked my pockets to find the one possession I hadn't burned. The folded photograph. I dusted off the yellow sand from my father's face. Bilal reached over to take a look.

– What do you have there? he asked.

– It's . . . why I've come, I said.

I handed it to him and watched as he brought it to his eyes, which seemed to struggle to adjust, having strained so long into the distance. He turned the photograph over.

– I'm looking for this place called Ayn Issa, I said. I know it's on the way . . . Not sure how far.

Bilal peered at the picture, the scratches, the frayed edges.

– Your father? he said.

I nodded. He gave me a thoughtful look.

– Your father does not look like you, he said, and handed it back.

I watched the big lad rise to his feet and prepare to set off.

– You said you'd travelled this way before . . . please, it's important.

The question seemed to unsettle him, Mister. I could see his shoulders shifting.

– You have people there at Ayn Issa? he called back.

– Maybe . . . I'm . . .

– You have people at that blue house? – *hurmp* – Sleep there? Eat?

I looked back at the photograph and read the inscription: *Abdallah's House, Ayn Issa. 1996.*

– I don't know . . . I said. If we find the place, maybe. We can ask . . .

Bilal turned and I saw him smile, his cheeks pushing his eyes into squinted slashes. He was suddenly buoyant.

– Zeinab! he called making his arms wide at me, Allah has answered your prayers! I know where is this Ayn Issa. I can take you, Zeinab. But we must go quickly . . . come, come!

With that he took up the small cloth he'd been sat on and made off with it around his neck.

I quickly scrambled up to follow him.

– This is the way, Zeinab! Must go quickly. I will carry you on my back if you need me. Ask me to do it, I will do it . . . Allah gives you protection, Zeinab. Come! Come!

I hobbled after him, Mister, tying a cloth around my head as he had for the weather. And we made for the mountains, me in his shadow, the imp and the ogre.

125. BILAL (MYTH) – I have tried two times to cross, Zeinab. One time car stops. Another time it was me, Bilal, – *hurmp* – who fell and stopped. I could not go with little food, little water. But this time we can do it, Zeinab!

I heard Bilal mutter a prayer for us. His eyes fixed to the path ahead. We were headed toward the green forest close to the foot of the mountains. Onward, settled into a rhythm, our sandals sweeping the ground, the sun mercifully hidden behind cloud. It started off well enough, Mister. But then, several hours later, I was forced to stop.

My ragged sides had gone, my thumping head with it, and my throat had become thick with dust.

– Just give me a minute, I sputtered.

Bilal watched as I sat on the ground rubbing my lower back. He came down and gave my legs and arched shoulders a concerned look.

– You are – *cripple*? he said, squinting.

I said I wasn't that. But legs first at birth, and so on.

– You are ever since like this?

– Yes, I said, but I manage fine.

Bilal glanced up at the darkening skies. He brought out his cloth and bag. He folded the bag to use as a pillow.

– Zeinab, here – you are untrained, unfit, he said. We sleep here for few hours. Then we walk in the early morning. It will be easier for you.

I helped make the fire. Put on my gloves and pullover to keep warm. We sat close to each other, Mister. And after we finished eating canned fish and hard white bread, we both lay back with the fire at our feet.

I tried keeping my eyes on the mountains as the sun set behind it. Bilal lay facing away from me. From where I looked, the slope of his shoulders seemed to match them mountains. I heard his voice then, low and gruff, strained from lying with his chin in his chest.

– Twice before, he said, I have met Britishers like you, Zeinab. All coming from cold countries and go the same way. It is very brave – *you* are very brave, Zeinab.

– I don't think so, I murmured quietly.

– Yes, of course it is brave! Because why, because look – there is war after the next border. You can definitely be killed!

I didn't reply. After a moment I heard Bilal snoring asleep.

It was strange to realise this lad had shared the same belief as them others. For him there was no doubt paradise was across this desert. His belief was resolute. Revelation awaited in them hills, Mister. Same as the half-cocked belief I'd heard before I'd fled. The same half-cocked idea I'd heard from them crowds, as well as the boy who'd given me my name. I fell asleep dreaming of them crowds. Them surging, trembling faces up at me. Most of that lot would have given anything to be where I was now, so close to the edges of everything.

Anyway, next day I awoke with my legs blue and swollen. I managed to get to my feet only with Bilal's help and encouragement. The path we were following had grown thin and scattered, and seemed in places to have disappeared entirely. When I stumbled, Bilal measured a bottle cap of water and held my chin as I drank. He seemed to believe, also, that I'd been put in his path for a purpose. And though he hadn't lifted me on his shoulders yet, Mister, it was that absolute conviction, that belief which still seemed limitless after so many hours, that pushed me alongside him.

Still, our progress wasn't enough to stop the visions from crowding again. I was dehydrated, Mister, and shapes and forms continued to appear to me.

And I swear it, Mister – I could see them.

These faces, bodies walking alongside us.

Some Mumtaz from London say. Some Abdul from Bremen. Muhammad or Sameer from Hamburg or Nottingham. Me and Bilal were part of some greater crossing. And although these visions made me uneasy, Mister, I couldn't help but smile as I staggered on. Bilal and I were not alone here. I even saw the big lad glance back once or twice himself. I thought maybe he could see them too, these travellers.

– Do you come this way for your father, Zeinab?

– Maybe, I said catching my breath, Maybe a part of me has, I suppose.

– You must be even more brave now, Zeinab. More brave, and you must be quicker!

Bilal stuck some khat into his mouth and started chewing. He offered me some. I took it and pushed a piece into my upper gums. It tasted faintly sweet.

– You are lucky, said Bilal, twisting his trunk-like torso. My father, he was a *fuck*.

Bilal spat at the ground. We continued. My eyes and ears

playing tricks. And to tell the truth, these visions didn't feel entirely my own. Even the *zoun ... zeen ... zeen ...* that I thought I heard in the wind, in our footsteps, sounded as if it was mocking me now, mingled with the breeze.

126. BLUE HOUSE It was disorientation, of course, from dehydration and sickness probably – and yet, I can't entirely discount it. There was a trace of something familiar, like a scent I'd smelled before. As we neared the dark foot of the mountains, I honestly began to breath in perfumes, Mister – peach blossoms, mint – fragrances belonging to my other Mothers' bottles. A soapy lemon arose as my feet crushed the first bit of greenery we'd seen in hours. And the scents conjured memories in a way that made me feel like impossible things might really be possible in the desert.

We came to a small village in the foothills. It was the early evening by then, and I could barely walk with Bilal's arms my only support. I saw derelict houses, abandoned buildings, and car tracks in the sand. Further on more narrow streets and trampled weeds. We'd come a long way from the dusty valley, Mister. Bilal stopped every few metres to read a sign, mutter something and heave himself up them white narrow steps to head further in.

It was only after we came to a small square that I noticed a few stalls, Mister. Spare carts were parked with dried fruit on display. I spotted other people there, elderly vendors, all men, in their crumpled shirts and sandals, sitting in the shade.

I watched Bilal walk over to one of them. He had my photograph in his hand. One of the men pointed vaguely in the direction of the brown hills. The other pointed the opposite way.

Bilal turned and led me into the farmland below. *Here . . .* he said with that same gruff certainty. And then later, *Here . . .* and then later still, *Here, now – behind this place . . .*

The lad seemed convinced he'd find this *Abdallah's House* from my photograph, Mister. Even if that meant turning every corner, and asking everyone we came across for the way. The mountains had crept into shadow by then, and the valley itself was beginning to be bathed in a cool light. I asked if we could stop again for a moment. I sat on a rock and drank from one of Bilal's bottles. The big lad mopped his forehead with his sleeve. He muttered another prayer now. It sounded more like a cuss.

Then, some old woman came up the road wearing a black scarf and carrying a cloth bag.

– I will ask this one, went Bilal, moving immediately across to her.

That woman's face, Mister, wrinkles baked in the sun, bashed-in teeth and pink gums. The way she glared at the ogre approaching her, with her face all scrunched up, reminded me of the way Mother Sadaf would glare at the house or the sky.

I watched the woman turn the photo over in her hands and peer with her tiny eyes. She nodded at Bilal in an air of recognition and pointed back in the direction from which she'd just come. Bilal thanked her and hurried back to me.

– Zeinab, here – the woman, the woman – she says there is a blue house in this road.

– She's sure? I said, lifting myself up.

– I could not understand everything. But she says maybe there, yes.

In a rush of anticipation then, we made our way down the road and turned into an alley. I was suddenly unencumbered by the pain shooting up my sides, and my swollen knees begging me to stop. We went on, and I watched Bilal bat away them low-hanging branches and climb the path upward. We came to an open area overlooking a cliff. There was a huge plain beyond, but what confronted us there, Mister, was only rubble and scattered ruins.

I spotted a white tree. Bricks, wooden frames. Beams that were mangled now, and half hacked to pieces. Black tape ran around the perimeter, fencing the site off from the rest of the road. There was no way of knowing, from what remained of it, whether this had been the same blue house as in my father's picture. It'd been a large house. That was obvious from the broken buttresses, and walls that had been all but crushed into white dust and splinters. There were blue-painted bricks mixed with it. But the tyre tracks hinted at some machine having flattened everything else.

– Nothing – *hurmp*, said Bilal, and he snorted, dejected.

The ground smelled of burning here, Mister.

– I don't understand . . . I said.

I looked up at the face of the mountains and noticed plots of abandoned homes in similar states of demolition along its ledges. I turned and looked past the hills and beyond at the parched river. The only thing I could see besides them ruins, Mister, was more weathered flatlands, and a few spare trees and lonely boulders. I felt very weak then. In my delirium, I imagined my Mother Sadaf among them furrowed rows. She was on her knees there, a carrier bag under her blackened arms, silently salting the earth, salting the entire valley to death. If she'd have looked up in that moment, no doubt she'd have sent me a scowl, sent me cusses for having come this far for nothing.

127. THE BOY The sound of tyres sliding over loose rocks suddenly made me turn. There was a small boy standing there behind us. He was leaning on the short stone cap where the gate had once been fixed. He was staring at us. The boy hopped off his bicycle and pursed his lips. He said something in a dialect I couldn't understand. Bilal took a step forward and replied. The boy repeated it, turned to his bicycle and sped off into another narrow road.

– He says we must follow him, said Bilal.

He shrugged his massive shoulders. The big lad's forehead was sweating now having searched in the heat. We went after the boy. He led us down a series of streets. The further we followed the more I could hear the sounds of the village. Sounds from other homes, the shuffling of carts and running engines and voices. I could hear children. We came to another area cleared of rubble. There were doors to shops that were mostly empty shelves. We turned onto a road where we found larger houses, and the smell of warm food in the air.

Bilal hadn't stopped praying since we'd left. I could hear his hurried breath rushing beside me. He whispered into my ears as we followed, *Zeinab, here – I can smell the lafah. It is in the air, do you smell it?* We turned into another alley, and the boy dismounted. I remember wheels spinning. Bilal and I watched as he ran into the entrance of another house. A blue-painted gate which swung as the lad went in. The boy was all loose sandals and black shaggy hair. Bilal whispered again, his low voice rising now, another prayer.

We waited at the gate, breathing in the scent of roasted pine nuts. The boy went up them steps, and a woman appeared at the door to embrace him. Was it his mother? This woman hurried the boy inside, scolding him as he went. She looked our way, Mister, and she smiled. She turned then, leaving the door open for us to follow.

128. THE FEAST There is no English word, Mister, for the Arabic *tusalem*. It's a word that relates to *welcome* but is closer to *receive* when spoken. The boy's mother approached as we removed our shoes to enter. She was repeating the word *tusalem* as we nodded and touched our chests in response. She had these long dark braids running either side of a loose scarf. We followed her.

The mother brought us into a room where a great spread waited, steaming dishes all laid out along a table. Plates were being served as the room began to fill with people, some of them carrying more plates. It was a family meal that we were being asked to join, Mister. Some large family, whose names were now being called – whistles for children, shouts for the elderly. Two little girls wearing Minnie Mouse bands bounded in from the garden. Several older men came in holding hot pots and plates, and behind them an older woman carrying parathas between fingertips. Bilal and I moved aside for children, who were being bustled away to wash and towel their hands. All around me, Mister, I heard voices and laughter, and that same dialect, blending in the air with the aroma of *charro*, chilli peppers and the scent of warm *musakhan*. I could see the outside kitchen from where I was. A large circular stove was there, and women were dusting flatbread baked over a hot stone. *It is a taboun*, Bilal said to me as we watched that round stone stove. *The bread is called fatah*.

Soon the feast began. Chairs were offered and Bilal and I sat among them. I learned that this house had been a sanctuary of sorts. *It is here for those who walk this path*, said Bilal, *the house, they say, is here for muhajirin. They give bread to fighters before they go on – it is Allah who blesses us, Zeinab. Allah who brings us here . . . we are blessed! We are blessed!*

I realised the people sat around us were used to travellers appearing at their gates. This was a sanctuary house, Mister. Similar to the one I'd grown up in on Forty Road – a last post for those in need and wandering. They'd feed travellers here, offer a night's rest. I noticed the portraits of young men on the walls. Men in military gear with dried flowers fixed to their frames. These were martyrs.

I asked Bilal about them but he only said: *There have been many wars here, Zeinab – their children are raised with war . . .*

All I remember, Mister, is that this family continued to pass plates our way with bottled water. I ate as much as I could. Even had to hold my hand as they offered, saying *No, thank you, enough*, my breath still sore but with every bite feeling my strength returning. I'd never eaten so well. Nor felt as welcome anywhere and made to feel so at home.

Later, as people started to finish, Bilal turned to me with a toothpick in his mouth.

– Zeinab, here – we must show these people we thank them, he said. This gathering of people is to remember one of their own, see there – see . . .

Bilal pointed to the picture of one of the martyrs hung above the main arch doorway. It was surrounded by coloured petals and chains.

– Their son? Did he . . .

– The old man's grandson – *hurmp* – only nineteen, and six years he is already dead. And your blue house, Zeinab, the one in your photo – it belonged to his father. Foreigners destroyed the house – *fiyuh!* – but Allah is very great, Zeinab. Because why? Because look – see there, there is the face we are blessed to find . . .

Bilal pointed toward the other end of the table. I looked and I saw an ancient-looking man. He was dark, with sunken, weatherbeaten skin, sitting low in his chair, Mister, sharing a whisper with a small child by his side. I nearly lost my breath when I saw his drawn mouth and realised who it might be. The older man in the picture. I was sure of it. This was Abdallah, friend of my father.

129. INSTRUMENTS OF GOD Coughing, spitting – it felt like I was having an awful fit as I sat there at the table. Bilal clapped my shoulders to make sure I wasn't choking. When I looked up again the old man was gone.

Was he another vision, Mister?

After the meal, we were taken to a small grove where a ceremony was to take place in remembrance of their grandson. It was clear the boy had been killed in a recent war. He'd joined the path and had died in battle. A portrait of the martyr was set on a table, flowers and letters placed neatly by his side, a chain of lanterns running along the fence. The grove itself might have been a proper garden once. Something had turned them bushes into an ashy white. The family sat along the walls, or on the grass and a few chairs brought out from the house. One of the older men started speaking. And as Bilal and I came out together I spotted the ancient face of that old man again. He was sat in an old wicker chair alongside small children, and a few older women.

I could only wonder at this gentle outpost, Mister. And this family here, mourning the passing of a boy at the bank of the valley, sipping tea together, in such calm grief. I sat and I listened to their peaceful conversation, though I couldn't understand a word. I assumed they were speaking about the martyr, Mister, as they were sometimes in tears, smiling through tears, as they remembered him.

It was later when a younger woman approached and introduced herself that I understood. She spoke English and said her name was Zakirah. We said *salaam* and gave our names, after which she called us *brothers*, welcoming us on behalf of her family.

– We have beds, she said. They are prepared.

I was suddenly very conscious, Mister, that both of us hadn't washed in weeks. I stank of the desert and sweat. I'd got used to it, I think. Our clothes had started to feel like a second skin. But we followed, a few paces behind. Her hair was very long, falling down to her hips. And like the other women, she wore a loose blue dress.

Bilal stepped beside her to ask about the old man in the wicker chair. Zakirah turned to me and smiled.

– Of course, she said, you can speak with my grandfather. Before he sleeps, come.

Zakirah led the way into the shade. There were a few stone

steps that Bilal helped me walk across. We were shown a stone bench where I saw a small boy carrying in a teapot and two cups. On another bench sat the old man, his head lowered, fingers curled around his *dang*, some polished wooden stick he used to walk with. Tea was poured as we sat. Bilal and I both held out our hands for the warmth of the steam and the clean smell of peppermint.

Zakirah shooed the children away. She then came and sat next to the old man. I watched as he bowed his head, slow and heavy, and whispered *salaam* in a quiet broken voice.

I couldn't help but stare. That familiar short beard, Mister. His lips drawn into the corners of his hollow cheeks. He looked like a ghost. I'd already convinced myself, without any doubt, that this was the man in my father's photograph.

The old man began to speak. Zakirah translated.

– My grandfather says you are welcome, she said. He says he knows you are here for *hijra*. But he asks why you choose to go across the desert at this time.

Bilal leaned forward and spoke in Arabic. I watched him and I could tell from his eyes he was speaking in terms of his commanding Allah, Mister. His calling to fight and protect. His duty to the *ummah*. Same as when he explained it to me, Mister, it was like Bilal's entire body had been awakened in answering the question. His reasons were fixed. And he spoke in total clarity about all of it.

The old man sighed heavily and pointed his *dang* in my direction. Zakirah translated.

– My grandfather says that this one looks like all the others. But you, brother, *you* do not look like a fighter. He says the desert is not for you. It will not protect you . . .

The old man's tone changed then. He wouldn't look at me. Zakirah touched his side to calm him down.

– My grandfather says that the people you want to fight are dogs. He says . . . he says you will die like a dog if you travel with them. Your friend too . . .

I could say nothing back, Mister.

Zakirah glanced at her grandfather and then back to us. She held a hand up.

– I'm sorry for what my grandfather says, she said. But always it's the same. Every time he tells them not to go. To stay and eat, sleep here instead. But they go . . . and it hurts him . . . you can understand.

Bilal leaned forward then, saying, *Sister*, in English, *if your brother dies fighting for the ummah – it is a very great blessing for your family*. And he nodded at me, and then closed his eyes.

Zakirah said nothing.

I could feel my fingers tremble, Mister. There was no way to explain why I was here. Not with Bilal here with me. Nothing made sense. For what reason would I have come, dragged my pale and broken little body into the desert, all the way from Poplar and East Ham, other than for death? I reached into my pocket. I brought out the photograph for her. And I watched as she offered it to her grandfather.

– I believe . . . I said, hesitating. I think, at least, that my father might have come through here once. His name was Marwan Bas.

The name was the only thing I gave, Mister. And I swallowed hard as I heard Bilal mutter one of his prayers again, some request of his imposing Allah.

Endless moments passed as I watched the old man peer at

the picture. Bringing it closer to his one eye at the side. He squinted at the thing, and I could hear his every strained breath. I leaned over onto my knees, Mister, sitting like one of them small children myself, waiting to hear him speak. The old man waved his hand and spoke a word to his granddaughter. He was shaking his head, no.

– I'm sorry, said Zakirah, My grandfather's memory is like water.

– He doesn't remember. What about the name?

She asked in Arabic, saying *Marwan Bas*. The old man shook his head.

– There are many men who pass here, said Zakirah. My grandfather looks younger in the picture. It must have been many years ago, yes?

She reached over and handed me back the photograph. I held it there stupidly in front of me as if in a kind of refusal.

– You are sad, she said, I'm sorry.

Zakirah rose to her feet, but then the old man started up at her. He began snorting, speaking through his beard, as if he'd just thought of something else. He gestured in our direction. I watched him lift the shawl over his head and stand, then cross over to another path and walk toward a second shelter. We followed him, Mister. Bilal helped me down a few more steps. And when we came to where the old man had stopped, we found a corner garden. A little space under the leaves of bushes with white petals. Something there was covered with black tarpaulin. The old man bent down slowly then, to take hold of the cover. Zakirah helped, throwing the sheet back and revealing what was underneath . . .

Ouds, Mister. All stacked on top of each other. Maybe fifty

or so beautifully carved instruments. They were laid out with their deep round backs facing down and strapped neck to hollow. Zakirah pointed at the stems of the ouds, their little bent heads, and the tiny inscriptions that ran along the bridge. The old man gestured at my photograph.

– Your grandfather's carvings? I asked stepping forward.

– Yes, she said, my grandfather was a maker of ouds.

– Not anymore?

– When the war started my grandfather stopped. And since my brother . . . his name was Jaffer . . . when Jaffer was killed, my grandfather made not a single more. He cannot feel the joy in his work. He thinks you will understand when he says this, brother.

The old man was staring at his work with a kind of bitterness, Mister. I followed his gaze and suddenly felt drawn to them. Them strings. Suspended as they were with tied bindings, completely still. I wanted to pluck one to see. Just so I could hear the sound it made. I raised a finger to do it, but the old man reached over and gently pushed me away. He said something in that heavy hardened breath. It made Zakirah draw the tarpaulin over them.

– These ouds no longer sing, she said and led us away.

130. ILLUSION Mister, you asked if any of this felt like a dream. That entire evening, you mean, sat there at the table, full-bellied and among all them smiling faces. And now this old man – who had suddenly appeared to me as my father's Abdallah, Mister, but whose memory of my father had fallen away.

I admit, at the time, it did feel like a dream. And still does, in a way. But I've come to realise also – as well you might understand yourself – that illusions, beliefs and dreams are similar. They ask us to accept things that might not be as they seem. And just like Bilal, say, maybe I'd come in pursuit of a myth and I thought I'd find something at that house. Something of Marwan, maybe waiting for me at Ayn Issa. But nothing turns out so tidily, Mister. Least not somebody's life story. And even here, as I write my life down for you, illusion blends into memory and gaps still appear as I tell it . . .

131. SONG CIRCLES It was the ogre who came to commiserate with me, Mister. Bilal laid his hand on my shoulder, heavy like some giant paw, and told me: *Zeinab, here . . . you did well for such an unfit man . . .* I took it as it was meant, and thanked him.

Bilal left for the desert a few days later. He'd learned that local drivers were crossing into the valley regularly, further into them mountains too, and beyond, into Aleppo. He told me he wanted to catch the next transport out. He left without saying goodbye.

The next day, Zakirah invited me to stay for as long as I needed. We walked into the grove as her family gathered outside on the grass that second night. Little children were tiptoeing around just as before. Zakirah explained they'd invited guests and neighbours for her brother's remembrance. I closed my eyes as I sat with them. Music began to play, and I listened. Nobody sang or recited much. We just sat there listening to the sounds bodies made in movement. There were men playing string instruments which looked to me like ouds but smaller. Some were playing pipes and other wood instruments, and a few were using their hands to drum a beat on the heels of their feet. We all swayed together to the drumming, an ascending rhythm . . . *zoun* . . . *zeen* . . . *zeen* . . .

It felt very strange to be alone again, Mister. These strangers had treated me like family, and yet when I sat with them I still felt very lost. My eyes couldn't help but follow the woman who'd shown me such kindness – that Zakirah. Her rounded face reminded me of my Mother Miriam's. And for a moment, with my body in song with hers, I imagined what it'd be like to live here with her and her family. With them younger lot, these other boys, with their pretty eyes and fair-coloured skin. They were there, all in brown and white linen, standing now to dance. I watched as they moved, Mister. Dancing in circles, their feet bare. I watched the shapes they made with their limber backs, arms slightly glistening in the heat. Their bodies came together, and as I watched them, I sat imagining just *if . . . what if . . .* , pushing at a sort of realisation that I was still too naïve, too rare in the heart, to understand, I think.

I felt, at the time, that I was in danger of drowning in other people's stories again. I knew I'd have to leave my father's memory behind, Mister. Just like them little fires in the desert, I'd have to leave some part of myself here. As I looked at the faces surrounding me, I felt I'd have to make the decision for myself. And learn, like this family had learned, that anything I'd claimed as certain, marked in the soil, or in memory, could just as easily be torn away from me. All that was left now was to choose. And so slowly, I came to my feet. I left the swaying dancers to their joyful mourning.

132. MARWAN BAS Every step so far into exile, Mister, had only shown up how unprepared I'd been for this path. Physically weak, *untrained*, *unfit*, inadequate in faith and otherwise lacking. Out of the number of young bodies crossing the caravan path into the desert that year, Mister, I'd have been the least promising prospect for martyrdom.

And yet – my father, who might well have passed through this place, might well have stopped at the oud maker's house, had carried on, had he not? And made it into the desert.

Following Marwan's myth had taken me this far, Mister. But I knew to go on from here meant I'd have to make my own way through it. And who was to say I couldn't? Hadn't I also been raised with war, Mister, the images of war and death, on that moth-eaten sofa, with my hard-eyed Sisi Gamal, who for years had taught me how to see, how to hear, how to *Speak up!* into the world at its most ugly and self-defeated? And couldn't my own Allah, Mister, have the madness in Him to catapult someone like me into further mystery?

After I left Zakirah that evening, I went to fetch a metal bucket from the pantry. I took it to the main gate with me, and while everyone was out enjoying the merriment in the grove, I sat down by the side of the road, and took out a box of matches. I gathered a few wood splinters, and made a fire. The wood caught instantly.

I reached into my pocket then, and pulled out my father's picture. I remember taking one last look at his face, Mister – Marwan and his Abdallah. Passing my finger over my mother's marks. My father's scribbled note on the underside. And then I threw the thing into the bucket and let it burn away. There was no ceremony to it. No ritual. I didn't even utter a prayer for my father. I'd realised, at last, Mister, that the footsteps I'd been following had been behind me.

In a matter of moments, the only image I'd ever had of Marwan was gone. It took a further few minutes for the fire to smoke out to nothing. And then I tipped the bucket over and let the ashes blow in the wind. Next morning, feeling just as firm and determined, I went to find the next transport out, and prepared myself, Mister, to head at last into the desert.

133. THE MOUNTAINS And so, to begin again – the obvious place to head was them mountains. Bilal had mentioned there were hidden campsites up there, where people usually ended up joining other fighters. The transport was at dawn, Mister. I rose early that morning, nabbing a flashlight from the house, as well as a blanket, a bit of bread and some water.

I remember casting the torch across them rasping crickets and buzzing flies. Another white van was waiting for me at the bottom of the road. It was parked near a fork, and as I approached, I realised this rusted shell and its driver were what would take me beyond the foothills among which the village nestled. I didn't know exactly where I was going, Mister. Bilal had said that the final transport would drop me at the foot of the mountains, but where exactly, and who would come and meet me once I got there, I didn't know.

The driver didn't say a word as I approached. All I could see was the back of his head. The man's marked knuckles were resting on the steering wheel, a lit cigarette between two fingers. He didn't even glance back when I slung a carrier bag full of *fatah* onto the backseats. I guessed he'd seen my sort before, Mister. But my heart began pounding as soon as I sat. I was frightened. I had to decide, then and there, that my fears wouldn't overcome me. Though, I knew the dark shapes and shadows wouldn't cease. It looked out the window like such a barren emptiness that it felt better to lob my burdens into it. And so, I said a full prayer as the engine started – and my new prayers, Mister, spoken silently, grunted or swallowed mostly, kept me from speaking my fears too loudly.

I felt the ground shift then, and we slid away into darkness.

134. THE DESERT Now, I'm sure, Mister, that at this point in my written record you're wondering whether I hadn't sense enough to know better. Or whether I really was foolish enough, in fact, to barrel on into such dangerous unknowns.

All I can say now, honestly, is that I knew it wasn't ordinary life I was after. To have been sitting there, in the dark, with that driver, represented one of the only choices I'd ever made in my life up until that point – and it wasn't out of bravery or foolishness, either.

I wanted to slip away from the bright-wide, slide into blankness, into the break, some cut in the world that would have nothing to do with anybody else's story except my own. The desert, the mountains, the cold, cloudless sky offered me that possibility.

I also knew that my Allah had sent me out here for a reason. Everything was so far away from any semblance of the West, and with my new name – *Zeinab* – and new prayers to utter, I thought I could sustain myself on another invention, especially if this new beginning would finally be one of my own making.

I was determined, Mister, I was steadfast. I still had zero faith that paradise lay in wait for me. But then again, you of all people should know, Mister, what it's like to follow ill-thought convictions so blindly.

135. THE FOREST We arrived at the forest only after two days' travel, and I was bruised and near delirious from the journey. The driver only stopped after we came to the shade. I went to stretch my legs as soon as we got there. I drew my breath and smelled vegetation again, the rustle of leaves. I heard the rush of a river somewhere, and the sound of circling birds.

I gathered my things, pulled out a blanket, and then rolled my coat into a pillow. The driver, who still hadn't said a word to me, made a little kerosene fire for us to keep warm and reheat dried meat to eat together. I eyed him suspiciously, his hanging belly and tar-stained teeth, while he tried his best to ignore me.

We slept back to back once we'd prayed, blanketed by the mist that came down the side of the mountain. I remember hoping, Mister, that I wouldn't dream. Everything in my head seemed already to be reeling, emptying into visions. Even the forest, with its strange sounds and odd yellowing light, seemed to shine as I lay there on my side. I fell asleep with the sense of something awful hidden beyond it.

136. GONE! *Pah!* I spat – it was the taste of earth that roused me. I'd slept with my tongue in the dirt and my mouth open. I reached up, fishing grit out from my teeth. The ground had been hard, Mister, but I'd slept the entire night out of exhaustion.

The brightness was somehow cool, and the wind was blowing. Slowly my eyes adjusted.

I could see the charred circle from the fire beside me. The trees, the desert and the rise of the mountains beyond them. I got to my feet and dusted off my shoulders. Rubbing my knees, I stared stupidly at the ground where I thought the driver had been sleeping. I looked around and there was no sign of him.

– Hello? I said into the air, only half awake.

His bag was gone. I turned. Only then did I notice that the white van had also disappeared.

I scrambled under my blanket and felt for my clothes, the bottle of water, the remaining parcels of food. My bag had been left untouched. The driver had left me there with my things, left me to sleep and wake alone – but why?

– Driver! I shouted.

I heard nothing but my echo. Nothing but the cracking wind and the eerie booming in the rocks and dry grass of the desert.

Gone. He was gone, and had left me to die.

A sudden fit of anger overcame me. Aimed neither at the desert, nor the conspiring forest, nor even the driver, Mister. I aimed it at the skies, them circling birds, and, there, at my spinning Allah above me.

I screamed, bellowing up at Him – something near to a growl escaped me, like a *youuuooo!* – and then I snatched up my shoe and flung it right up into the air above me. I sent it so hard, and high against my Allah, that I lost my balance and collapsed on my arse with anger. I rubbed at the soreness as the shoe landed flat beside me. I spat at the ground pathetically. I cussed at the air. The path of my choosing was being denied me.

I needed shelter now, Mister. The trees were the only option. I began weeping then, tears streaming, whimpering, and still, I was cussing the sky. But as shattered as I was, I found the strength to stand, scuffing my feet blindly toward the cover. I came to a parched yellowing wood, low branches rapping my shins as I went further, faster now, and aimless. I hoped my Allah could hear my cusses under that thickening shade. I wanted Him to hear me suffer.

137. ALLAH! ALLAH! Cusses, spits and blasphemies, Mister, turning again into prayers and tears. I went struggling on as the ground began to rise. The bark of the trees, the sharp *thwap-thwap* of branches snagging – the forest seemed to want to stop me from moving on. But I went on, trying for any ground that felt firm under my feet, my eyes darting between light and shadow, and watching for anything ahead of me, some clearing or shelter. I felt defeated, Mister. I began to have visions of every injustice that'd ever left me lost – every fist from a bully, every cuss from a Mother, anything hurled at my head as a boy, every face in a baying crowd, every sneering slogan, every wounding word that chased me out of your Britain, Mister, in your papers – but I sent these memories away, and when I knelt it wasn't out of an intention to pray, but pray I did – right as my foot hit a root or rock which sent me crashing to the ground in pain.

I gave out a cry. I realised I'd fallen into a decline in the forest. The ground either side of me descended into a thick mass of thorn bushes and green. And now, with my eyes reddened and stinging, I looked up in desperation at the clearing. I began to whisper another: *Allah . . . Allah . . .* but whatever I was trying to will out of me wouldn't come. Something had seized my breath. I felt my throat burn. I couldn't speak.

Frightened, I started scratching at my neck, scrambling to

my feet. But then, just as I stood, I stumbled again and fell. It was as if the earth had suddenly given way. I felt the loose gravel turn and I went hard down some kind of slope. I scrambled at them straggly vines, the leaves and stone debris that came down with me. I landed with a crack on my side which sent another howl out of me. My thigh was wet with what I feared was blood.

Nothing but woods, Mister. Only the rough face of them mountains above me. I found I couldn't see or hear anything except for the ringing in my ears and the slow whine of my breath blowing out of me. Everything fell into darkness.

138. BARZAKH My next breath – a gasp – awoke me. I was dry-mouthed and lying under that same green and yellow cover of leaves. The same ringing in my ears, Mister, and taste of blood in my mouth. The pain should have reminded me of the fall, but I was faint. I couldn't figure out the shapes and colours in front of me.

I heard myself question if I was still alive in my head: *Is this the barzakh?*

A beautiful word my uncle taught me – *barzakh* – meaning the middle world between life and resurrection. My Sisi Gamal told me it was the place where we all descend to awaiting judgement. *At the hour*, he went, *we all will go – the exact time, we don't know. The hour is known only to Allah.* I asked him how I'd figure out my time had come. He said: *If it is truly the barzakh, you will feel a great ecstasy – a rush of blood! As if you are drunk with living!*

Lying there I felt no senseless rush. All I really felt was a numbing pain, and some sense that everything inside and out had slowed down. I raised my hand to see my palm covered in red. I'd been bleeding from my side. But starved and bleeding though I was, Mister, I was alive. And it was then that I started hearing other sounds. Footsteps, voices, someone calling another name. I couldn't tell how far or close these voices had come. But then, suddenly, I felt myself lifted up. The taste of water on my lips. The coolness of something trickling over my tongue, into my mouth, and then the whispering of another voice beside me.

139. RESURRECTION . . . after that, only sounds and images, Mister. Like little shimmers of recollection. The touch of fingers say, brushing my cheeks and a soft stroke against my forehead. Drawing a warm wet cloth over my skin.

Mother Miriam . . . I thought, at first. But then I heard the murmuring of unfamiliar voices.

I slept, dreamed, and woke again. See my surroundings emerge like faces out of the shadows. A small window in a cement wall. The dark and broken ceiling. Crumbling walls and a little gas stove by the curtained door. See the wooden table with bottles all over it, blankets, towels . . .

When my other half-senses returned, I remember struggling to even think of the names of these things. Weeks might have gone by, and the words hadn't come. I felt warm soup poured into me, but I couldn't name the taste. The bitterness of the medicines dabbed onto my tongue arrived as a new sensation. I felt needles in my feet as the blood flowed back into my legs. But still, whenever I heard them bells, Mister, I couldn't imagine what might have made such a sound.

It would be days before my speech returned to me – *Who*

are you . . . ? Where is this . . . ? What do you call . . . ? How long have you . . . ? But had this been the *barzakh*, Mister, I don't think the answers would have mattered. As my Sisi Gamal might have said, quoting from his Ibn Abbas: *This world shares nothing with the afterlife except the names of things.*

140. RUSTUM *You are safe here. Worry not, stranger, sir –* this low voice belonged to a man whose reassuring presence I'd sensed as I slept. It was only once I became more aware of my surroundings, Mister, that I saw what he looked like in the light. He had on him a flecked and bristly beard. Squirrel-like, downward eyes under wild, furrowed brows. He was very short, and as far as I could tell, Mister, he had sat at my bedside for the longest time, waiting for me to awake.

– You are American or British? he said, raising his chin to stare down his nose at me.

I didn't answer. He made a kind of chuckle then, and pointed at me, wagging his finger.

– Look like American to me, sir. *Yes, yes* – like an American boy!

– English, was all I managed to say, wincing from a sudden sharpness in my sides.

– Britisher . . . *no, no* . . . okay, he said, leaning over me to adjust my sheeting.

– What . . . happened to me?

– You have broken ribs, sir. And your leg has a small fracture. You are healing okay, it is okay. You will be good . . .

– You saved me – out of the forest. Brought me here?

– *No, no* – the girl saved you, Ester. She found you there –

pah! kaput! – and brings me. I saw you there in the grass, stranger, sir, and I thought – *no, no*, the boy is finished. But we brought you here. And with what little we have we helped. It's okay: the hospital gives the – how to say? – dressing and the cloth. I do the stitching.

– You're a doctor . . . ?

– *No, no*, not a doctor. I was a nurse, sir, in Afrin. But now I am . . . other things here.

The man smiled and took a breath. He then reached over and rested his hand on my forehead. The coldness of his fingers made me flinch. He took his hand away. His palms, Mister, and his fingertips, I noticed, were stained with what looked like ink, a dark indigo, on both hands.

I tried to sit up and move toward the open window. There was a strong odour like a kind of engine oil or burning. Every so often I saw flashes of reflected light, as if cars were passing outside.

– You are in the Free City, said the man. To the west it is Syria. To the east it is Iraq. And to the north Turkey – understand, sir? There is army camp after the water. British soldiers are there with Americans, sir. They stop *daesh* from coming close – they are in the desert, sir, in places between. But the Free City here is built in the – how to say? – the ruins of the old city . . .

He adjusted my sheets and turned to stare at me.

– But you – you are here now, sir. In the Free City. You are safest here, okay? Only place you can be safe is here, sir – believe me, believe me . . .

He laughed and reached to knock on the table with his knuckle.

– We are a community here, stranger, sir. You will see – in time, you will see. But you must rest now.

I felt foggy as I listened to him. There was a distance between his words and my hearing them, Mister. I raised a hand to my head and realised one side had been bandaged. I turned and noticed a table at my bedside. White bottles were collected there. And a spoon. The memory of myself at the bottom of a ravine in the forest came back and assaulted my head. I started to moan.

The man drew my sheets to my chest and dusted where he'd sat. I noticed a limp as he stepped away from me, using the walls to balance himself before collecting a short stick to walk with. He returned then, with a white pad of paper and placed it next to my bedside. A black biro lay across it.

– This is for you, sir, he said. The girl Ester will be here to take care of you. Ester is deaf. She will not speak to you, sir. If you want to ask anything from Ester, you must write it here. Little English is okay, she will understand. But she will not speak!

The man put a finger on the pad and then to his ear. He tapped there twice.

– Stranger, sir . . . he said clearing his throat, nobody will ask what brings you, sir. When you are strong once again, you can thank us. And, *yes, yes* – you will hear rumblings in the night. Loud noises. Do not be frightened. What is your name?

I was listening, Mister, but the man's voice was beginning to drift now, and my senses with it. I must have muttered a name, I think, and I passed out just after I heard him say his.

– I am Rustum, he said. Good to meet you . . . Zeinab, sir.

141. FIREWORKS The first few days, my own cloudy senses were drawn to the rumbling Rustum had mentioned. Them noises in the night. It was half some desert away, but they kept waking me, Mister, drifting, as I was, in and out of my daze. When the sun was setting, and everything grew cool and still again, I'd notice parts of the sky light up in the distance. I'd raise my head and watch them lights follow the sound of artillery. Rustum would ask in the mornings whether I'd heard the *fireworks* in the night. Like it was all just a light show. Except the sound was enough to send faint tremors into the walls. And strangely, after a time, these vibrations became a kind of comfort to me. The dull thunder of distant shelling rattled my spoon every evening. And I suppose, since my own body refused to move, seeing the walls tremble became like a balm for me, lulling my muscles and disordered thoughts into sleep.

142. SLOW RECOVERY I was in a lot of pain, Mister. And my recovery, as much as I can remember of it, was slow and maddening. I soon realised I had to set aside whatever intention I'd had of chasing some distant desert and war. Wherever this place was, I was stuck. I'd have to get used to this strange and spare little room, Mister, and accept smaller measures for myself. Things like putting one foot in front of the other. Getting out of bed and managing my knees and my sides without falling. Both knees pounded insistently, like the drums from outside. But I began inching along at first. Using a pair of crutches Rustum had recovered for me. I learned how to lower myself to the floor for prayers – which, mercifully, my Allah allowed me to practise without His finger at my throat, or His tying a knot at my tongue. I prayed almost every day, Mister, and my thoughts would go to my mother Estella. I remembered how she'd been made to swallow all manner of bitter cocktails. Her blue room hadn't been so different to the one I'd found myself in – except with cracks and gashes in place of mirrors and frames on the walls.

I kept myself moving, Mister. Managed to do little circles in the room, just to ease my knees a little. Minding the tables, the odd distressed-looking wooden chairs. The next few months passed the same way. Me in circles and rounds, rounds and circles. All the while the girl Rustum called Ester – her with that thin, dirty hair which seemed to fall over her face to cover them scars at the ears – would follow me with her eyes, and smile as I struggled . . .

This is how we first met, Mister. A few glancing looks, little smiles. I remember Ester, at first, only helped once she figured I'd struggled enough. Only when I'd given in to the pain or collapsed on my arse from frustration. Then she'd come into my room with a kind hand and her shattering laughter – a gasped-back, grunt of a laugh, Mister, as if sucked out from her otherwise muted throat. But the girl – disfigured herself, and ever present – looked after me in them early months. She was also the supplier of my great fistfuls of unmarked caplets and my diet of endless soups.

143. ESTER I'll write more about Ester – for I've no doubt you've tried to track her down, Mister. Did your best to find her name in your records and so on. But the girl was strange, slight and able to evade my own imagining for the longest time. She'd have loosed the likes of you easily.

It was Ester, Mister, who forced me into finding new ways of saying what I meant to say. To complain, at first, and then ask for help. I'd grab the biro and send a flurry on paper and pad for *water . . . bread . . . an itch on my side . . . please more pills . . .* Sometimes she'd read my notes and ignore me. Other times she'd smile and carry them off to read on her own – I think she liked my handwriting, Mister. She ignored me when I needed ignoring, was there when I needed her most. And never, Mister, did I get the impression that Ester misunderstood me in any way. My own head was still banging at the time, and there was a constant ringing. And in some ways Ester's refusal to speak became like another inviting absence – ready for me to fall into, I mean, and begin anew.

I caught only glimpses of scarring behind them long tangles of hair on Ester. I tried not to stare, Mister. But she had no ears there. Her skin was severely hatched and wrinkled around the sides of her head. Whatever had happened to Ester had been horrific. Her deafness seemed no impediment, though. It was as if the world, with all its sounds and distracting rhythms, was a bother anyway, and she much preferred the pace of her own quick feet. And the way she ran about, I felt I could watch her for hours . . . And I did – I watched her skipping around with them rattling trays every day. Watched her rush over to ease me in and out of bed. Ester came to know every inch of me, Mister. The areas where I couldn't reach to wash – I washed in a little tin bath that was placed in the damp corner of my room – she'd take me by the hand and sponge and press cool water over me. That she couldn't hear my quickening breath made it easier for us both, I think.

I became so used to being inside that little room that I didn't notice much of the noise beyond them soothing rumbles in the night. There were no curtains in the windows. Only wooden slats that never kept the fumes out or the blaring racket. And it's difficult, Mister, to describe to you how oddly these months passed with only so much daylight. The seasons appeared as patterns on the walls. Winter made streams of blue across the ceiling as I slept. Spring peeled the floors into splinters which cut and pricked at me as I made my rounds. I'd recovered enough to feel stronger by summer. And eventually I joined Rustum and Ester at the dinner table, and we ate together.

Rustum would talk about the Free City. I could only half hear him, Mister, what with my ears still ringing – *This place is a wonder, Zeinab, sir – really you must see it, you will see it after you get stronger, sir, just wait* . . . I asked about the surrounding area, and Rustum told me it'd been devastated in the early throes of the war. The Western base had established itself across the sound since, allowing the area to settle enough for the Free City to flourish. He also told me, Mister, about how he and Ester had been expelled from their home in Afrin. They'd fled from the northern city which was close to the Turkish border. *We travelled here on donkeys, sir . . . I had to cover Ester's face in the mud so soldiers would not look . . . Now things are better. Yes, yes – she and me have travelled a long way* . . . But his stories aside, the quiet routine Ester and I fell into, settling into each other's silences, brought simplicity for me. I could listen to my thoughts alone, which came clear to me now, and calmer.

Many months later, it was Ester again – this odd girl with her uneven laugh and chasing energy – who brought me out into them teeming streets at last. And here, Mister, I'll write a little about them other faces I came across, amongst whom I spent the rest of my time in exile.

144. THE WRETCHED As I stepped into the open, it became obvious to me how close the fighting had been. I looked at these faces, these bodies, most of them as broken as mine, covered in dust and desert mud. I realised I'd been at home among the wretched. I was in a kind of camp here, Mister. A city made of tents. Made with threadbare fabrics, chicken wire fencing, and with people in and out of wrecked streets, under felled houses, holes in the walls. Ruins, the bones of buildings, rose all around me, Mister, suggesting that all this had been a city square before it became a settlement for the left behind.

The first faces I saw as Ester and I walked through the ruins belonged to a group of men sitting against a cement wall. It was some repurposed shack, I remember, similar to the one we'd been sharing with Rustum. White cracked walls and heavy-looking corrugated sheets for roofing. The men were elderly and clothed in worn white shirts and leather sandals. They had these yellowed arms too, all carved up with wounds browned over in the sun. A couple of them had bandages clamped to their cheeks, and were using caps to fan the flies away. They seemed to be counting what looked like electrical wiring, couplings and plugs at their feet. They stared at us as we passed, but didn't greet us. My legs had begun to really hurt, Mister, but suddenly there was so much to gawp at that I couldn't help but walk on.

Ester led me into another, suddenly bustling road. This road was pocked with holes, and uncleared scrap lay to either side of it. The street was full of the wounded and maimed. See one grey-faced man who came close to me, sucking water from a tin cup, exposing a mouthful of battered teeth. He had a bottle of what looked like watery milk balanced under his arm. There was another, sat on a porch, eating with his hands from a paper plate. He was speaking in short snorts to nobody next to him. There was a woman hunched thin, with her scalp totally bare, surrounded by what looked like a congregation of stray dogs at a doorway. The animals fought over the scraps, lapping at the ground at her feet. I was startled again when another man approached Ester. He placed both hands on her shoulders after she nodded at him and touched his cheeks in affection. I drew back when I noticed the lower half of him. His entire lower body was twisted around, Mister. If I hadn't seen him turn and walk with my own eyes, I wouldn't have believed it possible. He wore no more than a cloth around his waist, which did little to hide the scars beneath. The sight left me with a mix of horror and pity, Mister. The man painfully shuffled on.

Ester pointed to what looked like a hagglers' market near some other shelter and I followed her toward it. As we crossed the road, we were stopped by another wretch. This man, I'd find out later, went by the name of Arta. This one, Mister, who was proper bone-thin and contorted, went about shouting his name as he picked at heaps of trash. *Arta . . . Arta . . .* And this Arta hadn't anything I could call a face. Only grafted skin, smooth where his eyes should have been, and a distended, scarred mouth, from which he barked out his name – *Arta . . . Arta . . .* I watched him scuttle out in front of us blindly, somehow navigating the road on instinct alone. Or some other sense, Mister – smell, maybe, or the taste of the air – somehow he made his way around us and disappeared.

Ester had been watching me, I realised. She'd been smiling at me as I watched. And that smile – frightening in its own way, slightly downturned at the sides – was the first sign that this was only a taste of what I'd witness in this City.

145. FREE CITY (1) Worth staying with this for the moment – these pitted streets, Mister, these marked people – and for me to tell you how the Free City came to be. What I learned came from Rustum, who, over the course of several meagre dinners, would describe the impossibility of the place. He described it as a kind of refuge, Mister, protected from the war still raging hundreds of miles away in other cities. It was a place for people like me – *people like you, Zeinab, sir*, he'd say – to feel safe. It was with Ester, and once he felt I was fit enough to join him, riding around with Rustum in his repurposed truck, that I was able to piece it together. And while the City became more familiar, it remained for me a dizzying, astonishing place.

The story went that the Free City had emerged out of the guts of another. Some former municipality, Mister – a name like Fasili or similar, which would barely figure on any map – that had been pounded to next to nothing in the early years of the war. It was located near some large body of water in a valley which was deemed strategic. The fighting there had been fierce, Mister. The empty shells of buildings stood hollowed out around this central tent city now. Displaced people from all across the region had started migrating here a year before I'd arrived. They were looking for shelter, Mister, some safe place to hide. And with the near constant supply of food and medical aid streaming in from the bases across the water, the settlements began to organise themselves and extend into disputed territories. They were governed by a kind of civilian order. They even had their own councils, a government of sorts, and local militias within their bounds. Them foreign armies were kept at arm's length at the borders of the water, which was where their jurisdiction ended.

All around were makeshift homes, I remember, shacks made from mud, sheet metal and repurposed cement. Everything rebuilt using materials scavenged from nearby port towns, neighbouring cities, abandoned bases.

Rustum and Ester, I realised, were part of this communal sanctuary. *A new city remade, sir, from inside the old*, was how Rustum put it. And the thing about it was, Mister, the picture I'd neglected when I'd first come across all them bodies and their scars was that everyone seemed to share Ester's and Rustum's busy energy. Nobody sat idle. Everybody was occupied with some task or other. And while the war had left its mark on them all, Mister, they were animated with a proper sense of purpose.

The banging, sawing, hammering I'd heard from the window was a clue. The more able-bodied rushed from one task to the next. All the impossibilities Rustum had mentioned were on show here – civilian-staffed hospitals were being built. Schools were being repainted and reopened, and these kids all sat over their splintered desks, eagerly scribbling.

I passed a group of older children, many of them with leg injuries visible beneath patched garments, busy rehearsing some kind of dance routine under a tree. Their carefree smiles reminded me of Ester's. *The children are our responsibility, sir, we raise them together. One child has many fathers, many mothers, the community's children, these are . . .* I think Rustum enjoyed the little tours he gave me in his dusty old truck, stacked with rope-bound scrap. He had a habit of *tap-tapping* his fingers whenever he wanted to make something stick in the mind. And though he seemed to greet everybody with a *sir*, it was him who was treated as the City's unofficial mayor.

– All this . . . but how? I asked, watching the sputtering motorcycles and junked cars, trundling over dirt paths and semi-cleared roads.

– Zeinab, sir, in the beginning it was a big mess. No irrigation or cultivation, no sanitation. Nothing you see here was here . . .

We came to a stop near what Rustum called the Big Market. It was a massive hangar filled with many rows of moth-eaten fabrics, pots, pans, baby clothes and other used wares. I heard a proper throaty mix of languages there. People from all over, bartering like mad. *Like a pot* is how he described it – *bubbling pot, sir, mixed with Arabic, American, Turkish, Kurmanji . . .*

When we came to the gate, I saw that some of them wandering the aisles were armed, Mister. Men and women, as hard in the eyes as each other. Wearing long chains with pendants on and badges with symbols I didn't recognise. They were patrolling the tents under which hung donated clothing and fabrics. Rustum led me to another startling sight: a group of elderly women sat on a carpet with piles of artificial legs beside them. *Anything we salvage, sir, we share*, whispered Rustum to me.

These sellers had carpets unfolded, Mister. They were

displaying carvings, a few prettified wooden legs, intricately cut arms with wooden palms also, with patterns worked into them with their knives. Every carved appendage was ready to be exchanged for some other. And that was the thing, I realised – no money changed hands. I looked again at the boxes of batteries, the powdered milk. There were no prices. I scratched my knotted hair in amusement.

Later, Rustum explained to me that goods were only ever exchanged with other items. They did have paper notes in the Free City, but money was only meant for exchange with them foreign bases across the water. Rustum tapped his fingers on my shoulder, pointing at a small crowd. People were waiting on another woman, who'd perched herself atop a wooden box. She had a giant umbrella over her and a small table. What she was handing out to these people, Mister, was currency. American dollars. And as I stepped closer, I saw how she dipped every dollar she gave into a pot of what looked like inky vinegar. People came away from her with hands stained reddish brown and indigo. Rustum had been watching me stare.

– Disinfectant, sir. The money gives us dysentery, he said.

He shrugged, turned and threw his arms in the other direction. There was a bolshiness to the man, Mister, which seemed in harmony with the way all these people rushed about on their toes. Like Ester with that spring in her step, they all seemed so charged with having somewhere else to be. Carrying salvage on their backs or under their arms. One thing to barter in exchange for another. And all the while, the close signs of war, Mister, the collapsed upright halves of buildings, the brokenness of the people here, scars both visible and not, all of them carried by the same constant, rolling rhythm.

146. FREE CITY (2) On another day, we came to a ravine Rustum called the *Holy Quarry*. There was a group of men working to clear plaster and stone from the area. Large bits of debris had been scattered from a building that'd been bombed. Behind these men I saw a long line of others who were running metal buckets from inside the ruins out to the very edges of the drop. The area was adjacent to a steep decline at the foot of the mountain. These men were lowering buckets into the ravine.

Rustum and I came to the side of the road and could see down into the quarry. Rustum huffed at the harsh sunlight and pointed out at the men who were clearing.

– These men, Zeinab, sir – they come from all over. Those ones are Chechen. Others from Rus. These others here, sir, Chaldean. Eastern Christians inside. Armenians somewhere . . . and these are the Syrian Jews. And these ones – there . . .

Rustum pointed at a group of young men. Sweat was shining off their faces. They were shifting debris, in a drive to clear the place. I noticed how this group seemed to keep to themselves, away from the rest of the men. Most were big-chested, bearded and solemn.

– These ones here, sir, came to us as enemies. They were *fighters*. Some *daeshi* – him, there, and that other, were *daeshi*. But this is not a punishment, sir, that's not what we do. They left the fighting. And now, like everyone else, they want to help the community. No matter how they came, Zeinab, sir, they are welcome here – you can see.

I realised then, Mister, that Rustum had mistaken me for one of them *daeshi* deserters. I didn't say anything then, but I remember what I felt when watching these labourers under the sun. I had no pity for them, Mister, but there was a stirring of something else. A kinship, maybe – we'd all travelled the same caravan path to get here.

Rustum and I then walked down and joined another line of labouring men hauling buckets between the ruins and the ravine. The buckets were lowered with a pulley and rope, as I recall, bringing nothing up in its place. When I looked, Mister, all I saw were buckets filled to the brim with stirred concrete.

– It is *shit*, Zeinab, sir. There is shit inside with the concrete. It is to get rid of the smell.

Rustum explained it to me, Mister, and said the building they were clearing had actually been a place of ancient worship. It had been a Christian church. Them *daeshi* had used it as a latrine when they took control of the area.

This business of buckets and ropes and pulleys, Mister, was about removing the shit left inside, and restoring the church for prayer. *It is the only thing the daeshi left for the people here . . .* said Rustum, handing the last bucket over to me.

In the heat, Mister, under that burning sun, some of the men had started singing. They sang, I remember, in a dialect and rhythm I couldn't figure. I went inside and wandered around the desecrated church. I found broken pillars at its entrance, bits of painted ceiling strewn across the floor. There were red dots marked on some of them. Rustum had told me the markings indicated which should be discarded and which preserved. Some of the relics were loaded into Rustum's truck. Much of it was completely destroyed. Ancient frescoes and tiled art had been scratched with what looked like axes or knives. There was graffiti all over, red and black, and spray-painted in symbols I didn't recognise. The floor had been deliberately dug out, smashed with shovels to prevent prayer. I glanced back at the men lying exhausted outside. I realised they were clearing the church so that them Christians in the City could worship again.

And it lifted me, Mister. Rustum had often said that the Free City was a place for *people like me* to find a new way to live. To remake themselves even – begin again. He didn't explain what he meant by *like me*. But I could see for myself the way people reinvented themselves here. They reassembled in relation to one another.

147. FREE CITY (3) Over time I came to feel as if my ending up at the Free City had been a proper blessing. I'd been settling, Mister, making my way around on my own. As the months passed, I began to feel less constricted in my movements. I was able to walk with a straighter step. I felt looser. All them months spent in isolation had also allowed for a gradual change in my appearance – my hair had grown long again, and my beard, Mister, had returned with softer curls now, and they were thicker and darker.

I must describe to you the part of the Free City they called the Worshippers' Port, Mister. It was here, while them ancient ruins were being rebuilt, that people from both sides of the sound came to pray. It was called Worshippers' Port because of all the shelters erected on this side of the jetties. There were several shelters, Mister. Each designated for a particular faith. I visited the first time with Rustum and noticed two collared priests leading a group in ceremony. There was a Chalabi rabbi inside another. And among a more mingled crowd, Mister, there was an imam reading the Qur'an alongside an armed guard who seemed to be following along with the reading.

Most of them guards were female, Mister. They were part of some local militia who were ranging the mountains. I'd asked about it once, and Rustum had said, *And why not women guards? – They protect us from mostly men!*

Rustum had also told me that the Worshippers' Port needed protecting because it was where aid packages arrived from across the water. Rustum was in charge of all that. Sorting, distribution and salvage across the Free City.

When I looked, Mister, I saw jetties stretching far out into the water, and black dots emerging from where the boats were in the distance. These were helicopters coming and going from the bases. Over the next few months, I'd watch Rustum cross the sound on boats filled with large crates of collected material. Some special permit was required to cross. I stayed behind and waited. Usually, I walked along them jetties myself, Mister, and watched worshippers from afar. Seeing how they prayed, washed their hands, bent down, elbow to elbow, together.

Rustum asked me: *You don't join, Zeinab, sir? – Or does it still hurt to bend so far . . .* But it wasn't my injuries, Mister. I told Rustum I preferred to pray alone.

Truth was, I hadn't really prayed since them first few months of recovery. I remember lying in bed replaying memories of my Mothers' old house, my own mangy childhood, Mister, whispering invented verses into the cracks in the floorboards. My Allah felt very close to me then. He was silent for me now, Mister. I hadn't received a single vision in all my time in the Free City. Although, I could still feel the tremors of my Other inside. I'd started to mutter again. Mostly while I sat on them jetties waiting for Rustum to return. These weren't proper poems, Mister. And yet every time it happened, I felt the need to lift a bottle to my mouth, letting mouthfuls of water wash away whatever I'd been muttering into the sea.

148. DEAD TREE Which brings me back, Mister, one way or another, to Ester. It was toward the end of that winter, just after it began to get a little warmer, and I was back on my feet feeling spry, that we began to spend more time together.

She kept me busy around the house. Had me fixing walls, and broken flooring. Ester seemed to know exactly what she wanted, preferring bright colours to the cement, and handed me a brush. With her habitual quickness, and knowing the walls had already been ruined, we went about decorating the falling-down house in a kind of relentless flurry.

Every crack in the broken plaster was sealed with lacquer paint. I splattered the beams with little blue dots, making O faces out of the bullet-holes there. Ester grinned when she saw them, showing them mouthful of ridged teeth, her fingers fluttering at the walls. She was so pleased with how we'd managed to transform the place that she stood right up close to the walls as if she could smell the colour.

We chose the colours by pointing at tins, Mister. Scribbled weird little lines on paper to show patterns. And there was a boldness to the choices we made. We made them in silence. Chose the gaudiest shades, Ester's favourites, and covered them patched-up walls with it. We even headed out to them flapping tents, Mister, to the Big Market, to barter Ester's soups for ornaments, statuettes and little knick-knacks for the house. Her soups were prized for their saltiness. A taste which she'd managed, Mister, by using the saline pouches retrieved from medical packs from across the sound.

And Mister, I recall noticing how Ester ran about them stalls. Everyone seemed to know her. They'd greet her, Mister, by first touching her elbow. Ester would touch their cheeks in return. Sometimes she'd throw kisses on faces, pressing hard on cheeks and onto the lips, onto all the men and women there. She seemed so free with it, Mister, at ease in her own skin. See how she'd tug at their sleeves, jutting her elbow to indicate some little detail, before the bargain.

She exchanged soup for two wooden carvings that day. Two little figurines, Mister, which we both watched being made in front of us. A woman carved them from a block of light wood, balanced across her lap. One little figure we got was a roughly carved elephant, the other was either a goat or a gazelle – I forget. A few stalls down, I wanted to exchange a bowl for a set of photographs. I wanted to hang them around the house, Mister – writing to Ester on a paper I asked: *for the walls?* These were portraits of people I assumed had fled the City. I offered ten portraits for one bowl. I remember the man at the market saying he preferred dollars, but said he adored Ester, and let me have eight pictures for two small cups.

We covered one entire wall of the house with them faces. Didn't matter we didn't know who they were. They became familiar over time, and we gave them little nicknames like faces of family and friends. There was Uncle Vanya, a gruff-looking sort with his arm around a woman. Mary Magdalene we called her. Both in bathing suits and shorts, pictured stepping off a boat. Had our own Oliver Twist too, in a Kurdish kurta. And there, in another, some shaggier Mr Bean with a mole on his cheek. Captain Hook and Napoleon and a Kevin Costner, hiding their hands in each other's pockets. And a handsome-looking Gulliver, Mister, sitting on the bonnet of a silver car, an Audi, streets in the background recalling the former city.

When we stepped back we recognised how the streaks we'd made to cover the cracks had formed a kind of web behind each picture. Coloured lines, Mister, reached all around and under, like a tangle of wandering roots. On the pad and pencil then, I wrote to Ester saying the lines looked *like roots* to me.

Ester frowned, shook her head resolutely, and wrote instead: *no, dead tree*. She took a smaller brush and painted over the darker streaks, making little green leaves alongside them. It made them look like branches.

Then she wrote: *family tree*.

149. H–L–Q She loved that sprawling tree, Mister. I'd catch her every morning, standing on her tiptoes, wearing nothing under her nightie, looking at them portraits just after dawn. She'd bring a stool sometimes for the ones higher up. I liked them little half-smiles she made as she peered at the faces, scenes of family holidays, birthdays or other celebrations.

One frame in particular caught her attention. It was a picture of a group of young men. They all looked so clean-cut and well dressed in what I presumed had been the fashion at the time, sort of dusted jeans and massive collars.

Ester made a motion at me to come look. She glanced at my face and then the picture. She touched her chin, held a finger over her mouth. I didn't know what she meant. She rushed off to fetch a pad and pencil.

Ha-La-Qa.

Whenever Ester struggled to find the English, she wrote an approximation with the letters. Ester pointed at the pad and made the same gesture, once at my bearded chin, and another at the boys in the picture. I looked again at their clean-shaven faces.

Ester disappeared into the bathroom then, and came out with a circular glass and Rustum's razor. Ester wanted me to shave, Mister. I smiled uneasily. She seemed insistent, nodding along, and pushing the razor at me. I turned and looked at myself in the mirror. The face that looked back was only vaguely recognisable to me. My long hair had become thinner, and somehow straighter and more relaxed. It wasn't much shorter than Ester's now, falling at the sides. My beard though, had remained unruly. Ester stepped very close to me then and looked. She stared hard. Ester was quite a bit shorter than me, Mister, but when she stood on her tiptoes, our noses nearly touched. I suddenly felt a familiar hotness in my throat, and my breath held as she leaned forward. She quickly made a swipe at my cheeks with the razor and pointed to the bathroom door.

Well, I came out splashed wet and clean-shaven. I stood in the middle of the hallway, and she walked around, inspecting me, I think. At first Ester almost seemed offended. I looked nothing like them boys in the picture. But after peering close, she came and stood in front of me. She leaned forward then. Tilted her head, and raised her neck. She swept her hair back, as if inviting me to come close.

I didn't know what to do, really. I couldn't say anything, or write to ask. I stood instead staring at her little moles and the scars, and noticed the scent on her skin.

I realised then, there was something inside her, Mister, that Ester wanted to offer me in that moment, and which I had no idea what to do with. She wilted as she waited. And turned, finally, looking at me confused and a little irritated. She stepped back and blew sharply into my face, her breath smelling of sweet tea. And then she walked away from me. I could hear her laughing again in the next room, sucking back her frustration, whipping the sheets as she made her bed.

150. BANGING SKIES I felt embarrassed, I think. And annoyed with myself after that. At the same time, I recognised the look in her eyes, Mister, and was attracted by that odd, sudden impulsiveness in Ester. Anytime we came close again, however, she seemed to slip away.

In fact, Mister, Ester would even outright disappear at times. By which I mean, she'd leave the house when I was sleeping. Wouldn't tell me where or for what. I'd find myself alone again, and wondering. Sometimes she'd be gone for days, Mister. And when she returned, she'd simply pick up where we left off, brushing my hair, jutting her chin and asking my help with a bit of painting.

I came to expect these prolonged absences over time. I'd notice how she'd get irritated with me and become restless. I'd wonder what I'd done to offend her. But it was as if there were hot coals in her belly, Mister, and she needed to shift them. Like clockwork then, she'd vanish, gone with her bare feet, only to return again, suddenly settled.

Other times, I'd be blindsided by Ester's outbursts. Like the day I woke to her scampering feet. I went to see what the noise was, Mister, with the blanket wrapped around me for the cold, wondering what it was she was doing. I found the girl in her nightie, on her hands and knees, searching them empty drawers.

I waved when she noticed me there. She looked at the window, and then back at me. I went to close the window, but then Ester reached for my arm, and I saw that she had a steel pot and ladle with her.

I watched Ester bring out a pad, searching for a page to show me. She'd written in hurried lettering:

DRONE.

Ester suddenly pointed at the sky, jabbing her finger out the window. There was that restlessness again, Mister, which I didn't think I'd seen so expressed until that moment. Her whole body seemed to be shaking. She threw the pad and went past me still clutching the pot and ladle. She climbed the window ledge, sat down, and began suddenly banging the metal in a constant rhythm:

. . . *Passh* . . . *ta-ta-ta* . . . *boun* . . .

And there, Mister, others outside at each open canopy, faces peering upward, holding pots, plates, spoons, rattling the same sound outside.

. . . *Passh* . . . *ta-ta-ta* . . . *boun* . . .

It was a citizens' alarm, I realised.

A warning against an incoming threat – some drone.

The noise started getting louder, a hammering, becoming more frequent. It soon became unbearable to me and I had to back away from the window and pinned myself against the far wall.

It was a sight, Mister. Ester, in the middle of that cacophony.

. . . *Passh* . . . *ta-ta-ta* . . . *boun* . . .

See her open mouth, Mister, them bashing chords as if speaking aloud for her. She could hear nothing of that shattering noise, I knew. Them heavy crashing spoons, plates, and handles. And yet, it seemed as if she could hear, like she was leading them all in a kind of mad performance. And them terrified eyes, Mister. That mouth stretched wide in the air, completely silent, clutching them handles so bloodless and white.

. . . Passh . . . ta-ta-ta . . . boun . . .

It all ended just as abruptly. Everybody then, including Ester, quickly withdrew into their homes. The doors, windows closed. And above, the faintest of black moths appeared crossing the sky under the clouds. The drone, Mister, looked like nothing more than a low-trilling moth.

Then, down in the street below, another noise – a little girl. A little girl in a dress had broken free and had come rushing out, Mister. Her lone voice shattered the silence.

Ester and I clutched at the sill. The girl seemed as if she wanted to call to the flying drone, to summon its attention. We watched in horror as another woman came running out to drag her back inside. The little girl, screaming now, trying to explain the outburst, went on howling at the sky. She wanted to see it – the drone. Or for the drone to see her. The woman wrestled the girl back inside with her.

The door closed. The black moth disappeared into them darkening clouds.

The silence lingered a while longer. It took until evening for them carts, motorcycles and trucks to be heard again. Though Ester, who'd been so riveted by that civil alarm, Mister, that sudden eruption of excitement, as well as the vision of that little girl in the streets below, was still and silent for the rest of the day.

As for me, I could think of nothing else – that little girl and

Ester. Had it all just been a game to the both of them? Maybe something else. Even now, sitting here, I think of it.

How would it have gone, her story?

Maybe the little girl had been made an orphan by some previous apparition. Maybe she, by some childlike logic, wanted to show everybody else that they were also just playing along, Mister, as if this war was *bad weather*.

Maybe that was also what Ester had allowed herself the freedom to express. Maybe the little girl – who couldn't have been much older than four or five – had also reflected the same impulse. I don't know. Maybe she wanted nothing more than for that black moth to come for her, like it had for her mother.

Anyway, Ester returned to her quick self the next day. She went back to them walls, Mister. Began painting leaves on them branches again. And then, much later, Rustum told me the drones were only ever heading home to their bases. Most after mission completion, he'd said. But then, knowing that didn't make me feel any better.

151. SUSPENSION I think it's true to say that moments like that seemed to shatter the eerie suspension of the Free City. Most other days the constant drum of distant war seemed forgotten. Just as long as everybody kept busy, Mister, pushing broken bodies around, building something up, constructing, fashioning some trinket to barter, or something else to fill time. It was the only thing keeping it going, I think – that belief. The Free City existed because people here truly believed they were the ones holding it together.

Even Ester – see how she spent nights mending clothes by the light of a candle. One of her roles at the Free City was to sift through donations, Mister, deciding which garments were worth saving, and which to scrap. There was a kind of devotion in how she went about it. She was like a proper devout in her own way. Every time a new load of clothes came in, she'd spend hours matching patterns and organising piles. I couldn't help but admire the way she went about it. She was so careful with each item. And for instance, when sewing patches into children's clothes, she'd search for the same patterns for the patches. Just so every child at the City would believe they were receiving something new.

If you think about it, Mister – it's much the same with me and you. It's the same considerations I make as I write. Deciding what to take down, which threads to continue with, what to leave behind. Never quite sure how it'll all turn out, or whether it will all hold together in the end . . .

152. THE BLACKSMITH In a way, that feeling was true for every moment in the Free City. We were all deciding what to lose and what to hold on to.

I recall one day in particular, when I was out with them labourers, mostly Rustum's men, picking up bits of rubble near the ravine where a massive statue had stood. I kept picking up bits of stone finger and parts of a sculpted torso. I'd been loading a section of the statue's right arm, where you could clearly make out a stone sheath and a buckle, when Rustum explained the statue's local fame.

This was the strong arm of Kawa the Blacksmith, he said as we loaded it onto his truck. Rustum was marking the pieces with his red pen, trying to match the pieces together. *The story is told in children's schools,* he went. *The story, sir, tells of*

Kawa, who protected his son from a terrible king. The blacksmith forged a thousand swords for an uprising which burned the king's palace to the ground – he was a Kurd, this Kawa. He was very brave. Every Newroz, new year, we celebrate Kawa by lighting a fire in the City . . .

All that was left of the statue was the white stone plinth, Mister, the feet still fixed to the base. The deep engravings had been scratched away. Spray-painted symbols scrawled in its place. Rustum told me the area was being cleared now, and the City had planned to build a latrine close by.

It was a hot day, and the men were working into the evening. I remember we were interrupted at sunset by the arrival of a stranger – a Westerner.

The other men started murmuring and pointing at him. I turned and saw the man. He was crouching, wearing a white shirt and bright orange shorts. He had blonde hair, and slung around his arm was a long-lens camera. He held it up, aiming at the destroyed plinth.

The men dropped their heavy knapsacks, and stopped dragging the stonework and watched. I saw Rustum approach. He asked what he was doing here, telling him *media day* was tomorrow. I was confused, Mister, and stepped forward myself only to hear the foreigner speak in a British accent – one much like your own, high and lilted at the end.

– You, sir, come back tomorrow, said Rustum, holding up a hand.

The man grinned, looking away, and then pointed at the plinth.

– Can you tell me who might have destroyed this? he asked.

He rested a hand on stone sandals, the two iron rods sticking out of the centre of each foot. It was clear the thing had been torn down by someone.

– No, I cannot. This violence happened before, said Rustum. Maybe al-Nusra. Maybe *daeshi* – these ones do not like idols. Now, sir, please, you must leave this area, it is a place of construction, a place of –

The man looked over at Rustum. At his clothes. Started taking pictures.

– I've heard there are plenty of Kurds living in this sanctuary, he said. Are they not angry at who did this? Cultural heritage . . . all scattered across the ravine . . .

Rustum stepped toward him then, covering the camera.

– No, sir – not so much anger . . .

The journalist stepped past him and approached the other men. He started taking photos – their clothes, their dust-covered faces, bags holding stone artefacts and so on.

– So they don't want to . . . restore the statue, reclaim it . . . as it were?

The man sounded muffled, Mister. Speaking into his camera as he pointed.

Rustum followed him. Irritated now, I could tell, trying to turn the man away.

– It is just a statue, sir. He looked over at the remains of the plinth.

– These stone feet can belong to anybody, he went on. Kurd, Christian. And if you like, sir, we have very many in the markets. Wooden pieces, from clay . . . I can show –

The man turned again. He took another picture of the parts that were hacked off at the shins.

I'd been watching from the other side, Mister. And when he

spotted me there alone, exhausted-looking, standing at the mouth of the ravine, he raised his camera.

I quicky covered my face.

– No, sir! said Rustum, stepping forward, shielding me from his camera. Some of us do not wish to have our photos taken. So, please, sir – I must ask you to respect . . .

The journalist nodded. And then he turned away, Mister, and went on taking pictures of the empty plinth.

153. WESTERNERS Rustum tutted, *tap-tapping* the dashboard as we drove from the site. He seemed to want to guard me, Mister, against them prying lenses, I suppose. I'd gone so long without worrying about any of that, being seen that way. Being seen at all really, let alone photographed. And for Rustum to have jumped out to keep me distanced – I felt grateful.

The next morning, after having slept restlessly, I found the City overrun. Boatload after boatload had arrived, Mister, teeming with burned red faces from across the sound. Rustum said there had been a flurry of interest. A regular occurrence at times when the campaigns near the northern border had intensified. Press packs were sent to look around for a day, carry out interviews, shoot sequences and send footage back to bureaus abroad.

– Ah – but these people never ask about the latrine, sir, said Rustum, not the sanitation or irrigation – just statues always, and the holes in the walls . . .

I went about with the old man that morning. I spotted some of them in their white shirts and thin scarves, bottles of water fixed to their hips. Some in blue vests going about accosting citizens in the streets, asking for their story, their picture.

– What do they want with the City? I asked, as we reached the market.

– They think this is a very fun place, sir, said Rustum. We are very much a mystery to them. They do not understand why we stay, why we do not leave, why we continue . . .

I looked around again at them foreign journalists. See them eyes wide, Mister. Curious at the bustle of the place, pointing cameras, shooting faces, capturing what they could of the sights and sounds.

– But always they ask the same questions, said Rustum. They come, they look at our tents, visit our water tanks, talk to female guards, take pictures and go. Sleep in a hotel someplace else. But we still need their eyes, sir. Every Western eye brings benefits here . . . Better they are here now, with their military guns, military powers, than without . . .

Rustum put on a pleasing face then, and walked to greet a reporter. She seemed to be waiting for him. As for me, I had no intention of appearing on the evening news. It was easy to disappear in the market, Mister. But I was curious, myself.

I'd come a long way, after all, from sitting on that ratty sofa. There, in my old Mothers' house, Mister, watching the *Ten O'Clock News* with my uncle. I was out here in the desert now, in person, in the shadows again, but watching, listening along and up close.

See how them journalists approached these people for their portraits. See how they'd ask, Mister, and subtly tempt them all into spilling their personal stories.

My uncle had often recorded things like that. He'd scoff and cuss too, saying it was all just *weepy propaganda for the West* – all these soundbites, Mister, pinched from some war-torn face, some ragged body. The whole thing seemed suspect to me now, as I remembered it, and watched on. I knew the old man had been right.

These journalists already have some set intention. I watched them go about looking for it, Mister – stalking in boots, the way Westerners do – as if searching for sorry-stories alone.

I saw one reporter question Farid, Mister, who was one of the street sellers here, and told him to stand in front of some battered tower. They had him stand there, Mister, holding a tin windmill, and had him blow, making the blades turn as he smiled. They had him smile, Mister, showing his missing teeth. And had him wave, showing his burn scars, which ran like tracks all across his arms.

It made me angry seeing that, Mister. All these journalists wanted was to cast the City's people as the charming wretched of the war. And eventually I had to step away.

It was over the next day. Them journalists shuttled across on their dinghies and boats, and the City, as always, returned to its busy-work. I went to help them labourers again. I worked with them for the rest of the summer, Mister. Helping to lift the lighter loads mostly, sorting debris, and helping salvage parts with Rustum and his men.

154. THE PLINTH Many months later, with that latrine finally built, the area was clear of statue and stone. It was near winter, I think, and I'd eaten something rotten. I'd been running back and forth from that same latrine by the plinth all day. As for the place itself – they'd dug a giant void into the ground there, Mister, which dropped into the ravine under a cement floor so people could pass in peace. I crouched there, wheezing, and giving out, and I looked across into the long distance to where the blue sky scattered into a whiteness.

The view from that hole was spectacular. The colours of the shaded mountain lifted into a kind of golden haze. But as I sweated, sitting unevenly on my toes and my arches, my thoughts went back to them Western eyes on the City – how I'd kept to the shadows, watched them stalk about and said nothing . . .

I felt very ashamed of myself, I think. I'd even dreamed that night of my uncle, imagining the two of us sitting there, Mister, watching the telly together. I wondered if I'd ever see my Sisi Gamal again, and whether he'd have disapproved of my watching them Westerners and saying nothing. Them journalists were at the Free City looking for war, Mister. They'd come for the images of war, the faces of war – stories of war and destruction.

But then, catching my breath, I realised that this was one of the few times I'd ever really thought about my life back home – about my Sisi Gamal, or even my many Mothers – I'd been so busy. All them sweeping hours, salvage missions, pick-ups, running across the City with Rustum in his truck. I realised the strange, steady pace of the Free City was doing its work on me, Mister. Somehow, instead of ending up bloody, beaten or dead in some terrible war, I'd come upon more life.

I remembered that oud maker's house, them spinning, singing martyred kin, who had so openly welcomed us at the edge of the desert.

I was now beginning to ebb and flow myself, suspended, falling into the routine of this City. And while it was a strange thing to realise, Mister, while loosing a shit into the void, as I doused myself with the cup of clean water, I felt better for having forgotten my former life. It'd been more than a year since my recovery. And there was so much still left to do.

I finished up, taking a handful of yellowed grass, dropping it into the hole, along with several handfuls of sand, and the rest of the cup of water. And then outside, as I passed the white plinth, I recalled what Rustum had said about them stone feet belonging to anyone. I touched Kawa the Blacksmith's toes, Mister. I ran my fingers around them shaped-stone ankles, and them iron bars sticking out. It was another absence, Mister. And I smiled at that, for as long as nobody stood on that plinth, it meant that anybody could stand there, and that I could too.

And then – and then, it was out on salvage again, when with Rustum, only a few days later, I realised what that mad possibility could really mean for me.

155. SALVAGE There was a time, Mister, when I thought the closest I'd ever get to the war itself was in them telly reports, my uncle's tapes and hearing the clamour of pots over the City. But come that winter, when Rustum took me out to one of the nearest towns, I found myself face to face with the jumbled horror of it.

We were out on his truck, I remember. There were two other lads – their names were Hashem, who was bearded, with stained teeth and small. And Murad, taller, and with a nose that dropped at the end. Rustum said that the town we were heading into had been hit only months earlier. None of us knew how bad. But we knew the bodies had been cleared and survivors had already fled south. *We will take what we can of what's left*, said Rustum. *Salvage what we can, sir – take what is useful. And leave the rest . . .*

The approach to the town made us swallow any hope for it. Thin clouds of dust lingered over the path we drove on. It was very cold. Rustum had left instructions for everyone in the Free City to batten down for snowfall. I remember noticing as we crept toward the centre that the boardings and signs, even the roadblocks and bill postings, were burned black with recent fire.

With them *daeshi* banished, Mister, we knew this was the work of some foreign army. Them with the machines in the sky, I knew. I could see the rubble left from store fronts. Them bus stations and schools. Everything was reduced to chalk white now. And in the parts of buildings that were still standing, the rest having caved in, the collapsed floors were exposed like a row of jagged teeth. The blasted windows of apartment blocks looked like screaming eyes to me, and even the sparse trees and bushes were stripped and coated grey, matching the dirt of the ground and the dullness of the sky.

The telegraph poles were all that was left in some places. But wires lay about like slick rope, dangling from branches and across the backs of burned cars. Not a soul remained. And not a sound except for our engine and our tyres on the compacting earth. Rustum stopped the car. He turned and pointed two thumbs at the three of us sat there.

– Blankets, electricals – no food, like usual. Medical equipment – yes, this time take it. Take what you can – look for big houses, remember: big gardens, good tiles. We meet here – okay? We will collect the motorcycles after – go, go!

Hashem and Murad went for the military buildings and

abandoned shops. They'd look for non-perishables, while Rustum and I made for the private homes and office buildings. We clambered over together, keeping clear of the exposed wiring and glass on the ground. I helped heave a mattress onto its side to look underneath. We found a few dented copper plates and metal dishes. Rustum shook his head and suggested with a jab of his fingers that we move on. The homes we entered seemed to have survived the worst of the shelling. Some even had windows still intact and only pitted glass. A little way down an abandoned residential road, we found a house with only a few tiles missing. The interior seemed nice. *Rich family*, went Rustum as we stepped in. There was wallpaper, glinting ornaments and thick intricately patterned rugs that Rustum eyed as we stepped over them. He came away with two spools of copper wire from the second floor, some framed painting, and a box of bitten cigars. He stopped at an enormous clay vase by the back door. I helped to carry it out to the truck. *The clay is baked*, he said to me, *we can get a good price for this . . .*

After we'd loaded the truck, Rustum led me toward an area that had taken shelling. There was one house that caught my eye as soon as we came to it, Mister. It had a gash running down the centre of it. Almost as if someone had taken a giant cleaver and cut it down the middle. The two halves were separated, leaving a parting at the centre.

– This house looks like a cut cake, I said.

– A very rich cake, sir . . . wealthy man's house, said Rustum.

There was a slant to the floor as we stepped inside. Grand leather chairs were set in one room, while hanging fixtures and ornately gilded frames hung in the hallways.

Much of it seemed to have been ransacked already. Overturned carpets had been lifted off the polished floor. Metallic cups and expensive-looking dishes and cutlery had all been thrown about over the counters. I watched Rustum poke about, lifting things, peering close, and whistling to himself, inspecting this half of the house for forgotten treasures.

– Come here, Zeinab, sir, he called from across the crack in the floor.

He was looking into a glass cabinet in another room, where the chandelier fixture in the ceiling had been ripped away. The cabinet had baubles and ornaments that were left completely untouched. He knocked on the glass with his finger. I crossed the great gash to his side of the house and saw what he was pointing at. It was a little snow globe, Mister. It felt suddenly like a relic of some former life. There was a little Big Ben, with a double-decker bus and Beefeater painted on the base.

– They have visited your Britain, said Rustum smiling.

I nodded, looking at the other emptied shelves and disordered tables.

Rustum nudged past me, started opening drawers, lifting baskets, inspecting the wooden backs of shelving. He asked me then whether it snowed as much as it rained in London. I told him no, that it wasn't so cold, and the snow usually turned to sludge in East Ham. We stepped back across the giant crack where the opening in the floor reached up to the ceiling. From there we could see through into the upstairs rooms. Warily we made our way up the intact staircase. This side hadn't been as obviously looted, Mister. I went into a room with an old television set facing several plastic chairs. There were framed photographs on the walls. Faces of the family who'd lived here.

A father, mother, two sisters and brother. All framed next to university diplomas and shelves of books.

I wondered about them, Mister, whether they'd all sat together as a family in front of that telly, watching the news reports that had sent them scurrying.

– What do you think happened? I asked when we went inspecting the halls.

– Hard to know, sir, replied Rustum. Lucky if they escaped. It was a very heavy bombing a few months ago.

I glanced back at them portraits, coughing a little with the dust. I looked back and watched the old man shuffle through the wreckage, lifting broken stools and fallen chests of drawers.

– Rustum, I called after him, was it a bombing you and Ester survived? That did that to her – took her ears?

I heard the old man muttering, turning over shelves.

He glanced back at me, distracted.

– Bombs don't cut children's ears, he said.

He went over to another box, opened it, and gave a disappointed *pah* . . . Rustum turned, looking around seemingly aggravated, as if the room had somehow defeated him.

– Why doesn't Ester speak? I asked, looking through an old photograph album. Is it her voice . . . ?

Rustum waved me away and tramped through to the other room.

– Zeinab, sir, he called back walking away, this is the girl's story to tell you. But she will not tell it, unlucky for you. She will refuse.

I followed behind and caught up with him in the collapsed hallway. We began lifting bits of flooring. There was a jammed door that stood as if under pressure from one side. It proved difficult to push open, Mister, but it wasn't locked. Together, we used our shoulders to barge the thing open. It came apart on our fourth try. Inside, we found a dark room illuminated by the giant crack. The windows either side of the split were muddied. It was a child's room, Mister. We saw only a small chair to the side, and a few children's books on the floor. Dolls were left not discarded, but positioned, like in a game of sentries.

I walked over to the books on the floor. There were English books among them. Songbooks too, alphabets and numbers. On the other side of the giant split there was a crib, and blankets and pillows, left behind. Rustum stepped in and looked at the painted murals on the wall. Stars and zoo animals. Wild things with kindly faces.

Maybe it was because it was the only room in the split-apart house that hadn't been looted, Mister, but the gash down the middle seemed all the more violent to me, and the line of light seemed severe spilling into it.

– Is there anything, you see here, Zeinab?

– No. It just makes me think of when I was a boy, I said.

The room was nothing like the disordered mess I spent them clambering years as a lad, Mister. And yet, I felt a longing – the cot, the children's books, and the dolls set standing in the light.

– I see, sir – and now you must be thinking: *Why did I leave my Britain*. For what, sir! But don't worry. Young men do many foolish things . . .

I heard him turn for the door, and I realised the old man still figured me as one of them deserters, Mister. One of them who'd left the West for *the path* after some *big-eyed Allah* and His paradise and so on. And that he'd think that of me, Mister, after all this time, in that room, with all that was lain about us, I felt suddenly angry at the assumption.

– Wait, Rustum . . . I said. You have it wrong. That was never why I came . . .

I saw him turn back, sensing the change in my voice. He waited, watchful and silent from the door.

– The other men at the quarry, I went on. I should tell you that that's not me –

– Stop, sir . . .

– Even my name –

– No, sir – doesn't matter here . . .

– No, wait, wait. But of course it matters. I don't want you to think this way of me – you should know . . .

Rustum raised a hand, and I quietened. It was the sight of them stained digits, Mister, held in the break of the light.

– Zeinab, sir, he said, why must I know? Why must you tell me? And tell me what? What good can come if you tell me your story? Better we do not tell these terrible, these over-and-over-again stories . . . do you understand?

The old man stepped forward, wiping his mouth. The light caught him as he stood there, caught him in the eyes, Mister, but he didn't blink. He had on him such a fearsome look. He was almost glaring at me.

– This is the Free City, sir. It does not matter what you say. I can tell you nobody cares what you *say* here – what you *do* here is what matters to us, sir.

He brushed his beard with the back of his hand. He seemed to want to shake me, Mister. Break me out of whatever gabby state this still, quiet room had worked me into.

– You asked about Ester, sir. Do you think you know Ester?

Do you think you know me? And why? Because I told you the story of Ester and me at Afrin? That we were thrown from our homes, like dogs, down in the mud? And so what? If you ask for more, sir . . . what is left? What is left for me, and for Ester? *No, no* – better I lie to you then, and you can lie to me. We can keep our stories. Don't explain what you were before or even who you are today, ok? Tell me who you will be *tomorrow*, sir, and *after that*. And maybe then, sir, I will want to hear it . . .

The little man *tap-tapped* on the busted door.

– Make it up, Zeinab, sir! There are many surprises in war.

He turned then, and nudged back a bit of ceiling. He left me there, Mister. Standing alone in a child's room, devastated and confused, with only my muddied reflection in the window.

156. SNOW I'm trying to explain it here, but nothing I could say could really come close . . . I didn't understand all of what Rustum had told me, Mister, but it felt like a knot had come loose. It felt like a relief, honestly. And I wandered around the rest of that split-open house in a daze.

In the end, I came away with only a few silver frames, while the two other lads loaded the truck with hauls that were far more impressive. There were spice jars, kitchen appliances, bits of sheet metal. Rustum went climbing over it all, making his little dots.

I helped push a few motorcycles onboard too, and then went to sit with Rustum in the front. He didn't say much to me on the way back. I kept noticing how stained his fingers were, Mister. Almost black now. Black with ink, and that indigo staining. It's true there was still so much I didn't know about

Rustum. Who he'd been and how this war had changed him. I barely understood what we were salvaging for. I knew, of course, that most of it would be transported into sorting sites near Worshippers' Port. Some of it would be distributed into the markets and so on. But then, there were them other larger loads which I didn't think to ask about.

I didn't ask, Mister, where all them priceless artefacts were going. The stone heads and arms of historic relics among the remains. My thoughts went to them loaded boats and Rustum's regular trips across the sound. And his telling me that them military bases proved good *partners, paying tourists, who watch, sir, amused at our City . . .*

I didn't ask more. I told Rustum that I didn't think salvage was for me, to which he nodded and said, *I think not, also. But there are other things, sir – you will find your place, you will see . . .*

I stared at the white ruins as we passed. All them yawning walls, Mister. The desolation left behind from the shelling. I looked at the blanket sky above me. It was starting to snow. You could barely see anything falling at first, given the debris unsettled in the breeze – but there it was: snow drifting in like falling little lies.

157. MUTTERING AGAIN I'm not sure what came over me, Mister, but the next few weeks I felt much more intent on speaking to people. Jabbering honestly, to anybody who would listen to me. I came back from that flattened town wanting to make friends, I think. I did my best to mimic the rough dialect I'd heard around me. I started hanging out at the markets more. Stopping to speak to the old women at them carpets, calling out the day's wares with the men at the many rows of stalls. When I was alone, I noticed a few long-forgotten habits were beginning to return. I started muttering more often. Started doing a few rounds around the house trailing my fingers against them painted walls. I'd even catch myself reciting a few rhymes, Mister. No harm at the time, I thought. Not when I was with Ester in silence and making use of gestures alone.

Sometimes, I'd walk out with her, Mister, huddled and arms linked, and I was barefoot too, and if ever a word spilled out, I knew Ester wouldn't have heard me. I was cautious. Even asked to borrow a scarf to cover my mouth. I wore it like some of the women I'd seen, shielding from sand and the dust. I covered my nose and neck with it, wore it right up to my eyes, which helped during them dry winter months. Ester liked when I began to wear her clothes, Mister. She enjoyed dressing me, and going out together. Our long brown hair in the cold dead wind, flitting about with our feet uncovered. I even started to take some of her habits as my own. I used her comb, plied her soups in barter at them stalls, took some of that reddened khat she liked to chew, and made my teeth as blooded as hers.

We even began sleeping in the same bed together, Mister. We'd curl up late into the mornings, embracing each other as we slept. She'd even pluck hairs from my head sometimes – my hair was as long as hers by then, and she'd knit a few strands between the gaps in her teeth to chew on.

It was an odd thing, looking back. When I recall Ester, it's like I'm conjuring up a kind of ghost or apparition. It was like her thoughts were elsewhere, and never fixed. I remember trying so eagerly to impress her. Taking encouragement from her moods, or suggestions. The way she squeezed my hand, for instance, when we walked together in the markets. Or how she kissed me hard on the cheek now and then, whenever I showed her some pretty trinket.

And then there were days when we travelled all the way to the outskirts of the City. She let me follow her, Mister. Had me sit in front of a little house, and she'd disappear for hours at a time inside them. What she did inside for that long, I never knew. I assumed these were houses of friends. I'd always wait, face veiled and settled. She'd reappear, and I'd feel a warmth noticing how glad she was to see me. And we'd walk home together, Mister, passing the markets. And Ester, yawning and leaning into me, would pay dollars for the better fruit.

158. CUTTING WIRE Anyway, I'd promised Rustum that I'd find some other way to support the City. I went looking for work to busy my hands. I came to the women at the market, Mister, who agreed – after trading two bowls to teach me how to carve and whittle wood.

I began making little wooden pieces, Mister. Them idols which Ester had developed a fondness for. The statues, I realised, were all over the Free City. I'd spot them on desks at the local council offices, and in homes along with other furnishings. They were, as far as I could figure, a kind of local charm, and were among the only original things made in the City. Something not salvaged, I mean, nor from some other time.

The method was easy. And the tools were few. I had to learn at first to distinguish treated wood from the soft pliable sort.

For many hours, Mister, I'd watch the women carve their own false limbs with elaborate patterns. They'd use the same artistry on furniture and photo frames for others. People would come along with plain chairs, Mister, and I'd watch how they'd completely transform a varnished surface into some starry night. Their tools were thin filament wire and sharp blades. Sometimes a large razor to make the general pattern. Then the refinements were done using the wires and smaller knives. And I remember becoming intrigued by the little notes they'd make in the wood. The little figures or thorny little stems they'd cut.

I found a sense of calm in their company. Though they were a proper rowdy lot, these women – names like Bina Sameen, Bint Humera, Rabia and Nawal. All elder aunties with gold around their wrists and beaded necklaces. They wore bangles, little anklets and stone rings on their fingers – filched, no doubt, from some carpeted home. And they wore, Mister, this fragrant paste so everything swooned with notes of *rabahi* – a kind of camphor – and *yalanjuj* – the scent of aloe wood.

One of them, some rouged auntie, with puckered eyes, showed me how to carve a hollow into a piece of wood. The hollowed-out piece became a container for my tools. And, with some effort, I was able to fashion a little figurine out of a white speckled block that opened at the sides to reveal the inside hollow. I could keep a spool of filament wire inside there, the sharp thin little wire that I used to shave, and make indentations in the wood for my other pieces. I was able to make many figures after that. I'd pattern them with clothes, little lines for definition, and save the finest details for their faces.

Most of the time, the concentration would be enough to keep my lips tight, Mister. But I confess that I did sometimes whisper a few quiet words to them wooden figurines. It might have looked a little deranged to others – to see me there muttering like a child, working on these little miniature dolls, faces the size of my fingertips. But these figurines, Mister, delicately etched, became a comfort to me during the days Ester spent away. Or when Rustum would be out scavenging in one of the nearby towns. Despite my efforts, there was nobody else to talk to. Nobody else I knew, really, and even them perfumed women, with their bangles and laughter and stories I couldn't follow – their banter quickly became too much for me. And there were no books. Nothing to read worth a figure in exchange.

I also didn't bother displaying any of the ones I made. Not the way them others did, like little bodies across their stunted laps. I'd visit the markets to borrow sand files and things, their cutting wires, and then come home to line them up like they were my very own row of Yahoos, Mister. I even made one for Ester. And another for Rustum. Both likenesses made of light wood the colour of green olives. I made one for my own Sisi Gamal too, from memory, and another rounded bulbous Mother Sadaf – she, for whom I had to find the darkest of black wood. I kept these models for myself, Mister. Standing them like sentries on the sill. Sometimes I listened to them whisper to me as I slept.

159. ESTER'S SEAMS *Fat legs fat head* – was what Ester wrote in response to the figure I'd made of her. She spun around on her little feet to show me. She swiped another block from my uncut pile and was like *Go on then, begin again . . .*

I tried again, Mister. I watched her throughout the day,

taking my little block and knife to the kitchen table. I'd take it with me on my rounds with Ester. I whittled while I'd wait for her. At home, I'd watch her around the house, turning the wood along her lines as she danced about. She'd snatch away the thing at times, and inspect it, running her fingers along one side, trying to press, hide and pick at splinters. And I'd return to the thing, Mister, studiously paring, peeling, shaving away, whittling at the crook at Ester's knees, making little lines for fingers, always bringing my eyes back to the real Ester before me.

During the nights, when we were alone together, Ester would let me see her in the dark. She sometimes pressed my hand around the small of her back, and I could feel how it turned and drew a slow line downward. I would close my eyes, Mister. I could see clearer in the dark than I ever could in the light. It was as if the most delicate parts of Ester were illuminated for me, Mister. She led my hands down her spine and pressed. My eyes would be closed, though I knew hers would be open, falling to the side. My cheeks would brush her breasts, ribbons around her belly, the soft hairs at her pits. I learned all her contours this way, with her hand on mine guiding me. Every little ripple of her thighs, the hardness at her elbows. And so I refined my own image of her, Mister. Remaking the smallest scratch and imperfection in the wood.

When her belly began to swell, I made adjustments accordingly. Ester would take my hand each night and press so I could see how round her stomach had become. The first weeks the changes were slow and subtle. I'd shape the wooden thighs, the small of the back, and hands sat in roundness. Then two, three more weeks passed, and the roundness became a little bit more pronounced. And the figure in my hands, as I sat there in the shade of the window, whittling away as she slept for long afternoons that summer, changed with her.

160. RHAPSODIES It was clear I'd fallen into obsession again. Our silences became like rhapsodies in my head. And I noticed how I'd always get so restless whenever she wasn't there. Whenever she left the house, I found myself flitting about the same as her, imitating her, in some aimless repetition. I'd follow Ester's movements. Seized with a kind of giddiness, I think, a compulsion, or a serious desire to have her always present, even when she wasn't.

It was also happiness, I think. Something like happiness. We were in our little nest, after all, our hidey-hole – striped and dotted in all them primary colours. Her quickness had found its way into me now, a nerviness which I tried to focus into my wood.

It was like my poetry all over again, Mister. I'd have several likenesses on my sill by then. I'd made figurines of all the faces I'd met. All my bent and twisted companions, friends of Ester and Rustum. That scavenging Arta say, out there in the crowd, and Arafat the bootlegger, and them other painted faces in the markets and stalls. I'd even marked one towering stump for Bilal. I used a brown birch wood for him, and I found extra pieces for my lost brothers at the fountain: Moazzam, Hass and even Ibrahim. And for my many Mothers. I made them from my earliest memories, Mister. I made one for my father too, and for my mother.

My fingers became puckered and cut but I didn't mind it. Then, as I set down my wood and wire each evening, I'd find that my mind hadn't quietened as much as I'd wanted. My mutterings continued, and began to force a way out again. I started to stammer and hiccup, feeling the rise of whatever was longing. And like a child again, I started to wander about, making circled steps in the night. Past our wall of branched and entangled strangers, in and out of our little makeshift kitchen and stove, until Ester, annoyed at my wanderings, would bring me back to bed, my breath still quick and suffering.

And so I lay there next to her, Mister, unsure of what to do. I started whispering to her dreaming head in some attempt to lull myself to sleep. Had I prayed instead – had I found relief in my lost Allah, Mister, had Him hear me or had it out with Him at last – I might have avoided it. But at the time, it was all I could do to release my breath into Ester . . .

As it was, I spoke into the place I knew Ester could never hear me. Into them scars, into what remained of her ribboned ears. Far more than murmurs now, these were proper verses. Blue bright sentences formed on the tip of my tongue. They were painful to hear aloud, but I couldn't help but recite them, Mister. And I confess – I even went to whisper them over the curve of her belly – traces of poetry again, in recital for an audience of one – a child curling into the world from inside her.

161. THE CAROUSEL At the end of that February, when the City was lit up with lights and colour, it became almost impossible to distinguish between the coming thunder at the foot of them hills and the booming sound of drums, crackers and firing flares inside the Free City.

Rustum's committee lot had planned a carnival leading up

to Lent for all the City's faiths – *the people's feast, sir, for the Fat Tuesday, and Newroz, and something also for the rest, and the others* . . .

See them dragging long tables and dining tents, borrowing generators from across the sound. Tables and chairs were arranged in a broad circle in the clearing near the fenced-off quarry. The ancient church had been repaired by then. Its roof had been given corrugated sheeting. And the pillars, them chipped and hacked-at bearing walls, as well as a few defaced statues had been dressed now, with long tattered bedsheets, stitched curtains and patched-up clothes, and had been placed around the dining circle like standing monuments. The cooks were sorting food parcels, and rescue packages of rice and beans. And see them working a sweat, Mister, sorting dates for the salads, preparing meagre meat rations, and thin parathas, to stretch as far as they possibly could.

Rustum's labourers arrived with their sooty faces from them recovery missions elsewhere. Everybody had a go at dicing fruit and tomatoes and washing grain. It was lively, honestly. The entire City, working in favour of everybody. It was easy to see what Rustum had promised. All them crooked smiles, Mister, them patched-up people delivering plates to long tables.

Ester gave me another coloured veil to wear. Some beautiful fabric with blue and yellow florals. People from all over the City were dressing in all kinds of flowing colours. When we arrived on the night we were greeted by them bangled women. They took our arms and admired how we'd both made our-selves beautiful for the procession.

Ester and I had exchanged a few trinkets at the stalls that week, and were wearing little rings on our toes and bracelets called *hijl* around our ankles. Ester had tied what was called a *zunaq* under my chin. And for herself, she'd found some white ivory bracelet – a *kusbur*. We were both dressed in a light cloth called *qasab*, a flowing linen, which softened Ester's stomach and which I found very cool in the breeze. Still more approached the pair of us, said hello to me in their limited English, and placed their hennaed hands on Ester, smiled at her, and mouthed what I took to be blessing in the direction of her belly, feeling along the threading at the bottom of her hem.

Others were dressed similarly, and they were all beginning to gather now for a kind of procession, a great circle through the hills. They had painted faces, wore masks made from switches and bark wood. All them official-looking lot whom I'd spotted before at checkpoints and stalls were now wearing sackcloth and going barefoot, Mister, while others wore wooden crowns made with leafy twine to look like antlers. Musicians had gathered at the head of the line with drummers and oud players and so on.

Before the colourful walking carousel started, Ester and I were taken by one of the women who wanted to show us the little crook inside the church. I saw how some were refashioning a kind of Nativity scene. They were redressing it for a Lent now, with a few budding shoots set behind the bearded wooden Joseph. The white wood Virgin Mary wore a clove, and the hollowed cradle for the baby had fresh sprigs set into the rounded basket. I, myself, had made the ass, Mister. The beast was made to sleep on its hind legs next to the basket. I positioned it there, just under straw-bound Balthasar, and had its tail brushed alongside its behind. I was proud of him, Mister, and the forlorn expression I'd given him.

Outside the drums began to sound.

The procession had begun. We all hurried, laughing, collapsing over ourselves, to join the troupe. People were dressed as fools there, Mister, and spinning dervishes and decorated queens. My head swam with the sight as we approached. I was wearing my bright sequinned veil, covering my painted eyes. It appeared to me like a kind of vision. The music was loud and furious, with multiple bands at play, and somehow everything flowed through me, Mister. Like playing several parts of a song, with the drums going, and the flutes and the loud twanging sound of a familiar rhythm: . . . *zoun* . . . *dah-dah* . . . *zeen* . . . *dah-dah* . . . *zeen* . . .

After the procession, the people sat together on the floor, at the tables, and gorged on the delicious meal. The feast seemed lavish in that setting. One of the three priests led a service. The words were then related in the many languages of the City. And later, there was a moment when I looked past the crowd and spotted Rustum standing alone at the edge of the quarry. He was leaning over the bucket ropes that were resting over some plaster block. I wondered what he was doing there, Mister. All the people in the communes he'd helped revive were sitting behind him having a time. I think he was looking into that vast ravine. The ash-white limestone that'd once been excavated here – *a booming business not long ago* . . . He'd known, I think. Rustum had got the news ahead of time. The military presence, the whole sham protection that'd allowed this city to exist and forget, to live on despite the raging war on the other side of the mountains, had, at last, caught up with them. Your lot had decided to pull out and abandon the area, Mister. This was to be the last Lent festival at the Free City –

the last of anything, really. Had I known what was about to happen, I would have maybe danced, spoken to a few more people, instead of clutching hold of Ester the entire night. Everyone had been sat together, Mister, singing hymns, reciting *anashid*, telling old stories. And hundreds of them would be displaced within the fortnight. Sent to huddle again, Mister, at Worshippers' Port, waiting on passages to elsewhere. And it was there, Mister, that my exile also ended.

162. PRETENDING Mister, you asked if I truly loved Ester. And I did in my own way. I loved her in the way my Sisi Gamal quoted Ibn Arabi as having described it: *love is a force of the imagination* . . . My uncle once explained to me, Mister, that he was likening the feeling of love to the moment of First Revelation, when the Prophet was inspired to record the word of the Almighty. In this moment of ecstasy, it was only the angel Jibreel's voice that was heard, Jibreel was never seen directly. And so it was only in the appearance of language, Mister, the words on the page that proved the angel's presence.

My love for Ester was like that. I felt it in the consequences, Mister. Present in the ways I'd changed for her, the person I'd become. My love for Ester had felt so beautiful it didn't matter if it was real. Whatever I was allowed to believe in the Free City – suspended as I was, and so far from reality – the feeling itself became truer than true, eventually.

163. THE SEA *Leave* . . . went the scribbled writing. Ester held the words at me that morning, though for days now I'd known they were coming. The previous night we had not slept, watching them lights in the distance. Preparations for evacuations had been made. And to stay now, Mister, after the bases were being relinquished, meant facing whatever lurked hungrily in the desert. Everyone in the City was being roused from their sleep that evening. The decision was made. The Free City was being abandoned.

We found our transport with its engine running outside. All of our neighbours, Mister, were trying desperately to gather their bags and heave them onto the roofs of cars, clambering on top to fix them tight. The procession of vehicles was making its way around each commune. Ours was a white truck. One that had a deep scrape over the large door and seemed already at capacity. But then an older woman – dark-eyed and sitting alone, some mother who had no other family, it seemed – recognised Ester as we approached and asked the others to make room for us.

I pulled the door closed, nodding my gratitude to the woman. There was barely space to breathe, Mister. Our bodies and bags were piled in. Once we left the camp there was nothing but blackness outside on the road, and nobody could hear anything anyone was saying. Nothing but dotted lights and the churn of the other vehicles, Mister, heading in the same direction toward the port.

In the darkness, I tried to make out Ester's face. And I wanted her to see mine so that she'd feel safer, feel better. But it was pitch black. All I could really do was press her hand hard to let her know I was there. No one knew what the journey might mean for any of us.

I'm thinking now to myself, Mister, that I wish I'd asked the names of the other people in that truck with us. And I wish they'd known mine. I wished I'd spoken to that woman who'd made space for us on that journey, who'd given her seat to Ester. I wish I'd taken the time.

It was raining when we arrived at them jetties. See the great mass huddled under hastily pitched tents near the chapels and that. There were these officials with white faces dotted about, personnel from across the water, dressed in yellow vests. Some were trying to register people in the rain, trying to assign them ferries. I could see only a few boats in the blackness. Shipping equipment, radio antennae. I heard only shouts, orders, barked messages, all repeated in English. Beneath that, crying voices, the spluttering of engines in the wet mud, everything under the sound of the constant rain hitting the tarpaulin.

Ester nearly fell as she stepped out. It was the stranger who helped her. Ester had started retching, doubled over into a puddle. The older woman made a sign to me that meant to go and fetch water. I looked around and saw the tent near the worshippers' fountain. I found a plastic cup and quickly started pumping. I looked around me then. All these men, their clothes clinging to their skin. They were all waiting for a transport out, and the women rushing, arguing with yellow vests. The officials were only taking a few at a time, Mister. Speaking into their chests with their arms out, *I'm sorry – we can only do so much . . .*

I made my way to Ester with my hand over the cup. A yellow jacket approached and led us away, the stranger and us, into a smaller tent with a few dozen others. I looked over them. Some were faces I recognised. I'd seen them at the market stalls, Mister, them labour lines, and elsewhere. I knew some of them by stories they'd told, but very few of them by name. They were all sat together now, huddled and shivering as the rain continued outside.

The yellow jackets blustered in and out. I held Ester's hand tight in mine, the old woman held the other. Every so often an official came to check our names. Some young woman who seemed to be in a panic. She was handing out papers, trying to get people to fill them in. But was at a loss with her *English-English* and broken Kurmanji. Papers wilted in wet hands, as she tried to explain to families gathered around her: *We need a name, occupation – we need to know your place of birth . . . place of birth? – Where you lived before you lived here . . .*

She seemed in such a state, Mister, that eventually, I let go of Ester and approached her myself. I took the pen and paper and handed it back. I started pointing, and speaking into her ear.

– Him, he's a date seller, I shouted. And him, a carpenter – teacher – teacher – labour worker – for her just write Syria – him, Syria – for her, write Iraq . . .

– Thank you! she shouted back to me.

This yellow jacket was scared too, I knew. She was pale and cold. Once I was done, I pointed at Ester. I could see pity fall across the yellow jacket's face as she looked over.

Give me your names, she said, and I gave them.

Behind another tent we were given life jackets and instructions we couldn't hear. Each of us helping the other with large blocks of orange board. I felt the sides cut into my neck as I fixed it around me. I watched the faces around us, men and women, some carrying children, children holding hands, all standing as their names were called and following a yellow jacket into the loud darkness.

The older woman and I helped Ester to her feet. We walked out into the rain together. Hailstones, now. The wind deafened any directions them yellow jackets were giving out. I heard our names called near one side of the jetty. We made our way through the mud.

It was a small diesel float, Mister. Large enough to hold maybe ten to fifteen. I counted twenty among the group gathered there. Their faces all like pale stone in the darkness. I listened to the rushing sea beyond them, the cries of children sheltered under their jackets and masks. The sound of propellers cutting into water as other boats started departing.

Mister, there was no way of asking Ester whether she was ready or even able to board the boat. No way of asking if she was hurting too much, though it was clear she was now in serious pain. We crossed the ramparts onto the dinghy.

There was a place near the back where we sat with our backs against the side. The older woman, the good stranger, sat holding on now, holding Ester upright and feeling around the sides to ease her down into a place where she could sit.

When we pushed out into the water, I glanced at the road, beyond which lay that Free City, lost now forever. I turned back and Ester suddenly shook and buried her head in my chest. Something unearthly and guttural came out of her, Mister. I could only feel the scream against me. Under the noise of the roiling water. I kissed her hard. She tasted of salt. I put my hand on her belly. It was no longer just firm, but gripped by a proper solid hardness. Every part of me wanted to deny what was happening, Mister. I hoped that if I could only ease the journey for her, then we might even survive together. I even tried to tense and ease my body as she was tensing and easing her own. I watched how the stranger held on to Ester like a mother would her daughter. I watched how she searched inside her bag and brought something to Ester's mouth. The boat rocked forward and away, and the woman kept her hand there until she was sure Ester had swallowed it. The faces around us, I could tell, were looking away. But they were black contours to me then, orange blocks surrounded by darkness.

Ester pressed her face against me and turned to the sea. I felt her thin arms convulse for many long minutes then. Only the whites of her eyes visible as she grasped for something to hold onto. The rain lashed my cheeks as I watched. And as the engine pushed us over them foaming waves, Mister, I prayed.

I said a prayer into the dark. And then again into Ester as she pressed against me. She was astride me now. I was holding her back straight as the woman was crouched bringing my two hands underneath her. I could smell the blood mix with the water at the bottom of the boat. I thought about the water and the blood. Water, blood and memory. And I went on praying with the sound and smell, shutting my eyes against it. Ester's body rose and fell with that final push. I held my hands there. In the briefest light I could see she'd delivered. Some fleshy round shape. It was like a small heart or some bloodied floret. Some darkly burnished stone, still and lifeless.

She sank to the floor, and I saw the pain was over for her. I held the bloodied sac in my hands then, and slowly turned to lean over the boat. I felt my shoulders tremble. It was like cradling my deepest fear in my hands, or my guilt – yes, guilt more than any other feeling. Not sadness, not grief. Because I knew what I'd done. I'd spoken aloud during them winter weeks. I'd offered my poems into her, as we'd lain there together, Mister, over her belly in our bed. I'd invented rhymes to tell Ester how I'd felt about her.

I should have remembered my oath. The one made in the desert – *not a word ... not a word ... not a word ...* except I'd enjoyed the familiar rhythm. Same stirring in the flesh. But it'd been Ester's flesh this time, Mister, and her that'd felt it in the body.

I felt my fingers let go, and saw a darkness drifting out into the black water. I saw it sink down, the stone moving weight-lessly, allowing its own grace to carry it away. I imagined it, the smallness stirring, forming itself underwater. The water letting his body rise and drift for miles elsewhere. A body of a boy, Mister. A little boy soaked and alone, drifting, until, at last, washing ashore, finding a place to rest and belong among other bodies.

I sank beside Ester. My fingers searched to touch her fingers. I couldn't find the words to comfort her. I just sat there staring at the feet of them other passengers. Their faces turned away. And I remember, too, searching and suddenly realising there was nothing out there for us. Nothing but a line of lights in the distance, the shore on the other side of the sound.

164. AFTER THE SEA Upon reaching the far side we were told we'd be met by foreign soldiers. I didn't look up to see who was speaking, but I noticed the yellow jackets wore blue on this side of the water. Dawn was breaking in the sky, but it felt darker. Someone placed a blanket over my head.

How could I have done what I did next, Mister?

What overcame me, I don't know. All them others were standing behind us, myself, Ester and the older woman, shivering in silence. There was the fencing. Metal barriers. And them blue jackets with their clipboards and pens. They were going about getting people's names. Sorting people into tents and long lines.

Ester was so weak she couldn't stand. Some blue jacket helped her into another tent. I remember going with them. I remember where we sat and how Ester's wet hair made little patterns on her skin. I parted her hair, Mister. Made it smooth against her forehead as she sat there with her eyes empty.

A shout – one of the nurses. And then commotion, Mister, when a blue jacket noticed the blood on Ester's dress. The English nurse suddenly saw how pale she was, and how she couldn't bring herself to look up at her. My own instinct, Mister, was to take hold of my Ester now, and keep her away from them foreign lot. But she was rushed away, pulled into some other tent, where it was clear I couldn't follow. It was only a moment, Mister. But they were gone. I was alone again.

I stood outside, shivering, as the morning began to cloud over me. I glanced back at the brown tent into which Ester had been taken. It was closed and I couldn't see her. I felt somebody's hand on my shoulder. A voice: *Come this way . . . we can help you.* I didn't turn or say anything, Mister.

One of the blue jackets placed me among some other herd of soaking-wet strangers. I said nothing again when someone else appeared and began asking me questions. *English? Do you speak English? . . . Anyone here with you . . . ?*

I might have reached out a hand, Mister. I might have mouthed her name. But not a word came out of me. The brown tent had disappeared behind a crowd of other bodies. And, honestly, as I think on it now, Mister, had I drowned, had I sunk into the sound, with all them blasphemies on me, I might have been worthy of forgiveness. But I'd lived, Mister. I'd lived. And so, I said nothing.

The blue jackets were assessing everybody. Arranging us into groups, these hollow faces and desperate people. I was standing among them now, Mister. Some group the same age as me. Nobody looked familiar. They were all so wet and stinking. Some hadn't shoes and socks, and stood there with muddy pools of water at their feet. In another group I saw mothers sharing blankets with their children, or watching silently while their children played in the mud. Others stood shivering, weeping, or them ones unable to stand lay out like corpses on the ground.

I felt a sort of panic at having to stand with these people, to be counted as one of them. I watched them blue jackets going around taking names, asking questions. And I asked myself, Mister, soaked to the bone as I was, whether I'd been placed in the wrong crowd – why were we being herded together? And who were these others, these strangers I'd been placed with. What had I in common with them?

It's true that grief is something hard and hateful, Mister. But again it wasn't grief that fell into me in the moment. It was a cold numbness and a kind of terror. Terror at the thought of having to stay in this place a minute longer.

I began searching the crowd for a blue jacket I could talk to, some whiter face, Mister, somebody with a clipboard, a pen, ribbon around their neck. I saw soldiers standing around, and patrolling, guarding fences. I noticed the flags above the tents. And all these people surrounding them, hungry, cold, looking for loved ones. The panic rose in my head – *I don't belong in this line . . . Which line am I supposed to be in . . . ?* – and I jumped the barriers, Mister, shooting my arms out suddenly, grabbing a chair from beside them others, leaped to stand on it, balancing with my arms up, and screamed as loud as I could:

– I am a citizen! I'm British! I'm British! I don't belong here, not here, not here . . .

I shouted, Mister. I bawled my claim at every blue jacket I saw. *British! I'm British!* And then throwing myself from my chair, I grabbed one of them, Mister, some official, and shook her by the shoulders: *I am a citizen! I shouldn't be here . . .*

Eventually, the blue jackets conferred. I was sent to see another man, some proper Britisher, Mister, wearing Her Majesty's crest on his collar.

The man asked my name. I told him. I wrote it down for him. Out of gutlessness, and fear, and little else, I wrote my statement as fast as I could:

My name is Yahya Bas. I am a British citizen. I want to go home.

Yahya Bas

I am an octopus! . . . Mister, if I were to be asked again as a child, I'd have said that the animal I'd most like to be is an octopus. I'd stand on one of them classroom chairs and I'd declare it loud and proudly: *I am an octopus! My skin just as lucent, and in the end, just as spineless* . . .

And now, as I slipped my letter under the door and returned to sit and begin again with my papers, I thought to myself – here, what luck it was that the sea had brought me home. The sea and not the suffocating desert. The Qur'an says that water has the power to revive the dead. Coax barren land into living. It also offers a common mercy. Even for the cowardly and maladjusted. Like the many monsters, Mister, and other slippery creatures of the deep.

My own Allah prefers the sea to the desert, I think. The word for *water* appears over sixty times in the Qur'an. With *rivers* appearing over fifty. And *sea* over forty. And like the thing itself, the word spills into lesser forms like *springs*, *hail* and *rain* . . . Lucky, lucky me then, since my return could be seen as an act of worship. But then again, all this depends on whether a crossing like mine ends with a wade into known water, Mister, or into someplace unfamiliar.

165. RETURNEE Well, the Great Britain I'd returned to, Mister, with my tail between my legs, was a very different place to the one I'd left behind. My exile had lasted two years. And I soon learned my entry back was going to be contested.

I was among a sudden flood of *returnees*, Mister, whose right to asylum had been questioned. *What was I doing out there for so long,* they'd ask, *who was I with?* and so on.

I was told I'd be taken into a temporary facility until these questions were answered. How long for, I wasn't told. Bleaker House Immigration Removal Centre. A grey building just on the outskirts of London. It's also here that I lost my tongue, Mister. And also where I found you.

166. CITIZEN, CITIZEN Before all that, let me ask one thing: what do you think, Mister, happens to people like me when they return to Her Majesty's sovereign territory, having fled? Little welcome-home at your border checks, say, or at least a play-act of the same gesture – same document scan, same peek at my papers – but no, not likely.

Out of the men your lot fished out of the sound, me and a few others were taken and processed aboard some vessel. Our essentials were taken. My bag got taken away along with my little wooden idols, Mister. I was body-searched. And then locked in a room inside the lower deck. Eventually, my claim was confirmed – I was what I said I was: a British citizen.

Your lot kept me separated at first. And then them soldiers started to ask a thousand questions. *Where have you been? What were you doing out there in the desert . . . ?* I was happy enough to answer them, Mister, though any questions I had about Ester, say, or about where you were taking me, were never answered.

I remember when I complained about my legs – which were now beginning to play up again, and the pounding in my ears, which made the constant churn of the ship unbearable – they ignored me. And yet still, one after another, they'd come. Asking after names I couldn't give them. Places I hadn't been. Demanding a story I couldn't tell, Mister.

After a week of this, they threw me in with them others. Them who'd been labelled, ticketed and charged as asylum seekers, escapees, errants and the anonymous on-foot. I was desperate. They were stinking sat there and I stank worse. There hadn't been a proper toilet inside the room. I'd shit myself to my ankles. No pity was afforded me however, and we were left to suffer together in the same foul-smelling mess.

167. A CUP OF WATER So – to your England. Back home, Mister, returned like the lord of liars, near naked and afraid. Soon after we arrived, me and them other men were shuttled between two blacked-out vans with no windows. We were transported to some other location – I didn't know where, I was so disorientated. All I remember were motorways and the British radio going.

They had us sit in the back, huddled in like pigs, for the

entire three-and-a-half-hour journey. The smell was still awful. And nobody, not a face, spoke to another. I heard only terrified prayer and pleading in the dark. Frightened, ragged, these men seemed barely alive, Mister. Like pigs again, or cattle. Some had pissed themselves. I elbowed them, desperate to get away from the smell, though knew I must have smelled as bad.

I turned my attention to the rain outside, which smacked the metal roof as we drove. Although I couldn't see out, I could picture the overcast smear above me. Coming home to your Britain, Mister, among such company, the last thing I wanted was to glimpse that overcast sag. What could it offer me, Mister, or any of these other men, who'd been so blessed to sleep in the desert under them fire-lit heavens for so long?

Then the sound of gates opening. Metal rattling. Mechanical chimes signalling the end of my journey in.

It was a narrow, dark little room that greeted me upon my arrival – a prison cell, Mister. Although the walls did nothing to block the wailing and suffering and crying from either side. How long I was left alone in there, I'll never know. It was one of your own lot, one of them guards with scarred arms and scuffed elbows, that roused me enough to wake me. He'd brought me a cup of water, Mister. Only a single cup – just enough to drink or wash my own arse with. I sat staring at it, Mister. Feeling my body tremble as the guard left, my breath began to quicken, and I tried willing myself to pick it up, but I couldn't move. No matter how parched my tongue felt, I wouldn't dare drink it.

168. THE BOY IN THE SHADOWS I was stirred hours later. In my exhaustion I'd somehow fallen asleep again. I can't be sure what time it was, Mister, but I awoke with a sense that there was someone in the room with me. There – in the shadows.

Was I seeing things? Could the figure have been real?

I saw a boy sitting on the bed opposite mine. A small boy, dark-skinned and thin – I couldn't see his face. He was a little distance from me, Mister, sitting in the shadows. From his slight frame I would have put his age at fourteen, or maybe younger. He'd been brought into the cell while I'd been asleep. He had his arms wrapped around himself now, facing the wall, muttering to himself, and quietly crying.

I couldn't bear to imagine why he'd been sent here. And I tried to reach out, Mister, from under the thin covers. My own voice barely there, but I managed to speak: *Are you . . . okay?*

I tried to stretch my fingers to the lad, Mister, but I watched the figure retreat, and fall back into the darkness. I heard nothing more except for the slightest sound from his weeping.

I thought instead of my own terrors. My mind was sent into nightmarish visions. I saw Ester – her arms and tangled hair, white searching eyes, framed in that blue light. All of her body, pushing against the water . . . I must have heard the boy's cries, but as Ester's, Mister. I spoke aloud to her and to him: *It's okay – you'll be okay* . . . I said, tasting the salt on my breath as I said it.

I must have fallen asleep after that. When I awoke the boy was gone. The darkness threw me into confusion. I half wondered whether that lad hadn't been some imagined shadow. It's likely my fevered head had conjured him up.

I threw the sheets aside and sat upright, bringing my bare feet against the cold wall. There were sounds now, coming from outside. Loud voices, even laughing. The clatter of footsteps. I started hearing the shuffling of buckets and mops. I held my knees and attempted to properly stand, using the bed frame as support. I drew closer to the door. From the noise, the scrubbing of cloth, I realised it must have been morning. There was the sound of cutlery. The squeal of a food trolley. The loud yawning of other men. I yawned myself like a dog, and immediately felt a pang of hunger.

I slid to the ground and sat with my back against the door. My hands held my stomach. I heard more. Footsteps coming closer. And then some high-pitched buzzing above me, and a bolt being drawn back. The door suddenly sprang open. And I reeled forward onto the thin stained mattress as the light flooded into my cell.

169. DAYS, MONTHS, YEARS After the brightness settled, I made out a face: small, brown-skinned, balanced on bony shoulders. Bagged eyes sunk under black eyebrows. He came in rolling a bucket and a mop with his foot. He looked at me.

– New one, is it? He went.

He seemed to be calling back at a guard who stood just behind the door. The man's voice was high and faint. But then the pale, pink-cheeked guard leaned forward to look inside.

– Christ, he went, they're bringing 'em in at all hours, 'int they now . . .

I wanted to speak to them, Mister, ask where I was – but I couldn't.

The brown man sniffed, dusting the floor with his big dry mop, making a slow circle about the room as I sat there. His mop brushed against my feet.

– Mind out now, he muttered.

I lifted my feet. Bent my knees and withdrew.

I'd find out much later, Mister, that the brown man with the mop and bucket – this Shantih, his name – was just another detainee. Another inmate, Mister, in this colourless place. He couldn't have answered any question I had for him. But as a long-term resident, Shantih had been afforded his liberty, Mister, which are like privileges in this place. He earns a bit to spend for odd jobs. Cleaning, mopping, collecting rags and polishing banisters. All for a pound a day, which men like Shantih would get to spend on other liberties, like telly-time.

Shantih was a welcome constant for me in them early weeks. He visited every evening. And over time I'd got to know him, Mister. One of the first things I asked was how long he'd been at Bleaker House. I remember him saying something he's repeated to me many times since – and there's a quality to his voice, Mister, if you'd hear it you'd know – a quality proper truth tellers and seers have. He went: *You ask me how long – but we collect days here: we count upward, not down.*

And he pointed at the ceiling for me, his finger gloved in disposable plastic. As if the blankness, that concrete space above me, offered as much of an answer as any.

170. OTHER FACES I had few opportunities to glimpse the world outside my cell. The door was kept open during Shantih's visits, and during inspections, Mister, or when my food tray arrived, wheeled in by some officer. I'd spy the rest through the little clasped window on the door.

Sometimes I'd catch sight of these figures leaning over the banisters outside. I became curious about these men, these other detainees in the compartments across from me. They all seemed to be wearing borrowed clothes, and socks with holes in. Other faces, hard and young-looking, would stand outside sipping paper cups. Nobody noticed me slouching there in the door during inspections. And once I even leaned over far enough to notice two men eating together on the level below. They were sat elbow to elbow, totally at ease, in an area that looked like a canteen.

Other than these sightings outside, Mister, other than Shantih's visits every evening, I was alone in that cell. Strange thoughts would haunt me. And after however many weeks of isolation, my head started summoning faces and voices I'd known. I'd leap to the doorway convinced I'd heard one of my brothers. I'd see faces in the other cells – some familiar Fahim say, some Femi and Abdi there. I'd hear Hass, Moazzam . . . *Oi-oi, yeah-yeah – that you, yeah . . . ?* I'd keep my own voice quiet in case they heard, or ever answered. And even when one of the guards, one of them female officers, the one in her dark jumper and hair scraped back into bunches, when she'd walk past I'd sometimes whisper at her, into the walls rather, *Mother Aneesa, you'll not find me . . .* and I'd give a sniff for the bitter scent of vanilla on her.

On days when my head felt clearer, I'd find myself scowling at them back-bent guards, Mister, patrolling outside. There were no official badges on this lot, nothing that might reveal to me their names. I heard only voices as they stood outside my door, saying: *Where's he going to go? Just look at him . . . he'll get no liberties . . . no mixing with the other lot . . .*

It was only Shantih who pitied me, Mister. Each morning I saw him notice my sweat-stained clothes, my hair – thinner now and knotted – my ragged bleeding toes and fingers under filthy sheets. The guards shrugged whenever he'd enquire about me. The guard would go: *He should be so lucky. Got a room to himself, here – little prince here, Bonnie Prince Charlie. Should be grateful, him* . . . Shantih puffed his cheeks, and nodded at me, sending a consoling look before rattling over the steel floor as he left.

There was one time the clasped window was left unlocked. I poked my finger to open it fully and looked. I saw the rest of the inmates gathered, even Shantih pushing his mop along the far side. Some were playing games using bottle caps, Mister. I could see two others sat inside another cell. Them scrappers there, them labouring men. And the other, the date seller, the man who'd bartered soup for frames in the City. And then Rustum there, inspecting salvage. And in that striped cloth, the faceless Arta, there in the shadows, Mister, in the opposite doorway to mine. And there I was, the *idiot boy*, again, sat in my little hidey-hole on the uppermost floor, observing the bright-wide, as if I'd never been part of it.

171. MIMICS I could still do my rounds in that cell. See me trace the swept ground with my unwashed feet. I went with my splintered fingers, Mister, tracing them mattresses and that, them cold walls and the frame of the door. I'd found my injuries had regressed, my legs had bowed again, back into my boyhood gait. The nights were the worst of it. I'd awake every morning with a stiff right side. I cussed my body as I forced myself up. It was a battle, Mister, and it was getting harder every day.

I'd lie alone for so long that I had to find some way to occupy my mind. I'd mimic some of the sounds I heard in the night – some falling tray, the *chuk-chuk* of the doors closing, the tinny scratch in the piping. I even repeated the voices of other detainees. Little phrases I'd hear from the corridor: . . . *someone going to mop this up? . . . For what, man, for what?* I muttered these things over in the darkness, my mouth like a drip again . . . *You lot pack it in – pack it in! . . . Bunch of monkeys, animals . . .*

Sometimes the nightly guards would do the same with the foreign accents. Repeating their words back to them. I'd hear some East African voice, some Middle Eastern tone, saying to a guard: *Shut up! Shut up!* And then the guard, in laughter, would bark back: *Shout up! Shout up!*

I'd repeat myself, Mister. And some of the conversations among them too. That low British parlance among officers – *mate this, mate that* – and them going: *Mate, mate, I used to work in a car park before this – you?* These voices swam about in my head, Mister, they settled my nerves and kept my memories at bay. But they also fell out of my mouth sometimes in a cruel and pitiless babble. The quiet whimpering, say, the hard tremors in the walls. These were the sounds of grown men searching for ways to make it through the night. And I didn't know either, Mister, that across that second courtyard, on the other side of that wall, was a separate wing, for women, whose cries I couldn't hear, but made up anyway, and mimicked under my breath.

172. THE SKIES The grating of that platform under my feet was the first thing I noticed when they led me out at last. It was cold and I felt it sharp and prickly against my toes. I'd been woken up by some stocky guard. He opened the door at who knew what hour of the night and shouted at me: *Up you get, come on – you're being transferred . . .*

Had it been weeks? Months? How long had I been in there without a wash or more than a few minutes of light a day? There was no way to know it, Mister. And I still don't. But they were moving me, at last. Into another cell. Into a different wing and building.

When the guard asked me to put on that stained white overall, I did it without complaint. I changed out my underwear in front of him, Mister, and I followed him. Into the brightness, past a row of locked doors and the staircase down the hall. Them corridors were leaden walls, I remember. The paint was flaking the copper rails. I leaned on them to help myself down the steps. It's all I remember really. And the quiet. And the drying puddles all over the floor which stank of cleaning chemicals.

We stopped at a large exit door at the back of that building. I felt an ache in the knees but said nothing. I felt very lightheaded, Mister, and my breath was uneven.

The officer opened a small drawer near the exit. I watched him bring out an old light coat and a pair of heavy shoes for me. *Here*, he said, *it's chapping outside . . .*

I thanked him, Mister. Pulled on the oversized coat and zippered it. It had a fleece lining which was snug at least. I slid my feet into them heavy shoes and muttered to myself: *Like two pale fish inside a pair of pockets.* The guard, who hadn't heard me say a word, whistled as he turned the keys and opened the door in front of me. I walked outside, Mister. Out of habit, I glanced at the sky.

That whiteness came spitting cold sleet. The low sky – my

mother's *bad weather*. This was definitely Britain. The guard was busy giving me instructions: *Stay off the grass and keep to the kerb*. I followed him along the muddied concrete and over to the other side of the courtyard. You know the one – it's enclosed on all sides. Blue bars running along the walls in lattices, steel rails fixed to the ground, a short stone block at its centre, barbed wire along the perimeter. In my exhaustion, Mister, and near-blinded motion, the space resembled the court at the Ibn Rabah. It was a memory which, for the briefest moment, pinched a smile out of me.

I drew into myself as I walked on. And as we approached the red door on the other side, I felt the pull to linger a little longer, stay outside in the cold. I wanted to breathe the proper air, Mister, but the officer went on, leading me into another darkness, another room.

Once we were inside he switched on the lights. There was a short sound that startled me – some alarm that rang as we entered. *In here*, went the guard. And he touched my arm and led me through it. *This is you now, yeah* . . . he said, standing close as he flicked on a second light. *It's temporary obviously*, he said, *until* . . . and he waved his hand like I knew what he meant.

173. PRAYER MAT As I write now, Mister, the bed is still here in the corner. And here, the wooden desk is left by the wall. And my little window looks out to the court. There's a toilet, a small sink. And a low ceiling with a caged lightbulb at it centre, which still flickers, now and then.

This cell isn't much bigger than the one before. The toilet is cleaner. And I've more space to do my rounds. And at the time, I thought your lot had actually seen fit to offer me proper sanctuary. And I was grateful for it, Mister. I even turned around to the guard who led me here, to thank him, but he'd closed the cell door on me.

There was a prayer mat for me too. I saw that the thing was bound with elastic tape, it looked frayed. Proper worn out, I mean, and patterned with use. I went over and drew my fingers across the loose threads. There was a familiarity about it, Mister. Under that harsh light it looked like the one my Sisi Gamal used to pray over. It was like a memory to me, one I could touch and smell and hold on to. It was as though I was right back in our basement, kneeling and praying, feeling the presence of my Allah for the first time. I went to clean myself up. And when I did, washing my feet, my hands, the nape of my neck, I felt the stone in my throat lift again. I was compelled to kneel again, Mister.

It was the first time I'd prayed properly since the desert. I hadn't knelt at all in the Free City, not for this. But here, I spread the mat out, Mister, and let the words ring out of me, scented with *surah* and inventions as per, and allowed myself to feel the familiar burn again, that mixture of burning in the belly and a heavy tongue. The words arrived just as rich as in the desert crossing . . . and I was relieved, honestly, and felt calm afterward.

I sat in silence for a few minutes after that. I lay down on that softer, cleaner mattress, and I might have even wept . . .

But now, listen to me – I'm writing all this, Mister, as if you, yourself, hadn't had a hand in these new liberties of mine. This new room, I mean. This new mattress. I know now that *you* were behind all of it. And yes, I am grateful. I don't mind saying it – bad thoughts had been creeping in from inside the

343

walls at the time, ugly visions were beginning to emerge, I was beginning to see shapes in the shadows . . . But after you'd left me that mat, Mister, after I'd started praying again, I knew my Allah had returned. I felt calm again. I had someone to talk to, and in the weeks since. It's Him who's given me my peace. It's Him who sometimes whispers, incidentally, suggesting to me, hinting that proper liberty in a place like this, might cost a little more than a mop and a bucket.

174. 'ARE YOU DECENT?' I was told of your arrival the morning after. The courtesy allowed me by the guard who'd come to collect me, Mister – since he didn't barge in, but actually knocked – was enough to tell me something had changed.

Are you decent? was his question.

I could have answered the guard then and there, Mister. It could have saved you the trouble, I think. But the big officer came in and told me to put on my clothes, saying somebody had come to see me.

I had no idea who.

It was you, of course. You'd come, Mister. You were on your way to that room where we'd meet – with your folders, your photos, your maps, your plain white shirt, your thin white face. And all your many questions . . .

175. SPECIAL CASE First thing you said to me after you shambled in the door was *Forgive me* . . .

I remember you stooping as you came in, tucking in your shoulders. I'd been sat in the room for a little while, though nobody had told me what I was doing there. My first impressions, if I'm honest, didn't amount to much.

You looked taller under that low ceiling. And your thinning hair made you look older than you really are. That same black buttoned jacket, white shirt, them folders you carry under your arm. I noticed also the silver watch you wore. I remember how you slipped your watch off before saying a word to me, before you even sat down.

– Good to finally meet, you went.

You placed your watch next to them biros in a plastic cup. And then you sat down, Mister. You were all awkward elbows and shifted in your chair. You winced at the sound it made against the floor. I noticed the redness of your cheeks, and your slight, narrow eyes – which were blue, yet still somehow beady – but I've retained, honestly, nothing else. At the time, I remember thinking, Mister, that you looked like a hundred people at once.

You said mine was a special case – a *special concern*, was what you said, which was why there'd been a *special dispensation* in how I'd been apprehended. I'd also been returned *rather more quietly* than the usual chartered flight.

You also said you were a *special case worker*. And I remember thinking you were trying to tell me something then, as if there was some significance to our meeting.

Can I also say, Mister, that your voice sounded odd the first time we met – too high, perhaps, and a little plummy. I didn't know what to make of you. When you asked if the room was to my liking, I nodded. I didn't mention my previous cell, my journey in, and the agony of my return. I waited for you to ask me.

Except, you didn't ask me anything that first day. Though I did feel you knew more than you let on. I remember at one point, in the middle of your speech, you knocked the table leg with your foot. You seemed irritated by it. You acted as if the table, the chair, the room itself were not up to your standard, and you were embarrassed. One of your pens rolled on the floor. You stopped to pick it up, and when you spoke again, I could see that you were flustered. You went on about our proceedings then, and when you were done with your little speech, you stuck out a limp little hand for me to shake.

I stood, Mister. Confused, honestly. And then you told me you'd come back tomorrow.

– Good. Good, you said. It's important we get off to a good and proper start.

I shook your hand, Mister – do you remember? You sort of half smiled at me. And I wonder, also, if you noticed my fingers – my scabs and badly healed scars, from the many months spent carving faces into wood. I wonder if this was the good and proper start you wanted. Because nothing else in these many months since has seemed to satisfy you.

176. QUESTIONING That next day you started with your questions. All in that same prying method I've become accustomed to. Sort of kindly at first, informal yet direct, your sleeves rolled up, and your fingers laced and your pen down, your watch on the table. And then you'd wince at me, Mister, with that snappish half-smile.

And then you began.

First thing you asked, as I recall it, was about my name.

– Unusual, you said, *Bas* . . . Peculiar. Tell me, where does it originate?

You did an odd thing then. You brought your hands forward

and cupped them, like a kind of priest. You seemed impatient with me, like you were suffering me. But I was curious.

The way you acted, it seemed as if you felt I owed you. But what could I possibly owe, Mister, or offer in exchange? You must have understood, Mister, that asking anything of me in that state, shell-shocked and sunk as I was, wouldn't have amounted to anything.

I shrugged in response, and kept shrugging at everything you asked me.

– All this must be difficult, you said, I can understand that, of course . . .

You repeated that often. Kept saying you understood me, Mister, how difficult it was for me to speak. I wonder if you knew how strange and threatening it sounded to me at the time. Like you were playing, teasing and toying, until you could find the moment to say what you really wanted to say.

You knew me, Mister. You knew my face, my name, knew everything about me but acted like you didn't. And then, after a few more shrugs them questions of yours started to sound like statements.

– You were raised in East London, you said. Attended primary school there, and remained close for the rest of your secondary. You spent your entire life, it seems, in the same little place. Is all this correct?

You drew a circle with your fingers, as if all East Ham could fit inside it. I didn't reply, Mister. And then you looked down at your notes, raising your voice as you went on.

– You lived with your mother – Stevens, Estella. And uncle – Bas, Gamal.

You weren't looking up any more. You tapped lightly with

your fingers whenever you found a note to read out to me. And after another hour of that, Mister, you let go the effort of waiting on my answers. I noticed all them lines around your eyes begin to disappear, and how you eased, dabbed at your mouth with your thumbs.

– What I am wondering, you said, and here you leaned back into your chair, Mister, just as certain as I was that you were getting to your point – I'm wondering why someone like you, who is British, who has an English mother, who has lived all his life in this nation, this country, would turn his back and end up hating your home. Leaving the only place you've ever known. Never looking back – until, of course, you had to . . .

Then you let out a little breath, like a little laugh. And you looked at me, offering another pause, waiting for me to say anything in response.

But I said nothing. And then you tugged at your collar and started collecting your things.

– I think you'll find that speaking to me is, in fact, in your best interests, Yahya. I can help you. If you'll allow me. I'm here to help, that's the point. I can see you've sustained injuries. I can see you get the care you need. All we need from you is information – your story, in effect. I want to hear your story, Yahya. Hear for myself. Though, I can understand, if it's difficult. Sadly, it is necessary.

You said a bit more, Mister, but I can't recall the rest – I'd expect you remember every word. Probably you've spoken them a hundred times or more, sat in that same chair opposite your other cases. Even the *special cases* you've kept. You did say there were others – other young men who'd *fit my profile precisely*. Men who'd *returned home*, you said. Just as sick. Just as busted as me, ragged out of the sound. Men and young women, Mister, who'd come crawling back from the desert . . .

– Now, Yahya, you may choose not to talk. And you would be well within your rights to say nothing. Many of you choose to say nothing – at first. But then again, I have a feeling you'll surprise me. I think you may well surprise us all.

You wagged a finger. Then I watched you stand. Watched how you strapped your watch back onto your wrist. Brushed your knees with them folders. Drew your mouth down wide, turned and left with that uniformed guard holding the door for you. Holding the door, Mister, like you were a proper somebody, making an exit.

I went to my cell after you'd gone. Pushed off them plimsolls they'd given me, drew the mat out and prayed again. I did my rounds again, Mister. Barefoot circles in my cell. I tried turning my shoulders, twisting them painfully backward and across, thinking, childishly, that maybe the next time we met, Mister, I'd be able to sit up straighter and face your questions properly.

177. MISTER'S TERMS The thing about what you asked me, Mister – the part that really bothered me – you asked for my story, your pen poised, as if only a single page was needed.

What made you think you had any right to it, anyway?

Or expected me to tell it, Mister?

I did speak up the next time we sat together. I was determined to talk. No doubt you felt you knew me. I'd suspected it, Mister, because of the way you'd flinch whenever I'd reach for anything – a cup of tepid water, say, or shifted in my seat. How you'd watch me. That little tell in the eyes, in your fingers. I'd see it whenever I'd make a sudden movement or raise my voice higher than a whimper.

You made no bones about the fact you felt you had me figured out. Started telling me things about myself, Mister. Claiming you knew all there was to know about my botched budding as a boy, the people who'd pulled me up by the collar and into education. You even said you knew a bit about my father too, and about my – as you put it, the way you painted her . . . *your poor, troubled mother* . . .

– I can read here, you said, your mother has been received at Hahn Routledge – a care home for . . . And your uncle . . . resides close to her. Lives alone. And your mother – here, it says your mother worked as a primary school teacher before she met your father – is that correct? It's what our records hold. But perhaps you didn't . . . perhaps this was before you . . .

You went on like this. Picking apart names, places, and then hinting, tapping at all the names I'd left behind. You consulted your records, said it had been hard to piece together a childhood as muddled as mine. As if my life was no more than the sum of your notes, Mister.

Your tone shifted after that. Your face soured. Dropping your head, you tried again:

– It must have been very difficult for you, Yahya. I understand that completely . . . but we have records here – of your father . . . Bas, Marwan. Arrived in Britain from Iraq, 1984 – the entry is here. Then he seems to have disappeared. No records at all after 1991. The same year you were born – dear, dear . . .

And then you opened one of them brown folders. You

pushed a plastic wallet with your pen. Inside, there was a photocopy of a photograph.

– But there is this . . .

It was the same photograph of my father, Mister, the same picture I'd burned in a bucket in the desert. It felt as if the room had fallen in. It was my father: them big shoulders, thick hair, stood with that Abdallah by his house. And there: his eyes scratched and cut away. How was it possible?

– Where did you get this? How?

– I understand it must have been difficult. The circumstances of your father's departure. I have records here, showing school administration fees, payments. All indicating a communal home in East London – no place for a boy your age, not at all. Especially with your disability. It must have been very difficult.

I looked at you, Mister. Proper looked at last.

– I want to know how you got this, I said.

– Oh, it's really of no consequence. What is important, Yahya, is that you give me precisely what I need from you – places, dates . . . and so on.

– Why? What's all this for? – You haven't even told me. You make me come here and listen to you talk, and I've no idea . . . I don't know you, I don't know what all this is about.

I clutched at the sides of the table, Mister. You saw me do it and leaned forward as if you had me exactly where you wanted. And then calmly, as if you were done teasing, you collected the papers you'd spread between us. I watched you, wanting desperately to cuss you, feeling my belly, twist and contract.

– Things haven't been easy for you, Yahya. And it's important to say so. Establish the case, do you see? That way we can get a different picture of you.

– Different . . . to what?

I watched you pick up your watch. And you stood up, hunched, brushing your lap with your folders. You gave me a look then. A look of almost disappointment. You wanted me to fill these silences, I think. But I refused, knowing that was what you wanted. I only slouched in my chair in front of you. I think you figured you'd get nowhere with this method, Mister. And the fact you thought any different was your mistake. That you thought you might have understood anything about me, who I really was and where I'd come from was absurd.

178. FACE IN A CROWD That was the last time I met your gentle manner. It was the bullying, cussing, Mister, I met at our next meeting. You came in with your box, Mister – do you remember? It looked hefty, full of folders and zip-locked bags. And can I say now, also – your voice, Mister, which had sounded so high and clear only days before, had somehow become coarser. You went on with your show-and-tell for me.

– You might think, you said, with breath that smelled of morning coffee, that your silence keeps you safe. I can tell you now, it is quite the contrary. There is a great deal you will have to answer for, Yahya, if you intend to get back into ordinary life – as a citizen. And, clearly, as you may well have guessed, you were not unknown to the authorities. We were watching you. Listened to you speak, heard you sermonise and spread your message.

The first few folders, Mister, had stains and were frayed at the edges. You threw a few open so that the contents fluttered to my side of the table – photographs, photocopies of photographs. There were thin strips, cuttings from papers, all stuffed inside them wrinkled wallets. I spotted newspaper articles, *The Times*, the *Guardian* and local rags, one from the *East London Advertiser*. Highlighted lines, torn pamphlets, more pictures. You picked out a few and showed me.

– I trust all these are familiar to you?

I felt my stomach turn when you pointed one out to me. The photograph was unclear. A copy of a copy. But it was familiar to me in all the ways images of Al-Bayn are familiar, Mister. That same stance legs apart, and index finger. The picture was taken at a recital somewhere, some early rally. You were watching me from across the table intently, I remember. Searching for some recognition as I looked.

– At Faisal Aswan mosque. In Clapham, 2013.

With your pen you picked out another. Al-Bayn again, similarly half slanted to one side, shawl fallen, revealing my black keffiyeh, eyes mad, lifted up at the ceiling.

– And here – Al-Muriyya Islamic Centre, 2014, July.

You then put three pictures in front of me. All had faces looking up, illuminated by park lamps and glowing spotlights. These were my crowds, Mister. All organised into pages of several records. Someone had made red circles on them. Red dots marking points of interest, faces, bodies, groups of people.

– Do you recognise anyone here?

These faces were dark blurs to me, Mister. Figures half in shadow, faces gurning upward in the direction of the light.

I shook my head. But I'll admit it, I swallowed hard at the sight of all these gaping mugs again. I could see them strained, arms lifted, reaching out from the huddled crowd. It all put me in mind of my final recital in the domed hall before I'd stumbled out into the alley. I didn't tell you that then. I just let you continue, Mister, shaking my head, shrugging. I was silent.

From then on you grew more agitated. Them lines around your eyes had returned. Then, you started throwing photos at me. These images, Mister, of my Al-Bayn, and them seething, hungry crowds.

I shut my eyes when you started shouting. Started pushing me, Mister, recalling Al-Bayn's verses. You'd copied some down and wanted to recite them back to me. Extracts from my poems. The bold stuff from the pamphlets – you tried to read some aloud, Mister, but I couldn't listen. I covered my ears. Then you knocked over your pens again. This time you didn't bother picking any of them up.

– There are gaps, you said, blank parts to your history. All of it needs to be accounted for. The people you met, the places you travelled. *Names*, Yahya. *Affiliations* . . .

That's when you got out the folder, Mister. The blue one from inside the separate box. The one you'd kept to the side. A new folder this time. You opened it in front of me.

– And so, these last two years, all that has happened since. The terrible events that have taken place during your disappearance – while you were *exiled* as you claim. Do you really expect anyone to believe, Yahya, that you were unaware of the attacks? The attacks here in the UK and in cities across Europe?

I should have paid more attention. When you showed me the face of the lad in your folder, it was, honestly, the first time I'd seen him, Mister. But at the time you wouldn't hear it. You kept pressing a finger at the face, saying his name aloud, and insisting. It was only when you pointed at them others circled in crowd that I saw – it was the same face circled in the other photos. The same face in the parks, crowded halls and mosques. That same dark, thin face, Mister, completely struck by the light and looking up.

– Younes Hassan . . . you went, your face drawn, looking at the photo. Six days ago, this young man killed four people in Hamburg. Bystanders. Innocent people, three men, one woman. Attending a local festival. His choice of weapon, you should note, was a kitchen knife.

You didn't bat an eye, Mister. Neither did I.

And now I wonder whether you still believe I knew this man at all. Hardly think it matters now. All you wanted was for my story to match your own, Mister, having already made up your mind about how my story ended.

179. HAMBURG Here, I'll write what you said: *Of course, you did know*, you said, setting down your watch . . .

Let's not pretend, play around, waste time. Of course, you knew, Yahya. Knew full well what you were leaving behind when you left. The likes of this killer, this Younes Hassan. And others – Muslim boys with no history, who liked to attend and listen to you speak. No criminal activity on Hassan's record, no pick-ups, no nothing. Lived his life peacefully. With his mum, dad, a little sister. Lived in the suburbs out there. Attended school there. Decent student, okay marks. Made friends easily. He was well liked. German police were completely undone, they said. Didn't know what to make of this boy. Younes Hassan. Good son. Immigrant son – father from Yemen. His anger, his violence seemed to come out of nowhere . . .

Look, here – this is an image of the square right after his attacks. On any other day this is a spot for tourists, shoppers, festival goers, music. And look here – I always find it interesting to see what people leave behind when running for their lives. Dropped clothing, the mess of street food, bags scattered – look, a kid's balloon and somebody's very expensive coat. All of it lying on the floor like rubbish. This sort of thing used to be the exception in Europe. And now Hamburg is only the latest exception. One doesn't shake the sight of terror and abandonment in Europe's great capitals do they, Yahya – or do you prefer Al-Bayn? Paris, London, Barcelona. These cities belong on postcards, don't you think? Not the *Ten O'Clock News*. The families of the victims are marked as well as the rest of us are marked when we see things like this – and I think you know this about people.

I do think you are sensitive to it. I know you are, having watched you. Having listened to you speak, and after reading, as much as I could, of what you've written.

Your poems have made a lasting impression on me.

I'll just take a few lines and read them out for you now – though you should know I'm no poet. I don't have your, shall we say, flair for oratory. But even so, if you'd allow me, I think it'll be useful to have these read back to you – fresh ears, as it were – I'll do my best . . .

In 2011 you write on an online forum: *Raise their bodies to bury, For there is no Heaven for them, Only the pointed edge, Of your pious knife* – yes? In two other poems you mention, or actively suggest, the acting out of mass violence. For instance, in 2012 a poem was circulated that has since been credited to your alias: *They will say 'forbidden are those who trespass against us', But Brothers show might to the meek, Seek them in their streets and pave the ground with their fallen bodies.* This same contempt, Yahya, the same hatred spills out of every line –

can you hear it? The same year, you write: *You are meagre in number, You have the weaker voice, But you have been forever victorious since the battle of Noah, You will be again, my brothers.*

Brothers, you called them. And here, in 2013, just before you stole away, you spoke to these brothers directly. In a poem entitled *Brutes*, you write – *Brothers, wield your martyrdom! Leave behind the story of your life! So that you may keep living in its recount!*

I could go on. But you can see that I've filed several accounts of your works – the files are here, and here, just look – all indicating your *premonitions*, shall we say. Acts of terror, hatred and violence, which have since manifested across our cities like a rash, like a scourge.

And it's the last poem, Yahya, on the subject of martyrdom, which was found on scraps written in Younes Hassan's hand. Your poem was found in Hassan's bedroom. The boy was a promising poet himself. Hassan liked to use Al-Bayn's words as practice. Perhaps he thought it would help put into words what he felt about his own country.

The boy took his own life shortly after murdering those others. This is why I find you fascinating, Yahya – you seemed to have foreseen the whole thing coming. You seemed to have identified the anger, the hatred, simmering in these young men. And you wrote about it. And whether intentional or otherwise, it was these very men who read your words and found themselves reflected. Of course, they read you. Came to see you. They felt heard by you, and seen. And now, we all have to live with the consequences.

Which brings me to my point. I'll likely never have another

case like yours, Yahya. There is so much to document, record, a lot of which can be traced back to your writings. Except now, as I sit here, giving you a fair hearing, you refuse to speak!

I find it perplexing.

Tell me how you became who you are to them – and who the people were that helped you, were responsible for you. Names, dates, is what I want. And you will eventually give me your testimony, I can assure you of that. Because, while I don't take pleasure in saying, it is within my power to detain you indefinitely. I can see to that if you force me – I am capable of it.

But I'll take my leave of you now . . . As for – as for . . . the next few days, you might come to enjoy these facilities – nice room, good shower. Use the courtyard if you like. Get your lungs some air. And in time, you will come to understand the obvious: it is a privilege to have me listen to you. It's a sanction to have your story set down in our records. Therefore, I trust you'll become more forthcoming with me. That you will open up. Show a bit of manners. There's really no need to fight the system of justice that seeks to protect all British citizens – and that includes you, Yahya. This is your country, after all – this . . . *this matchless land, happy and glorious . . . for England means as much to you as England means to me . . .*

180. CITIZEN'S BARGAIN At the end of my pen, Mister, parts of me pass into you. You can see how easy it is to invent you. It's the same method I used to invent my Al-Bayn for my poetry. I can hold you here, in my ear, and here – on these pages – I can even make you sing . . .

Rest assured, I did listen to what you said to me. And you were true to your word about it. I was, indeed, let out for an hour after you left. Them guards let me walk into the court-yard with them, like you said. It was bright, I remember. The skies had cleared. I could see a clean patch of blue behind them towers.

My head became dizzy from the light, I think. I remember reaching out to the world as soon as I stepped into it. Walked out in a kind of delirium. First time the others had a good look at me. Them other detainees, I mean, whom I'd pass in the aisles and outside my cell, whom I knew only as names – names like Namdi, Olumide and Saqib. I noticed how they looked, dressed, went about together, speaking in huddles. I seemed to be the only person sitting alone.

The guard kept me separate. I couldn't hear what they were saying about me. Some of them would look over and stare. Curious as to why I had someone guarding me. There was a grassy area, and I took my plimsolls off to walk across it. I knelt, Mister. Felt the grass and the hard ground under me. I bent to touch the ground with my forehead and felt the wet and the coldness in the dirt. That felt properly rare after so many weeks alone. I nearly wept, honestly. Just to have my tears touch the earth as I knelt.

For the full hour, Mister, I sat crossed leg-over-leg on the uneven grass and kept very still. I let my knees tremble under the discomfort of it. I listened to my ears ring in my head, and let my tired, starved eyes look around at my surroundings. Nothing but walls and barbed-wire fencing, Mister. Grey surfaces took up most of what I could see. And them towers, and the patrolling officers, passing each other in them heights. I focused on the faces. The murmur of voices from them other men. Shuffling about during their idle hours.

That one sitting there at the stone centre, for instance, could have been Hass, twisting his wrists as he did in class. And them other small, swaying bodies who were standing against the painted gate – were they dressed all in black together? Bearded and baggy-eyed, reciting their own verses out of tune? Big-shouldered Moazzam was there, walking past the other side of the court. Surely it was him – brushing his bald head and beard as he went. And there, I nearly shouted at the sight, Mister – for the tall man, out by the long path, could have been my Ibrahim. I recognised his long and elegant strides, as if he was about to glide over. The stooped old men walking along the stone barriers – that one had my Sisi Gamal's long nose on him, the other Mother Sadaf's shabby clothing. And any one of them, Mister, slow-walking and shambling, might have worn the same old face as Abdallah. There – my Mother Aneesa's fat ankles patrolling the far wing. There – my Mother Miriam's moon-face on that boy in the corner, sitting with another boy, whose face wasn't familiar. There – my Bilal sharing shoulders with my Zenab. And there, Mister – could I have really seen him? – watering the plants by the far black wall was Rustum, lumbering along the outer bank.

Apparitions everywhere I looked. It made me yearn to be heard again. Seen by them. But then, the guard gave a grunt and nudged me. And it made my heart sink.

Once back, I wanted to come to a decision about what you asked me, Mister. Did a few rounds in my room, making circles under that flickering light. I realised there was nothing I could possibly say to satisfy you.

My story, for your purposes, could have easily fitted on a list:

1. Born Bas, Yahya, British-Iraqi, Iraqi-British.
2. Disabled. Delinquent – raised in poverty.
3. Radicalised against Western intervention in Iraq.
4. Gains notoriety promoting works of anti-Western hate.
5. Absconds from the UK – abandons known family.
6. Spends several years in exile. Stateless. Displaced.
7. Returns a pariah. Tail between legs.

You'd know now, of course, that nothing numbered here could have told you anything about me, Mister. At the time I don't think you really cared. You never were interested in what I had to say. All you wanted was to settle your own story, Mister, one in which I could play your preferred part.

I remember going around in circles that night, trying to think up ways of getting through to you. I knew simply replying to your questions wouldn't do. I needed to do something that would get attention. I needed you to look, Mister. And proper see me, in the same way, I suppose, the lad in Hamburg made you see him, same as in Paris, same as in Tavistock Square – for it's only then that the likes of you really look. Only then are you unable to look away.

And that's what I wanted from you, I think – I didn't want you to look away.

I made a short prayer for you that night. And then I took my seat at this table, having decided, Mister, that I was going to make a trade with you – a sort of citizen's bargain, for which I'd need something from you in return.

181. THE ASK And look – the confusion on your face was funny. You'd thought I'd maybe ask for something more, something bigger. Maybe you weren't really expecting me to go for it at all. You acted like it was an imposition at first. Started going on about the bureaucracy you'd have to wrangle to fetch the thing. But I insisted on it, Mister. Saying it was the only possession I wanted in exchange. It was my wooden figurine. The one I'd brought in from the desert. My last piece of carved wood. It was the figure your lot snatched up upon my return. And I promised that if I'd had it back, I'd trade with you my story.

Still, you blustered. Still, you blew your cheeks. But you said you weren't without your mercies, Mister. And I could see how it pleased you to say you'd try for me. *I'll make no promises*, you said. Which made me laugh. And then, once I got back to my quarters, I prayed for you a second time. I knelt, rose, muttered my prayers into a tattered cloth. I laughed again. Laughing as I prayed, turning my laughter into prayer.

182. THE FLINCH I've also – if I may mention it, Mister, before I go on to recount what must follow – wanted to tell you that I've noticed something about you. Something revealing about you, Mister, which actually makes me think that you and I, despite our differences, need not feel so distant.

It's something I noticed from the moment you avoided my eyes. And from how, on every occasion since, you've turned away whenever I've tried to speak back.

Mister, as you know, you can tell a lot from how a person listens to what others have to say. You have to pay attention to the patterns, of course. Especially in the way the other person replies. How they speak. Their little *ums* and *ahs*, repetitions, hesitations and involuntary spills. People are made of language, Mister. You can even get a sense of a person from if they don't say as much as what they do. There's a lot in silences alone.

It's why so many of your fictions too – your novels, fairy tales and uneven histories are stuffed with people with unforgettable faces. I remember my rounds reading on them buses as a boy, noticing how your heroes were similarly drawn, Mister, and how your monsters read so familiar. All them big noses, Mister, mad hair, and disfigured bodies.

It's why I don't blame you, honestly. Reading all them English books has helped me read you better, Mister.

For instance – your flinch.

It's what I've noticed about you. The fact that you flinched the first time the guard shut the door and left us alone together. I noticed that little jerk in your shoulder too, which you tried to hide with a hand at the side of the table.

You're hardly the first, when faced with a mug like mine, to flinch, wince, or scan for a sign of bad intent. But I wonder, Mister, whether you've ever considered why you even flinch at all. Could it be that you sense the anger, the stuff unsettled in me, and in all the bellies of the beaten. And maybe the instinct behind your little flinch, in some unspoken sense, is common to that recoil provoked by any black or brown body in a public square, a British street, or any European city.

Because deep down, I think, you understand, Mister, that there have been things done in your name that have been unforgivable. It's why while all them British bombs fall far enough away, you still flinch here at home. Because even here,

Mister, among your own, you sense the possibility of vengeance.

You know that them same black and brown bodies who went to the same schools as you, played in the same parks, and even share some of the same memories, Mister, might not stand with you now, or protect you any longer. And you understand why, of course, because in your heart you wouldn't blame them.

It's this that terrifies you most, I think. And I can understand it. But at least your terror means we share a common language, Mister.

. . . I see now that I'm running out of paper. If I'm to continue, I'll need you to bring me more. I'll only add to this letter, Mister, that you were right about one other thing: you said that boys like Younes Hassan seem to come from nowhere. And yes, it's true – they always do. I know it, Mister, because I'm from a nowhere place myself. There are nowhere places all over your Great Britain. Emptied-out ends where your neglect is obvious. Bits of East London feel like that. Like nowhere to me. And there are entire towns where resentments have settled into the bodies of people. Into how they perceive everything, in the way they appear to each other, and the way they move and breathe and even speak.

And while I know you'll keep harping on about my ditching this country for the desert, Mister, it's worth remembering, that it was this country, and them who lead it, that abandoned the likes of me first. And anyway, honestly, it's not something I'm all that ashamed of, nor feel the need to atone.

183. THE CUT It'd be a further two weeks before I heard from you again. I spent the time on my rounds, Mister, working up the strength in my legs again, and preparing myself for a longer stay. I was determined, now, to do it.

I was thinking very seriously about spending some indeterminate time here. How I'd survive the *drip-drip-drip* of the running tap, the one that plays a mad little melody in my head with the rest of it, the *click-click-click* flickering light, and the slow dull sound in the ceiling, which comes out in an *mmmmm* . . .

When I heard the knock on the door it came as a relief. It was your package. You'd found my wooden figurine. The taller piece, crafted from the softer whiter wood. You'd found it for me, Mister, had it delivered and I was grateful. Immediately, I placed the thing in the niche of the square window, I had to stand on the table to fix it . . .

After admiring it for a few moments, Mister, I brought it down again. Held it in my arms as I said a prayer. I sat for long hours like that. Just holding the thing in my arms. Nothing else I'd rather have with me here, honestly. It reminded me of my desert, the people there, and the knowing, Mister, that for a moment I had glimpsed the possibility of a life lived otherwise.

See me sat under the yellow lamplight. The caged and weak little bulb above me. The light, Mister, which had that night started flickering again, off and on again, all in time to that dying scattering sound in the ceiling.

I remember looking down at the piece of wood in my hands. And it was then that I saw, Mister, under the light, how the shadow would cast different shapes over the same surface. I could see at once how the face I'd carved was recognisable as my father. His dark low brow, and fat lower lip. Small scratches in the crevice of his eyes. And then, as I turned it at an angle, it was more like my Sisi Gamal. Wider face and rounded shoulders. And then, another flicker made the same figure seem fatter, rounder, like my Mother Sadaf. Turning again I saw my Mother Miriam, thicker in the lower half.

I turned again, Mister, and felt underneath.

The soft impression, an indentation in the hump of the back, made it feel more like a vision of my own body. With a last little flicker, a turn to the side – it began to look more like Ester . . .

Ester – that sharp little jaw and them cheeks. It might have even been the figure Ester herself had watched me make. I brushed the side of its unworn head, and with the tip of a nail scratched at the small motes at the earlobes. I smiled then. She looked just like I remembered. I'd thought of her every day in this cell. And I uttered an invented prayer, then, Mister, for forgiveness. And then I felt with my fingers along the side of the wood and found what I knew would be there.

The seams at the sides sprang open. The wood split into two halves in my hands. Inside the hollow I found the small filament. The wound-up wire which lay thin and sharp. I placed down the two halves and spun the blunt ends inside both palms. I pulled at the ends and made the filament taut. I pulled the wire wide so that the razor flashed in the light. I opened my mouth. Brought the wire around my wet tongue. And pulled as the light flickered off and on above me.

184. LIFE AND TIMES The rest you know. It was Shantih who found me. Shantih himself who gathered me up with them bony arms, and ran me out into that courtyard for help. He'd sworn at the sight of me thinking I was already dead – *Thought you were gone, friend, there was blood the likes of which on the carpet* . . .

He'd kept my limp body awake by talking to me: *It's me, Shantih* . . .

And had me repeat his name to keep me conscious.

Not an end, Mister. Not quite a beginning. There was a hospital. It was there that I recovered. Much of it I don't remember now. My mouth was stuffed with swabs and stitches. I remember the nurses who cared for me, but the drugs have mystified the rest. I think there might have been another room somewhere, in some brighter wing. And it's there I stayed for what felt like weeks, but could've been longer, until I was well enough to return.

And here – I'm able now to feel around for what remains, Mister. I don't think I'll ever get used to the ache in the hollow. I still wear my swabs. The stitches itch every time them cotton wads get caught. I've been told to wash everything I eat down with a flask of bitter liquid. And in the mornings, Mister, after the medical men visit me and leave tidily enough, I'm subjected to a series of inspections. The guards come at midday. Turn the place upside down in search for hidden trinkets.

I began to wonder what had become of you. You stopped visiting altogether. I'd thought you'd be curious having heard what had happened in your absence. I kept sending requests. Later, I realised they'd gone through. Because it was then that I started getting your pages. Great stacks of blank paper in through the door. And I knew, finally, that I had your attention, Mister. I knew you couldn't look away.

And so, *chop-chop* – it was time for me to keep my end of

the bargain. Though I fumbled my first go, writing many false beginnings, before beginning again.

For the first attempt, I wrote a quick account. I described the parts I figured you'd favour – skimming my busy childhood, cutting past them wonder years, going straight to the names I knew you'd prefer – Gamal, Ibrahim, Zenab, Bilal – but I tore the thing up, Mister, threw it away. And then I wrote a second, quickly, to get it all out in one go. This second telling traced a thin outline of my father. I even added a few lines about my years at the Ibn Rabah. The books I read there – under the arch, in the court – and the boys who read beside me. I touched only lightly on my time in exile. That part was difficult for me to write altogether. Eventually I gave up. At every turn, Mister, it seemed like the story of my life would unravel.

It took some time, and over many nights, doing my rounds, making little scratchings, going over revisions and corrections, on torn-away sheets of paper. In the end, however, I came to a kind of understanding.

I realised that if I was going to have a proper go at it, to *speak up! speak up!* at long last, and go loud with it, I was going to have to write into silence too.

Into my own silence, Mister.

And the silence that holds between me and you.

Clutching my mouth during them early first drafts, I started writing in circles, into winding lines on the page, and began telling my story as a kind of masquerade. I knew all I had to do was keep going. And that I – if I kept playing along with a certain truth in the lie, I could show you, Mister, prove to you, that even the likes of me, some nobody from nowhere, would-have-could-have, lived a full life worth a proper show!

I knew I had your attention when you started writing back to me. Your little notes, Mister, sent with more blank pages, asking for clarifications on this, that, and the other.

But it was too late by then – I was off to the races with my big life, and it was all I could do to keep writing. Page after page, Mister. Until many months later, here I am: wondering if somewhere along the way, you've recognised yourself reflected in my story, Mister, and in me, your ugly Other.

And now, for the rest of my days, I'll sit here and pray, and say not another word to anyone. I'll be happy with that, Mister, once I'm done. I'd be over the moon. And I can just picture you, lifting them beady eyes from my letters, sticking your feet into crosses, blowing your cheeks and declaring, in imitation of me:

Now that's a life! . . . Cor, what a life!

Stories like mine, Mister. As told by an idiot – or a king, or a beggar – or in whatever guise it comes to you next, I hope by then you'll want to listen. Because someday, some other teller might sit where I sit, and whisper stories like mine forever. They'll make every *tomorrow and tomorrow and tomorrow* sound like today, and maybe then you'll listen.

Maybe then you'll read again, Mister. As if your life depended on it.

As mine still does, in a way – in the telling and re-telling of my story.

In fact, tell you what . . .

I'll tell it again – bring me some paper!

185. PARADISE Here, look – I'll change the names around this time, have people play other people. I'll write a story the likes of which . . . And it'll be an unruly, clamorous thing. Where names and origins don't matter. Where I can tear away pages or skip entire acts. I'll use what's at hand, and the books in my head, to construct it. I'll look out the square window and have them bodies out there play free men. In the gridded court, with them towers and barbed fences around. I'll make a paradise here, that's what. I'll dig an estuary and begin. My Mothers will arrive swapping dialogue. Even my Sisi Gamal will breathe better, and speak in mottled improvisations. But more than this: I'll turn everything around on its head. Let me paint the faces of them others as my brothers – give Ibrahim the part as Paul, Moazzam as George, Hass becomes Ringo and I'll become John. And we'll make popular songs the world won't fail to dance to. I'll even have my Mothers play their lovers. I'll cross every line in the book. I'll spirit you up something ancient, Mister, and beautiful, and busy and new. And you'll be frightened of it. I'll have Zeinab play Bilal, and Bilal play Zeinab, and have the boy haul an ogre across a spinning bike. I'll have my Mother Miriam turn a corner too, and discover, hidden there, some bullet-riddled tree, in front of a hundred other runaways like her. And my father – maybe his writing had been girlish enough to assume my mother's hand. And maybe my mother could play the poet next. My father left to mime. I'll have my mother fish out lyrics from the future, while my father whispers to the past. And me – and me, and me, and me – I'll be a thousand and one things at once. I'll be an adventurer, a sailor, a tailor, a thief. I'll be a peer, a lord and a queen. I'll be a butler, a prince, a drone operator and a flyer of multi-coloured kites. I'll be a British soldier, a minister, a pickpocket and a saint. I'll make implausible things sound plausible then, and I'll have a bone to pick with the times. I'll still find a moment to write my way back here though, Mister – this, here, back to England, back to Blighty, and back to this cell from where I write . . . only, inevitably, I'll write my way out again. I'll throw a prayer mat over the barbed-wire fencing. Make a break for it that way – but to where?

To an ending, to the sea . . .

To there, look – I'll stand shivering on a white pebble sweep somewhere. Waiting for ferries, dinghies and rowing boats to arrive. I'll sit there, crossed leg-over-leg, fugitive, deserter, holding a flag with a message in tight golden lines: *Welcome!* – and with that, I'd be ready to receive any Tom, Dick and Harry in need of a night's sleep. Any Maalik and Amaal too. Or Abdul Ali. Or Abdel Fattah. Or Maher or Paulina, or Kemi or Nneka, or Seleem, or Tasneen, or Zineta, or Yara, or Nazeeh or Ahmed, or Taha . . .

In almost every language in the world, Mister, the place where the river meets the sea is called a *mouth*. And so I'll be able to invent a new word for *welcome* when the tide comes in. It'll be a crime worth committing. And then, and then: I'll sit and I'll wait for the rest of you lot to come and join me. Only the mad and the good and the seditious will be left, sat on the shore beside me. But that wouldn't matter, Mister. We'd all be braver by then, and bolder . . . I'll put my pen down, take a breath, and leave the rest, and what it all means up to you. Whether I turn out to be the hero of my own life, or the villain of yours, these pages must show.

Acknowledgements

My thanks to the heroic efforts of my editor Mary-Anne Harrington and the team at Tinder Press including Ellie Freedman, Emily Patience and Joe Yule, as well as to Mark Handsley and Kate Truman. My deepest thanks to Hamza Jahanzeb and Tam Hussain, whose guidance and advice have been deeply appreciated. Sophie Lambert – thank you is not enough.

Adrian Poole, my friend, for your kindness and embraces in the Great Court, which I really needed at the time, and for so much more, thank you.

Ali Smith, you put your hand on my heart on a day I felt most defeated. Every Thursday that you offered your time, you made me, and this book, braver – thank you.

For those who offered an ear when all I was able to do was try to talk my way out of what this book could be – Nilesh Bell-Gorsia, Raymond Antrobus, Nikesh Shukla,

Adam Westbrook, Parwana Fayyaz, Carlos Fonseca, and Hampus Jakobsson – thank you. My gratitude to Zenab Ahmed and everyone involved in the London Learning Co-op whose foundation in Islamic Philosophy will last a lifetime.

I am also indebted to the writers whose works have become sources of inspiration, revelation and at times utter exaltation – thank you Paul B. Preciado, Jack Halberstam, Fred Moten, Stefano Harney, Homi K. Bhabha, Houria Bouteldja, Saadallah Wannous, Maggie Nelson. And to those whose vivid genius lives on in their monumental works: José Esteban Muñoz, Derek Jarman, Idries Shah, Édouard Glissant, Nawal El Saadawi – thank you.

And because all this, days sunken, gifted, lost, recovered again, feels like a conspiracy between what I hear, what I know, and what I don't – thank you ANOHNI, Meredith Monk, Sons of Kemet, Colin Stetson, Perfume Genius, Caroline Shaw, Björk, Andrew Norman and Anna Clyne for keeping my mind alive and brimming with possibilities. Your music floods within.

Mister, Mister could not have been possible without the generosity of Trinity College, Cambridge. Thank you for the space and the time to complete it. It was the only place it could have been.

My gratitude remains with my family, Heidi, Emi, and Lily. You three are my only hope. For everything, everything, everything – thank you.

A Note About the Author

Guy Gunaratne is the author of *Mister, Mister* and *In Our Mad and Furious City*, which won the International Dylan Thomas Prize and the Jhalak Prize and was long-listed for the Man Booker Prize and the Orwell Prize for Political Fiction. Gunaratne was a Visiting Fellow Commoner in Creative Arts at Trinity College, Cambridge, and is a trustee on the board of English PEN. They have also served on the judging panels for several literary prizes, including the 2019 Goldsmith Book Prize and the 2023 Rathbones Folio Prize.

14 Day   10-23

JC